T0247941

Exiled Shadow

NORMAN MANEA

Exiled Shadow

A NOVEL IN COLLAGE

Translated from the Romanian by Carla Baricz

A MARGELLOS
WORLD REPUBLIC OF LETTERS BOOK

Yale UNIVERSITY PRESS | NEW HAVEN & LONDON

The Margellos World Republic of Letters is dedicated to making
literary works from around the globe available in English through
translation. It brings to the English-speaking world the work of
leading poets, novelists, essayists, philosophers, and playwrights
from Europe, Latin America, Africa, Asia, and the Middle East to
stimulate international discourse and creative exchange.

English translation copyright © 2023 by Carla Baricz.
Originally published as *Umbra exilată* © Norman Manea, 2021.
All rights reserved.
Epigraph by Dylan Thomas from THE POEMS OF DYLAN THOMAS,
U.S. copyright © 1952 by Dylan Thomas. Reprinted by permission
of New Directions Publishing Corp. UK copyright © The Dylan
Thomas Trust.

This book may not be reproduced, in whole or in part, including
illustrations, in any form (beyond that copying permitted by
Sections 107 and 108 of the U.S. Copyright Law and except by
reviewers for the public press), without written permission from
the publishers.

Yale University Press books may be purchased in quantity for
educational, business, or promotional use. For information, please
email sales.press@yale.edu (U.S. office) or sales@yaleup.co.uk
(U.K. office).

Set in Source Serif type by Motto Publishing Services.
Printed in the United States of America.

Library of Congress Control Number: 2023931272
ISBN 978-0-300-26572-9 (hardcover : alk. paper)

A catalogue record for this book is available from the British
Library.

This paper meets the requirements of ANSI/NISO Z39.48-1992
(Permanence of Paper).

10 9 8 7 6 5 4 3 2 1

For Cella, my beloved, my sister

Do not go gentle into that good night.
Rage, rage against the dying of the light.
—Dylan Thomas

Contents

Exiled Shadow

THE PREMISE, OR THE PAST
BEFORE THE PAST

Exile begins the moment one is expelled from the womb. A mother, in turn, is cut off from a grandmother's womb. A grandmother, a grandmother's grandmother, and her great-grandmothers have all experienced the same earthly debut.

The applicant sent a request to National Geographic's Genographic Project (as well as to other global projects specializing in such matters) to analyze his saliva. Since his payment for expert analysis was received on time, we are able to trace the genealogy of his maternal ancestors.

His ancestors' migration encompassed vast spaces. DNA results show that they belonged to a genealogical tree known as a haplogroup. This group contains the subgroups U*, U1, U1a, U1bm, U3m, U4, and U7. The map of their wanderings demonstrates that all began their journeys in eastern Africa. Of course, such journeys occurred over tens of thousands of years.

Descendants of the applicant's maternal ancestors, the majority of the haplogroup, survive to this day. We have at our disposal 569 letters of the mitochondrial sequence—the letters A, C, T, and G, representing the four nucleotides—the chemical building blocks that are responsible for life and that make up the DNA of the applicant. From time to time, a natural, usually random, and mostly harmless mutation changes the mitochondrial sequence of the DNA of the applicant's ancestors. We can think of this as a pronunciation error: one of the "letters" in the sequence changes from a C to a T, or from an A to a G. If this sort of mutation happens to a woman, she passes it on to her daughter and to her daughters' daughters. She also passes it on to her sons, but they cannot pass it on further.

Analyzing the mutations, we can compile a list of "begats," ancestor by ancestor, for the applicant. The list of those who abandoned Africa begins with a first, furthest removed ancestor. Who was this furthest removed ancestor, where did she live, what was the story of this Eve? We do not know. Proceeding down the list, toward more recent times, we note the movements of each of the applicant's predecessors: the first would have lived between 150,000 and 170,000 years ago and would have been the woman whom anthropologists call "mitochondrial Eve." She would not have been the first human woman. Though *Homo sapiens* had existed for some 200,000 years already, at some point, approximately 150,000 to 170,000 years ago, we know there lived a woman, this Eve, from whom we are all descended. This would have occurred 30,000 years or more after *Homo sapiens* evolved in Africa.

We now turn to the haplogroups and the mutations that occurred in Eve's descendants: L2 into L3, then the first Group M, resulting from a migration toward Ethiopia and then toward Australia and Polynesia, and, at last, the appearance of a second Group M, which reached the Sinai Peninsula, where Group N appeared, which subsequently wandered through Asia, Europe, India, and America. Haplogroup R then appears, originating with a woman who lived 50,000 years ago and from whom the European, North African, Indian, and Arab subgroups are descended. Haplogroup U5 is limited to Finland, while U6—a derivative of haplogroup R—branches out from the Middle East toward Scandinavia, as well as toward the Caucasus Mountains, to the Black Sea, and then toward the Baltic regions and western Europe. Like the ancestors of the members of groups M and N, the particular ancestors of this haplogroup who might interest our correspondent come from Europe and the eastern Mediterranean and make up approximately seven percent of that population. We repeat: seven, nearly seven percent. According to our research, this is the result of a series of migrations taking place over hundreds of years, one exile following the next.[1]

A BRIEF STOP AT THE
RED STAR LINE MUSEUM

The first great empires of the Middle East appeared about 2,300 years before the Common Era, around the same time that the wars between them and the resulting mass displacements of population also began. The famous mathematician Pythagoras was the son of an immigrant and himself a wanderer through Egypt and through Italy, where he died around the year 497. One might also point out the Silk Road (200 BCE–1200 CE); the large European and Arab migrations between the years 375 and 1000 CE; the Crusades (1095–1271); João Ramalho, the Portuguese who founded the Brazilian metropolis of São Paulo; the European exploratory expeditions (1418–1580); the importation of millions of African

slaves into the Americas (1510–1888); the European migration due to urbanization and industrialization (1815–1930);
the migrations after the First and Second World Wars; the
colonization of Africa (1870–1975); the independence movement and the partitioning of India (1947); the hiring of seasonal workers (1950–1970); the Eastern European migration
(1989–present); and so-called "illegal migration" (1970–present). They are all moments of a "frantic dialectic of change,"
as Bertolt Brecht once described exile. In relation to the
Russian ports, to Danzig in Poland, and to Hamburg in Germany, Antwerp became an important transit point for such
European migratory movements, the place where the wanderer who sold his shadow—a character in a famous European Romantic fairytale of the nineteenth century written
by Adelbert von Chamisso—also seems to have landed.[2]

THE INCARNATION

Peter Schlemihl,[3] who will accompany our hero on his adventures, owes his name to a burlesque juxtaposition of the
Christian and Judaic traditions. Peter, his Christian name, alludes to Saint Peter, one of the first apostles of the Church. A
Jew born in Galilee, in the Holy Land, a close friend of Jesus
and his brother, Saint Peter had to contend with Saint Paul, a
Greek Jew from Tarsus, a visionary who promoted Christian
internationalism and mass conversion. Peter maintained
that in order to become a Christian one first had to be a Jew
like himself and the Messiah, while Paul, with propagandis-
tic fervor, argued for opening the Church's doors to everyone.

The character's family name, Schlemihl, can be found in the Babylonian Talmud, in the chapter on Moses, and means "beloved of God" in Hebrew. However, the name also has a clownish connotation, as Adelbert von Chamisso, the author of the famous Romantic fairytale, took note of and desired for his literary hero. The name Schlemihl connotes the doltish Jew, both unlucky and in dire straits, a bewildered jester fit for public mockery. A harmless Auguste the Fool and Patches the Clown.

Jewish tradition bestows sacred attributes on this imbecile and fool, a Dostoevskian and un-Dostoevskian "idiot," who must be regarded with indulgence and protected. The Talmud tells the story of how poor Schlemihl became involved with the wife of a rabbi and was caught and killed. What others had managed to do, probably many times, Schlemihl, a clown of failure, couldn't manage at all. From the Hebrew *schlemiel* (goose, ignoramus), the name later veered into Yiddish, the argot of exiles, becoming *schlimazel* (luckless, hapless, and unlucky), a Schlemihl. Jewish texts say these lost ones are loved by God.

THE BEGINNING OF THE FICTION

Once upon a time, or every time, or at no time ever, there was a morning wakening.

One eye open, the other shut. He saw, or rather glimpsed, the door, a yellow envelope stuffed under it.

Lately, he would spend a long time sleeping, and wake only with difficulty, never fully, quickly falling back into the abyss, into prolonged lethargy. He shut the open eye, fell back asleep, woke up. The yellow envelope reappeared. Then, a repeated rap at the door. The woodpecker was impatient, the red-painted door irritated it. The slumberer had painted it red, the official color, to provoke irritation, or disgust, or fear. In the half-open door: a messenger with a yellow envelope in hand. He wore a drab suit, well cut, covered in lapel pins, and a fanny pack, with a large, green buckle, was slim, well proportioned. The suit was tight in the right places. Black hair, thick and disheveled; a thin mustache, also black, shiny, slicked with shoe polish. He turned back toward the half-open door and whispered to an unseen companion: "He won't get up. He's a deadbeat."

"Who are you, what do you want?" the sleepy one inquired.

"You'll find out," the messenger answered from the doorway. "You'll find out, yes, yes, that's the order, to find out."

In briefs and undershirt, the sleepy one got out of bed and headed toward the bathroom. In the bathroom door stood the messenger's twin, who had entered—when? how?—through the open door. He was holding a paper full of official-looking stamps.

"Now don't get antsy. You'll stay in the house. You can't go out. You're being arrested. You're under house a-rest. That's what it's called: house arrest."

The lanky one in the drab suit pointed toward the bathroom door, which stood half open. Beyond it, his slim twin with black, disheveled hair and a little mustache slicked with shoe polish (dressed in a similar fashion, it seemed) was now sitting on the toilet seat cover, immersed in a text. On his knees, a second yellow envelope. The sleepy one had risen, was now on his feet, now standing in front of the look-alikes carrying identical yellow envelopes, who were shamelessly contemplating the captive's torn briefs of finest cotton gauze.

Arrested without any justification! Arrested! Now of all times! And he had just gotten up, was now just waiting for his sister to bring the usual steaming cup of coffee with milk and the croissant, freshly warmed in the oven as usual. "Tamar!" he wanted to call out. He was choked with fear. Don't we live in a People's Republic, a constitutional one? There is peace and harmony in the world at large, people everywhere love one another, laws are respected, intruders have no right to rush willy-nilly into the legal place of residence of a peaceable citizen who pays his rent and taxes on time. Hesitating, he turned toward one of the twins, holding his hand out for the envelope, but the official extended his own hand and shook it delicately.

"I'm Ed," the aping one whispered, bowing. The other, the twin, did so as well. Hard to say whose hand he had shaken, or who had tenderly shaken his hand.

The slumberer kept trying to wake up, couldn't tell if he had. One eye open, the other shut, as before, as an hour or two earlier, or god knew how long ago. He'd been sleeping a lot recently, waking only with great difficulty, never fully. After a while he opened both eyes, saw the door under which someone had slipped a yellow envelope. Having finally decided to wake up, he opened both eyes wide, rubbing a damp, sweaty forehead.

"Tamar!" he wanted to shout, to beg for a sip of coffee. But he remembered that he had not lived with Tamar for a long time. He remembered this fact and so must be waking up, must have woken up.

The official notification was brief.

THE MINISTRY OF THE INTERIOR
STATE SECURITY DIVISION

Esteemed Comrade,
You are hereby summoned to our headquarters: 27 Arenei Street, Room 22.
Comrade Colonel Vladimir Tudor

Yes, yes, he'd had misgivings the past few days. Something was bound to happen. I am Ed . . . and the other one also Ed. And now Colonel Tudor! Who the hell was he? Previously he had received messages only from captains, and once in a while from a major. Never from a colonel, and they'd never summoned him to the headquarters of the feared institution before. Rather, it had always been bizarre addresses, shadowy dwellings. No, never to headquarters. The dream, yes, yes, the dream, he had not forgotten it: the nervous woodpecker at the door, the text the man had read in his bathroom. Ed and Ed standing before the culprit. The culprit, indeed. It was becoming true and was no longer a supposition. It was becoming true, and it was not a surprise. Surprises had lost their cachet, nothing was surprising any longer, no one could afford astonishment anymore.

A few days after the strange dream with the yellow envelope, the sleepy one stopped asking himself about guilt. It no longer seemed important which of his guilts was preoccupying the comrades who kept watch over the country's peace and order. The citizens of the Republic harbored plenty of guilts. Though only some were chosen for the guillotine, everyone was a suspect.

At the counter inscribed RECEPTION, the military officer's cap drooped over his left eyebrow. "I've been summoned by Comrade Colonel Tudor. Today, Friday, four P.M., room twenty-two." The officer straightened his cap and held out a little blue cardboard square on which was typed "RE-CEPTION 22."

The colonel was not in uniform. He wore an elegant suit of a rabid, wind-blown color and a silk tie with a Chinese print. Short and chubby, black hair combed over with brilliantine. Glasses with thin, fragile lenses. Large, immense hands. The culprit was made to feel awkward by the modest height of the agent, as well as by his own long, thin, body, shaped like a board. He—the accused—had a shaved head and was dressed carelessly, in a black vinyl bomber jacket over a shirt that had at one point been white.

"Eh? You like my tie? A gift from the wife of a colleague who visited the Great Wall of China. I'm crazy about everything oriental. Extremely oriental."

The easy-going manner of the colonel seemed suspect. It wasn't the brutality of the captains, who would summon him to always new, always different privately owned apartments that they had keys to and that they would use during the times when their inhabitants were not at home. Maybe the small, pomaded man with his officer's stripes would switch quickly from informal address to formal politeness, and then back to informal address, so that you'd forget how to speak to him.

Comrade Colonel Tudor gestured toward the armchair opposite him and opened a silver cigarette case with oriental incrustations. Extremely oriental.

"Thank you, but I don't smoke anymore," whimpered the spindly one.

"They're Kent cigarettes. Imperialist. Marvelous."

The culprit knew the brand of American cigarettes preferred by officials, a sort of elitist symbol, a bribe to be given to doctors, butchers, lawyers, limousine mechanics, gas station attendants, and other intermediaries without whom the everyday world could not function. The elegant colonel lit a long cigarette. His guest persisted in staring at the imposing furniture.

"Yes, it's not a typical office. I see you admiring the furniture and mirrors. They match the position, like my own attire. Passport Services! You made a request for a passport once."

The agent's immense hand was too massive for the thin cigarette and its wisp of circling smoke.

"Ah, that was a long time ago. A very long time ago. My application was denied several times, then I gave up."

"What about now? Would you still give up now?"

The interrogated kept silent. In fact, long as he was, he barely could be seen, lost in the trough of the armchair.

"Now the situation in this country is worse. Right? A real disaster! That's what you proclaim to everyone."

"I do?" the shadow in the armchair whimpered.

"Yes, of course, that's what you tell everyone. Friends

and strangers. Friends who I dare say aren't the most peace-loving."

"But how . . . " the spindly one stammered, increasingly distraught.

"Just so! You are known to mix more and more frequently with groups that pretend to be patriotic, too patriotic. Hence suspect! Increasing squalor, the blabbermouths say, increased surveillance, the tyrant's hijinks. That's the kind of clichés you soak up."

Comrade Colonel had a pleasant voice and a piercing gaze; he had just lit another Kent cigarette, which he held between two thick fingers. Collapsed in the armchair, the citizen was silent. His gaze took in the mirrors on the walls, which stood in place of the standard official portraits. Not a single portrait here, not even of that Most Beloved Son of the People, or of his wife, Bitty, with teeth and a sickle of gold.[4] Only mirrors in bizarre frames.

"Let's drop it. That's not why I've summoned you. You are not being investigated, the investigations take place elsewhere. This is Passport Services. Ah, yes, let's not forget! Another cliché you propagate is that informants have multiplied. That's why you've painted your door red, like the warnings on high voltage transformers—Danger of Death! Childish things. It's not a coincidence your colleagues claim that you're childish. If informants have multiplied, they won't be scared by a little proletarian red."

The wispy Kent rings raised their smoky eulogy to the dramatic sketch being acted out. The officer was cordial, elegant, slicked with all the oils his role required.

"A catastrophic multiplication, that's what you maintain. Mushrooms after the rain, a rain of hail, poison, and brimstone, that's what you say. One in four citizens? A quarter of the Republic's population? And who do you think would process such a mountain of information? What division of analysts, psychiatrists, and propagandists would have sufficient personnel to study the files that choke our cabinets? How many daily arrests do you estimate possible, given so many denunciations? How many? Have you thought about that? Have you ever mused on that unsolvable mathematical dilemma? A reduction unto death, that is how the trick is usually explained, but does that explain the lack of arrests? Have you ever thought about us, the poor operators, suffocating under the weight of an archive that grows hour by hour, exponentially? Or of the frustration felt by those unable to act? Are we intelligent enough, patient enough, calculating enough, are we Buddhist enough to keep everything in check, on the down low, until the appropriate moment? What do you think? After all, we are not allowed to act, those are the instructions! All we can do is provide adequate storage for the information and keep it up to date. We don't need media scandals, like the ones they have in that putrid Occident . . . We're no longer living under Stalinism, our operational strategy is no longer based on arrests. You've figured this out, and you profit from it, and God be praised! We don't arrest anyone, but we store information. People know this, or rather the kingdom of subjects knows it, given that we have one informant for every four citizens, if it's as you say. So. What if, let us say some of your friends, patriots all . . . might be among the one in four citizens who have become informants? Wouldn't we know everything you gossip about in that future's backstage of yours?"

The colonel was right. The long-as-a-board captive made

himself smaller and smaller in the armchair which did not protect him.

"That's not why I've summoned you. Not because of that. The passport has been approved. That's the big news! Meaning, we've decided to give you a passport. I won't explain, but it's not by chance. It's not a matter of chance, the enviable news is not a chance matter."

The dumbstruck one tucked away his amazement into the armchair. He hadn't expected such a blow. The nightmare with the two agents and the yellow envelope had prepared him for a meeting of this kind, but of course the bloodhounds could sniff out even dreams and had prepared a blow to match—not delivered by the expected captain or major but by this quasi-actor reflected in the mirror-like walls of the sacred precinct.

Could the big news be a trap? A trap meant to increase the number of informants? The speechless, spindly one co-opted?

"I've told you that I've given up," the astonished one stammered at last.

"Why? Because your application was denied a few times? That's standard. Vanity has no place here. The endorsements are few, even your playmates know this. Don't you want to see your sister again? As far as we know, the pair of you have a close relationship. A *very* close relationship. The relationship with your sister overseas is *very close*."

"Agatha?" murmured the little one in the armchair.

"Wasn't it Tamar? Or Tamara. Term of endearment Amaretta, no?[5] Or Mara? I'm joking, yes, only joking. I know you baptized her Agatha. That's how you refer to her in the letters you send, and we have decoded this moniker!"

So, the informants. One out of four honorable people knew of the close, too close relationship between him and Agatha, though they did not know its real meaning. Tamar, called Tamara; they had no idea how Agatha really figured in, they didn't know all of it. Mysteries accessible only to the initiated. This was indeed significant news, well worth the visit to the headquarters of the State Security Services.

"Yes, yes, Tamara, not Agatha."

"You're giving up then? Really giving up? Maybe, by some chance, you find yourself unable to leave behind your patriot friends, or the homeland foundering in squalor and tyranny, or the idiot informants and their idiot bosses?"

"Yes, I give up," whimpered His Muteness.

The colonel was sucking on a new capitalist cigarette.

"Just like that, you're giving up? You'd rather stay here under the terror? That's what your friends say, that the squalor and terror have increased."

"I can't leave the country, not now. Together to the bitter end, this country and I."

"You've chosen to abandon your own sister! Or you urged her to abandon you . . . Save yourself, that's what you told her. And Günther? What about him? Your friend Günther, the communist unhappy with our communism. Balkan, is what he used to say, not communist. And now, the so-called free press, meaning the press in the pay of the capitalists, writes that we are expelling the two minorities that are, after all, essential to this country: the Germans, sober and hardworking, and your coreligionists."

"I don't have a religion," grumbled the Member of the Minority.

It had become quiet, then completely quiet. Not even the

stirring of a spider could be heard, nor did the words manage to reach the agent.

"So you don't wish to leave the country that's persecuted you? True heroism! Leave your country? Leave *that?* But how could you? Are we little children, comrade? We are big kids, comrade, we both know this! Even though some are babies given to mischief and pranks, and it won't end well for them, even if they have an identity card and a union card, maybe even a Party one. Oh, you can't abandon the poor dissident children? What does your brother-in-law say, comrade? For a few years now, he has made strenuous efforts—in both a personal and official capacity—to have this passport approved."

"But it hasn't been approved despite all his efforts. It was not approved."

"Now it has been! We, too, fix our mistakes; we're human, not monsters as your friends seem to think. We make mistakes, then we fix them, then we make others, and we'll fix them. But whatever you want! You decide. I've notified you that it's been approved. You can see your sister and brother-in-law again. Nothing more to it. Maybe even Herr Günther. Or Genosse Günther. Isn't that how it goes among Marx and Engels's offspring? Genosse Günther."

The Authority had risen up on its short legs, and its guest had stood up as well. A long, thin walking stick. He was asking himself if this meeting had something to do with his patriot friends, or his Yankee brother-in-law, or the Marxist German.

"And, naturally, you'll come back here! After a month or two, you will come home. To the homeland. To your friends. The point of departure is also the point of return. And one's birthplace is irreplaceable. The geography of one's birth: a unique place! Which you are attached to, don't we know it. And you prove that. Very attached, it's obvious. Like your friend Günther. He, too, was one of those who didn't want to abandon the homeland of his ancestors—which they colonized eight hundred years ago! He wanted to stay, oh yes. He wanted to criticize us, he insisted we're all mixed up, that our communism is a primitive put-up job. A play, a circus. Behold, the two of you have something in common!"

The suspect was silent. The cigarette smoke was thin and perfumed, like an illicit pleasure.

"You have some time to think about it. The passport will be waiting for you here. Your stay abroad can be extended at our embassy, if you feel that you need an extension."

The passport was not a chance occurrence, but how would the generosity of the Authority have to be repaid? Did the American brother-in-law have to pander to his wife's homeland?

The cigarette was at an end, the hearing was at an end, and the smoke was thinning. The colonel was no longer smiling.

"Do you still go to the theater? Increased squalor, increased tyranny, but the theater endures! Extraordinary theater, some of the best in the world, right? So many talented people—wonderful! The national stage is always lively, even in hard times. The stage is lively, the street is lively, like the football field, the restaurant, the markets, and the songs and jokes. Admit it, even the jokes. That's how we mend our spirits, at the bodega, the markets, and in the steam baths. And at the circus, naturally. I've read your essays on the circus. I've read them carefully. I know they're not easy for the average person. I read them with pleasure and objectivity. I didn't look for any subtext. I don't go in for that, I don't lay traps."

The state-paid Actor continued to wait for the man he was investigating to answer, while at the same time, continuing to honor him with provocative interpretations. The anticipated replies were not delivered.

"Our people tried to contact you several times, you didn't seem enthusiastic. We understood, we left you alone. In the not very peaceful peace of unpeaceful friends. So, what do you want to do about this passport? The much dreamed of passport, the much dreamed of sister. Or the Berliner Günther, the implacable communist, the dreamer. The incurable dreamer."

"I will think about it. You've been very kind, thank you. I will think about it, it's an important decision."

Yes, it was important. Had become important ever since the theater had also . . . it wasn't just the squalor, but the theater, too, which had become grotesque. He paused, while the tiny colonel watched him from below.

"Could I have a cigarette?" The subject of the investigation smiled.

The colonel did not smile but promptly produced the cigarette case from his pocket.

"Of course. It seems you've decided then. The passport means fine cigarettes. Of course. Though, I did think Doctor Sima had broken you of the habit some time ago, several years ago in fact. The four-eyes with the thick, bifocal blinkers, Edward, who also treated you for that illness, or syndrome, some syndrome, I can't recall. No, I do recall, it was RP, yes, I think that's what it was called. Reality Phobia, yes. RP. A fear of reality, I think that's what it was deemed. Doctor Edward Sima thought that an adventure by land or by sea would be the definitive cure. You haven't talked with him in a long time. Maybe too long?"

The mute one felt paralyzed, frozen in place. The final blow had been powerful, masterful. He saw he had forgotten about the cigarette, though the comrade colonel's lighter continued to burn. He bent down, lit the cigarette, and bowed again to thank the Authority, which had extended its large white hand.

THE LONGEST NIGHT

On the night of his suicide, which did not occur, his relief came in the form of a pack of cheap cigarettes (strong, stinking shag), a cheap bottle of wine (plonk, as it is called among the people), and long pauses between unanswerable questions. Until dawn, when the answers made questions unnecessary.

The end masquerading as a new beginning? Another exile . . . after how many? He had become accustomed to exile in his own birthplace, which, in turn, and little by little, had annihilated his emancipatory reflexes. He saw again the all-knowing smile of the comic opera colonel.

"You have suffered since childhood, we know this. Like your sister," the all-knowing colonel had informed him. Like your sister or *like* your sister?

"Enough," mumbled the sufferer.

"Did you say something?" the Actor inquired.

"No, nothing," the walking stick answered, repeating, in his mind, "no more enough no more."

No more Comrade Tudor, given that I still have the where-withal to walk, eat, sleep, and even listen to a proposal for liberation at the headquarters of the State Security Division! A therapeutic solution, it seems, according to the opinion of your collaborator, Doctor Edward Sima. The specialist should have told you that the reflexes necessary for rebirth cannot overcome the reflexes of the larva. But you know this, you've trained us both, taught us the lesson of drifting off, of dozing in pointless waiting in the little cell with the bloody door that bars unwelcome guests. I got my diploma of autodidact-stoic waiting, wandering among books and nightmares, disdaining the frantic pursuit of riches and adventure, of joy's phantoms. RP syndrome? Yes, I proudly brag of my successful diminution, my loss of vitality, of survival instincts. To make my way in the world . . . whereto and why? My isolation in the red cell sires infinite imaginary vistas, and they are boundless and inaccessible to the poor conquerors of the quotidian, dizzy as they are with the smoke of gilded cigarettes.

"We know, know all too well what the nightmare of the concentration camp where you lost your parents has meant to you. Wartime, what can one do . . . We know, and, more importantly, we can imagine. Our profession obliges us to imagine."

"Yes, comrade colonel, with the passing of the years the captive has become indifferent to captivity," the silent one had wanted to answer.

"Did you say something?" the professional questioner had asked again.

"No, nothing," had answered the one under questioning,

continuing to repeat to himself silently that comrade Tudor was right to disdain the illusion of change, and that the passport could be the only honorable change. There, on another shore, waited Tamar, dubbed Tamara. "Mara Amaretta," whose brother was the only one who had any right to conflate her with Agatha, the mystery's code name.

He thought her departure had redeemed him from feeling the still-fresh wounds to their familial ties, but he had not ceased longing after the ghost of Agatha, as he secretly called her. Though he had not confessed it to himself, had not had the courage to confess it to himself. Now, in the endless night, in the cigarette smoke, under the influence of the loathsome wine's poison, he was thrown back again into the past that had not passed.

Exile, then! An exile that was not the exile of his childhood of barbed wire. Exile! Liberation from squalor and tyranny, a parting of ways with the spies who had multiplied like mushrooms after the rain of false promises. Rebirth, the nth, who could keep count! Rebirth after his long, unfinished death, and a regression toward infancy. He remembered the day he had left the concentration camp, the end of the war, the cheers of the captives, the long and bony arms of Deborah, mother of Tamar, the baby. Debi, the aunt who had become his mother, held him tight against her chest, wracked by sobs. Aunt Debi the younger sister of his mother, who had died after a few months in the camp. Debi, who had become his father's lover, his father the widower who had also been swallowed up by the fiendish night a year later. The wretches kept changing death's name. First typhus, then cancer, then tuberculosis, then *inanis,* inanition, inanimation, they themselves no longer knew what to call the curse.

The sudden appearance of the angel Tamar, born of Deborah and her brother-in-law, who had become her lover, had been the sacred sign of hope. The sobs of the ghosts mad with joy could not be forgotten. Debi's sobs. Debi mother of Tamar, who had become stepmother to the orphan who, frightened, clasped her hand so as to not lose her, so as not to be lost, so as to not have happen what already had happened to his mother and father swallowed up by nocturnal tigers.

No, he would not go! He would stay. He would stay to the end by his mother Debi's graveside, wrapped in his sister Tamara's letters. With her he had gone from one orphanage to the next and from her he could not part even in sleep, attached to the same placenta, like conjoined twins. Here, in the country of his birth, he had become an initiate in the connivances of submission. Here, he had fallen in love with words and had deceived himself into believing that he lived not in a country but in a language. No, no he did not feel prepared to surrender to deafness and dumbness in the Paradise of Prosperity, even if Mr. Brother-in-Law at last had yielded to his wife's demands to bring her little incestuous brother to the World Beyond and World to Come.

He sucked on the cigarette that stank. He could have gotten hold of Kents like those of Comrade Tudor . . . They were sold on the black market at ten times the price, like the good wine, stolen from the luxury cellars of the Authority. No, Comrade Doctor Sima, I no longer try to protect myself from our stinking shag, nor from their perfumed shag, no, nor from this sour, poisonous plonk.

"There's not enough poison," he had grumbled unheard when Comrade Investigator had found an opportune moment to be compassionate toward one of the survivors of the Final Solution. "Since early on you have suffered, just like your sister," the Authority had recited, without expecting an answer. It didn't bother to come.

Enough, Comrade Colonel! The venom of suffering was inefficient, given that the one who had been raised from the dead persisted in playacting the quotidian and dozing in the large armchair of the State Security Division. The concentration camp? The persecutions? No, not a word! I will not take part in your hypocritical scenarios! I will be silent, like someone dead, like someone executed and rendered up to the crematorium, I will not give you the chance to perform the libretto of opportunist compassion, assign you any verse of lachrymose discourse.

The colonel had been taught meticulously when and how to use the musical score. It was no longer about a passport but about one's relationship to the powers that be, that was why a colonel—rather than a captain or a major—had been chosen. Someone schooled in polite manners and polished behavior, someone ready to make a good impression on the future defector, be it Günther, evacuated to his fellow Teutons, or this expert in the world of the circus, who at the very end had been honored with the "Sima blow," so that he might be driven mad.

Edward Sima? Ed? No! It could not be! The brothers Ed had been dark haired, their hair and mustaches slicked with shoeshine, whereas Doctor Sima was bald and paunchy, blue-eyed like an angel, perfectly reputable.

Maybe a premonition, is that what the Ed twins had heralded? But who could have guessed that the nightmare had been a premonition? Doctor Edward Sima had impeccable integrity, no one would have been foolish enough to doubt it . . . the psychiatrist, who it now appeared was also a police informant, zealously guarded his reputation and fee schedule.

The name Agatha was the only thing the hounds had not sniffed out. Too complicated for them to search through libraries for the volume that had inspired the man under investigation to consider himself "a pariah without qualities" with a sister rich in mysteries. "Have you forgotten who deported you and killed your parents?" Agatha had asked him after he refused to follow her.

"But I would never have known you otherwise," the two-bit player had grumbled. "Hatred toward the Messiah's killers, the sidelocked money lenders?" the brother had asked rhetorically, annoyed. "I know about this, I knew what hatred means both before and after the camps—the perpetual suspicion, the perpetual persecutions and envy that define our current hell."

He had not followed Agatha. The cynic had stayed behind to study the history of the circus and to scrutinize the national performance of utopia as farce. Though, in fact . . . no—this had not been the reason. A fear of the nameless, FN, but also of the too well-known named Agatha. "Yes, I'm staying behind, I couldn't stand becoming a wanderer, as I've been told time and again that I am. Should I be a speck in the desert, my only identity conferred by a salary defined by American pragmatism?" the doctor in art history and the history of the circus had replied to the American journalist turned brother-in-law. Bitten by a stray hound, the journalist had been laid up in the Hospital for Infectious Diseases, where he had come upon a beautiful lady doctor. The victim of canine rabies became a sleepwalker in thrall to her blinding radiance. Her brother now saw Agatha in the glass of yellowish plonk and through the poisonous smoke rings, repeating, over and over, the same humble refrain, which she herself had taught him: "But your mom and dad, and your uncles and aunts, all left behind in graves in foreign forests? Do they not matter? How about my mom, who became your mom and made us orphans in the home for strays?"

He sucked from the poisoned cigarette and the poisoned wine again, scrutinizing his sister, who had strayed throughout the waters in the glass, which shook in his sweaty hand.

"I don't want to carry those shadows with me into a foreign world. I'm staying put, in the squalor and terror. Among friends, spies, and policemen whose deportment equips them to play the quadrille of adaptation. I'm used to them now, and I don't have enough strength left to learn the manners of prosperity." Then, he had murmured without conviction: "If I stay, you have to stay, too." He had heard the glass's whispered reply and did not want to hear it: "If I leave, you, too, have to leave."

He had not left, and it was now later than before. What did he have left to sell on the free market, what skills did he possess, what could he offer and to whom? The doctorate in the history and art of the circus? He was not a real doctor like Agatha, nor was he blessed with her charm. The bottle was empty, the pack of cigarettes was not yet empty. Agatha was still there, shocked, as on previous occasions, by the whims of her little brother who had made up his mind to gulp down the guilt of having survived without having suffered enough—as he insisted—without having died enough, like so many others, to the last drop. "I'm no longer able to compete, little sister. Perhaps I've never been able to. I am the shadow without qualities, like the author you deny used to say.[6] I can't be a house painter, or a driver, or a magician, I'm caught in the chains I've created for myself. I'm not nostalgic, I believe in the vanity of the ash we will all become after we have passed through the ovens of our illusions. Yes, you're right, we'll talk on the phone, as usual. And we won't have the courage to atone. Once again, we won't have the courage or the decency to end the farce, to tie ourselves up with the TNT cord of the telephone, wired to the explosives of longing."

Agatha smiled silently at his old claptrap. The well-known irresistible smile shamed the stutterings of the circus player who would soon run toward the airport, sweating, toward freedom and adventure, and toward the future named Agatha, baptized so by a reader who considered himself to have no qualities. But no, he wouldn't leave. It was only the putrid, sinful wine that had made him insolent, ready to spew up all his uncertainties. Stretched out naked on the floor, near the bleeding door, he listened to the glass, which hissed furiously, in a staccato voice: "You can't compete, that's what you think, you two-bit player? When, as godless orphans, we began to swallow textbooks whole, to work at anything, sleep anywhere, eat what fell from the sky, when we refused to give up, where was the apathy to which you now dedicate yourself with so much callowness? Commonsense questions, little brother! All you have to do is look around and take in the market fair of lying slogans to find the strength to break through the bloody door and abscond far away from the country that bore us and tossed us into the abyss and then resurrected us for its dressage of experimental animals. Have you turned stubborn again, as when you were a child, when you had discovered your own weaknesses and shut the door firmly against everyone? I think you've forgotten my name. I'm no longer Tamar. Not Tamara, Tara, Ara, I am Agatha, and only *you* know this. From now on I'll only be Agatha, as you decided once upon a time, when we spoke the same language."

The same language? The language of the past, which continues to disappear by the second? No, leaving doesn't solve anything! A Fata Morgana, a new illusion in the desert. Further vanity. "No, don't hang up, listen to me, believe me, you're just putting things off again, straying even further away. That's all, all, please do understand me, you who understand everything and could not fail to understand now."

The face had disappeared from the glass, but the voice persisted, faintly, more faintly, he tried not to lose it. "I am not Agatha! I'm not a character in a book but a human woman in the flesh of my mother and your aunt. I am real even if far away, far too far. I'm not Agatha but Tamar. Don't drive me away into a book, farther away than I already am, just so that you can meet me in the void anytime, clasped by shadows without qualities rather than by you, my real brother, with real qualities and real defects. You can't leave the sepulcher of books in which you've walled yourself up! Their leaden covers! They're really what you can't bear to part from, yourself you cannot part from! The vanitas of your walls!"

Stretched out on the floor, near the door, he extended his hand to find the pack of foul cigarettes and didn't find it. As he had desired, he was drunk that night with miserable alcohol and poisoned that night with miserable cigarettes in the squalor of the paradise where he had been sent to die, then resurrected, suspected, spit upon. He could not leave.

"It's yourself you cannot part from, isn't it?! Yourself! That's the curse!" His little sister knew him well. "Everywhere you go, you're still yourself. It's the bookshelves that are the *vanitas vanitatum,* little brother, not the adventure of finding me once more. You are offered a magical chance at a life after all this, the afterlife! *Vanitas* next to Agatha! Rebirth! Once happy, you will regress to ages past. And you'll see as you did before, grow up again, as before, next to Agatha!"

He heard her, and he did not hear her. He was drunk and tired, and he could not find the cigarettes he had not tried for more than a decade. He could not manage to get hold of the pack. His hand only grazed, again and again, the empty wrapper and the empty bottle that had rolled near the corpse that had not succeeded in dying.

THE DICTIONARY

exile, n.

1.a. Prolonged absence from one's native country or a place regarded as home, endured by force of circumstances or voluntarily undergone for some purpose. Also: an instance or period of this.

1.b. Banishment to a foreign country, or (more fully *internal exile:* see *internal* adj. and n. compounds) to a remote part of one's own country, according to an edict or judicial sentence.[7]

———

wanderer, n.

1.a. A person or thing that is wandering, or that has long wandered (in various senses of the verb); one that is of roving habit or nature. Also *figurative* or in figurative context.

2.a. Zoology. Used as translation of various modern Latin terms of classification; a bird of the group *Vagatores* in Macgillivray's system; one of the wandering spiders (*Vacabundæ*).[8]

wander, v.

1.a. Of persons or animals: To move hither and thither without fixed course or certain aim; to be (in motion) without control or direction; to roam, ramble, go idly or restlessly about; to have no fixed abode or station.

3.a. Of persons (or things completely, or in part, personified): To deviate from a given path, or determined course; to turn aside from a mark or object proposed; to stray from one's home or company, or from protection or control.[9]

wandering albatross, n.

1. large white albatross (*Diomedea exulans*) of southern oceans that has black outer wing feathers and a wingspan of about 11 feet (3.4 meters).[10]

Brazilian wandering spider, n.

1. any of a genus (*Phoneutria*) of large, venomous, nocturnal spiders of tropical South America that do not build webs and actively hunt prey by traveling on the ground. NOTE: Brazilian wandering spiders adopt a characteristic aggressive de-

fense posture in which their front legs are raised straight up into the air.[11]

"Wandering Jew" in *wandering,* adj.

n. A legendary personage who (according to a popular belief first mentioned in the 13th century, and widely current at least until the 16th century), for having insulted Jesus on his way to the Cross, was condemned to wander over the earth without rest until the Day of Judgement. Often referred to as the proverbial type of restless and profitless travelling from place to place. Cf. French *le juif errant,* German *der ewige Jude.* For the application to trailing plants see sense 2e. In the earliest form of the legend, the Wandering Jew is called Cartaphilus; in the best-known modern version his name appears as Ahasuerus, but other names also occur.[12]

refugee, n.

1.a. A Protestant who fled France to seek refuge elsewhere from religious persecution in the 17th and 18th centuries, esp. following the revocation of the Edict of Nantes in 1685. Now *rare* (*historical* in later use).

1.b. gen. A person who has been forced to leave his or her home and seek refuge elsewhere, esp. in a foreign country, from war, religious persecution, political troubles, the effects of a natural disaster, etc.; a displaced person. Also *figurative* and in extended use.

1.c. In negative sense: a person who is fleeing from justice, deserved punishment, etc.; a runaway, a fugitive. In later use only with *from,* esp. in *refugee from justice.*

1.d. A migratory bird. *Obsolete. rare.*[13]

AND THE EVENING AND THE
MORNING WERE THE SECOND DAY

The calendar performed its appointed task: once upon a time, or every time, or at no time ever.

A feast day: Uprooting. A clear, cold day, the sky far off. Having retrieved the green passport from the Authority's service counter, he heeded the dictums of prudence and confidentiality as required. They protected him both from envious friends and from the nagging questions of spies. He knew that the offer—chance, trap, privilege—could be rescinded anytime; he also knew that the laws of suspicion that kept the apparatus of power in motion would not evaporate once the captive had escaped, that the marketplace for souls and rewards would continue to send its middlemen by land, by sea, or by air, anywhere they might be necessary.

The ritual of Customs had proceeded slowly but without incident, the suitcase ransacked item by item, shirts, ties, scarf, gloves, shoes, slippers, pajamas, the atomic bomb nowhere in sight. At last, he faced the final official, who regarded him carefully, silently. The passenger stared in turn, trying to guess whether his hippy looks would arouse suspicion. He was freshly shaved, both head and face. He wore freshly washed jeans and a white shirt, dry-cleaned, under a slick bomber jacket, navy blue with large chest pockets. On his face: gangster movie sunglasses.

"Passport, please."

The hand moved to the left breast pocket of the jacket: a thin yellow booklet, notebook-like. Quickly, he pushed it back in place.

"No, no, please don't rush. Let's see what you have there."

Intimidated, the traveler held out the yellow booklet.

"What's that? What in god's name is that, you freeloader?"

Like the guard, the "freeloader" kept silent, his heart pounding. A long, shared silence.

"A guidebook. For the trip," ventured the traveler at last, stuttering.

Insulted, the guard woke up.

"What did you say? A guidebook? Something that small, that tiny, tiny enough to be hidden in a pocket? What kind of guide can it be? Is it code? Maybe it's in code. Is that it? Is that it!"

The yellow booklet was now being held up, was nearly glued to the intense gaze of the vigilante who had decided to decipher it.

"A-del-bert. A-delbert," the official syllabized. "What's that? What the hell is that? It can't be a foreign passport."

"No, no, pardon, I mixed up the pockets," stuttered the unlucky one. "This is just, well, just for reading, on the plane. To pass the time . . . on the trip."

"What is it? A travel guide? How to sway in the big sky bird is it? How to weather any storm is it? Wunder. Wundersa-me," syllabized the soldier.

"It's a story, a fairytale for children," the suspect answered calmly.

"For children? Did you say it's for children? A guide for children? But, if I'm not wrong, you're no longer a child. No, I can see you're not."

The official took his measure of the guilty one top to bottom and bottom to top, then gazed at him sideways. No, he was not mistaken: Little Bo Peep was no longer a child. An idiot maybe, but not a child. He turned to the other officer, who was inspecting the suitcase of a corpulent old lady.

"John, get your butt over here!"

John wandered over, pink and plump.

"What do you think this is, John? German? Do you know any German?"

"Nah. Let's show it to Comrade Captain. Comrade Captain Dobre has one of those big German dogs, a Doberman. Charlie Doberman. Maybe he knows German."

Official Number One seemed to find Official Number Two funny, but he turned, looking even more suspicious if such a thing were possible, toward the liar who was no longer a child.

"Re-claim, Phi-lipp Reclam. Jun. Stutt-gart. Universal, Universal Bi-Bibliothek."

And then, suddenly, a trick! The little brochure disappeared into the back pocket of the shiny official uniform.

"Not allowed! No printed matter can be removed from the country without prior approval. The approval of the appropriate authorities! The Ministry of Internal Affairs! Especially not foreign publications in foreign languages. Not without approval! You can file a petition and wait for approval!"

The passenger did not protest. The unlawful object would be safe in the Official Pocket, protected from chance and accidents.

Official Number One took another vigilant step, snapping the flap on his back pocket. He was now examining and re-examining the passport photo against the original who stood before him. A minute examination. Time enough to exercise your memory.

It had been a rainy Saturday, there was a long wait at the photographer's that day; the client was armed with a pack of Kents, German chocolate, and fine soap (French)—one of the marvels would have to work. The photographer, however, did not even look up at the client. Nor did the blonde, fat cashier woman, to whom he had tried to explain that he needed a photo without any touch-ups. In no case was he to look like a babe in the cradle still in love with fairytales, as he had in other photographs by other photographers. He needed his wrinkles and age spots fully on display. At the final frontier, the photo had to inspire trust.

Smiling and plumping her peroxided curls, the cashier had listened to his demands and at last had allowed herself to be convinced, as by a capricious child, receiving (clearly touched) the Kents, the soap, and the chocolate. She rose heavily from behind the cash register and circled the owner trembling and shaking. Bing bang boom, and the photo was done! The professional had moved on to the next customer. Now, pursing her lips, the obese cashier tried to temper the objections of the walking stick. She was sweating due to the excess effort and pounds, repeating that a little forbearance went a long way, especially when one finally saw oneself in a high-class photo. Small discrepancies between an original and a reproduction were normal, expressive, and yes, thank you very much for these fine cigarettes, my sister smokes and she'll be in seventh heaven, and yes, I've also heard of this famous brand of soap, I'm thinking about tonight's bath, and the chocolate, of course, I'm a reprobate, I can't help myself when it comes to sweets, but don't worry, really, there's nothing to worry about. The lips are ironically half open, as required, the thick eyebrows indicate your daring and strike a fine balance with your more timid side, though naturally you are not timid, after all your ears are small, fine, and your eyes, what more can one say, you have a gaze that will pursue me when I make use of the swoon-worthy pleasures you've so kindly given me.

The passenger was holding the passport that had reappeared—how? when?—in his hands.

"Nomad, eh? That's what they call you, right? Or at least, that's what they used to call you . . . "

The nomad made a noncommittal sound. Was that how the spies referred to him? In his student days his classmates had nicknamed him "Suitcase," because he kept moving from one rented room to another. Might there have been informants among his classmates or landlords? Why not, why ever not, but a long time had passed since then, pointless time. Maybe time that stood still in the archives of the bloodhounds. Yes, Suitcase, that's who I am, that's what my once-upon-a-time colleagues used to call me. Destiny always speaks through the mouths of sinners, and here is one, disguised as an airport official.

Should he ask him if he was called Ed? Password: Ed? The Nomad! Had it been a premonition of some sort? Nomad . . . Premise, premonition, predestination . . . Ed, the poor Cerberus, was right to laugh at the dumb mug of the walking stick with half-open lips and eyebrows raised in surprise. That official grinned, he grinned beneath his red mustache. No, he didn't grin, the venom had not yet become a grin, it was only the thin, predatory sneer of someone in authority.

"Good to go. Everything A-OK! We declare you OK, we are letting you go forth into the world," the officer announced, gesturing to the Nomad to walk forward, toward the bird that would carry him any which way.

Did he bleed entering the airplane? Not at all. He had imagined his departure from himself as a kind of bleeding out. As if, in exchange for his passport, he had agreed to a surgery that would cut off his tongue. Now, the team of professionals was gathering up its barbaric instruments. The old blood would issue forth again. No anesthesia? Rusty, barbaric instruments. He waited, tense, for the blood to spurt from his brain, heart, belly—and why not—from his eyes, from the gaze accustomed to a lifetime of the same scenery, from the ears that had become so accustomed to the phonetics of his biography. Yes, he waited, both resigned and horrified, but nothing happened. Nothing. Nothing. Who could have imagined it?

He swayed, climbing the boarding stairs; he appeared dizzy and, in fact, was so. Undone, he burrowed into the narrow window seat. Head tightly gripped in sweaty palms, suitcase heaved above dizzy head. Exhausted, the passenger rested in the womb of the flying beast.

He flew, left, escaped, was liberated, unshackled, uprooted. Toward nowhere.

"You don't feel well?" the stewardess asked.

The pallid passenger did not respond. He concentrated, trying to remember the first words in the little yellow brochure confiscated at Customs. The first sentence, at least the first. *Nach einer glücklichen . . . einer glücklichen, jedoch beschwerlichen Fahrt . . . jedoch für mich sehr beschwerlichen*

Seefahrt . . .[14] So, on the sea, a trip by sea, not by air. Lucky, yes, it appeared to be lucky, but very arduous. No mention of where from or where to, no mention of either. *Nach einer . . . für mich sehr beschwerlichen Seefahrt erreichten wir endlich den Hafen.*[15] A port, yes, the foreign shore, the shore of his uprooting.

"Let me give you an aspirin. We have special aspirin for those who have difficulties flying."

The pretty woman held out a pill and a glass of clear, crystalline poison. The patient wasn't astonished by this. He seemed asleep. The old Soviet plane shook maddeningly, as if trying to wake him, but no one seemed capable anymore of waking the Nomad, pallid as he was, withdrawn into himself, eyes closed, insensible and ascending. He was alone, alone, he hadn't succeeded in thinking his thoughts to Tamar, not even now, when he had so much to tell her.

He was speaking to the stewardess. He would speak to her when she brought him another glass of distilled poison and a cyanide capsule. He would speak to her.

"No, believe me, I didn't want to be a nomad. Neither did my friend Günther. You bestowed on him the great gift of belonging to his former fellow citizens from the German Empire, who paid for his passport, and it was pointless. I didn't know that Doctor Ed Sima also considered this a kind of therapy. I tried out adventure at a young age, as an innocent, and it didn't agree with me. It didn't agree with me at all, but I never managed to throw it up, it's still stuck somewhere in my guts, it's infected the entire nomadic machinery. It didn't agree with my beloved little sister Tamar either, nor with our parents, nor with others. Though I prefer defeat, and if it is necessary, I prefer the illusion of defeat, but, no, I didn't want to become a nomad again. I don't believe in Ed Sima's therapy. Here, in the place where I suffered and loved, where I learned how to speak and to write, and, most important, to read, here I saw the sea. The dispatcher of destinies will only send me the DNA of a wanderer, I know that. But I wanted to stay in one place. I don't believe I've suffered enough. And I'd gotten used to the tricks, the compromises, the compensations, the songs that replaced prayers, the old jokes made new for an improved hypnosis. Yes, I'd become used to it all. Only Tamar was missing. I admit it, I miss her. That's why I got drunk."

The stewardess had left but the patient continued to speak to her both in his mind and out loud. Difficult to stop him.

"Yes, I got drunk until I could no longer recall Agatha or myself, drunk with cheap wine, sick with cheap cigarettes. A long, toxic night to cure me of my stupidity. To throw me at long last out of that happy purgatory. To remove me far, far away into the afterworld, heaven or hell, whichever it might be, far away in any case, as far as possible. But, unbelievably, at the break of day, I woke up stupider than ever, surer than ever that I would be stuck in that paralysis of routine all my life. That simple arithmetic . . . I understood the doublespeak, the triple-, the multiple-speak, so many fluid meanings. I had even discovered the pleasure of probing the charades of survival. Taking precautions with metaphors, though tempted by them. I savored the slippages from fawning and sweet talk to fury and rancor, the humor of the enterprising, the code of the poets, the sensuality of women, I had friends and books and mountains and the sea, real joys."

"Did you call me?" the young woman with the perfect set of teeth inquired. "You've revived? I see that you've revived."

Yes, the lamentations once again. Befuddle Muddle was not at all sure about his decision to uproot. The lunkhead did not believe in resurrections, nor in rebirths. He had been initiated into skepticism and apathy, and he felt how the plane was removing him, removing him from himself, as he was: old, full of sores, and orphaned as he was. "It's unbearable like this, it's unbearable," friends and spies had repeated. "That's it! I've reached my limit." They were all exhausted, the spies and the friends who had become spies; the demonic absurdity of it had tired them all, at last. "What if you have another pain in your kidneys, like two months ago, when you couldn't find a taxi and that pig Mitu saved you, that informant with a car and all the schemes going on?" He shut then opened his eyes, as on the morning when he woke in the shadow of the two bloodhounds and the yellow envelope.

"Stop tormenting me with these memories, Agatha! Don't oppress me with your warnings, all I want is a little water. Water, water, just water from the sink, that's all."

Then Agatha had disappeared, like Tamar. He felt again the velvety hand of the official lightly touching his neck.

"All over, we're here. The others have already deplaned but it's good that you've had a chance to rest. You've revived. The rest took care of your panic."

Yes, there was nothing left to decide, the plane was empty.

THE PRIMORDIAL BED

Spinoza renounced his inheritance altogether except for one item: his parents' bed. The ledikant *would accompany him from* place to place, and he would eventually die in it. I find the fixation on the ledikant fascinating, by the way. Of course, there were practical reasons to keep the bed, at least for some time. A ledikant is a canopied, four-poster bed with heavy curtains that can be drawn to transform it into a warm, isolated island. In Spinoza's time, the ledikant was a sign of affluence. The common bed in Amsterdam houses was the armoire bed—literally, a bed inside a spacious wall closet, whose doors could be opened at night. But imagine holding on to the bed in which your parents conceived you, in which you played as an infant, and in which your parents died, and deciding to sleep there forever, live there, practically.[16]

Never mind how welcoming Amsterdam was, one cannot imagine Spinoza's young life without the shadow of exile. The language was a daily reminder. Spinoza learned Dutch and Hebrew and later Latin, but he spoke Portuguese at home, and either Portuguese or Castilian Spanish at school. His father always spoke Portuguese at work and at home. All transactions were recorded in Portuguese; Dutch was used only to deal with Dutch customers. Spinoza's mother never learned Dutch. Spinoza would lament that his mastery of Dutch and Latin never equaled that of Portuguese and Castilian. "I really wish I could write to you in the language in which I was brought up," he wrote to one of his correspondents. Manners and dress were another reminder that, prosperity aside, this was exile rather than the homeland.[17]

The recent history of Sephardic Jews forced Spinoza to confront the strange combination of religious and political decisions *that had maintained the coherence of his people through the centuries. I believe the confrontation led Spinoza to take a position on that history. The result was the formulation of an ambitious view of human nature that might transcend the problems faced by the Jewish people and be applicable to humanity at large.*[18]

THE REUNION

Einer glücklichen, jedoch beschwerlichen Fahrt.[19]

A lucky though arduous journey. He descended from the plane as unsteadily as he had ascended. Once again, he was going to see his former companion from Pioneer summer camp, Günther Buicliu, rebaptized Becker, after his German mother who had brought him to Berlin, beyond the Wall of Death between the East and West. Günther had been a zealous activist, one whom the boyish comrade destined to become a nomad had nevertheless succeeded in getting close to. Thus, little by little, he had found out some details regarding the private life of "Comrade Pioneer" Buicliu.

He was the son of Aristide and Ilsa, former owners of a beer factory renowned in the multicultural province of Transylvania where they lived. As if this weren't sinful enough, he had participated unenthusiastically in the Hitlerjugend, whose harsh physical exercises, rather than its ideology, had made him feel humiliated. After the war, embarrassed and guilty but proud of his party card, which redeemed him from his past, Günther had become a volunteer on a large construction site alongside other young communists. "With two Nazi uncles, I had a lot to make up for." Later, in the capital, he had reencountered his old teenage friend at the university. At one point, the latter had dreamed enthusiastically of a communist paradise, but since then had turned into a skeptic, a reader whom the bureaucrats at the Romanian Institute for Cultural Foreign Relations felt they needed to watch.

As might be expected, the pair's youthful comradery had survived; they saw each other often, and their heated discussions continued unabated. A former party activist, Günther had evolved, joining a singular and eccentric group made up predominantly of Germans and known both to themselves and to the secret police as "leftist dissidents." He invited his former friend to a few of the secret meetings, but later stopped doing so, so as not to expose him to danger unnecessarily. Günther's group was a true anomaly in a country where critique of the system came primarily from the nationalist right wingers and never from the leftists, who were allogeneic and quasi-invisible, a group that considered itself to have been betrayed by the officials in power.

Günther was contemplating the departure of his parents, redeemed as foreign exchange goods by the German State, which had lost the war but won on the peacetime bourse. He did not guess that he would soon follow them though he unexpectedly received an undesired passport, paid for by the West German capitalists at the behest of his mother, who had settled in Munich. His refusal to bend to Colonel Tudor's flattery, or to consider the offer of a Western Gomorrah passport had been pointless. At last, he surrendered. His self-appointed role as a good German communist—a rebel against comic book communism—suffocated him, as did the pantomime of small-time graft on the Wallachian street corner. Could there be Purity of Dogma in that burlesque bedlam? So he had left. His childish stubbornness had not helped him, so he'd gone without having found an answer to his dilemma.

Before departing, he had met with his former friend from the Pioneer group; he felt the need for a symbol on which to hang his departure. He asked for a commemorative exchange. Not of their old red Pioneer ties, but of another kind.

"Listen, buddy, this is what my frazzled brain's demanding. I want something to remember you by. Tit for tat, I promise."

In that historic moment in his friendship with Günther, the historian of the circus did not suppose that he, too, would one day depart for the abyss.

"Yes, yes, something to remember you by. I want your tallit, from your bar mitzvah. I'll give you my little Catholic necktie from my confirmation."

"I'm truly sorry. I haven't had that for a long time. I'm surprised you've held on to your scrap."

"My mother, she held on to it. Okay, I'll give you my necktie then."

The friend had examined it carefully and subsequently placed it in his closet, among some shirts, where he hoped that, eventually, little by little, its sacrality would diminish. After his turn came to accept a passport from the same Colonel Tudor, he was tempted to take Günther's necktie with him. He hesitated, however. What if the customs officers recognized the symbolic object? Naturally, he had not suspected that the mix-up at the at the border would come in the form of a German fairytale written by an agnostic Frenchman, the romantic poet Chamisso; agnostic, yes, like so many of his own friends. "No printed matter!" Customs Official Number One had informed him.

In the meantime, Günther had proven pigheaded even in Berlin. Having been contacted promptly both by the leftist anticommunists and by a famous writer who promised to launch him in the social-democratic press, he turned away both, refusing to declare publicly what was expected of him regarding the opportunism and tyranny of the homeland that had given him the boot: "I don't shit where I've eaten." At last it seemed that he had found a small group of independents who were not shy about critiquing both the left and the right, both depraved, rotten capitalism and state socialism, corrupt and criminal.

And now? Handsome Günther had gone gray, that's all that could be glimpsed from his growing bald spot. He smoked vehemently, his nicotine-stained fingers hinting at his failure to adapt and his cheeks deeply lined. They regarded each other nostalgically: their youth was long gone but they were still alive and standing in an enviable manly embrace. Günther led them toward the small anticapitalist car, a coquettish dwarf-sized box on wheels, just right for two bohemian immigrants. They sat down on the two aged seats. Günther felt like talking.

"You know where you've landed, don't you?"

"How could I forget. The curse of the nomad began here, in the Reichstag. It followed me, though I was still only at the age for playing hoop and stick."

"For now, let's forget about Adolf and his little mustache. There were eight hundred thousand inhabitants of this place in 1871; today, there are two million. No other city besides Chicago has ever experienced such rapid growth. A European Chicago, that's what Mark Twain thought. A dynamic, ugly city, a strictly functional one. One architect referred to it as 'the house without eyebrows.' Commerce took off quickly, in American fashion. Businesses, banks, luxury, hotels, brothels, modernism, mass industrialization. Until the locomotive became heavy artillery."

The passenger listened without paying attention; he understood that Günther was trying to put off starting the engine.

"The Beloved Adolf wanted granite buildings that would last forever, like himself. Granite probably quarried in the concentration camps. There were debates here at the time regarding the problem of skyscrapers. If we're Chicago, we can't avoid the Yankee stilts, many said. Even the Galician Christian convert, Joseph Roth, dreamed of resolving the lack of housing this way. The dilemma of the Tower of Babel. We will defy the heavens, we will defy the Omnipotent!"

"Where are we going?"

"To my place. A small monastic cell that will force us into untested proximities."

"Rathenau-Platz?"

"How did you know?"

"The address on your envelopes. The famous Jewish minister who was assassinated by the Teutons avenging Jesus. I once read his mother's letter to the assassin. Very moving."

The engine had started, the city awaited its guest with both commotion and elegance. Many parks, no skyscrapers.

"I once met Herr Rathenau."

"How? Before your birth? Did you dream of him?"

"I met the character Arnheim, described by Musil in *The Man Without Qualities*."

"That book's too thick! Those books . . . The novel's too long. I didn't have the patience to read it. But I know the biography of that liberal Rathenau. After his assassin was released from prison, he saved Jews. Maybe it was because of the letter from the victim's mother. Walter's mother, the man who was killed."

"Musil didn't have the chance to find that out."

"Prophecy was lacking among his many qualities. But he had others, hardly marketable ones."

"Did you know that in 1902, at the beginning of the century, Minister Rathenau wrote about the most beautiful city in the world? The Berlin in which you live."

"There wasn't a Wailing Wall between the East and West then. There were, however, the disabled playing barrel organs. The child Walter saw them when his grandmother took him to applaud the Emperor exiting the Palace. He imagined that the barrel organ player who had charmed him would offer up the song *The Most Beautiful City in the World* . . . He was admiring the street of the great Friedrich, not suspecting that in the future it would divide the city in two. And the Hercules Bridge and the famous Church of Saint Nicholas. Nabokov, too, praised the city during his exile in these parts. He saw myths in the sky and the stars of posterity, he spoke of his friend Pilgram, the entomologist, after whom the *Agrotis pilgrami* is named. He dreamed of distant islands and forests full of butterflies."

"Unbelievable, I'm really impressed with you. You have a room stuffed full of books. I can see that you've made many friends in your solitude."

Günther's dwarf-size room was full of books and cassette tapes. At the top of the building, no elevator, two minuscule windows. True bohemia, befitting the leftist professor of music.

"I see you've brought almost no luggage. That suits my birdcage. We have room for a mattress on the floor, on which the host, meaning myself, will sleep. You'll have my narrow ascetic's bed. We'll figure it out. The trick is to not spend too much time in the birdcage but to wander around Rathenau's most beautiful city instead. Meaning, around the capitalist half. I suppose you're not interested in the Eastern other half, in Germany's tyrannical utopia?"

"I might be. The famous Pergamon Museum, the other monuments . . . But I'd be afraid to pass over to the other side. The Stasi might grab me and send me on to Moscow."

"We'll limit ourselves to this side of the city then, sequestered as it is from the socialist kingdom to the east by Chinese Great Walls. The Western Vitrine! Perfect for spies and artists, and thus inspiring. Besides, that's what we'll do today, too. We'll go along the wall. Our side is covered with graffiti and full of impertinent slogans, as befits a newborn democracy. On the other side: machine guns. It's getting dark, we're nearing the end of the year, you'll see the fairytale lights of the city. It will do you good; I hear that in the Balkan Little Paris from whence you hail, the streets are dark."

"Yes, and the houses are freezing. An education in stoicism. An infirm, military socialism with a golden future."

The festive lights were, indeed, vividly on view everywhere. The city floated in lights and holiday garlands, the display windows were full of gifts and warm greetings. Only the Wall signaled that, on the other side, the scenography was more serious, that it had to be defended with guns. A small bodega in the Turkish quarter reminded the exiled pair of the good times of their youth and the gastronomy of their native places.

On the way back, Günther removed the magical object from an aged case and offered his interlocutor Telemann's *Fantasien für Flöte* as an homage to their meeting once again.

THE TEMPLE

The morning seemed welcoming, and the sleepy pair had decided to leave the birdcage as quickly as possible.

"Where to?" the voyager inquired.

"I propose the synagogue. Or the church, the mosque, whatever you want."

"But you know that I'm not . . . "

"I know, of course I know, but that's the traveler's job: to visit museums, churches, parks, it would only be a part of the ritual . . . Tourist sights, let us say."

Right at the bottom of the old apartment building in which Günther lived, on the first floor, was the headquarters of the bank where he would withdraw his spending money. A few clients stood at the counters, several more were lined up and waiting.

"This is the Temple of our times! The bank. Behold them!" Günther urged the newcomer. Parishioners waiting intently, praying to the God of the Bourse to bless their accounts . . . Yahweh, Buddha, Christ, Mohammed, Confucius, whatever pseudonym or coded name he might deign to take. They are shy, the parishioners. Yes, behold them! Unsure, restless, mute, tense . . .

In the sacred silence of the bank, indeed, they were. Lowered, pious gazes.

"I hope you're not tired, and we can attempt a first touristic incursion. I've set aside these few first days just for you. I suspect you're curious to see the relics of great Adolf."

"No, I'd prefer the Botanical Garden."

"The Botanical Garden? I didn't think you were a nature lover. I suppose you've fallen in love with Mr. Chamisso."

"Yes, I'm looking for the relics of the former botanist. First a poet, then a botanist. Von Chamisso. I've told you about the events at the airport and how they confiscated the fairytale of the shadowless man. I hope to replace it here, in some bookshop. Until then, I want to see what's left of Adelbert von Chamisso's memories. An exile, like us. A French nobleman, driven away by the French Revolution, landing on these shores as a young man in the service of the queen. Then the army, then his studies, and so on and so forth. It's said his entire circle of friends was from someplace else."

"Okay, we'll hit the Garden, too. Maybe I'll educate myself a bit more about the planet's flora. But since we're talking about the earth, we'll stop at the cemetery first."

"The cemetery? A tourist attraction?"

"That, too. A large cemetery where you can see the entire history of this glorious, sad nation inscribed."

It was quiet and clean in the metro, as in the immense cemetery with its large pathways and ancient trees. Famous names, princely tombs, grandiose inscriptions. Truly, the entire history of the kingdom. Beneath the sumptuous stones slept the elite of a great nation, capable of grand disasters.

"The majority of these long-departed superstars were nomads, like you, or fugitives and vagabonds, like me. They became generals and procurators, renowned doctors and bankers, well-known swindlers and high-end courtesans, medalist MPs and circus jugglers. Even highly esteemed church fathers. After all, the Führer, too, was a stranger, even if not one from distant parts."

Günther kept straightening a rebellious lock of gray hair.

"You're a writer's writer. The cemetery reminds us. An epigone at the beginning of a new cycle of migration. Cyclical like all beginnings. With a finale to celebrate here, in this place of eternal rest."

"Your humor didn't use to be morbid when we were Pioneers. We joyously wore our red neckties and chanted the slogans about our faithfulness to the great cause of Lenin and Stalin. Now we no longer have either slogans or faithfulness."

"You've retained something of that."

"Not from the infantile slogans. And yet . . . the illusions . . . progress, isn't it?"

"A progressive dissident? An exile rather. I've been exiled to the homeland of my ancestors from eight hundred years ago, who in turn had self-exiled themselves to the Balkans as colonists and colonizers. Exile and again, exile . . . Your coreligionists eventually got used to exile, didn't they? They kept trying it out, they even created values based on it . . . aspirations."

"Coreligionists? I don't have a religion, you know that."

They sat down. Günther looked at the tourist, who looked at the trees and was silent.

"I suppose you were hoping to see the bunker where the

Führer drank poison together with the undeflowered Virgin," Günther said, trying to restart the conversation. "Or perhaps the place where the officers' attempt against the parvenu failed. Or the place where he held forth hysterically. Hysterically but hypnotically, as is well known."

"No, no, the Botanical Garden was my tourist attraction. Louis Charles Adélaïde de Chamisso. Adelbert. The famous botanist . . . more famous than the poet he was also."

"We'll go tomorrow, I promise. These solemn trees as my witness, these sacred stones as my witness, I promise, and I'll keep my word. Tomorrow. But we'll take the Berdichev rabbi along."

"No, because he doesn't like atheists. The story goes that one Saturday, on the way to the synagogue, the rabbi meets the village hooligan, vagabond, lowlife. Atheist, too, of course. He is smoking serenely and inhaling the smoke with pleasure. 'What's this?' asks the rabbi. 'Smoking on the Sabbath? Don't you know it's forbidden? Did the doctor recommend it? You have some illness? The cigarette is a medical treatment?' 'Not at all,' comes the response. 'I smoke because I enjoy it. I only do what's enjoyable. I don't like doctors or rabbis. I'm an atheist.' 'An atheist, you say? And pray you, at what seminary did you study? Which yeshiva? You can't give up on something you don't know anything about. So, what yeshiva? What yeshiva made you an atheist?' That's the anecdote. A joke. It's a joke, and it's not a joke. What kind of atheists are we?"

They were silent once again, Günther once again straightened his lock of hair. No answer. Was he waiting for another question?

"Tell me why you're showing me the graves of well-to-do

German Jews? Jews who were more German than the Germans? Are you still obsessed with anti-Semitism?"

"Sure."

"The story about your mother's gynecologist? You told it to me one night at summer camp in Lipova. I can't remember the details."

Günther was silent. The question floated off into the surrounding treetops. After one, two, perhaps twenty-one, twenty-two seconds, the question delicately descended again toward Günther.

"That's not the only time. Not the only time I started having doubts. But if you must know, after the anti-Semitic persecutions began but before the expulsion of the Jews from our Transylvanian town, there was an interdiction in place forbidding Jews to work. This included doctors. My mother didn't want to give up her gynecologist, who was a Jew, and this was a problem for our family. You know, of course, that ethnic Germans like us sympathized with the Führer. Well, not quite all, my uncle Rudolf was an antifascist, and he almost got himself in hot water. In any case, on occasion, my mother's doctor, a pallid, myopic guy with a Viennese diploma, would show up late at night, secretly, and sequester himself in the bedroom with his patient. When it was time for him to go, my mother would shut the door carefully, having checked the street to make sure no one had seen. The whole affair is engraved in my memory both because it intrigued me, made me start to wonder about who we really were, and because it coincided with a period when I was no longer able to handle the physical exercises our class of young Nazis was subjected to. Then came the much-lauded peace! All the display windows featured photos of the concentration camps. Lies, of course! Winners' lies about the losers, as always . . . "

Günther stopped, winded.

"I went humbly to the pastor. He cared about me, his favorite student. I knew where he lived. 'We are executioners, murderers, we burned people alive because they were Jews.' The pastor listened to me and stroked my shoulder. He took me into the library an took out a large volume with a leather cover. 'Behold what we have written, we ourselves and not our enemies have recorded it. The German medieval chronicles offer ample details, both convincing and horrifying.' The German guilt, time and again! I carry it with me, as you know. I fight it, we cannot be separated. And now, I'll ask you: What is your illness called? Autism? Does it rhyme with mine? Autism, anti-Semitism? Meaning anti-anti-Semitism. Philo-Semitism?"

"No, not at all. They're not at all alike—our fixations. I am preoccupied with the circus. Exhibitionism, if you wish. It's essential. Essential to my earthly journey."

"And the Holocaust? Yours and ours . . . You've been stubbornly silent about it for years, as if it wasn't your story. I kept meaning to ask, but I couldn't find a way in writing." Günther had leaped up in anger. The bench shook briefly. "Never! Not one word about survival! Or the camps, the memories? You don't let Tamar talk about her mother or your mother either. Absolute silence, you weren't even there, it's all Greek to you, you understand nothing, you've never heard of it."

"Others speak out, many. A kikeish farce, they say. Jews are declared to be liars, profiteers, manipulators. A circus spectacle with noisy actors—victims and executioners with innocent-seeming masks instead of faces."

"Why should you care? The truth is what matters."

"The truth? It can be found at the circus. That's always been so. We perform flying trapeze acts and swallow swords, no?"

"Is that why we're atheists then? Me with my bleak obsession, you with your infantile game? Both godless, mythless? Reality and only reality?"

"It seems to me the chronicles of anti-Semitism have taken over your life. It's a long-lived virus, eternal. Do you have room for it in your monastic cell?"

"As much as I can, as much as I—not the space—can take in."

And the evening and the morning were the second day. Tomorrow.

THE BROTHEL

"So, you have a plan for today, too."

"Yes, the Brothel."

Günther was calm, he refused to notice the former Pioneer's consternation, and then, in the taxi, refused to explain. The building in front of which they alighted was tall and severe looking. A philanthropic society? A bank? Or both?

"No, I'm not taking you to a sex shop. Not yet. We should try the door there, too, you don't have that kind of therapy in multilateral socialism. But this is the proper stop after the cemetery . . . Eros and Thanatos. Or Thanatos and Eros. You can go to the sex shop alone, you don't need me. Here, however, it's good to come with someone."

Hulking and impassive, a man in livery bowed ceremoniously before the clients; he opened the heavy, massive door with golden letters saying KAUFHAUS DES WESTERNS, the Western Store. The Planetary Store.

"The Western Brothel? Everything is done in broad daylight?"

On the ground level, cosmetics and perfumes, lingerie, jewelry, and trinkets; on the first floor, toys and children's items; on the second floor, travel; on the third, women's shoes; on the fourth, men's apparel; on five, women's fashions; on six, men's shoes; on seven, household items, and so on, until floor ten with the immense display cases with thirty-eight kinds of fish, forty-nine types of cheese, fifty-one brands of salami and ham, and eighty-eight vintages of wine and other drinks from around the world. And meat, naturally, dear consumer, let's not forget the meat in this vast shrine to consumerism: beef and pork and rabbit, tiger, swallow, and goose, turtledove and squirrel, bear meat, viper meat, veal and vulture, hundreds of elegant coffins with elegant labels in the many elegant languages of global massacre.

"The brothel! This is it. The Brothel of Gluttony! The pornography of the well-to-do and their gastronomic whims. You can't set off on your great adventure without acquiring this most fundamental education. The democracy that caters to all tastes and incomes.

"In the postindustrial epoch, everything is an industry. The industry of pornography, say (dizzying profits), or the food industry, the clothing industry, the weapons industry, industry after industry, everything potentializing global consumption, commerce and competition, the masses . . . and individuality with its great needs and aspirations. That is, if you're lucky enough to live in the capitalist promised land, far away from the ruins of the third world with its dearth of water, bread, and aspirin. Take it all in, dear traveler. What time did you get up under socialism to get in line for a liter of milk? Or toilet paper? Or batteries for your heater?"

The traveler seemed to be paying no attention, or rather seemed to be waiting for the moment when his conversation partner would stop to catch his breath. "I can see you're once again turning into the Pioneer you once were. Hungry for knowledge, you haven't been disabused of your logorrhea in the paradise of the well-to-do. Boyish nostalgias."

"And that's not all. It's information. A useful orientation for a migrant. Emigrant. Immigrant."

For a moment, they stopped to look at each other.

"Information and observations, that's all. Did you see the packaging? The packaging industry! For chocolate, for shoeboxes, for boxes of condoms and cosmetics and bottles of brandy, for bras! A major industry—packaging! The label is always essential! It defines the epoch. The prosperous and sinful epoch. At the store, at church, and in parliament, the industry of trivialization delivers each day's narcotic carefully prepackaged. Carefully packaged and marketed. Opium for the masses, like Marx's dialectic taught us. Packaged ploys for profit. Naturally, for profit. That's the eleventh commandment, which has become the first. The surplus value of Uncle Karl. Embroidered on the diva's panties and on the minister's tie and on the hats of assassins. Didn't our homeland kick us both out, one after the other, both the superior race and the inferior race? It didn't kick us out, actually, it just let us go."

They stopped again; they looked at each other again.

"Here I finally understood that everything the liars there said about the liars here was true. And that everything that the people here make up about those behind the Iron Curtain and the Wailing Wall is also true. Don't think I've forgotten that man is the most precious form of capital, as Marxist dialectic taught us. We used to get up at dawn for a place in the breadline and milk line, a quarter of a TB-ridden chicken, or three rolls of so-called toilet paper. That's what it was like, no? In the winter, the frozen 'precious capital' sits on the couch, bundled up in blankets and sweaters.

"And the masses . . . the masses continue to swallow shit, get in line not only for oil or cheese, but for newspapers in which you can barely find a true statement. I know, I haven't forgotten that world, interesting as it is, more interesting than the pragmatic boredom here.

"Interesting, yes? You don't know if your friend is a police informant, if your lover reports there, too, or if the listening devices are hidden under the lamp, in a fork, or in the mattress where you jerk off. Interesting, no? I unmasked the hypocrisy, and they screwed me over. They didn't like my communist protest against their masquerade communism. They thought I was provoking them, dangerously so. I don't do a bad job fending off the locals either. The security services here are no better, they're just better equipped. But tell me about Comrade Tudor. Comrade Colonel. He sang me the serenade of departure, too. He was glad I had been bought by the capitalists, whom he knew I hated just as much as the Marxist swindlers on the Danube."

The Pioneer did not answer him, he didn't feel like talking. Only after they had sat down at a back table, in the great food court of the store full of dishes, drinks, and cake, did he become amenable to broaching the subject, a frown darkening his whole face.

"Comrade Tudor? Plump, elegant, and weaselly. He makes deferential gestures. Then, once he has you in the palm of his hand, he turns ferocious. The new professionals! Incomparably more crafty, subtle, and better trained than those of our parents' time. They're scared even of their own shadows . . . The shadow, the informant's nickname. The shadow was always among us, silent and feverish, all eyes and ears. Without an ideology, with only a methodology. In the end, I didn't understand what the colonel wanted—for me to leave, to not leave? I didn't even understand the final blow, I only know it baffled me."

"Meaning?"

"Doctor Edward Sima, whom I hadn't seen for years, made his appearance suddenly as the colonel's collaborator! Not a recent development, a very old one. From the time I used to see him."

"What kind of doctor?"

"Psychiatrist."

"Ah. I understand."

"Just so. Only Mr. Sima was universally respected, clean as a whistle, immaculate as a tear. *Lacryma Cristi* . . . A colleague of my sister's, at the hospital. She sent me to him as if he were a priest. A saint. A sacred healer."

"And did he heal you? What did you have?"

"A syndrome . . . "

"Anticommunist? Anti-Communist Syndrome? Is that why he turned you in to the colonel?"

"I didn't know anything about the colonel then, it hadn't even crossed my mind. Who could have imagined that gentle, polite Edward was in service to Colonel Tudor? Edward was thought to be an angel. Always ready to help."

"He'd even help the colonel. When you're nice, you're nice to everyone, aren't you? So, you had a syndrome. If not anticommunist, what was it? What's it called?"

"I don't think it had a name. Edward called it RP. The colonel reminded me, that fiend. The doctor told him that going abroad would cure me. Would you believe it . . . So, you could say the cure has begun in your left-winger monastic's cell."

"RP, what's that?"

"Reality Phobia. Fear of the real."

"Your doctor is a man of letters. I haven't heard of this illness."

"You're hearing of it now. Edward's theory was that the concentration camp wounded me deeply, then communism deepened the wound. So that I no longer trust reality. I've replaced it with books."

"Interesting. Very interesting."

"Of course, as you put it so well, everything there was interesting."

"And exile? How would exile resolve it?"

"It would impose reality on me. Because I'd lose my language, and therefore the books. Reality would become inevitable."

"You can find books here, too, some even in your own language. Your language from back home. It's not a problem."

"I'm only quoting Saint Edward on this point."

"Did he recommend any other treatment?"

"No, he was against pills. He said it would be enough for me to recognize the situation, to understand it, and the cure would come on its own."

"Is that what happened?"

"If you mean was I cured of books? No. As you know, I have my doctorate in the history of the circus, not in the dark streets of shining socialism. But let's go see the plants now. You promised. The reality of plants, not books, not even books about the world's plants."

"Tomorrow. We can only go tomorrow. I've had a chance to review the history of the aristocratic polymath. Monsieur von Chamisso: Romantic poet and researcher, explorer, savant. I know all about him. It's I who sent you that little fascicle with Schlemihl and the shadow. Adelbert was also a husband and the father of legitimate children, four or five of them. And I've read up on the Botanical Garden. Not during the night, when you were sleeping like a dead dog, but before your visit. That's how I also discovered Kadú, Adelbert's friend, native of I-don't-know-what islands where the ship of the expedition round the world landed. Adelbert became friends with Kadú, the native, and dedicated a moving eulogy to him."

"Where did you read that?"

"In the book about Chamisso's journey around the world. You can find details about his amazing journey in the Botanical Museum and the Botanical Library. That's where I discovered Adelbert and Kadú. Yes, you'll have time to read in the museum library. In complete accord with RP syndrome. But now, to the pub! To the Teutonic pub!"

THE GARDEN AND THE LIBRARY

As usual, the visitor readied himself through preparatory reading, though Günther proved a well-informed guide.

The Garden had been founded in 1679 by the Great Elector and had moved to its present location at the beginning of the twentieth century, when the collection had become global in scope. Now each of the plants bore two names, like all of humankind and like their great baptizer, Carl von Linné.

The organism with blood red petals surrounding a pistil of multicolored bulbs (white, green, red) recommended itself to the world as *Euphorbia pulcherrima* and had come from Mexico; so had *Selenicereus pteranthus,* the white princess-of-the-night, erotically unfurled for pollination above a bed of sharp, thin, green leaves. Sumptuous, strange adventurers, like all allogeneic beings.

"What about the 'Wandering Jew'?" the tourist asked the man in the overalls, who accompanied him after Günther had left.

"Are you referring to the *Zebrina pendula* or the *Tradescania albiflora?* Both are called the 'Wandering Jew.'"

"I'm not sure, I'm not exactly sure. I'd like to find out," the tourist answered.

"They're not in this greenhouse but in the oval one farther off. They are no longer considered to be exotic or tropical plants; they've been assimilated by the modern world. In the oval greenhouse, you can also see a special, thought-provoking exhibit conceived by our associate Ms. Trude. She makes artificial flowers out of animal organs. Morbid, superb flowers. She has a doctorate in art and a gallery in the city center, where iconoclastic artists exhibit their art."

"What artist isn't an iconoclast?"

"Well, not all of them, surely. Trude works two days a week here, in our laboratory, where she has her own space, but at the moment she's abroad. Her flowers are perverse but provocative."

"Animal organs? What do you mean?"

"Skin and organs. Kidneys, lungs, liver, tongue, bladder, heart, ear. And the sex organs, of course. She stretches the limits of what is considered aesthetic, that is what her catalogue, titled *Bestial,* states. The slaughter of animals happens anyway, for food. Our friend Trude combines fragments of dead animals or birds that are still fresh. She photographs what she produces, then destroys it. It would rot anyway. The photograph becomes an artistic document."

"So, photographs."

"Photographs of the hypothetical, that is what she says. Conquering nature, as man always seems to do. Fantastic, carnivorous flowers. As, for example, the *Vagina pilosa.* An orifice with carmine lips barely half open in the vaginal cleft. Around the point of temptation, an envelope of thin fur, surrounded by thin, white bird feathers, like tufts of tangled hair."

Intrigued, the visitor looked up at the guide. The gentleman in the white overalls and glasses with thin, gold frames, was impassive: a scientist reciting a text known by heart. The silence lengthened. The guide lost his patience, tried to change the subject.

"If I've understood correctly, you have decided to visit all our greenhouses, as well as the library—for the Chamisso documents—in the week to come. Yes, he was one of the founders of the Garden. Here he found both peace and eternal rest. Shall we sit a while in the shade, on a bench, and talk?"

The shaded bench proved to be just ahead.

"In 1943, we lost four-fifths of the Herbarium to the bombs. After the war, international trade became possible again, and we received seeds from around the world. A remarkable individual in the history of the Garden was Mrs. Elisabeth Schiemann, the first woman scientist to work in the Botanical Museum, who published *On the Origin of Cultivated Plants*. Like other eminent botanists, she had been fired from the university due to the Nazis' racialized politics. In 1943, the SS installed an underground defense system in the garden, but the Russians destroyed it. The reconstruction of the exterior gardens began in 1949 with aid from the Marshall Plan. Forty years later, we were the first to open a garden for the blind and partially blind. It allows them to perceive the uniqueness of each plant through smell and touch."

The conscientious guide guided, the listener listened, and the sun allowed itself to be cast into shadow by clouds of ashy cotton.

"Oh, yes, about the great Chamisso," the guide in the immaculate overalls at last remembered. "At first he was a curator at the Royal Botanical Garden, under the directorship of Heinrich Friedrich Link. An exile, that Mr. Chamisso, as you well know. The emigration of the French nobility had begun even before the Revolution. The young Adelbert arrived in Prussia in 1798, where he was page to the queen, the wife of Friedrich Wilhelm I. He then completed his military training and, during the Franco-Prussian War, he was forced to fight against his own lost homeland. Like all exiles, he was torn between two national identities."

Again, he had spoken as if by rote, with downcast eyes.

He looked up then, to see if he was being listened to. He was, eagerly.

"Chamisso was obsessed with the idea of a journey around the world. He was only able to undertake one in 1815, when he participated in the naval expedition on the Rurik led by Captain Otto von Kotzebue, who was the son of the famous playwright, you see. After rounding Cape Horn, he arrived in the Caroline Islands, where he was fascinated by the multitude of reefs and corals, as well as by the animals and plants native to the place, though also by the dwarf-sized, childlike inhabitants and their innocent, idyllic lifestyle. There, among the childish natives, whom he adored for their intelligence and candor, he found a friend—Kadú. He took Kadú with him to Kamchatka. Chamisso also traveled to the Russian territories in America and Asia and was shocked by the inhumanity with which Russia treated its populations. At the end he even journeyed to Petersburg. Though naturalized as a Prussian, Adelbert remained a French gentleman to the end. He was horrified by despotism."

The explanations, too, seemed to be at an end. The caretaker accepted the tourist's thanks with a quick nod and assured the stranger that, if the need arose, he would be at his disposal again in the days to follow.

Alone again, the traveler headed toward the library in search of information that could only be found between book covers. It would be enough to open each in turn.

I am a Frenchman in Germany and a German in France; a Catholic among the Protestants, Protestant among the Catholics;

a philosopher among the religious [. . .], a mundane among the savants, and a pedant to the mundane; Jacobin among the aristocrats, and to the democrats a nobleman [. . .] Nowhere am I at home [. . .]![20] This was Adelbert's lament at Mme de Staël's table. Infatuated with the famous writer, he asked her: *What will you do with me?* The famous writer replied: *What you are; a man of strong heart and charming manners, unsociable and timid in the world, a man of status and culture.*

When, in 1801, the Chamisso family decided to return to France, Adelbert did not accompany them, for lack of money. The young officer, an avid reader, consoled himself with extensive perusals of Rousseau, Voltaire, and Schiller. His displeasures and depression seemed to evaporate in the clean country air. Finally, he decided to go to Berlin to study natural history. He crossed the Alps on foot, gathering plants.

Books . . . open on the lectern. Moving confessions about friendship and a precarious mental state, but also about the book he is working on, the one about *the lost shadow . . . In this manner I entered decidedly into the story of Peter Schlemihl. I wrote that summer to unwind and to gladden the children of a friend. To my surprise, the story was well received in Germany and England. By chance, I found an article about a Russian expedition to the North Pole at my friend Julius Hitzig's house. Hitzig sent letters to Privy Councilor Kotzebue and soon received a response from his brother-in-law, Admiral von Krusenstern, then a captain in the Russian Imperial Navy, deputed by Count Romanzov to undertake the expedition.*[21]

Was his homeland the source of the thrill of the journey? Parting and returning home, the longing for faraway places and for home, and always the one longing calling out to the other. In this dim wavering, the lack of a shadow wasn't discernible. *Who are you, in fact?* [. . .] *I'm a nobody, a scholar without a title; neither a poet of the soul, nor anything else; I don't have anything, not even a homeland, which even the poorest man has. I don't have a shadow* [. . .] *Nor do I want to have one; soon I will take up my hiking staff once more.*[22]

The times were not as forgiving as they had been around 1800. The age had passed when, a few years earlier, the diplomat and the scholar Varnhagen von Ense, with whom Chamisso had edited the *Berliner Musenalmanach,* had given his heart to the allogenic Rahel Levin, who had converted to Christianity . . . Now was the time of the great terror descending from Frankfurt and Würzburg and other places in Germany. Cries of "Hep! Hep!"[23] were heard, stones were thrown, the Jews were beaten and driven away, Ahasuerus's pale, drawn face threw an immense shadow over Germany.

Adelbert believed in Christ and in Germany, which, being Christian, could only be humanely noble. Why were no opposing voices raised, why had everyone gone mute? Goethe was silent, though what he had to say would have kept things in balance; as a Protestant theologian, Schleiermacher had to keep his distance, though he mixed in Semitic circles and endorsed the baptism of Jews; and Wilhelm von Humboldt fought with his lover Caroline, a ferocious anti-Semite. But Adelbert believed Germans to be humane and cultured, and if this was so, then surely there was no reason to worry. He and Edward Hitzig, a Jewish convert to Christianity and his closest friend, talked frequently. *Jews have a lot of options,* Humboldt had said with skepticism. *Each option is difficult, has its good and bad parts, like almost everything they do that differs from what others do. They are strangers par excellence, and they have it tough—they are a burden to themselves as well as to the nations where they live. [. . .] The way that you have taken [becoming Christian] seems to me like the righteous crowning of the Emancipation of the Jews; you have placed the seal of Christian religion on their [civic and political] equality; you have led an authentic Christian and German life, one exemplary in its humanitarian effects. You have grown up in an environment you loved. Nevertheless, the destiny of the Jews is unavoidable since they are mixed up in hostile situations and conflicts. The other path, that is, remaining faithful to their sacred identity, would have led to unimaginable consequences, to a national reevaluation of a two-thousand-year-old history. I am shaking my head thinking about this.*

The tourist copied assiduously, and now and then translated a phrase or two in passing, so as to have it, to live it in two languages, that of the author and his own: *Both for himself and for those in whose midst he has lived and will live, the stranger carries his destiny around his neck like a millstone. Compromise solutions will keep them always in a state of hostile tension. In everything, they present us with a problem, which they cannot resolve, but it is this very lack of solutions that is valuable and profoundly human.*

He had twice underlined Humboldt's words. He was sorry that the university that bore his name was on the other side of the Wailing Wall.

He had underlined, twice, in red, the following idea, too: *It is difficult for us to consider them righteous. Perhaps, after so many sufferings, they should become priests and saints; but they continue to see only to their banal, human pursuits. A disappointment that can also be a source of hatred.* Priests and saints? RP Syndrome, that illness invented by Sima, the security services man, and reported to his superiors to prove his fidelity and skill as an informant?

I don't hide my doubts that a community of these ancient wanderers that would be fully observant would be protected from the misunderstandings of those around them. I sympathize with them, Humboldt told the Christianized Jew, Hitzig, looking him straight in the face. *The meaning of their extraordinary history is a unique epic of suffering borne on behalf of all peoples and nations. But Judaism is lost,* he continued, addressing the Jew who had lost his Jewishness. *This loss, the consequence of the confrontation between the blessing and the curse, is their way of being chosen.*

The chosen people? Chosen for suffering? But what about suspicion, Herr Humboldt? What about the scapegoat? With eyes downcast, but tearless, the tears already having been wept, Ernest, Adelbert's son, related that he had been told that his father was a *schlemiel*, not a true German, and among the morose Frenchmen from Bell-Alliance, some maintained that he, too, was a Jew, which was even worse. Could this be Ernest, Adelbert's son? That is what one would have to assume . . . After all, he was not protected from the cloud of suspicion that surrounded his father, the aristocrat Louis Charles Adélaïde de Chamisso, who had been cast out of the family's noble castle and had become a wanderer, a pariah, a stateless person chosen for suffering.

Without much conviction, Chamisso tried to comfort his son. "*Schlemihl* is a fairytale, just a fairytale." Greatly moved, he embraced his son, feeling his young heart beating. "Is it true that Schlemihl is a Jew? That is what the professor said." "I don't know, Ernest. But if he were, his story would express the pain of losing a homeland. The lack of a homeland. The suffering of a stateless person is profoundly human. The one who suffers must be accepted and protected. In this cruel, banal world the stranger needs to be protected. This is what your professor should have said." He felt that the boy only half understood him and had not calmed down, he wanted to keep him from suffering further. "It's not shameful to be a Jew, it's not even a bad thing. It's only very hard, if what I've seen and heard is true. To be a human being is not shameful."

It's not shameful, Monsieur Chamisso, is that what you really think? And if so, where does RP syndrome come from, Sima's pathology of the camps and postcamp traumas? Isn't it shameful to be a man among these so-called men?

Not so-called, but real men, alive, lively, vulnerable on the earth they have populated with skyscrapers and dreams and the horrors they perpetuate in their millenary delirium.

"I've bought the little yellow book you wanted from Reclam," his friend Günther welcomed him, opening the door to his monastic cell and handing him the gift. "Here it is, recovered."

"Yes, that's it," the wanderer agreed. "Philipp Reclam jun. Stuttgart. My own copy was confiscated at customs. 'For the reading delectation of Herr Doberman,' the socialist official said. Their humor outlasts their misfortunes. Does it encourage my Sima Syndrome? Books, books. Reality Phobia . . . "

"I wouldn't say so. Quite the opposite, it's the hunger for the real. But how was the Garden?"

"Fabulous. Uncontainable and indescribable. Fantastical

plants, the imagination of an unbridled, boundless creator, I'd even go so far as to say a maniac. I plan to go back, it's an essential experience. You learn to see yourself as insignificant. Mundane. A number."

"I allowed myself to open the little pamphlet. It's like a pocket-size travel notebook. At the very beginning, I discovered the botanist's dedication to his hero. As if it were addressed to us. *Der Zeit gedenk ich, wo wir Freunde waren, / Als erst die Welt uns in die Schule nahm.*[24] Is this Peter a relative of ours?"

"A distant relative, I'd say. But Adelbert is a wanderer, like us."

"Expelled, exiled, an adventurer? How old was Peter?"

"We don't know, it doesn't say. He's not Kafka's immigrant, Rossman, newly arrived in America because he slept with the servant. And he doesn't have a senator uncle. Just a letter of recommendation."

"To whom, from whom . . . I don't remember."

"To the rich Mr. John. Naturally, the letter mentions the qualities of the sojourner. But Mr. John opens his eyes to reality: here you're a man if you have a million dollars. Then the Man in Gray appears and buys the wanderer's shadow for a bag of money that never runs out. In other words, the aforementioned million."

"Oh, yes, I saw that on the first page. I am often asked about the shadow we so frequently lose when our consciousness retreats into shadow. Under socialism, the shadow was the Informant, who followed us to report as much as he could. The spy. The Shadow in Colonel Tudor's service."

"After he sells his shadow and becomes wealthy, the wanderer becomes suspected by all."

"The deal with the devil?"

"Not quite. The Man in Gray is not the man in black, he's only an intermediary. A broker, a dealer. A hero for our mercantile times. The devil made banal and trivial, accessible. Democratic and populist."

"Man is the most precious capital."

"A definition fulfilled. This only becomes possible under capitalism. Straight out of Marx's *Das Capital.* Before turning into a hermit and scholar of nature, Peter lands in the hospital as patient number 12, dubbed 'the Jew,' or, perhaps, recognized as one. Different, a plague, a number. Have you heard of *schlemihl* literature?"

"I don't think it was discussed in our Pioneer meetings."

"I've only discovered the term today, at the Botanical Library. Seventeenth- or eighteenth-century Spain. *Picaro* or *schlem.* A portrait of society told through autobiographical wanderings. In other words, the Jew eternal. The etymology of the word *picaro* goes back to Jewish tradition. *Schlem* in German corresponds to *picaro* in Spanish and is related to the Hebrew *Aas,* the sign of the *converso,* the return of a converted Jew under the Inquisition. The picaresque journey progresses horizontally in space and vertically through society. That's what I discovered. Uncertainty rules everywhere."

"Well, yes . . . Uncertainty. I got you something else from a used bookshop. A novel by a Czech, Natonek's the name. Something about Chamisso's life. Behrendt Verlag, Stuttgart, August 1949. *Mich drängt aus Europa hinaus, sagte er zu Hitzig.*"[25]

"You're not a converted Jew, you aristocrat. Hitzig converted in order to give his children a stable future. You don't have children, or a wife. Or a beloved, as far as I can tell."

"No, but I'm a leftist, as you say. Hence, a Jew. Long be-fore the Holocaust, Hitzig advocated for a Jewish spiritual and political separation from Europe. He was already seek-ing something else. Africa, the far reaches, the desert. And he was a German nobleman, not a pariah."

"A separation from Europe also to assure a stable fu-ture for his children. The nobility had been expelled from France, and Chamisso was not too sure about Germany ei-ther, though he wasn't a Jew. Only stateless. He would go on to get married, however, this Monsieur Chamisso . . . out of love. He became the father of two boys and a girl. I found out about one of the boys, Ernest, today, in the library."

"Two boys and a girl? What about Peter?"

"Yes, three children and a ghost. The fictive son. Fictive and not entirely fictive. His favorite, probably."

"Yes, but today I've also found you an English teacher. It's a global language anywhere you might go. She's agreed to take you on. It's just a matter of how long you'll be staying."

"I don't know. Tamar is having problems with the di-vorce. Maybe it's even because of me. Mister Brother-in-Law couldn't put up with me from the very beginning. He consid-ered our relationship excessive. Tamar promises that she'll rent me a place nearby and come visit, that we'll talk on the phone, blah, blah, blah . . . It's not a happy opening act. But it does have an aura of mystery. You know I'm afraid of the boredom that accompanies prosperity. Though now I see that excitement might be possible."

"We've had this discussion before, when I left the social-ist slum. I said then that you can't have total boredom any-where there are people; they take care of that."

"I didn't want to leave. I only spun you tall tales. And

why should I leave? For the fabled Hesperides? That's how I would talk, but you kept going on about the experiment of freedom. I don't feel like writing an ending to the story. What's certain is that it would be better to wait here a while longer. Not too long though."

THE ENGLISH LESSON

Günther had informed the tourist that Jennifer worked at an American army center. He had also given him the necessary preliminary information: address, phone number, and a short, hardly encouraging description . . . A young, unsociable, shy woman, slim, disheveled, and energetic, with shining eyes. The tourist tried to get in touch over the phone, but displeased with the laconic nature of the conversation, finally decided to meet in person at her workplace, curious, too, to see what the German school for uniformed Americans looked like. "Yes, Jennifer speaks perfect German, you'll be able to understand each other," Günther had assured him, repeating that the young woman, his friend, had agreed to initiate the wanderer into the mysteries of the language of the New World. She would not accept any payment, considering this voluntary act of charity the too-small price to be paid for all the disappointments that her arrogant and egotistical compatriots had caused the poor captives beyond the Wall.

"Jennifer?" the visitor asked, bending slightly toward the desk where a young woman with short hair and blue-rimmed glasses was writing assiduously in a register.

"Jennifer Backer, *ja, ja,*" the teacher answered promptly, without bothering to look up.

She blushed before meeting the searching gaze of the stranger. She had stood up, tall, in a white tank-top that was tight over her generous chest, and taken off her glasses. She had large, dark brown eyes, which sparkled, or shone, as Günther had said. She gestured to a colleague, who brought coffees, and told the Wanderer that she was from Boston, and that early on she had fallen in love with the German spoken by the Romantics, as well as with the history and life of this fascinating city. She was planning on staying another few years to teach the members of the occupying army the language of the Teutons they had defeated. She didn't feel much like returning to the competitiveness of America, though Boston ("as I'm sure you know") was a kind of little Europe.

Behold! After a short conversation, she was no longer laconic. When she saw that her guest seemed satisfied by what he had found out, she took a napkin from the table and wrote down another phone number.

"We'll decide on a schedule when you call."

She lived in a four-story apartment building, next to a park near the Opera. Floor two, no elevator. The shock was immediate: in the doorway, the host received him with open arms and an amical smile completely devoid of shyness. The guest stared at the host's long arms and beautiful palms, at her long, bare feet. She was in black jeans and a short top. She was still standing there with open arms.

"Please come in, don't hesitate. I'll take care of everything."

She didn't seem interested in her student's astonishment, nor in not having anything to hold in her arms.

"Reality Phobia? Let's get real. Meaning, let's not. Günther told me about your exotic diagnosis. Monsieur Sartre called it *la nausée.*"[26]

The Nomad was already in the room. It was almost devoid of furniture: a wide bed and wide table, piles of books on the floor. He felt himself suddenly being pulled toward the cheerful explainer, who was speaking in staccato tones, repeating: "This is my job, don't worry. Don't be surprised. Give yourself up to me."

Jenny began to undress him slowly, methodically, from top to bottom, smiling encouragingly. When she finished, and they were both naked, facing each other, she took a step back to contemplate the aroused member. "It's nice. And not shy at all," she smiled affectionately, taking a step toward the large green bed.

"Günther doesn't have to know," whispered Jenny during their final embrace. "I understand the nausea of reality after the concentration camp and after the quagmire of dispelled illusions that followed. I'm a pragmatic person, despite these heaps of books, even though I've actually read comrade Sartre."

The student smiled too. Behold! Surprised by the unexpected opening act. The mundane nature of the adventure.

"You still seem amazed. You don't have to be. Attraction is simple, natural. We'll have time for English, too. And for a real conversation."

"Yes, we will. I'm convinced."

"You were here, present, I felt it. You still are. It's not your shadow following you, it's the present."

"I'm not sure," the student answered after a time. "I hadn't expected Günther to tattle. Germans are usually more discrete than the progeny of the Balkans."

"Günther, too, is from the Balkans, even if he's German, and there's nothing wrong with that. You're much more full of life than people around here. But he didn't do anything disrespectful to you. We're good friends, we know each other, we trust each other. He was convinced that we, too, would be friends."

"A seer, a prophet . . . What else did he tell you?"

"About your sister. That you're in love with her."

"In love? Love is an error of attribution, says one of the books on your floor. We are close, yes. Two orphans raised together. Each with and for the other. Estranged from the world, if not completely against it."

"I hear she's married."

"Yes, she's married. I'm not a husband. She can't divorce me. And she wouldn't want to."

"And what is she called?"

"Tamar. Tamara."

"That is what I wanted to hear. To understand if you trust me. You don't. Not yet. You will. We will be friends. Tamar is something other than Agatha."

"Agatha means RP syndrome. Reality Phobia. Evidently, Günther has also told you this."

"He was sure we'd become friends, that's all. But I don't like RP Syndrome. It needs another name, another metaphor."

"Does it seem metaphorical? It was a doctor's definition, his diagnosis."

"A frivolous reader. Susceptible to playing cheap tricks."

"What do you propose then?"

"I'll think about it. We have time. I understand that you put off going forth into the world."

The vestal one undertook the erotic ritual with imagination and ardor. She was persistent, there was panting, there were brief, shameful, shameless cries and tender and torrid caresses. A sort of quiet, tenacious, irresistible therapy. Yes, irresistible, her partner was trapped in this delicate, expert communion. He was no longer sure if the shadow was acting on his behalf, nor did he care, caught up in the electrifying game of the moment. Two bodies thirsting for joy, one was his, or so it seemed, and he couldn't pull away, nor did he want to any longer. Jenny was entwined in him completely, and he was in her, tethered together, shackled, once and again and again in joy. Attentive and perceptive, the teacher was fully dedicated to the exalted bodies.

How will the English lesson go, the student asked himself after he had recovered from the hypnosis and lay, exhausted, gazing up at the ceiling.

The pause lengthened. Like the silence of the satiated bodies, the silence in the room was perfect. Jenny was no longer in bed or even beside him—the shower could be heard from the bathroom. It seemed she wasn't in a hurry, the student had time to arrange his outfit and thoughts for the pedagogical experiment to come.

She hadn't changed her overall appearance, she was still in jeans and still barefoot. The captive stared at length at the beautiful arches of her feet and at her beautiful hands. He was ready to confess his infantile obsession with feminine hands and feet. The blouse, however, was no longer of voile but of thick black linen buttoned up to the neck, nun-like. The stranger resigned himself to contemplating the large room again, ready to ask the teacher if the erotic exercise could be moved to the end of the lesson the next time. On the table there were now two cups of coffee, notebooks, books, and pencils.

The lesson unfolded perfectly, in a friendly and professional manner. No frivolous deviations. At the end, Jenny embraced him amiably and patted him protectively on the shoulder. They would see each other in three days, at the same time and in the same place. He didn't have any time to ask about the ritual being moved from the beginning to the end of the lesson; he would do it the next time, three days later.

At their second meeting, the surprise was just as great as before. Jenny appeared in the same outfit, with the same cordial disposition, but lacked eagerness. Perhaps she was waiting for her partner to take the initiative, but he didn't make a move. English seemed like an ample enough domain for both their curiosities.

The same happened in the weeks that followed. The global language of the global epoch augured a new adventure and a new refuge, but the Nomad was a novice and could only hope for a beginner's familiarity with the new phonetics and a few choice slang expressions, which Jenny endowed him with enthusiastically.

They went out together on a few evenings, their conversation tackling many of the volumes on the floor to the evident satisfaction of both. No allusion to their closeness on that first day! As if their first meeting had not taken place at all or had been only an errant shadow of lost time. The cerebral exercises, undertaken with the same competence as the erotic ones, reunited them, however. They found closeness again in books that they had both read in different places and in different languages.

It was as if their conversation borrowed its complicit intensity from its earlier erotic counterpart, reestablishing the pair as a couple. It had nothing to do with Reality Phobia; it was about another reality altogether, a deeper one, which the tourist thought about unceasingly. Jenny, who had described and confirmed herself as pragmatic, was no less preoccupied with their bizarre meeting than her student was.

AT THE LIBRARY: THOMAS MANN

This poet whose name was so early familiar to us, this German author who was set before us boys as our first and best model, was a stranger, a foreigner. French songs were his lullabies. The air, the water, the nourishment of France shaped his body, the rhythm of the French tongue was the medium of all his thoughts and feelings, till he was half-grown. Only then, at fourteen, did he come over to us. He never managed to converse with fluency in German. He reckoned in French. Tradition says that up to the last, when he composed, he first recited aloud in French and only after that poured his inspirations into a metrical mould—but after all, the result was masterly German.

It is amazing, it is even unheard-of. True, there have been cases of gifted men who were so drawn to the genius of a stranger folk that they changed their nationality, immersed themselves ut-

terly in the ideas and problems of the people with whom they felt this affinity, and learned to use their pens adequately, even elegantly, in a tongue their fathers did not speak. But what is correctness, what even elegance, compared to the deep intimacy the artist must have! The knowledge of the ultimate mysteries and refinements, the uttermost control of his craft in tone and movement, in the reflex workings of words on one another, of their sensuous appeal, their dynamic, their special stylistic, ironic, pathetic value; that mastery—to put in a word what, after all, is unanalyzable—of the delicate and powerful mechanism of language, which produces the literary artist and is indispensable to poet and writer. He who is born and called one day to enrich the literature of his land will quite early find himself peculiarly concerned with his mother tongue. The Word: there it is, it belongs to everybody, yet it seems to belong to him more in particular, in a more inward and gratifying sense than to anyone else. It is his earliest wonder, his first delight, his childish pride, the field of his private and unpraised efforts, the source of his strange and undefined superiority. At fourteen years, if the individual sustains this unusual relation to the Word, there may already have been some private beginnings. And then, at this age, to be set amongst strangers speaking strange thoughts in a strange tongue! Even though some latent, unexplained sympathy were already present; even though there was some unconscious adjustment to the German tempo and German laws of thought; still, and even so, how much conscious labour, how much wooing for the favour of our tongue was needed to make a German poet out of a French child!

He was a tall, mild man with long, straight hair and noble, almost beautiful features. Capable of friendship with children and savages, he loved to remember the Radak Islanders whose guest he had once been and whose beauty and nearness to nature he praises in the style of Rousseau. The Ulea-Indian Kadú, who served him in the South Seas, he considered "one of the finest characters" he had met in his life and one of the human beings he "loved most."

For the over-delicate and the brutal are complementary cravings of the romantic temperament. It is precisely this contrast that places Chamisso's works with all their Latin clarity and definition in the category of the romantic in literature.

The Marvellous Tale of Peter Schlemihl was, to begin with its literary history, written in the year 1813. At that time the poet, in a state of desperation, both personally and politically speaking, was botanizing on the estate of his friends, the Itzenplitz family. He himself said he undertook the work to distract his mind and amuse the children of a friend (Eduard Hitzig).

Peter Schlemihl has been called a fairy-tale. [. . .] That it is not. However indefinite its terrain, it is too much the novel; with all its whimsical vein, it is too modern, feverish, too much in earnest to come within the rubric of the fairy-tale. [. . .] The story begins in a quite realistic, commonplace vein, and the real artistry of the writer lies in his knowing how to keep up the realistic bourgeois atmosphere to the end, all the while relating in the greatest detail the most fabulous and impossible circumstances. This in such a way that Schlemihl's adventures impress the reader as "strange" in the sense of a destiny seldom or never before visited upon an erring human being by the will of God; but never actually "strange" in the sense of an unnatural or irresponsible or "fairy" story. The autobiographical, confessional form, as contrasted with that of the typical fairy-tale, contributes to emphasize its truthfulness and reality. So, if I were challenged to classify Peter Schlemihl, I think I should call it a fantastic novelette or long story.

No cloven hoof, no demonry, no diabolic glitter. An over-courteous, embarrassed man, who blushes (a pricelessly convincing touch) when he introduces the crucial conversation about the shadow. Schlemihl, hovering between horror and respect, treats him with aghast politeness. What this extraordinary amateur offers him in exchange for his shadow are good old familiar things: the genuine magic root, the mandrake; magic pennies; thieves' thalers; the napkin of Roland's squirrel a gallows-mannikin; Fortunatus' wishing-cap "newly refurbished." The story here refers to familiar and taken-for-granted paraphernalia of saga and fairy-tale, and this sustains its atmosphere of the legitimate and reliable. The befooled Schlemihl chooses the lucky purse; and then follows that priceless moment when the grey man kneels down and with admirable deftness loosens Schlemihl's shadow from the grass, lifts it from head to foot, rolls it up, folds it, and puts it in his pocket.

But now, of course, everybody—man, woman, and street Arab—straightway perceives that Schlemihl has no shadow and overwhelms him with scorn, pity, and horror. On this point, I am not quite so sure as I was in the matter of the lucky purse. If a man meets me when the sun is shining and he casts no shadow, would I notice its absence? And if I did, would I not simply conclude that there was some peculiar optical factor unknown to me that made him seem to lack one? Well, no matter. Precisely the impossibility of checking up on and deciding this question is the real point of the book; granting the premise, everything follows with shattering consistency.

For what comes next is the portrayal of an apparently advantaged and enviable but actually romantically miserable existence, dwelling solitary in its own mind with a sinister secret—and certainly no poet has ever before succeeded in bringing home to the reader the emotions of such a man or depicting them with such convincing simplicity, realism, and sympathy.

We see the wealthy Schlemihl leave his house by night and moonlight, wrapped in a voluminous cloak, with his hat drawn over his brows, driven by the tormenting desire to test the general opinion and read his doom out of the mouths of passers-by. We see him cringe beneath the pity of the women, the mockery of the young, the scorn of grown men, especially the portly ones, "who themselves cast a good broad shadow." We see him staggering heartbroken home when a sweet innocent child chances to cast her eye upon him from close at hand and at sight of his shadowless state veils her lovely face and passes on with an averted gaze. His sense of guilt at this incident is boundless.

Schlemihl tries to adjust himself more or less to his affliction. To his valet, a sturdy fellow with a kind face, he has in a weak moment confided his shameful infirmity; and the good soul, although horrified, conquers his feelings and, defying all the world, remains loyal and helps Schlemihl all he can. He supports his master, walks everywhere in front of him, and, being taller and broader, he covers him at critical moments with his own imposing shadow. Thus, Schlemihl is able to go among people and play his part in society. "I had indeed," says he, "to pretend to many oddities of conduct. But all such eccentricities become the man of means." Defeats and humiliations are not lacking and presently comes that touching episode which is an immortal theme of romantic poetry: the love of the marked man, hunted, infamous, accursed, for a pure and unsuspecting maiden, to whom he turns like any simple, bourgeois human being.

I mean the unhappy idyll with the forester's daughter; there we have all the typical elements of the theme; the simple, foolish, match-making mother; the decent, distrustful father who does not look so high'; the tender attempt to penetrate her lover's secret and her woman's cry: "If you are wretched, bind me to your wretchedness, that I may help you bear it." The old tale is told with such freshness, such convincing gravity, such veracity and detail, one loses sight of the fact that the premises are fantastic, since the poet himself seems wholly to have forgotten it. Nowhere is the story so little a fairy-story as here, nowhere so entirely a romance, reality, serious life.

One would like to tell the whole story over again, put one's finger on every paragraph; but here is the rest of it. Nothing happier than the last chapter where the Evil One, "as though used to such treatment," silently bows his head and stoops his shoulders and lets himself be thrashed by the faithful servant Bendel. [. . .] And no finer conclusion imaginable than the one invented by the poet. It is a good and soothing end, though at the same time an austere one, remote from the childlike optimism of the fairy-tale, where everything ends in wedding bells and "if they are not dead they live there still."

Schlemihl, "shut out by early sin from human society," never returns to it and never regains his shadow. He remains solitary, he goes on doing penance. But he finds in nature a substitute for bourgeois happiness. By a fortunate chance, he is drawn to contemplate her and spends his life in the service of natural science. The author accompanies with a wealth of accurate geographical detail the account of his hero's travels in the seven-league boots— here again employing the method of supporting fantasy with realistic detail. [. . .] Now a grotesque figure magnificently satisfied with his lot, Schlemihl covers the backbone of this earth, striding and studying. He establishes the geography of unexplored regions, he botanizes and zoologizes in the grand manner, and he will take care to have his manuscripts submitted before his death to the University of Berlin.

And what does it mean to have no shadow? People have racked their brains over the mystery ever since the book appeared, they have devoted theses to it and answered it all too clearly and precisely by saying that the man without a shadow is the man without a country. But that would be to narrow down too much the deeper meaning of a motif which in the first instance was only a grotesque fancy. Schlemihl is no allegory; Chamisso was not the man to whom an intellectual idea was ever the primary thing in his production. "Only life," he said, "can recapture life." But precisely because that is true, he would not have been able without some basis of experience to fill out a comic idea into something so full of life and novelistic veracity. Need of distraction, avuncular *benevolence, could never by themselves have enabled him to write the tale if he had not known himself to be in a particular situation that gave him power to animate it with verisimilitude out of his own personal lot.*

But again, what was this peculiar and personal lot? Chamisso wrote a charming forward to the French edition of Peter Schlemihl. *Towards the end of it, he says that his tale has fallen into the hands of thinking people, who, accustomed to reading in order to be edified, are troubled because they want to know what the shadow was. And then, with a straight face, he proceeds to quote in French from an old tome the definition of the shadow:* De l'ombre [. . .] L'ombre considére sur un plan situé derrière le corps opaque qui la produit n'est autre chose que la section de ce plan dans le solide qui représente l'ombre.[27] (René Just Haüy, Traité élémentaire de physique, 2 vol., chez Courcier, Paris, 1806. §§ 1002 et 1006.)

C'est donc de ce solide, *Chamisso comments,* dont il est question dans la merveilleuse histoire de Pierre Schlémiel. [. . .] La leçon qu'il a chèrement payé, il veut qu'elle nous profite et son experience nous crie: songez au solide. [. . .] Songez au solide![28] *Here then, is the ironic moral of the book, whose author knew only too precisely what it means to lack solidity, human regularity, bourgeois stability. [. . .] He knew the torments of youth, the problems of the young man who, without any normal future to look forward to, cannot test his powers. Wounded in his ego, he sees mockery and scorn wherever he turns, especially from the stout and solid, "who themselves cast a good broad shadow." He had perhaps even stranger insights into the fluctuating unreality and precariousness of his existence. By birth a Frenchman, he had made Germany his home and could say to himself that if chance had so willed, he might* just as well have made it anywhere else. Somewhere in his writings, he expressly declares that he had discovered in himself the gift of feeling at home everywhere. His extraordinary talent for languages was no doubt part of this feeling—we know that he possessed not only German but all sorts of other tongues as well, even Hawaiian. What was he, who was he anyhow? Nothing, everything? A creature, not a person, uncircumscribable, everywhere and nowhere at home? There may have been days when he felt that out of sheer vagueness and unreality he himself cast no shadow.

The shadow has become, in Peter Schlemihl, a symbol of all bourgeois solidity and human belongingness. It is spoken of as money is spoken of, as something which one has to respect if one wants to live among men; which one can only get rid of if one is minded to live exclusively for himself and his better self. The ironic summons: Songez au solide! applies to the bourgeois, as we would say today, to the philistines, to use the word of the Romantics. But irony almost always implies making a superiority out of a lack. The whole little book is nothing but a profoundly experienced description of the sufferings of the marked and solitary man. It tells us that young Chamisso knew with painful vividness how to esteem the value of a healthy shadow.

It is the old story. Werther shot himself, but Goethe remained alive. Schlemihl, shadowless, strides booted over hill and dale, a natural scientist, "living to himself alone." But Chamisso, after producing a book from his sufferings, hastened to outgrow his problem-child phase. He settles down, becomes the father of a family and an academician, master of his craft. Only the eternally bohemian finds that stupid. One cannot be interesting for-

ever. Either you die of your interestingness, or you become a master.—But Peter Schlemihl *is one of the most charming youthful works in German literature.*[29]

ARPEGGIONE

The wanderer appeared with a bouquet of flowers for his final lesson. The teacher was waiting for him in the doorway. She was no longer barefoot nor sociable.

"If I understand correctly, you're off to your sister's."

"She was the cause of my self-exile. She needs me. And I, her. In fact, I, her . . . We don't have any other family."

"Yes, I understand. But leaving so soon? If I knew you well, I'd say you were capable of suddenly disappearing one night. Perhaps you've already decided to."

Watching her, the exile was silent. High heels, beautiful white hands, her smile.

"Before parting, I suggest we wander around Berlin, my favorite city. I have concert tickets. We have three hours to wander around, time enough for melancholy. The program includes German and Austrian composers. As far as I know, Bukovina has ties to Austria. For sweet Bukovina we have the sentimentalist Schubert, his *Arpeggione Sonata* is listed on the program."

"I'm familiar with the *Arpeggione Sonata*. I first listened to it many years ago, played by a Russian cellist."

"The elegant Franz is a sentimentalist."

"Perhaps, but I don't consider that a defect. I know from experience that vulnerability flows out of melancholy. It's one of the pieces he wrote shortly before his death. He was gravely ill and desperate. *La mélancolie, c'est le bonheur d'être triste,*[30] Victor Hugo says, and Herr Schubert knew this."

Leaving the concert hall, the Traveler kissed the hand of his teacher in the old continental style.

"The concert was fabulous. Thank you for the musical evening and for everything else."

"So, you're leaving soon."

"Yes, soon, I have plane tickets. But before that, we could have dinner? It's our final evening together, after all. I hope it won't be forever."

"You'll come back again to the Old World?"

"Who knows what the future holds. All my life I've lived in uncertainty, I'm used to life's mysterious byways."

They entered a small Hungarian eatery nearby. The wanderer picked at his roast and emptied two bottles of red wine. The teacher contemplated him silently, smiling. When she opened the door to her apartment, she bowed toward her guest and threw her shoes in the corner.

WALLED IN

There might have been a shy knock at the door, but the sleepy one was too tired, he couldn't move. Then a second, louder knock, a yellow envelope under the front door. The sleeper didn't have the courage to open his eyes and waited in the same position, paralyzed. Then the two fat twins in evening wear entered and, bored, scrutinized the small room and the guest in his eternal slumber. Now the yellow envelope was no longer under the door, but under the table. Where was Günther, why didn't he come to report the home intrusion?

Without any reason or apology, Günther had been absent for more than two days, and the voyager felt increasingly uneasy in the narrow studio, in the big, foreign city, constantly bewildered as he was by the many attractive novelties. He had been alone for two days, and still he couldn't get up the courage to call the police. He waited for his host to reappear. Nocturnal phantoms overwhelmed him with summons to present himself urgently to the appropriate authorities, to justify his stay in a foreign capital. Each time, they assured him that nothing bad would happen to him, that the investigation would be perfunctory, that the Trial would not take place, that the democratic bureaucracy was slow and inefficient, just like the undemocratic one. And when, at last, a Trial did of course take place, it would not be public. There was no reason to worry. It would be secret, it would be held behind closed doors, it would be proper: sealed Teutonic army tribunal proceedings.

And behold! The blond one took off his large felt hat and opened the yellow envelope while staring fixedly at his brown-haired twin brother, as if there was no one else in the room, only the two of them, sent by Colonel Tudor. The sleeping witness was the yellow envelope's addressee.

"My dear patient and friend," the first line of the summons read. Patient and friend? Meaning what? How had this double greeting come to be? The wanderer tossed and turned. Who had invented this nightmare? Where was Günther to protest against its staging? "I advise you to visit me periodically. Not because I'd like to reestablish contact with Dr. Tamar, my colleague at this Balkan institution. Not at all! For your own good. Because of your illness, if we may call it that. We may, you conceded this. You conceded it, don't forget, you agreed, and it's good you did so."

The envelope had passed from the blond one's hands to his brown-haired brother's, continuing to spell out its message from the informant doctor.

"I hope you remember your diagnosis: Reality Phobia. Product of the camps and a period of increased hypnosis after the camps. I remember you didn't like the disease's name. You contested it vehemently. You may call it whatever you'd like, Refusal to be Complicit, the Privilege of the Lair, Absent Without Leave. Any name will work, what's important is that you pay attention to it. You promised, don't forget. Don't forget! Even though you'll be far away, at your sister's. Far, far away . . . The Colonel told me he gave you free passage."

Without opening his eyes, the sleepwalker tensed and raised himself up on his elbows to confront reality. He waited a few minutes, blinked his heavy eyelids with difficulty. Nothing, no one. The same as yesterday, as the day before yesterday! The actors masquerading as the police had disappeared as if they had never been. They had even taken the envelope with them, so as to leave no trace. Yes, they had taken the yellow, lemon-colored, hypocrisy-tinged envelope with them. The wanderer collapsed again among the pillows but could not fall back asleep.

Everything had been set off by Günther's absence, but yesterday's message had been the real cause. How . . . and when had he snuck out into the night from his monastic cell, silent, on tiptoes? Instead of the usual morning coffee that Günther took special care to prepare every morning, the Wanderer found only the smallest sign of life. A message with a brief injunction in red ink: "Read the papers!" It suggested that the former instructor of Pioneers had returned in secret at night, when he knew his dead-tired friend would be asleep after the long day, and then had disappeared again, as on the previous evening.

The papers were indeed alarming, though the alarm, which rendered comprehensible the general panic, sounded different in their various pages: "The Russians Arrive Tomorrow"; "The Americans are Coming!"; "The End of the Second World War"; "Holes in the Wall"; "We'll be Reunited!"; "Kennedy's Homage: Wir Sind Alle Berliner"; "The Czechs and Hungarians Send Us a Message"; "The Third Global Massacre on Its Way"; "Everything Now Depends on Kremlin's Misha Lemonade";[31] "Stock up on Food and Portable Radios"; "Now's the Time! It's Between the Yanks and the Siberians." The traveler asked himself if he should immediately return to the place he had left or if he should become a spectator to the pranks of History from his current, privileged position. He had only just left and could go back to his rebel friends and to Colonel Tudor. Or he could stay here, between worlds, participating in the pathetic political meetings Günther was involved in and chanting the slogans of freedom. Or, maybe . . . the third way: he could fly faster toward nowhere, where Agatha waited on a painted branch.

Feverish, restless, he'd been infected by the hysteria of

the moment. Confused, he was on alert, like the passersby on the streets who spoke only of the apocalypse. He must lie in wait for Günther, take advantage of his brief reappearances and try to understand what was happening, ask for his advice, as an old and trusty companion from their teenage years. His sleep was restless, the nightmares succeeded one another without rhyme or reason. On a stormy night, in the small room, maybe yesterday, or the day before yesterday, or even today, he had again seen the two visitors who had come to notify him of his arrest and of the impending Trial prepared for him: the same twins: one sitting on the toilet seat, the other at the small table near the window.

After they disappeared, would he find a message from Colonel Tudor again? Yes, there was a yellow envelope on the floor, under the table, but it had no address. Inside was a message in rushed handwriting: "I advise you to visit me periodically, like any good and conscientious patient. Not because I wish to reestablish any kind of collegial contact with Tamar, though I know you've taken refuge with her. No, I have no such intention, none at all! It's about your illness. I've called it Reality Phobia, and that's what it is. You can call it what you like: Obsession with Solitude, Refusal to Hope, Infectious Suspicion, the Reading Addiction. Whether it's the result of the camps when you were a child or of what followed later is no longer important. Look me up before you leave. I insist. I only wish what's best for you . . . as your doctor and friend."

What's best for me or for Colonel Tudor?

The sleepwalker hesitated with one hand on the phone, ready to call Jennifer, or the police, or the hospital. In Günther's narrow studio there was nary a mouse, nary a fly, nary an umbrella from which he could seek advice. His dilemmas had neither simple nor easy solutions. He had wrestled with similar ones for years, for decades, under the gilded shadow of the hammer and sickle. Having withdrawn into the matchbox-like little room, he nevertheless put in a regular appearance at the debates organized by his accomplices in rebellious rhetoric. Had it all been just another routine? The polar opposite of the routines the state had stolen for itself, nationalized, and subsequently reimplemented? And if so? Nothing. Nothing. He had ended up in the same place, far from the madding crowd. In a foreign capital with a dubious past, having withdrawn into the library and garden of Mr. Adelbert von Chamisso. And now, when the explosion had finally reached the Wailing Wall between the East and West, would the Nomad run away again from what was happening, which he had not dared hope for, only because he no longer had the courage to believe in reality? Because he was armed against bright, sparkly traps? What would the wailers from the East do once they reached the other side of the Wall? Or their fellow countrymen, for that matter, who had ceased to be their fellow countrymen decades earlier, concerned as they were only with taxes and tariffs, rather than with any kind of protest or the future of mankind? And what would these individuals do when their new Eastern neighbors, who at last had jumped over the walls, filled the streets and stores and churches that they previously hadn't had access to, demanding shelter, food, and job training? Poor sods come late to the table of plenty, forced to teach the arrogant children of the Nation and the Banknote that the enemy is not necessarily the inferior race, but can even be a member of one's historical family, someone who had wandered for years in the desert of deception and terror. Ach, let's see them together then, blood brothers of the Hooked Cross! And I, the eternal wanderer, where and how will I find refuge, suspect by definition on every side, in any territory I may find myself?

He had learned to shave every morning, but on this rainy, festive morning when the Wall shook much like himself, he felt the need to protest against the game of gods and of chance. He reseated himself at the table and contemplated the black circle of the coffee, waiting for the two twins on a mission. He watched the cup and the clock, allowing for the requisite amount of time. Then, having doubled the amount, he stood up solidly on his long, thin legs. No, today he would not shave! Not today, he had more important things to do. Before closing the door, he snuck the passport with the proletarian emblem into his briefcase. On the table was his message to Günther, in case the latter reappeared after his guest's departure: "Thank you for everything. I am forced to leave your marvelous, fractured metropolis just as it is becoming whole and glorious again. My much-beloved sister is getting a divorce. I can no longer dawdle. So, I'm putting on Schlemihl's flying boots, and I am gone in the blink of an eye."

IN FLIGHT

The one-time Pioneer and his friend, the instructor, sat down on the bench, just as once upon a time, watching each other sympathetically. They were waiting for the boarding announcement. They were roused to intense debate.

"I won't insist if it's truly a family issue, though I doubt it. But we're not talking about a simple trick of history, as I think you'd like to believe. In fact, it's an extraordinary event, something we've all dreamed of. A unique chance to be in the here and now, at the heart of the explosion! I'm not convinced by any of your arguments."

"I wouldn't be convinced either."

"Does that mean you'll stay? At least a month—a week? I think the Wall will bite the dust in a week, and we'll get to hear the cheers."

"It would be presumptuous to stay. I haven't contributed anything to the great victory. And I don't feel like celebrating it here, here where my sickness—all my sicknesses—hail from. Not just the cross I bear, but the Hooked Cross."[32]

"It's not all just Karl and Adolf. There's also Chamisso."

"He was French and an aristocrat. An exile. He doesn't have anyone to join him in his rebellion."

"You should stay, even if only for me . . . Join me in that great embrace on the Day of Restoration. There'll be plenty for you to see as a student of the circus. The long dreamed-of Teutonic reunification . . . The prosperous Westerners and the famished Easterners fallen on hard times. An extraordinary lesson! The Germans don't only hate the Jews; people can also hate their compatriots, those of the same blood and the same faith. You're a human being, aren't you? The Westerners are all afraid that their brothers from the East will diminish their incomes and taint their beer—those dirty boors raised by Honecker, Comrade Ulbricht, and their ancestors Marx and Engels. It will be some show, believe me! The thrill of unification will fizzle out as soon as the Westerners look in their wallets. You'll see what national unity—what historical identities—really come down to. The Easterners will raise the flag of surplus value discovered by another German, though—it's true—an unclean one! The grandson of a rabbi, Herr Karl *der grosse* Marx . . . "

Günther continued his plea with diminished passion. Finally, he took an envelope out of his rucksack.

"I kept hoping you'd change your mind. I've put off giving you this. It's from Jennifer."

"A certificate of virility?"

"You could skip the sarcasm. Jennifer is a wonderful person. I know her well. Honest, brave, enlightened. I understand you've dropped out of your lessons?"

"Recently. After I decided to schedule my flight. I didn't tell her anything, but she knew."

"Yes, she has extraordinary intuition, you know."

"I know. She's generous with surprises. I'd expected everything but the initiating lesson and the final one. I told you about the initiation. Surprisingly, a perfectly scholarly and chaste period followed. Nothing, not a single gesture of closeness, not a single allusion. I kept wondering whether it had all been a dream or one of the nightmares that often plague me. Or, more likely, just disappointment. As you know, I'm vulnerable to doubts. But then, boom! When I had stopped expecting anything, recently, after we went to the concert, came the recapitulation of the debut. The initiation lesson taken up again, just the same! As if there had been no break. An identical beginning and end: pathos and passion. And professionalism, I could add, though you'll say I'm being sarcastic."

"You are, you are! That's the issue! She wrote to her uncle at the university."

"What uncle? What university?"

"She has an uncle who adores her. He is the president of some Yankee university or college, I don't know. She wrote to him about the wanderer from the East. A kind of letter of recommendation. She says this uncle has never refused her anything."

"Another reason to take off. So, what's in that envelope?"

"The address of said uncle and something to read on your flight. An English lesson, to make up for lost time."

Günther removed the small, thin, yellow gift from the envelope.

"*The Schlemiel as Modern Hero.* Look here—at the chapters: 'Ironic Balance for Psychic Survival.' And further down: 'The American Dreamer' and 'The Schlemiel as Liberal Humanist.' And the publishing house: The University of Chicago Press. Chicago & London. Your world of bookworms. A phobia, or reality's inherent potential?"

"Yes, yes, but they're announcing the flight, and it's about time. A last question, since I don't know if and when we'll see each other again. I won't ask you about the three Semitic wives you've divorced, or why, or what kind of terms you're on with any of them. The first was Zimra, who changed her name to Zoia. Zoia Kosmodemianskaia, the heroine of the Soviet Union. Next Shulamit, whom you'd taken to calling Sula. Then, lastly, Erika—no? None of them succeeded in curing you of Jews. Why are you so fascinated with the Jews, to the point of obsession? Is it the persecution? There are others, always others who are persecuted. Don't forget you're a progressive and a universalist, a cosmopolitan, an internationalist. Why the Jews?"

"German guilt. I'm German after all, even if I was raised

between the Carpathians and the Danube. Of course, there are always others who are also turned into devils and who are hounded and driven off, but the Jews keep their place of honor. Always and always. Before and after Jesus, before and after Hitler, Stalin, and Haman the Persian. First place in the rankings. I foresee only additional proofs, not improvements. Even in our idyllic times when the compass points are getting closer and bleeding into one another. But you? I won't ask you about the circus, which is also immortal. I'm asking you why you keep running away from yourself? Why you plug up your ears anytime you hear anything about the Holocaust, pogroms, ethnic hatreds?"

The voyager was silent. After a time, he looked at the watch on his left wrist. It was late, the steel bird had started its engines.

"Pride, Günther. I refuse pity, I hate the wailing. I leave it up to the others . . . those who massacred and burned us . . . to explain themselves."

"Meaning me? Me? That's what I do, and I see it annoys you."

"There's also the fear of having to relieve reality. Once is enough."

"You'd leave the task of ransacking the German past and the history of the persecuted to me?"

"I no longer believe in a task. I don't want to weigh you down with anything. It's all the same to me."

"Can it be a matter of no significance to you, of all people?"

"It can be, *mein Herr*. Especially to me, the expert on clowns and the circus. Is this what you wanted me to say?"

"Not at all. We are at the airport, we are parting. It's not by chance that we are here together."

"Maybe not."

"Then tell me when you became blind and deaf. Are you prepared for exile? Exile in the country of exiles?"

"Perhaps. Your dialectics defeat me but don't convince me. They defeat me, and they resurrect me for a fraction of a second, but they don't convince me."

"What would convince you?"

"A meeting between Karl and Adolf, the shadows that haunt us. Or, rather, haunt you. I'm immune."

"How did that happen? Since when? For how long?"

"Repeated immunization. The quotidian burlesque."

"That's too easy! Just rhetoric! I don't even recognize you."

"An advantage for us both. It makes saying goodbye easier."

A long, lengthening silence. Predictably, the traveler said nothing, but his friend could not keep quiet for long.

"Can I write to you? We're in the free world, aren't we? You'd write back?"

"I don't know. The future is uncertain."

"Should I write to your sister?"

"Under no circumstances! She's not a part of this."

"She could be."

"No, I'd prefer you keep her out of our disputes."

"Then I'll write to you."

"Whatever you like."

"I'd like to, I'm a stubborn German."

"Then I promise to read your Berlin missives."

"But you won't answer?"

"I don't know. I can't speculate."

As at their first meeting, the pair embraced one another in a brotherly fashion, supplementing feeling with a manly shoulder pounding, as if the future deserved just as much desperation as the past.

Hesitating, the traveler climbed the stairs to the future, grasping the metal handrail, not looking down so he wouldn't get dizzy.

And again, it was the second day. His seat was near the window, the neighboring seat was free, the stewardess thin and blonde.

Had he bled climbing up into the plane? Not at all. Only a slight dizziness, as before crossing the Styx. He was curled up in the narrow seat, lost in the belly of the flying beast.

"Don't you feel well?" the stewardess asked.

The pallid walking stick did not answer. He felt well, really, no reason to worry, only a bit of emotion, as on one's first transatlantic flight. The flying fortress was American, it was familiar with oceans and crossing them. The passengers were few and in good spirits. No reason for concern. The stewardess served orange juice, and the whiskey, too, would come, as well as the flavorless soup . . . our client, our master, we worship you! The client did not seem interested in the menu. He had taken out the little yellow scrap from his pocket along with the slightly bigger book, which was also yellow, trying to defend himself from the boredom of the prolonged trip.

Nach einer glücklichen . . . jedoch beschwerlichen Fahrt . . .[33] Chamisso's fairytale warned. The reader looked for the episode with Mr. John's banquet and its warning to the wanderer that he needed a million to become an honorable citizen. Then he looked at the ending, with the magic boots that could take you anywhere in the blink of an eye. Mr. John? Yes, yes, it was John, wasn't it, that the girlish Jennifer also had mentioned. John-something-or-other. John, yes, John Patrick Johnson was written on the note stuck to the first page of the monograph he had received as a gift.

Mr. John Patrick Johnson, that's my uncle. He already knows all about you, the dainty polyglot had written. Then, the address of the college president, J. P. J., his home and work telephone numbers, and the name of his wife, formerly a Swedish widow. Then the academic title: Doctor of Philosophy. Ah, such a fitting dessert for a bookworm's lunch!

The schlemiel *is a character of folklore and fiction [. . .] He stands in the age-old company of fools, embodying the most outstanding folly of his culture: its weakness.*

The schlemiel *is vulnerable and inept. The* schlemiel *is neither saintly nor pure, but only weak. The sleight of hand of his comedy is intended to persuade us that this weakness is strength. In much the same way, the technique of adaptation required of the Jew that he reinterpret his weakness as its opposite, for how else could a weakling survive?*

The refusal to be defined by others is not merely a convenient pose that can be assumed by anyone wanting to turn the tables on his oppressor. The tight internal structure of the Jewish community and the intricate code of behavior by which each individual governed his daily life produced this strong sense of identity

as one of its by-products. Interestingly, in modern Jewish litera-
ture when the individual moves within his own community, its
stultifying and repressive tendencies are emphasized; once the
Jew emerges from this community to confront the wider world,
his background is translated into a source of individual worth,
strength of identity, even personal freedom. For many reasons,
some odd, others natural, this unlikely hero, the schlemiel, be-
came a recurrent figure in American culture during the 1950s.

The proliferation of the schlemiel *has not gone unnoticed.*
However, like so much else in America, he stands cut loose from
his roots, and neither he nor his audience seems aware of his
origins.[34]

An elementary English lesson? It demanded rereading, again and again. Jennifer's student had not met his teacher's high expectations. It was worth trying the exercise once more. But the passenger was sleepy and exhausted; he hadn't slept all night, what with celebrating Günther's reappearance in his lair and their incipient parting.

All night the talk went on, about what would come after the Wall, what other Walls would spring up in their place (where? and how? what kind?). After all, people would never give them up, would they? A provocative question from the wanderer who knew walls all too well. Just as in years and ages past, the liveliness of the conversation was genuine and deserved to be celebrated.

Except now, on the narrow seat of the flying beast, he

would have liked to fall asleep. He didn't have the courage to, he wasn't sure that the twins wouldn't put in an appearance to remind him of the elegant colonel and the doctor who served him.

The most detailed etymological inquiry into the term schlemiel *(schlemihl, shlemiel, etc.) can be found in Dov Sadan's Hebrew article "Lesugia: shlumiel" [On the problem of the schlemiel] in* Orlogin *1 (December 1950): 198–203. Professor Sadan establishes the currency of the word in German usage before the nineteenth century, citing in particular Grimm's dictionary in which the word is traced to a Jewish underworld slang, and to the Hebrew word* schlimazl, *meaning luckless. Bringing numerous examples from Hebrew and Yiddish writing, Professor Sadan shows that the term generally refers to the good and devoted man who has no luck, who is either accidentally or characteristically a prey to misfortune.*[35]

Unfortunately, the subject could not be brought up with Günther . . . Hysterical, he had exploded after the first, timid attempts: "You've taken this up now, now when the Wall is finally about to fall? Of course, there'll be others! Of course, Walls are inevitable! But at least one of them is about to blow up! Now, here and now, where there have been walls on top of walls, all the time walls!"

Although Professor Sadan cannot substantiate the claim that Chamisso thought of his protagonist as a Jew, he analyzes the book to show that Peter Schlemihl is subconsciously modelled on the figure of Ahasuersus, the wandering Jew, and the lack of a shadow (which all other men possess) is the closest metaphorical equivalent for the lack of a homeland (which all other men possess). He also shows that in the works of many of Chamisso's

German-Jewish contemporaries, the term schlemiel *came to be used in a fairly specific way: not for the simple bungler, but to represent the man fated to be different, homeless, alien, and Jewish.*

Of course, Professor Sadan also refers to the most famous etymological explanation for the term, Heinrich Heine's bogus claim, in Hebrew Melodies, *that the name originates with Herr Schlemihl ben Zurishaddai, head of the tribe of Simeon (Numbers 7:36), who was killed accidentally by the irate Phineas as he was trying to assassinate Zimri, thereby introducing for all time the type of the hapless victim. Heine called all poets the descendants of that first* schlemiel. *Professor Sadan says wryly that the creator of the prototypical* schlemiel *was himself its embodiment—Heine's statue, like Peter Schlemihl's shadow, being banished from his native soil and finally finding refuge only in the unlikely harbor of New York.*[36]

The words were shaking, and the reader dozed, despite the fact he was only at the beginning of his journey to far and distant lands. Heine's statue, Peter Schlemihl's shadow, New York's implausible shore . . . he turned the leaves of the little yellow book. Dizzily, he tried to peruse it, drawn in by familiar names. Don Quixote, Menahem Mendel, Oblomov, Herzog, Dostoevsky's idiot, Nabokov's Pnin, the Prague Samsa, and Ulrich, Musil's solitary Man without Qualities, together with his sister, Agatha, the Trieste Zeno, Monsieur Meursault and Monsieur Berenger, he couldn't find any of them . . . The author, Ruth Wisse, concerned herself only with wanderers from the Eastern European diaspora. But then in the chapter "Holocaust Survivor," on the *schlemihl's* relationship to the survivors of the darkness, there was André Schwarz-Bart's *Le dernier des justes,* yes, though Gimpel the Fool was no survivor, despite being a *tam,* meaning a fool, naïve. But where was Singer's Herman, the survivor who had burned in crematoria for the rest of his life? No, not there. Neither was Bassani's Grosz, nor Tišma, nor Kertesz, nor Kiš, Levi, or Celan. He was falling asleep, he was asleep, the two twins sent by ben Zurishaddai from the tribe of Simeon were lying in wait for him, to let him know that the Trial had been delayed far below, on earth, at a low altitude, in the always incomplete guiltlessness of guilt.

In the air, however, the traveler seemed to be on a visit to his teacher's uncle, John. He has prepared himself by reading about Peter Schlemihl's visit, the appearance of the go-between, the Man in Gray, and the latter's proposal to purchase Schlemihl's shadow.

"Is it for sale?"

Stupefied, the emigrant quickly came to his senses.

"Sale? Why not. It's no use to me. Do you pay well?"

"Wondrously well, you'll see."

Sleep, yes, the optimal therapy, the paradise of apathy! Ornamental angels, Jennifer the affectionate, the doctor and the airport officials, the Library of Alexandria with all the books in the world, and you let yourself be carried forward on the night sea breeze, free and unharmed, without a compass or watch, floating in the clouds of salubrious amnesia to a shore blue as the sky, where good luck waves its handkerchief in welcome.

He was coming nearer, yes, he was approaching the diaphanous shore where hope fluttered, he could not ready himself and had no reason or means to, but could only let himself be carried on by the perfumed, deceitful breeze. Inertia, yes, inertia, that was all, apathy and disillusionment, that's all. It could last however long, time and duration no longer existed, absence could last and would do so as long as necessary.

Angels' diaphanous fingers touched him. He didn't have the strength to open his eyes, to wake up who-knew-when-or-where, alienated from himself. No, it was better not to, the plane's slight shaking felt like a touch, the angels touched him, they had found him, they . . . Slowly, ever so slowly, he opened his eyes so that others could know him for himself.

"Don't you feel well?" the stewardess asked, her ethereal hand on his shoulder.

She was just as before: slim and blonde. He didn't have the strength to contradict her, the words died on his lips.

"I noticed you were sleeping very restlessly. I was worried. Would you like something to drink? Water, tea, coffee, whiskey, wine? Whatever might help . . . "

"Yes, yes, whiskey. I hadn't thought of that, but it would be just the thing."

The slim, conscientious blonde retreated so as to return with the poison. The traveler fell asleep again, instantaneously. Only the stewardess's diaphanous touch, skin on skin, persisted, as in his childhood dreams and in his dreams years later, when Tamar would curl up in her brother's seashell, or eggshell, as they called it, or spoon, or lair, and they would fold themselves into each other, naked, skin on skin, silk on silk, two felines folded up, inseparable, one, as they wished, let the years, assaults, ages, and torrents pass over them. Nothing would touch them, untangle them. As in the long ago past, the traveler had curled up to make room for his sister in the hollow of the airplane seat made only for her, then, now, and for ages upon ages, past and passing. Torpor, celestial rocking. Again together. One body, as before, as always, one body, the unhallowed and overpowering vertigo. He was blinded. By the light of her hands, which were tightened like a snare around him, by the perfect lines of her feet, which clung to him in tenderness, like vines come to life, and by the deep, clear voice that always translated for him the Destiny of the implacable double, triple, multiple paths and byways of exile.

The emptiness of deception, endless. The plane's shaking. Soon, there would be a second diaphanous, angelic touch, which would ask him to open his eyes.

"You fell asleep again . . . I'm glad. Now you're better. I've brought the magic elixir. The others have already deplaned. I can help, if you'd like."

By no means, we are in the Promised Land, every man follows his own star!

The burn of the alcohol was efficient. It traveled the length of his body, like an electrical charge. A moment of bewilderment. Boom. Boom. Then wakefulness.

THE REUNION

He had descended the airstair slowly, had waited patiently for the appearance of his suitcase, had headed toward the exit without rushing. He quickly identified the silhouette and face of his sister in the waiting multitude. He no longer walked forward, nor did she run toward him, as the screenplay suggested she might. They stood at a distance, watching each other.

The traveler closed his eyes to see her better: a young girl, then a young woman, standing next to her tall, slim brother, who, bending slightly, embraced her shoulders, then much earlier, the two of them in identical pajamas, when he carried her in his arms to their beds in the orphanage. Then later, at graduation, when he had waited for her, roses in hand, to walk down the front steps of the university building, the *infanta* from the story standing next to her brother dressed in a tracksuit. Then again, a teenager in a skirt that was too short, in love with her brother, then the doctor in a white coat, all grown up, then the marriage to the journalist, then the visit to her mother's grave, searching for redemption from past and future sins.

He opened his eyes: his sister was a step away. She was neither Schlemihl's Mina, nor Jennifer, the polyglot. Simply Agatha.

"Agatha," the traveler whispered, picking her up in his arms.

"*Not* Agatha," the cherished one whispered back. "I'm Tamar, your beloved sister. Beloved. The only. Tamar. Tamara. That is what your aunt named me, my mother."

They didn't kiss. They each waited timidly for the other, overwhelmed with feeling, trying to keep it in check. They wandered toward the taxis holding hands. Then they were together in the taxi. Then, on their way to the hotel. Silent, distant, each had turned inward.

———————

The room was not large, but it was airy. On the table: a bottle of wine, two glasses, a photograph, the brother and sister at the age at which they became b'nei mitzvah. Solemn postures. Two shy prospective spouses frightened of the eyes of the world. They turned toward each other suddenly, in a fierce, painful, everlasting embrace.

"How long can this go on? How long?" Agatha sighed.

"Until we are a single body again."

"Leave the suitcase, you can take it up to your room later. It's just one floor up."

"My own room? What's the point? Are these the rules here?"

"Not at all. I . . . it's just what I decided. It's better that way. Or maybe it's better."

"Can the better be preferable to the good?"

"I think so. And you do, too."

A long, very long silence followed.

"Okay, whatever you want. We agree again."

"I was sure we would. I felt it. So, maybe it's better."

"Yes, yes, the better that's preferrable to the good."

Tamar was laughing, her full, young laugh filled the room as her brother filled the glasses. They toasted, they looked at each other, they couldn't get enough.

"What kind of wine is this?"

"Made special for a doubly important event like this."

"Doubly?"

"Yes, my divorce and your arrival."

"Really? I thought you were putting it off."

"It *was* put off but not by me. There were long debates. Much too long. We don't have children, I was not caught in

111

flagrante delicto, nor was he, there are no difficulties regarding the separation. But he won't forgive me. He feels humiliated, and he will never forgive me that. But I'm standing on my own two feet now. And they're still lovely . . . "

She pulled up her skirt to show him the silky, soft, enchanting skin. Then she continued:

"Nevertheless, he wrote you a letter of recommendation."

"To whom, Colonel Tudor?"

"No, to a great university in this country."

"He hopes to get me as far away from you as possible."

"Yes, that's right. He was suspicious from the beginning."

"No one asked me whether I wanted a letter of recommendation to the Balkan hellhounds or to the Yankee academics."

"He asked me to speak on your behalf, in your name. He wrote to a former college friend, who is now the president of a major university. As for the colonel, anything was worth the price of getting you out of that place. Or don't you agree?"

"Yes, yes. Of course, I agree. And I did get out. Meaning, I was allowed to leave. The circumcised Wanderer wandered forth in the footsteps of German Günther! And now I'm here, with you. But let's drop it. What are we drinking?"

"It's special. Prince Cantacuzino. To remind us of the history of our common homeland.

"So let's drink to the past."

He bent down to kiss her, but she put her hand over her lips.

"I said the past, to the past. Our past! Our kiss, our pact. The good, only good things," the brother insisted.

Tamar glued herself to him, as in the past. She had again put her arms around his neck, and she kissed him at length, as in times past. They drank the bottle of wine in silence.

"Take off your shoes, I want to see your legs from top to bottom. And your hands and your arms up to your shoulders." That was his obsession: hands and feet. Tamar threw her white blouse onto the bedspread, she was in her bra and panties as long ago, she . . . but the private viewing came to an end.

"Do you remember how you used to kiss your hands, your own hands, in your sleep?"

Her brother was pale and growing paler, it was obvious that he was having difficulty controlling himself. "Yes, and you got scared. You were next to me, awake, you thought I'd gone crazy. And I thought they were your hands rather than mine. Another kind of madness."

"No, a lesser one. We both laughed at how you gave yourself away in your sleep."

"Not only in my sleep. You shook me so hard, you tried so hard to wake me up. You didn't know I was kissing your hands."

"No, I didn't know, it was not my nightmare. It was yours. You were kissing my hands, you thought they were mine, but they were your own hands. A nightmare?"

Her brother did not answer, contemplating his sister's, his other half's hands and feet. It was not the nightmare past but an ongoing one.

"We'll go down to the restaurant. Then you can take your suitcase to your room, and we'll go to sleep. Each of us safely anesthetized in our own rooms and beds."

Her brother watched as she dressed, slowly, ever so slowly, and did not answer. The restaurant was nearly empty, and they ate without pleasure and spoke very little.

"I reserved a room for you on a different floor. It's for

three months. You'll have the time to take a language class for newcomers. You have to confront reality."

"You know what I think about reality."

"I will always be by your side, literally and figuratively, as you well know."

"I had almost forgotten. I thought that's what you wanted, for me, for us to forget."

"You're not allowed to. I won't either. And I don't want to. The rooms are a floor apart, not a continent. Colonel Tudor would be happy to know that you don't get along with this reality either. But it's a different reality, you'll see. Your phobia is an old one, but so was the reality it was responding to."

"A new reality. Of course. But still reality."

"It deserves a chance. It's an experiment with amnesia, a new beginning."

"I'm ready. I bought myself a guidebook in the airport, written by a stranger like me."

"Books again! Books and more books! I am not Agatha, I told you. I am Tamara, or Mara, as you like."

"You know what I like. But I'll take your decision into account."

"It's for the best, you're not the brother without qualities either. Let me see the guidebook."

A pamphlet made its appearance on the table: *In Praise of Shadows*. Jun'ichirō Tanizaki.

"The Japanese author maintains that our shadows disappear in this practical, mercantile world. All we are left with is an emblem of the past, the kind of thing Far Easterners seek. A different aesthetic. Perhaps even a different ethics, compared to those of the capitalist marketplace. Here, even shadows are on sale. The shadow like everything else—kidneys, heart, sperm. A great carnival of capital, of perpetual change. You buy and sell. And after you've sold what you have to sell, you buy again. Even money is bought and sold in our modern temples of international, global banking. I wish I could deposit my shadow in a metal safety deposit box and send you the key in the mail."

"Those are clichés."

"True to reality."

"Perhaps. But they're still clichés. All the lacunae, the mysteries gone. All the ambiguities. Whatever could have seemed most interesting, most inviting about this place. But let's not think about it anymore until tomorrow. You're tired, of course."

"I am. Though not tired enough. Never enough."

"I plan to stay another week to help you adjust. I'm afraid I can't stay longer than that." At dawn, he heard the diffident knock, like a rat's scratching. The nocturnal ghosts' double. Had the two ghosts of the past returned? The shadows sent by Colonel Tudor to search the premises of the Wanderer's new refuge? The two trusty agents capable of finding him anywhere?

"Yes, it's me," Tamara whispered. "Here to welcome you." The nightgown had already slipped to the floor, his sister was naked, naked like at the beginning of time. Tempting, as always. Her brother kissed her hands, her hands and feet, as he had long ago, as he had always.

And, again, the evening and the morning were the second day.

A stroll through the city. Agatha clinging to the walking

stick's long arm. A reunited couple. Sunlight, that infant's happiness.

In front of the White House, her long fingers held him back.

"Don't rush. Look carefully at that statue."

The visitor looked attentively at the statue of President Washington, the symbol of the capital.

"That's a statue of Washington, his coat is missing a button.[37] Have you ever come across something like that before? The president of the country! Of the New Empire! Symbolic statue. National Symbol. Can you imagine something like that set in stone anywhere else? By the British Imperial Crown, the German Reich, the great French Republic, tsarist or Stalinist Russia? It's not an accident. It's not even iconoclastic. It's pure realism, authentic, inevitable. The accepted imperfection of the real. The tie between the nation's chosen people and her common citizens. The Novelty of the New World."

Obviously, Tamar was recounting from memory, or perhaps only ransacking the frontiers of imagination. "This is where you've landed. Where we've landed."

"And where can I hide?"

"Nowhere, you don't have any way to. But you could disappear. If tomorrow morning you disappear without a trace from the hotel, we'll see each other again in twenty years when you miss me again. In the meantime, the devil find you. Though you never know, the devil could be in possession of the map of this continent, with its little colored flags marking the lairs where refugees from reality are hiding. Though I think Sima made that diagnosis only to protect you from the Colonel and his bloodhounds."

"Hardly. The Colonel knew about my meetings with the dissidents."

"So reality represents something else, not a phobia, but something else."

"Both something else and phobia. In Berlin, my friend Günther couldn't understand why I didn't want to see the fall of the Wall. I just can't trust illusions anymore. I can't. That's the phobia."

Her brother looked at her. She was the same as always, as long before, and yet she was not the same. She also looked at him with an excess of concentration. She had relinquished her usual shyness and that discretion that became her so well in favor of an Anglo-Saxon bearing. She was even more elegant than she had been on the day of their reunion, though her elegance was simple, as usual, and became her, as usual, as if she had not been born in a concentration camp and grown up in squalor, under terror.

Tamar halted in the middle of the path, scrutinizing the snail who had halted before her shoe tips. "Look, we have a companion! He is barring our way, letting us know that he exists and that he wants to come with us. Oh, what a meeting . . . I never wrote you about my depression, did I? A colleague from Chile at the hospital brought me a book about a snail who, simply by his presence, healed a young woman who had been ill and bedridden for a long time. A mute, enigmatic presence. A therapeutic one. The wandering snail has returned to welcome its exiles, wanderers like himself. Frightened, he is prepared to retreat into his shell at a moment's notice. An accomplice if not a relative, this messenger. Look, President Washington even took care of this: he sent us an American to welcome us. A wanderer. In solidarity with the wanderers of the world who have gathered here to pay homage to the president with a missing button. Let's sit down. Here, on this green bench."

They sat down. Tamar held the snail in her palm, in a large white handkerchief. "I'm taking him with me, this small witness to your return. Or do you want him? He'd keep you company. He's unobtrusive, eats very little, makes no noise."

Tamar had already snuck the snail wrapped in the handkerchief into her purse.

"You've noticed that I'm not shipshape," the brother murmured at last.

"Who is this day and age? Everyone has their own shipwreck."

"I call it the Schlemihl shipwreck. As for poor Peter, the main character in the story I told you, we don't know where he came from or where he went. All we know is that, in the end, he retreated into a cave, far from the joys of human companionship. He took up the study of nature, like his creator, Herr von Chamisso. Not human nature, but the nature around him. The journey had clarified the problem of his fellow humans for him long before."

"I'm not shipshape either, and I wasn't referring to literary shipwrecks. It's probably your arrival, but maybe it's also my arrival . . . toward you. Perhaps you remember, I used to have those cyclical breakdowns, or depressions, especially in the summer. For no particular reason. Only the nothingness, the void, which it made worse. I'm reliving those summers, the summers of the past."

"The past barely in the past. But it's no longer summer. The fall rushes headlong into winter."

"I know. It means the cycle has been altered. Its frequency has changed. Or increased. I'm sorry, I wish I could be clearer, more collected here, at our reunion."

"I'm not either. But we still exist, we continue to exist, don't we? That's the most important thing. We're part of the same landscape again. When will your divorce finally be over with?"

"I don't know; it won't be easy. He was pleading, then adamant, then threatening. He won't give up easily. He promised me infinite freedom, I don't have a reason to leave him."

"What about the freedom to take me in?"

"The freedoms he had in mind were of no importance to me. I want to be alone and to rediscover myself. That's all."

"So we can't be together even after the divorce."

"It wouldn't be wise."

"You called me. I came."

"You had to get out of that impasse. And I'll visit you, and you'll visit me. We'll see each other."

"For coffee."

"We'll have as much time as we like or can stand."

"Perfect. That's fair."

There was no reproach in her brother's voice.

And the evening and the morning, and night, it was night, the night of departure.

"For this night of departure, I've supplied us with a new bottle of Prince Cantacuzino. It's hard to find, expensive. It's also the snail's first night with us. Meaning, with you. I'm going to relinquish my claims on him. Not so that he'll replace me, but so that, mute and blind as he is, he'll be with you. A

119

gift to you from me, not from the president with the missing button."

After the glasses were filled and emptied, the voice from the long ago past spoke again.

"Do you remember that Soviet film *The Shadows of Forgotten Ancestors*? Parajanov, wasn't it? I think that was the director's name. It had something to do with the Carpathians, didn't it? We saw it together, I was sitting on your lap. What happened to us, so early on, led to this, too. Alone, orphans, the two of us were left alone in the world. We burrowed into one another. Reality Phobia was it? Our reality. We had decided never to speak with anyone about ourselves ever again! The past was barely past, as you put it. We erased the words harassment, pogroms, camps, Holocaust, hatred, persecutions, Judah from our vocabulary. We didn't want to accept the roles that had been written for us."

"Is this what you want to discuss? Is this why you've invited Prince Cantacuzino?"

The night of her departure, which should have been the night of their reunion, proved to be long and hard and difficult to forget. Her brother acceded to her wishes as he always had.

A week after his sister's departure, the brother phoned President John Patrick Johnson, Jennifer's uncle. Agatha no longer wanted to be Agatha. The library cannot save anyone from despair.

When that overwhelming shade
From its talons lets me escape

Yawp! I shout
Yawp! replies the smothered echo.[38]

MR. JOHN

He was halted at the gate of the imposing property by a man in a black suit and tie. He showed him the invitation, then the man made a phone call, curtly pronouncing the strange name of the guest syllable by syllable, then nodded, pointing toward the garden where the pleasant trill of the guests' conversation issued forth. A clink of glasses and youthful voices toasting, it was a sizable gathering. The invitation underscored the nature of the festivities: the president's wife had just returned from Hong Kong together with her son from her previous marriage, whose entry into adulthood was being celebrated. Surrounding the happy family—the handsome president, the beautiful blonde, the young man in a white suit and white shoes, hair jet black, slick with brilliantine—a group of elegant guests fought for prominence.

"Oh, it's you! The eternal wanderer! The Nomad! I'm glad you accepted the invitation. Jenny's recommendation was more than convincing. She's my favorite niece, you know. I might even call her my daughter. My brother, the great neurologist, didn't really have much time for her. She never writes letters like that one, she's very serious and despises any kind of involvement on others' behalf. I trust her completely. So, let me show you around. A refugee, aren't you? Newly escaped from the Red terror, if I recall?"

The newly arrived guest shook hands with the ladies and gentlemen surrounding the jovial president and seemed both moved and unconvinced by the kindhearted welcome of the audience, who smiled at him encouragingly.

The president did not seem to consider the conversation closed, however; he wanted to incite curiosity and prolong the good mood of his guests.

"My brother is a celebrity. And as usually happens in these parts, celebrity also means money. Steve is very wealthy, it's true, but this has never mattered to Jenny. I could even say that she's defied wealth, even scorned it, though her father's wealth was the product of hard work and well deserved. She's an ascetic in every way."

The refugee had begun to find the host's disquisition interesting; he was waiting to hear more about the asceticism of the president's niece, but Mr. John abruptly changed course.

"Forgive me, we've already come round to money. A vulgar, American subject, don't you think? It's not our fault, not even our choice. It's pure conditioning. Pragmatism built this great nation. Often, tough consequences, too. It's not like Paris, where you can get by in a crappy garret. Here, if you have a million dollars, you can live well. And if you have two, well . . . I'm not trying to discourage you, I'm trying to bring you up to speed. On the other hand, anyone can become anything. Popular democracy. You'll fit right in, you'll see."

The Nomad was silent. He felt completely out of his element. He tried to agree, nodding, miming as exiles do.

"The real issue is whether your virtues, as Jenny outlined them, can be sold on the open market. If I understand correctly, where you come from they couldn't be, not really. Here that remains to be seen. Something to think about. You'll have plenty of that to do."

The stranger took advantage of a moment when the host's attention drifted toward the guest of honor to head toward a path that led into a small wood, where others also seemed to have wandered off. On a bench, obscured from view by a bush, sat an elderly man with long hair and glasses, wearing an impeccable gray suit. The nomad sat down beside him.

"I heard John's introduction. A very intelligent man, the president. And well meaning, you should know. It's not always easy to see, he doesn't brag about it, but he really does help people. Let me introduce myself: Charlie. Lawyer. I deal with immigrants. With their paperwork, their resettlement. You won't need my services. I think they'll find you a place at the college."

"I doubt it. As he said, my few qualities are not marketable. They weren't in my country either. Then there's the language to think about. You saw yourself, it's a kind of stammering. In this place, I'm still deaf and dumb."

"This nation has room for everything and everyone. All qualities and all defects. It's not like the place you come from, with its single owner, the State. Or, the Party, right?"

The Nomad turned toward his interlocutor. Beneath the heavy gray suit, he wore a black woolen vest, and, hard to believe, he had gloves on. Next to him on the bench, a cane with a silver buffalo head for the handle, and a large black hat.

"I have nothing to sell. No one will buy my soul. Goethe and Faust are no longer in fashion. Past their expiration date."

"That's true. But if it doesn't work out with John, come see me. We'll find you something."

"Kardash" said the business card. Konrad Kardash.

"How did that turn into Charlie?"

"That's what people call me; it's easier. A nickname. But I'm from your part of the world, too."

A Hungarian? A Turk? And how did the tiny man know the Nomad's place of origin? Did Mr. John warn his guests that among them would be a newly arrived refugee from such and such country? The exile had already slipped the rectangle with gilded lettering into the many-compartmented wallet he had received as a gift from his sister. He watched the lawyer walk away with small quick steps into the rainless, sunless afternoon, hunched beneath his huge, pointless umbrella.

After a month of waiting and hesitating, he knocked on the door of Charlie Kardash's tiny office, on the top floor of an old building without an elevator. Inscribed on the door: Konrad Kardash-Greyhound (Charlie).

The small Greyhound wore terrycloth slippers and a thick red-and-green-striped sweater, over which he wore a thick black vest. He sat at the table, a cup of black tea before him. Small, freckled hands and the same minuscule glasses.

"Ah, welcome! So, good master John did not manage to find a place for the wanderer. Though he'll eventually find one, I'm sure. Of course, for now, we'll have to make do. Please take a seat in my inhospitable cell."

The client sat down on the stool facing the table stacked high with papers.

"So, what can you do? Or, rather, what could you do before?"

"Nothing. I don't even know the language. I can only make small talk. I'm taking a class, my sister enrolled me. An elementary language class, completely elementary that is, to help me get oriented."

"Aha, so you have a sister, you're not completely lost. Though you're not saved either. I understand, I understand. What does your sister do?"

"Doctor. Pediatrician. She doesn't have a license here, she wasn't able to . . . to have it accepted. She is a head nurse."

"I understand. And what did you do in the country you came from? What was your profession?"

"I worked at a research institute."

"What did you research?"

"Art. Art history."

"Yes, I remember what you said at John's party. That you didn't really have anything to sell there either. The soul, art, well, they're not in-demand products. What kind of art? What specifically in the history of art?"

"Spectacle."

"That might be worth something. Spectacle has filled us up and fills our life. You could expand your area of research."

"I was interested in the circus. I've even published a few things. A dangerous subject in my country. Dangerous but topical. Bread and circuses. Circus everywhere, bread hardly anywhere. The censors were afraid of the authorities, especially in the last decade. I was discouraged, I was working on a book. In secret. I have a list with the excerpts that were published in foreign journals."

"Interesting, interesting. That could be useful. PR. Do you know about PR? Public relations. Nothing happens without publicity. Our meeting is PR work. Networking. The network. Advertising. Packaging. Do you have any censored manuscripts? Illegal ones, I mean?"

"No, you couldn't leave the country with anything in writing, nothing printed."

"Ah, interesting," the lawyer agreed, sipping his black tea. "This, too, can be a PR detail. Meaning, it can be used as PR. I have to do some reading, some thinking. There are colleges here for clowns. Only a few, but they exist. You've also dealt with clowns?"

"Clowns especially. From the earliest to the most recent. The articles published in Italy all focused on this, on the art of clowning and on clowns. And about their place in society and in art."

"Perfect, perfect. We already have the outlines of a biography and a bibliography. I'll make inquiries, I promise. I'll find out and help you find out. Leave me your sister's address, I suppose she's the more settled one."

"No, no. Meaning yes, she's settled, but I wouldn't use her. I'll call you here to find out."

"How long have you been here?"

"A month."

"And what do you live on? You're staying at a hotel, if I've understood correctly."

"Yes, my sister booked me the room for three months. A modest hotel, but pleasant and well-situated."

"And your daily expenses?"

"She also sent me some money."

"Aha, so you're close."

"We've always been very close, since childhood. Only a half-sister, but life has strengthened our bond. We've always been together and fought for each other."

"And how are you managing?"

"I'm friends with the hotel porter, an Indian. He found me some dogs to walk. It's well paid. I wash the patisserie windows, organize the bottles of pills at the pharmacy, and so on."

"Real life! Are you interested in reality?"

"Not really. But domestic reality doesn't bother me. As an orphan, I got used to it, I survive. What I can't stand are manipulations, illusions, slogans, utopias, hope."

"Aha, so you work a little here and there, as best you can."

"I don't want to overburden Agatha."

"Ah, a beautiful name. German?

"Austrian rather."

"And how do you occupy your days? I understand you don't have friends."

"No, and I'm not looking for any. When I have free time, I go to the library here."

"Aha, so work . . . Okay, we'll keep in touch, call me in about a month. I'll find you something, I assure you."

Agatha didn't seem enthusiastic about Charlie's promises, and when the latter, at last, made a concrete suggestion, she truly seemed to panic.

"Far away, in the mountains? In a little isolated town?"

"If they hire me there, I won't stay long. A year, let's say. I'll learn more of the language, get more used to Americans. And I'll return to Mr. John on my knees, bearing Jennifer's old letter in my mouth along with a new one from the clown college."

"A year, two . . . " Tamar murmured, overwhelmed. "An

exotic clown college, hidden somewhere up in the mountains, far away from any metropolitan area. I'm sure it can only be reached on the back of a stubborn donkey, and I don't see myself riding up to your cabin."

"It's not far away from any metropolitan area, it's near a health spa. And the donkeys are only used in acrobatic acts, so you don't have anything to worry about there."

To Tamar's disappointment and the refugee's own stupefaction, the hiring interview at Buster Keaton College was wholly unconventional and took place under very favorable circumstances. The president of the college, Stephanie de Boss (small, thick-set, with curly, red hair), was European and generous.

"My parents are French, the name is my first husband's. The second one was short-lived. Now, I'm married to the college. I've dedicated myself to the circus, and, as I understand it, we share this passion. Or weakness. Are passions weaknesses? I don't think so. I was a passionate trapeze artist, and now I'm a passionate administrator. But we, the passionate, in fact are extremely serious, right? What do you think?"

"Too serious," murmured the candidate.

"In Bordeaux, my parents had friends from your beautiful country. Friendly jokesters. They said that they hailed from a wonderful country, too bad it's inhabited . . . Inhabited by clowns? That might not be so bad. Spectacle, staging, farce, magic, slapstick, acrobatics, why not? Here, in the country of all possibilities, spectacle prevails. Democracy means multitudes, and the seduction of voters. You seduce them, you buy their votes by promising them things, you accomplish all things through spectacle. Democracy? Only a quarter of the population votes . . . The majority of a quarter is next to nothing. But it's still better than the yoke or the hammer and sickle under which you all lived. I've looked over your list of publications. It's not bad at all. But your bibliography doesn't include any recent scholarship."

"There was no way of accessing it."

"I understand. Only the global circus is up to date. The global game. Do you have a favorite clown?"

The candidate was silent. His silence was impolite, but Stephanie did not seem annoyed.

"Chaplin? Or our mentor, Keaton? What do you say?"

The candidate found the courage to reenter the conversation only with difficulty.

"Peter Schlemihl. I would teach a course about Peter. He was a clown and he wasn't, that's actually the interesting part."

"Peter? Saint Peter? He wasn't a clown at all. He wasn't even funny," Mrs. Boss replied. "*Petros* means rock in Greek. Rock. I don't know what it is in Aramaic, maybe the same. Jesus named Simon Bar-Iona just that, the rock."

The refugee listened open-mouthed and kept his mouth just so, open, waiting for the enchantress's next surprise.

"I see that I've amazed you. Did you think a trapeze artist is by nature illiterate? I was a trapeze artist, and I've stayed Catholic. Catholic school is quite serious. Before acrobatics, I was taught by the sisters, and since I haven't been a trapeze artist for a long time, I've managed to find the time for books. As for your Peter, I've never heard of him. Never."

"He's not exactly a clown. The name in Hebrew refers to a befuddled person, someone who is tangled up in his own movements and thoughts."

"Hebrew . . . a Jew then?"

"Not necessarily. The name combines the Christian saint, the former Jew Peter, with the unlucky nomad and Jew Schlemihl. Only identified as a Jew when he reaches the hospital. The illness unmasks him. Depression. Anxiety. Illusions and disillusions. Alienation. Meaning, the wandering. A suspect minority figure, a marginalized man. A stranger. Excluded. Harangued. What do the bureaucrats at the hospital know about that? They saw him, his beard grown overly long, and that was that! They numbered him among the damned. The Talmud tells us that Schlemiel the Baffled got into a predicament with the wife of a rabbi, a wife who wasn't entirely pious; he was caught, dunce that he was, and killed for the sin that so many others had committed with that very same woman."

"Here we don't have a rabbi, or a rabbi's wife."

"But you probably have a pastor. Peter is a sacred name for pastors."

"Who is the author?"

"A French Catholic. A great botanist and Romantic poet. Exiled during the French Revolution. Born in the castle at Boncourt, in Champagne. He was an exile, a wanderer, an accomplice of wanderers, and a child of nature. He also visited these parts, California, where he conversed with flowers and trees. His hero was likewise a wanderer, a symbol of migration and globalization."

"I don't know if that kind of thing works for our students. Or, rather, I do know. It doesn't."

"The text includes a magical element. It, too, is connected to our mercantile age. Schlemihl sells his shadow."

"His shadow? Who buys it? I once read a Soviet work, *The Shadow,* it was called, by Evgeny Schwartz. It came to us because it was considered subversive. The shadow rises up against its owner, against his authority. But no, I don't see how this subject would fit in our curriculum. Perhaps, more suitably, you could teach something connected to your experiences or your biography? I know Charlie Kardash, who sent you to me. Though actually we're really not at all close. Perhaps that's why we know each other so well."

"I, too, am a stranger. We all lose our shadows. Even if we don't sell them."

"Well, our students learn how to wear the mask of the comic and tragic buffoon and merge with it to the point where they identify with it; they learn how to get bopped on the head, to walk in enormous clown shoes, to do triple somersaults, juggle and mime. A class like the one you're proposing would be unusual; I need to think about it. In the end, perhaps it wouldn't be a bad thing to help them improve their self-esteem. But what about clowns under terror? The French and Russian revolutions, the Holocaust, the Gulag, the church, the mosque . . . I've read your biographical note, you know these topics well, you've lived them, in fact. I came upon another such case here. A family of dwarfs deported to Auschwitz. From your Carpathian Mountains. I hosted them for a time, here at the college. They even put on performances, left documents in our trust. I've made use of their lives. The college needed and needs donors . . . I think you understand me. In this country, charity goes hand in hand with financial largesse."

"An original idea. Somewhat cynical, perhaps—I'm referring to the dwarfs. Grotesque."

"The grotesque is an integral part of the circus, as you well know. As of life. I'm not that original, reality is much more so. They had survived hell because of their disability. Yes, a grotesque disability. They were protected, chosen as experimental subjects, but also as mascots for entertainment. I hosted them with pleasure, I filmed them. The Auschwitz test, they called it. A test, not a crematorium, or a hell, or a horror. Mengele spoiled them; they remembered him as a beloved dressage master. Siberia, Cambodia, the Islamic tyrannies, Auschwitz, all great universities of terror. The Circus of Terror. What do you say, will you teach it?"

He was attracted to the notion of being hired at Keaton College. When he shook the president's hand, he observed, belatedly, that Mrs. De Boss had unusually large hands. Could it be due to her acrobatics work? He felt ready to ask Schlemihl, the hermit, who had hidden himself away in his cave to study nature.

THE REFUGE OF THE LIBRARY

The bourgeois romanticists, from Novalis onward, are people of the type of Peter Schlemihl, "the man who lost his shadow." [. . .] *The literary man of the contemporary West has also lost his shadow, emigrating from realities to the nihilism of despair.*
—Maxim Gorky[39]

But the true fable-poem is that which contains the whole of its meaning in itself, like any romance, story, play, or lyrical poem, because the fabulous or prodigious elements, from which it is woven or which are interlinked within it, make no difference whatever in respect to art. For this reason, Peter Schlemihl is a little masterpiece, and since it is a masterpiece, should be read according to its own unique meaning, its literal meaning, with a mind cleared of all the innumerable hermeneutic researches as to the real nature of the shadow, of the seven-leagued boots, and of Peter Schlemihl, and as to what can possibly be the real signification of this slice of his life which he is introduced for the purpose of narrating.

—Benedetto Croce[40]

To read Peter's story in terms of an allegory is to take a false lead. We must take the shadow "for what it is worth." It is worth nothing in practical terms, but its absence makes Peter a marked man. In this way, the missing shadow can serve as a symbol for anything that can produce such an effect on a man. The shadow in question, however, is not just an ordinary shadow. Since the devil has a hand in the business, it assumes magical properties. It can be manipulated, rolled up and unfolded for display like a substantial physical object. A second characteristic of equal importance is the fact that when Peter shows himself in the open, its absence is noticed by everybody at once. Such attention to an attribute of totally negligible value runs counter to all observable habits of human behavior.

Perhaps the most ingenious feature of our whimsical story is the two systems of value presented. They may be ranged in a single mathematical series as (1) the shadow, (2) gold, (3) the immortal soul. In this series, the shadow appears as the equivalent of zero value, the inexhaustible purse is a finite value, and the immortal soul, which we can render as personal integrity, is of infinite value. In discussing this graded series of values, the devil deftly turns the three on the central axis to an angle of one hundred and eighty degrees. The purse, the finite value, is left unchanged in its central position while the other two values are reversed. The shadow takes on the value of infinity, while the immortal soul, personal integrity, takes its place at the zero end of the scale. We remember how the glib salesman refers to the soul as this unknown quantity, this "X." A neater reversal of the values of the world and those of the spirit cannot be imagined.

Consider the squeeze that the devil applies to Peter in trying to make him rescue Mina from Rascal's clutches. He appeals to Peter's warmest, noblest human impulses in order to induce him to agree to the absolute renunciation of his personal integrity in order to achieve a limited good. The motif of the sacrifice of self is posed here in its most paradoxical form. Peter's logic, of course, is too untrained to penetrate the maze of this dilemma. Speaking tongue-in-cheek as the simple man of feeling, he leaves the logic to us.

—Herman J. Weigand[41]

I fear the dilution of the comical and the potentializing of the lament—for, in fact, the story consists of a+b, the Ideal and the Caricature, the tragic and the comic elements taken together.
—Adelbert von Chamisso[42]

KEATON COLLEGE

Signs at the college gates:

Coming events cast their shadow before.—T. Campbell's
epigraph to Byron's poem *The Prophecy of Dante*
We adhere to yesterday's and today's commedia dell'arte.
Better a witty fool, than a foolish wit.—Shakespeare, *As You
Like It*
Jesters do oft prove prophets.—Shakespeare, *King Lear*
*The purpose of playing, whose end, both at the first and now,
was and is, to hold, as 'twere the mirror up to nature, to show
virtue her own feature, scorn her own image, and the very age
and body of the time his form and pressure.*—Shakespeare,
Hamlet

Situated among the mountains, in a superb, silvan enclave in the tradition of Herman Hesse's *The Glass Bead
Game,* Keaton College is a unique cultural repository that
combines the highest form of dramatic art—following the
famous principles of Stanislavski—with the burlesque inven-
tiveness of farce and satire, in the classical and modern tradition of film and theater. The faculty includes film directors
and well-known clowns (including members of professional
circuses), as well as eminent commentators and critics, authors of much-appreciated works in the history of artistic,
theatrical, and cinematic representation. In collaboration
with members of the Latino-American & African Institute of
Film and of the Museum of Brazilian Art, they offer a variety
of theoretical and applied courses on the grotesque, on satire, humor, and melodrama, as well as on tragedy and pup-

petry. Students are introduced not only to the art of clowning but also to the historical and aesthetic contexts of the clown's role from antiquity to the present day, in the form of spectacle and as part of daily life. They learn that carnival and masquerade are not recent phenomena, but eternal facts, and have their place even in the era of television, demagogic, political populism, and the boundless commercialism in all spheres of life. They are encouraged to see the grotesque and the clown's tears as life lessons. Together such phenomena make up the sentimental education of the spectator and the actor.

The instructors at this unusual School of the Arts represent a coming together of many great talents. They aim to encourage students to grow in character, to develop their originality, to be boldly and incisively creative, and to pursue an individualistic approach to existence regardless of the spiritual or professional choices that might follow graduation from this prestigious academic institution. The college and its faculty pay special attention to the relationship between the events of contemporary history and current political and social realities, as they are reflected in the act of artistic creation and in contemporary literary and artistic criticism.

The college also organizes summer camps that offer a sampling of the educational opportunities on campus, while also taking into account the participants' collective interests and current aspirations.

ON THE WALLS OF THE COLLEGE

Feinstein: [. . .] *Mr. Keaton, it has been said by many that the secret source of humor is not anything pleasant, but pain or pathos. Commentators like Sigmund Freud and Mark Twain have made that same point. Freud called humor "the loftiest of the defense functions"; and Mark Twain says somewhere in* Pudd'nhead Wilson's New Calendar *that "Everything human is pathetic. The secret source of humor itself is not joy but sorrow. There is no humor in heaven." And since you mentioned Yiddish humorists, a lot of Yiddish humor has been explained by way of its intrinsic sadness. To come to the medium of film, one humorist, Al Capp, has written about another, Charlie Chaplin, that Chaplin is only funny because his tramp is a professional victim and is so truly pathetic. Capp says we laugh at Chaplin's* City Lights [1931], *"because we are eternally delighted at the inhumanity of man to man." Now, in view of your own brand of dour, deadpan humor, Mr. Keaton, would you agree that human pain, not pleasure, is at the bottom of the most successful humor?*

Keaton: *Yes, I'm afraid I do to a certain extent, a great deal of it because an audience will laugh at things happening to you, and they certainly wouldn't laugh if it happened to them.*

Feinstein: *In* The General [1927], *the boy is a* schlemiel.
Keaton: *In* The General, *I am an engineer.*[43]

Thomas: *Tell me, how did the business of the frozen face come about, the dead pan?*
Keaton: *That came from the stage. As I grew up, I was the*

type of comedian that the minute I laughed at what I did the audience didn't. So I just automatically learned to take everything seriously, and by the time I was—oh, something like—ten or eleven years old working with a sober face was mechanical with me—never even thought about it. So, when I went into pictures, I was twenty-one, and I got the reputation immediately [of being] called "frozen face," "blank pan," and things like that.[44]

That comedy is a difficult and meticulous art, no one (except Chaplin) could have said it any better than this exemplary man, intelligent, exceptionally gifted, who created a "personage" having an intense poetic face with a certain sense of the absurdity of the world, and who would have been "Kafkaesque" (before Kafka) if he had not always had, underneath his "blank-page countenance," a warmth of heart, a noble tenacity of spirit, a faith in men, yet none of this with a smug boy-scout style optimism . . . In 1920–30, Keaton was prodigiously modern, and he has stayed that way, this cantor of the irrational, this lyric eccentric, this grand poet who the surrealists would place in their pantheon besides heroes from Lautréamont to Jarry.[45]

DIDACTICA NOVA (I)

It was not quite that hot in this country to which a man of learning had come from the colder north. [. . .] On[e] evening, the stranger sat out on his balcony. The candle burned in the room behind him, so naturally his shadow was cast on the wall across the street. Yes, there it sat among the flowers, and when the stranger moved, it moved with him. "I believe my shadow is the only living thing to be seen over there," the scholar thought to himself. "See how he makes himself at home among the flowers. The door stands ajar, and if my shadow were clever he'd step in, have a look around, and come back to tell me what he had seen." [. . .] The stranger rose, and his shadow across the street rose with him. The stranger turned around, and his shadow turned, too. If anyone had been watching closely, he would have seen the shadow enter the half-open balcony door in the house across the way at the same instant that the stranger returned to his room and the curtain fell behind him.

Next morning, when the scholar went out to take his coffee and read the newspapers, he said, "What's this?" as he came out in the sunshine. "I haven't any shadow! So it really did go away last night, and it stayed away. Isn't that annoying?" [. . .] This was very vexing, but in the hot countries everything grows most rapidly, and in a week or so he noticed with great satisfaction that when he went out in the sunshine, a new shadow was growing at his feet. The root must have been left with him. In three weeks' time he had a very presentable shadow. [. . .] The learned man went home and wrote books about those things in the world that are true, that are good, and that are beautiful.

The days went by and the years went past, many, many years in fact. Then one evening when he was sitting in his room, he heard a soft tapping at his door. [. . .] "Ah," said the distinguished visitor, "I thought you wouldn't recognize me, now that I've put real flesh on my body and wear clothes. I don't suppose you ever expected to see me in such fine condition. Don't you know your old shadow?" [. . .] It was really remarkable how much of a man he had become, dressed all in black, with the finest cloth, patent-leather shoes, and an opera hat that could be pressed perfectly flat till it was only brim and top, not to mention those things we already know about—those seals, that gold chain, and the diamond rings. The shadow was well-dressed indeed, and it was just this that made him appear human.

"I saw what no one else could see, or should see, [the shadow said.] Taken all in all, it's a wicked world. I would not care to be a man if it were not considered the fashionable thing to be. I saw the most incredible behaviour among men and women, fathers and mothers, and among those 'perfectly darling' children. I saw what nobody knows but everybody would like to know, and that is what wickedness goes on next door." [. . .] "How extraordinary," said the scholar. [. . .] "Alack," said the scholar, "I still write about the true, the good, and the beautiful, but nobody cares to read about such things." [. . .] "You don't know the ways of the world, and that's why your health suffers," [answered the shadow]. "You ought to travel. I'm taking a trip this summer. Will you come with me? I'd like to have a travelling companion. Will you come along as my shadow?" [. . .] "This has gone much too far!" said the scholar.

The learned man was not at all well. Sorrow and trouble pursued him.

Finally, he grew quite ill. "You really look like a shadow," people told him, and he trembled at the thought. "You must visit a watering place," said the shadow, who came to see him again. "There's no question about it. I'll take you with me, for *old friendship's sake. I'll pay for the trip and you can write about it, as well as doing your best to amuse me along the way." [. . .] So off they started. The shadow was master now, and the master was the shadow. [. . .] At last they came to the watering place. Among the many people was a lovely Princess. [. . .] That evening, the Princess and the shadow danced together in the great ballroom. She was light, but he was lighter still. Never had she danced with such a partner. [. . .] His knowledge impressed her so deeply, that while they were dancing she fell in love with him. [. . .] Tactfully, she began asking him the most difficult questions, which she herself could not have answered. The shadow made a wry face.*

"You can't answer me?" said the Princess.

"I knew all that in my childhood," said the shadow. "Why, I believe that my shadow over there by the door can answer you."

"Your shadow!" said the Princess. "That would be remarkable indeed!"

So she went to the scholar in the doorway, and spoke with him about the sun and the moon, and about people, what they are like inside, and what they seem to be on the surface. He answered her wisely and well.

"What a man that must be, to have such a wise shadow!" she thought. "It will be a godsend to my people and to my country if I choose him for my consort. That's just what I'll do!"

The Princess and the shadow came to an understanding, but no one was to know about it until she returned to her own kingdom.

"No one. Not even my shadow!" said the shadow. And he had his own private reason for this.

Finally, they came to the country that the Princess ruled when she was at home. "Listen, my good friend," the shadow said to the scholar, "I am now as happy and strong as one can be, so I'll do something very special for you. You shall live with me in my palace, drive with me in my royal carriage, and have a hundred thousand crowns a year. However, you must let yourself be a called a shadow by everybody. You must not ever say that you have been a man, and once a year, while I sit on the balcony in the sunshine, you must lie at my feet as shadows do. For I tell you that I am going to marry the Princess, and the wedding is to take place this very evening."

"No! That's going too far," said the scholar. "I will not. I won't do it. That would be betraying the whole country and the Princess too. I'll tell them everything—that I am the man, and you are the shadow merely dressed as a man."

"No one would believe it," said the shadow. "Be reasonable, or I'll call the sentry."

"I'll go straight to the Princess," said the scholar.

"But I will go first," said the shadow, "and you shall go to prison."

And to prison he went, for the sentries obeyed the one who, they knew, was to marry the Princess.

"Why, you're trembling," the Princess said, as the shadow entered her room. "What has happened? You mustn't fall ill this evening, just as we are about to be married."

"I have been through the most dreadful experience that could happen to anyone," said the shadow. "Just imagine! Of course, a poor shadow's head can't stand very much. But imagine! My shadow has gone mad. He takes himself for a man, and—imagine it! he takes me for his shadow."

"How terrible!" said the Princess. "He's locked up, I hope!"

"Oh, of course. I'm afraid he will never recover."

"Poor shadow," said the Princess. "He is very unhappy. It would really be a charitable act to relieve him of the little bit of life he has left. And, after thinking it over carefully, my opinion is that it will be necessary to put him out of his way."

The whole city was brilliantly lit that evening. The cannon boomed, and the soldiers presented arms. That was the sort of wedding it was! The Princess and the shadow stepped out on the balcony to show themselves and be cheered, again and again.

The scholar heard nothing of all this, for they had already done away with him.

—Hans Christian Andersen[46]

In 1814, three decades before the publication of "The Shadow," Adelbert von Chamisso had published Peter Schlemihl's Miraculous Story, *a story about a man who sells his shadow to the devil in exchange for a bottomless wallet. Andersen's story was prompted by Chamisso's, and he refers to it in "The Shadow":*

"He was very annoyed, not so much because the shadow had disappeared, but because he knew there was a story, well-known to everybody at home in the cold countries, about a man without a shadow; and if he went back now and told them his own story, they would be sure to say that he was just an imitator, and that was the last thing he wanted."[47]

The quality that we call beauty, however, must always grow from the realities of life, and our ancestors, forced to live in dark rooms, presently came to discover beauty in shadows, ultimately to guide shadows toward beauty's ends. And it has come to be that the beauty of a Japanese room depends on a variation of shadows, heavy shadows against light shadows—it has nothing else. Westerners are amazed at the simplicity of Japanese rooms, perceiving in them no more than ashen walls bereft of ornament. Their reaction is understandable, but it betrays a failure to comprehend the mystery of shadows. [. . .] The hue may differ from room to room, but the degree of difference will be ever so slight; not so much a difference in color as in shade, a difference that will seem to exist only in the mood of the viewer. And from these delicate differences in the hue of the walls, the shadows in each room take on a tinge peculiarly their own.

Of course the Japanese room does have its picture alcove [tokonoma], and in it a hanging scroll and a flower arrangement. But the scroll and the flowers serve not as ornament but to give depth to the shadows. [. . .] Most often the paper, the ink, the fabric of the mounting will possess a certain look of antiquity, and this look of antiquity will strike just the right balance with the darkness of the alcove and the room.

The lack of clarity, far from disturbing us, seems rather to suit the painting perfectly. For the painting here is nothing more than another delicate surface upon which the faint, frail light can play; it performs precisely the same function as the sand-textured wall. This is why we attach such importance to age and patina. A new painting, even one done in ink monochrome or subtle pastels, can quite destroy the shadows of an alcove, unless it is selected with the greatest care.

Whenever I see the alcove of a tastefully built Japanese room, I marvel at our comprehension of the secrets of shadows, our sensitive use of shadow and light. [. . .] The "mysterious Orient" of which Westerners speak probably refers to the uncanny silence of these dark places. And even we as children would feel an inexpressible chill as we peered into the depths of an alcove to which the sunlight had never penetrated. Where lies the key to this mystery? Ultimately it is the magic of shadows. Were the shadows to be banished from its corners, the alcove would in that instant revert to mere void.

This was the genius of our ancestors, that by cutting off the light from this empty space they imparted to the world of shadows that formed there a quality of mystery and depth superior to that of any wall painting or ornament.

The darkness in which the Nō is shrouded and the beauty that emerges from it make a distinct world of shadows which today can be seen only on the stage; but in the past it could not have been far removed from daily life.

A phosphorescent jewel gives off its glow and color in the dark and loses its beauty in the light of day. Were it not for shadows, there would be no beauty. Our ancestors made of woman an object inseparable from darkness, like lacquerware decorated in gold or mother-of-pearl. They hid as much of her as they could in shadows, concealing her arms and legs in the folds of long sleeves and skirts, so that one part and one only stood out—her face. The curveless body may, by comparison with Western women, be ugly. But our thoughts do not travel to what we cannot see. The unseen for us does not exist.

We Orientals tend to seek our satisfactions in whatever surrounds we happen to find ourselves, to content ourselves with things as they are; and so darkness causes us no discontent, we resign ourselves to it as inevitable.

Our ancestors cut off the brightness on the land from above and created a world of shadows, and far in the depths of it they placed woman, marking her the whitest of beings.

I have thought that there might still be somewhere, possibly in literature or the arts, where something could be saved. I would call back at least for literature this world of shadows we are losing. In the mansion called literature I would have the eaves deep and the walls dark, I would push back into the shadows the things that come forward too clearly, I would strip away the useless decoration. I do not ask that this be done everywhere, but perhaps we may be allowed at least one mansion where we can turn off the electric lights and see what it is like without them.
—Jun'ichirō Tanizaki[48]

THE PRIVILEGED TRAUMA (I)

As to Peter's past, we know very little, meaning nothing at all.

Why and how he abandoned his home and family, his friends and books. If he did so of his own will or was forced to by circumstances. If he was a social or political pariah, or if he was in danger from or in open conflict with those around him, or if he was ill, or had no means of earning a living, or if he did it out of a spirit of adventure.

The story that the good author (the botanist himself) dedicated to Hitzig's children, to help them sleep at night, is told in the words of an "honest" *narrator fully trusting in both the integrity and the friendship of the author.*[49] The poet-botanist acknowledged that he did not sufficiently value its comic potential, and even worse, that he did not realize that actual living people might be recognized in its pages. Employing a romantic device that by then had become banal, the future Berlin botanist maintained that the pages of Peter's autobiographical manuscript had been brought to him by *an extraordinary-looking man, with a long grey beard, and wearing an old black frock-coat with a botanical case hanging at his side, and slippers over his boots, in the damp, rainy weather.*[50]

We are not told anything about the narrator's social class. Nor whether this individual could eventually return to where he came from. On the other hand, we do come to understand that Peter's migrations most likely took place in the same country and language of his birth, given that the tale does not mention passports, border controls, frontier crossings, or problems of communication with one's new fellow citizens. This might have lessened the trauma of dislocation from his old biography for the character, though even in the German Reich of Adelbert von Chamisso and Edward Hitzig, the differences between Protestant and Catholic areas should not be underestimated.

Rather, Peter seems young and unfamiliar with the torments of suffering. The haste with which he accepts the proposal of the gray messenger demonstrates not just his taste for adventure, but also his impatience to explore the unknown and to take advantage of the opportunity he has been offered by an unprecedented event. As in so many traveler's tales both recent and perennial, the trauma of this change is not self-evident, nor is it explained. It is as if, as the beneficiary of a wondrous change made possible by emigration, the refugee comes to inhabit another world too quickly. It is only the unfortunate consequences of this that finally allow him to take his place where he belongs, among the great mass of luckless nomads, of men without a country, of the hapless and ill-starred of all places and of all times. His neurosis, if it could have been called that in his age, sends him to the Schlemihlium Sanatorium, a kind of hospital-asylum for vagabonds. There he comes to recognize in the charitable Ms. Mina the woman of his dreams, and in the philanthropist in charge of the institution, his former devoted servant Bendel.

As a patient, identified by the number 12 and nicknamed "The Jew," his only obvious connection to his cast-out ancestors is a beard grown past all limits and the impression he makes on others. These others see in him the perpetual wanderer, the once-and-future suspicious character. In the end, his cursed state gives way to the fortunes of a hermit cast away in a cave of solitude. A perfect point from which to observe the global comedy set in motion by the ephemerality of all things. Animals and plants and even—more than once—other individuals playing marionettes animate the theater of his disappointments, between darkness and triumph. In the end, everything seems a nightmare of chance. The fairytale exhausts its illusions in the asceticism of the study of nature and of one's own nature that take place far away from the cynical conventions of a world turned banal. Far away from the world of men.

Justo judicio Dei judicatus sum; justo judicio Dei condemnatus sum, states the note found in the Man in Gray's pocket, which is never empty. *I was judged by the right judgment of the Lord; I was condemned by the right judgment of the Lord.*[51] It is the only invocation of the divine in the narrative of the poet-botanist, and it is not sardonic by chance. When it comes to the invisible Omnipotent One, the narrator is a skeptic like all those who probe nature's mysteries. At the same time, the suspicion aroused by the unprecedented speed of the protagonist's acquisition of wealth, as well as the suspicion generated by his lack of shadowy dealings, his pristine reputation, are age-old. So, too, is the resentment toward strangers and the outsider's retreat from the world. However, here such suspicions are different in both consequence and kind from what might be called a zealously cultivated suspicion, or from the reprisals of a totalitarian state against those it considers hostile and dispensable.

In the era of globalization and the most lethal kinds of weapons, the Nomad is inevitably conscious of the new reality in which he lives and of the new dangers hanging over his head, no matter how far Colonel Tudor might have allowed him to escape from the prison camp universe of his own history. Picked apart for decades by the tyrannical system that he eventually became accustomed to, the Nomad sequesters himself in his lair of books, though they offer him only a fictitious and frivolous kind of protection. Though of uncertain age, he does not seem old. Rather, he is a "latecomer" who has made his way to the gates of the free, competitive, and individualistic world long after the game was up.

The little yellow booklet printed in Goethe's tongue and confiscated by the border official retains its place of honor in the chest pocket of the traveler preparing for takeoff: for an exile like him, from a cosmic and metahistorical perspective, the self-confession of the hapless Schlemihl, who belongs to the vast family of haps of all places and times, remains a burlesque, classic text in which existential farce finally finds its proper language.

In the original, the fairytale is the exile's guidebook. Then, in translation, it becomes the textbook with which he teaches his students about the adventure of becoming an Other. Beyond its social and political dimensions, beyond the social and political focal points of persecution, the solitude it encourages, like dislocation and deprivation, gives exile a language; it lays the foundation for an apprenticeship in the earthly dialectic of change and in the metamorphoses of renewal.

GÜNTHER

My Dear Wanderer,

You likely never anticipated that Comrade Colonel Tudor would evict you from your monastic cell of books to send you off to be reeducated not in a work camp but on the other side of the world (so that you'd understand who you really are, who others are). As you well know, I once met him, too, when he attempted to exercise his flattery on me, to domesticate me, anticipating my future in the West, unsatisfied with my former menage in the East I was leaving behind, having been bought by my co-nationals of eight hundred years ago. In other words, he was worried that later I'd smear the country where I was born with mud and shit, betray it to strangers more than it had already betrayed itself. It's too bad, really, that you didn't want to take part in the fall of the Wall. Your lack of trust in History and its promises isn't enough of a reason to recuse yourself from an event like this. Or from its unpredictable consequences. (Predictable ones, you'd say.) I confess that I let myself become dizzy with hope, as I often had when I was young. Maybe also because I was doing everything I could to bring down the Wall, as I had in times past.

And now there you are in the New World. Of money made and spent? An essential truth, no? *Songez au solide!*, your good master Albert warned us with his stories to sing children to sleep. Solid reality—the Dollar, no? Is your beloved sister helping you grasp the nature of the place where you've ended up? All ideologies are suspect, your Americans probably say. Especially utopias, right? Can we do without them? And, if we can, is that for the better? Now the new missionaries of the crescent moon in their şalvar pants have come on the scene, who pretend to be in permanent contact with their Lord and who behead people in the name of Purity! The Teutons here don't give me much hope either. After they yelled and chanted for Unification (and I along with them!), they are now muttering against their Eastern brothers, who they say are lazy and backward, who drive up their taxes and sabotage the prosperity of the Homeland. Squirrels and whales and storks don't worry about these things; we're the only ones. And we're said to be made in the image of the All-Powerful, would you look at that!

You don't reply to my letters. Is this a good sign or a bad one? I asked Jenny what she thought. She didn't tell me, but she did let me know that her uncle, John Johnson, from the university, has retired and is moving to Australia with his new wife, who was the widow of some wealthy guy. Mr. John won't forget you, she's sure of it, and anyway she'll remind him. It would be useful if you at least kept me up to date regarding that.

I'd like to think you remember the red Pioneer's pledge: "Fighting for Lenin's and Stalin's cause, forward we march!" And the answer, in chorus: "Forward, ever forward!" After a while, the slogan became "Be prepared to fight for the cause of the workers' party!" And the answer, just as prompt: "Always prepared!"

As an old friend with a red tie, both militant and well intentioned, I can only wish you: Forward, always forward! With chance as your only compass. Un-ideologically and without God. Without a reason, really. Like life. Jennifer agrees with me. As you can see, neither of us has forgotten you. G.

A NEW WORLD RABBI

Mr. John disappeared without really disappearing. He retired and became even wealthier, a member of the administrative council of the college. He moved to Australia.

Nevertheless, he continued to maintain a residence in his optimistic and pragmatic homeland. This address was the address to which the Nomad continued to write to him, as he had promised at their first, brief meeting, when he had pledged to keep in touch until he applied again to that formidable institution of higher learning. He wrote to Mr. John with the aid of the dictionary that sat in front of him on the table. He minded this humiliating solution less than the even greater humiliation of sending letters into the unknown, to anyone anywhere, begging for refuge and charity. Mr. John would answer briefly, but promptly. He gave no signs of being impatient or bored. The exile had gotten used to this routine; perhaps even more conspicuously than his experiences at Keaton College, the exchange confirmed to him his own presence in the new world and gave him a vague hope for the unexpected. And indeed, at a certain point, he received an unexpected letter from Mr. Luca Lombardi Formenton, distinguished Professor of Anthropology and Dean of the small elitist college. An invitation to an interview.

The elegant dean looked at him pointedly through the thick glasses that kept sliding down his freckled nose and informed him that it would be a group interview, in accordance with such democratic procedures as those that repudiate oligarchies of any kind. He was immediately led into an adjoining room. Six future colleagues waited for him there, all seated around a long, rectangular table. He answered their questions for two hours, as laconically as possible, to avoid any possible linguistic mix-ups. There were questions about his complex biography—from the Nazi camp of his childhood to the communist one of his much-delayed adulthood, about his dead parents and about his sister. About his bookish pre-occupations, the history of the circus, and the psychology of the immigrant; about the history of censorship and its modern forms. And, most of all, about the risks he would be exposed to if he were to return to the Homeland he had avoided leaving for so long. The investigative committee assured him that this homeland would soon experience radical changes, which would propel it toward its much-dreamed-of democracy. "Oh, hardly," the candidate hurried to answer. He did not believe in change. Not in any change that could be predicted, anyway. The tyrannical system of "highly developed multilateral socialism" had perfected its survival techniques, having converted even the rot into an advantage. As to the risks, yes, they should be considered, but he couldn't evaluate the risks a return would expose him to. The risk can be terrible, yes, or it can simply disappear, postponed to a future moment and its new methods of torture.

At that moment in the conversation, he felt himself struggling against the need to evoke the presence of the elegant colonel, pomaded with the multifunctional ointments of a chameleon, who had staged the Nomad's conversion to . . . "detachment." Behold, he was already detached, indifferent, absent. He seemed to wake up only when he was asked what he could teach the students of affluence. Hurriedly, he enumerated alienation's authors and themes. It was the same list he had already used at Keaton, but it didn't seem to make much of an impression on the audience.

After a long silence, a blond, corpulent man rose from his seat. It was Professor Parker, who was chairing the gathering. He explained the financial difficulties the institution was experiencing, noted that it had been difficult to obtain the budgetary allocation for refugee intellectuals, and said that it should be used with the greatest care. "As I believe you know, our college receives nothing from the government. We don't want to have to depend on anyone." In the phrases that followed, it became clear that, as part of another of the college's many factions, Professor Parker was hostile both toward Mr. Lombardi Formenton and toward the honorable Mr. John. The game was evidently lost, but the dean diplomatically avoided a definitive refusal. "We will inform you of our decision," he told him when they parted, affably shaking both of his hands.

For two months, the candidate received no news. He didn't want to write to Mr. John yet, though it seemed like the only option. He knew no one else, but he didn't feel comfortable with the uncle whom the generous Jennifer had put him in touch with. He had to rely on others, that's the way it was, to rely on chance, rely more than ever on acquaintances he did not have and strangers wearing inscrutable masks.

Of course, there was Tamar, but he was avoiding Tamar. Pained discretion after their last conversation. Had he requested her help in any practical matter, his sister would have rushed in to prove her devotion—to the point of self-effacement. But he preferred to rely on himself, to shoulder the full burden of the change.

In a short letter to Mr. John, he described with restrained irony, in the most polite terms he could muster, his adventures with Luca Lombardi Formenton and Professor Parker. He received no reply from Australia. However, after some time, he received a new invitation from Dean Formenton to a new—and this time "definitive"—interview. Mrs. De Boss again proved to be very understanding, giving him a week of unpaid leave.

This time, he was met not by the dean but by one of his assistants. A young man, carelessly dressed and obviously uncomfortable with having to explain that the deliberations had taken a long time, that the full committee had been present, all six professors, and that everyone had expressed their appreciation that, with impeccable manners, the candidate had refused to take advantage of the committee's compassion and had not mentioned the fact that it was impossible for him to return to the country where he had previously lived, and which, newly freed from its dictatorship, was now experiencing a dubious transition toward nowhere. Because of this, he was being given another chance to sell his shadow in return for a position and a salary that might rehabilitate his self-esteem. Self-esteem was a new concept for this immigrant, but a beloved, well-worn one to those with whom he found himself interacting.

The new test was structured around eight meetings of half an hour each, with professors from different departments. This would be followed by a last meeting with the dean in her office. The student who would take him to each of these eight meetings and then, four hours of conversation later, deposit him back in the place she had found him, was already waiting for him.

The first meeting began auspiciously. The social sciences professor was a Belgian woman and spoke French, an expediency that seemed to have been designed especially to please our wanderer: at last, he would speak the lingua franca, the argot of rich loafers. After the polite preliminaries, the professor posed the essential question: "If you were to join us, what could you teach? As I understand, you've never been a professor before." Without any delay, the novice answered that he studied the history of the circus, the theater, and other such cultural subjects. As to the social sciences, his life experience and his deep reading centered on the two great European themes: Nazism and communism, Holocaust and gulag. "The Holocaust?" the agitated Belgian professor replied. "What kind of books do you have in mind?" The survivor of the camps listed a few of the canonical titles. A great long silence followed. "But you realize . . . I, I am the one who teaches the Holocaust here!" came the unyielding voice of destiny at last.

Other meetings followed: with the tall, arrogant Moroccan professor who taught French, with the gentle, mustachioed professor who taught medieval English, with the fat, voluble Ukrainian who specialized in the Russian Revolution, with the teachers of Spanish, the history of sexuality, Marxism, postmodernism, Japanese for beginners.

Having safely been returned to the assistant dean, he came to understand that the decision had been made even before he had finished: he would be the beneficiary of a decent fellowship, two semesters long, and be allowed to live in the house of a chemistry professor who was on sabbatical for the year. He would teach two courses in the spring and two the following fall.

Happily surprised, he received the congratulations of the young man who was surveying him without hearing his question.

"Are you going to the train station? Taking the train?" the official assistant repeated.

The traveler nodded.

"That's what we thought, too. At the entrance, there is a red car waiting for you. It will take you to the station."

"I'm leaving then?" the traveler asked.

"We'll need to wait a little longer first. We're waiting for the rabbi. They'll be going with you to the train station."

A quarter of an hour later, the rabbi appeared. A miracle! A young lady in jeans, with short hair and a large bag full of books. The young woman was ready to talk to the taciturn passenger, who was visibly intimidated by her young body and transcendental mission. The train was coming from Canada, and there would be a two-hour delay. Time enough for an initiation into celestial mores? Or into the psychology of American youthfulness?

"How did you choose this profession? Or vocation, rather . . . A young, cultivated, attractive, modern woman . . . Why this of all things?"

"I've always been concerned with community."

"*Com*-mu-ni-ty? I lived for forty years in a state that called itself *com*-mu-nist. I can't stand the word anymore."

"What would you have us replace it with? Do you have a better idea?"

"Individuality. The supreme value. Long live the individual! With his shadow or shadows."

The young woman had stretched out on the back seat, taking off her shoes and propping her curly head on the bag of philosophical texts.

"Speaking of shadows, do you happen to know if they have a mystical meaning? Or a religious one?"

The rabbi did not answer. She simply smiled, revealing her teeth in their metallic armature.

"No. Sacred books don't deal with shadows."

"That's sad. I would have thought that the Omnipotent would offer us the key to all mysteries, fit for any question. Is your family religious, too? Concerned with community?"

"No, not at all. We're a scattered family."

"Who scattered you?"

"Our own wills. Our own helplessness."

"And your parents? What do they do?"

"High school teachers. They split up when I was twelve."

"Puberty. A difficult age."

"All ages are difficult. But these books help. And connect me to those like me."

"The true family. But what about that earlier one? Brothers, sisters, aunts, grandparents?"

"A sister. I have a sister."

"Likewise married to the Man Upstairs?"

"My sister is a Buddhist. She lives in California and raises horses."

"Horses? Not rabbits? Does the horse have some significance in the Bible?"

The rabbi did not answer. Offended, she opened one of her secret books. The wanderer's aggressiveness irritated her. But after a time, she looked up again.

"I work with refugees. My grandparents came from far away."

"Where from?"

"Lithuania. I studied the Great Jewish Tribunal in Vilna,

the Vilna Gaon,[52] their Supreme Authority. There's also the famous Jewish Theater of Vilna. No rabbi at that time looked like me. We are no longer of those times, we live in the land of freedom. The land of unlimited possibilities, as the politicians say. I know you're not used to rabbis like me . . . "

"No, I'm not. But I'll get used to it. I've already started to get used to this, to everything . . . Even to train delays. As in the Gaon's time, as in the world from which I come."

"You're from Lithuania?"

"No, from another Eastern place. From where those Hasidim excommunicated by the Gaon were from originally. I don't think you're up to speed with that."

"I know what you're talking about."

When the train arrived at last, the rabbi hurriedly took her leave from the wanderer, but not before holding out a business card.

"As I said, I work with refugees."

"I already have a rabbi. Dr. Adelbert, the rabbi of plants and exotic vegetation. But what is your name, if I may? Lamm? With two m's? And Rebeka? With k or c?"

"Yes, with two m's. Rebekah with a k and h at the end."

Without any hesitation, he gave little Rebekah a brotherly hug. Dr. Rebekah Lamm, graduate of the Theological Seminary and the Department of Psychology, the little yellow piece of cardboard indicated. He was grateful to her for the orientation she had provided to his new place of residence. He understood better now the nature of the world in which he had landed.

ATTEMPTS AT FITTING IN:
OLD MRS. CAROLINE'S VISITS

"I've imagined what your first meeting with Mr. John must have been like. I should have been there, well hidden under a regal hat." This is how the distinguished, white-haired, mannequin-thin lady presented herself. She had not rung the doorbell but merely pushed at the door with the pointed tip of her boot. Obviously a former beauty, highly styled, with large blue eyes which became even larger as she gazed at the Nomad.

"John is brilliant, and his value will never be truly appreciated until he leaves this small, prestigious college for a position that gives him more visibility. His new Australian partner could be a solution." She respected the silence of her host, allowing for a longer pause.

"You seem distracted and unfocused. I assume you did not notice that after quickly scanning his niece's letter, he gave Rita Agopian a discreet sign. That lofty, lofty diva, you'd think she was on stilts, nicknamed the Giraffe. Rita is the eminence grise of the college. Executive vice president, expert bookkeeper, expert economist. Without her approval, nothing can get done. An endearing sense of dependency on John's part. He's so intelligent, so eager for recognition. Knows so much and seems not to know anything. If he ruled the world, what would it be like do you think?" She respected the resident's new silence. Her still large eyes and her thin, wrinkled hands confirmed her impatience. "We can disagree on this matter at the party that Caroline Olson Dodge is inviting you to—that is my maiden name and my widowed one. Former wife. I offer myself to you as a new potential conversation partner. It's your first winter among us, after your apprenticeship at that monastery of clowns, and I am the first in this community to invite you somewhere. I feel it is my duty."

Winter. The first day of the new year. An epistolary explosion.

Born into the family of a pastor, I grew up in Switzerland, in Zurich, where I read Dürrenmatt with the sadistic ardor of a young girl. Then Canada, of which I have fond memories. I was worldly, well known in college for the soirees that brought together not just fellow students but the teaching elite. Like the New Year's soiree you attended, where you met my niece Eve. You were timid and mysterious, as usual. You drank somewhat too much, glass after glass. The new year started off on a frivolous note, I'm well aware. Perhaps you got out of bed in the morning troubled, hung over. Please don't worry, you'll forget all about it. Here's the shoe you left behind at the party, you can walk about on the streets with it or step right into a fridge full of cake and bacon.—Caroline O.

A winter's dream: our poet laureate and I have an erotic encounter in the aisles of the concert hall. He asks me what he should do with his life. I tell him: wash floors. Indirectly, I was citing Auden, who maintained that poets and philosophers should scrub, carry heavy loads, do hard labor to es-

cape their thoughts. Is an erotic encounter not hard labor?
Caroline

Still winter.

The best part of this frigid week was the superb liturgy of the Russian Church, Saint John Chrysostom's—Saint John's the Golden Mouth. I'd go see it again anytime. The spirit is willing but the body is weak. I also saw the soloists from the Bolshoi Theater. Remarkable. The pianist reminded me of a marionette, though her interpretation was not at all wooden. The bassist seemed like someone from a Soviet poster, the tenor had long, gray hair, the soprano was sweet and gentle, the alto had coal-black skin.

My friend Alexandra is converting to Judaism. She has the zeal of a *chabadnik*. The rabbi does not seem too convinced by the authenticity of her choice, seems to think that the pious fiancée is the real reason, and he, paradoxically, seems less like a pious man and more like a fanatic.

I'm a kind of Buddhist by affinity, as I've told you before. I've also been Catholic and then Protestant. My deceased husband was Irish, his family has been here for many generations, and he was a kind of Buddhist priest or guru. I've become so used to their sense of calm.

Spring, torment. Who was I before I left the forests of the North and became myself? And who will I be when I am no longer myself?

And so, without parents, friends, great loves and betrayals, only the quotidian, earthly curse remains. Stones, rocks, trees. I suppose you can't identify with this extreme viewpoint.

But I can. I identify with all things, as the Adamic snake suggested I do . . .

We, too, had our ill-matched evening. You drank too much, you felt good among your new colleagues. After everyone left, you still had a full glass in your hand. I thought it was the right moment to take advantage. It's said that our exodus begins the moment we abandon the womb. But how does incest begin? Our reentry into the womb?

I'm not that old, and I am still passionate. Imprudent, immoral—I am still all those things. My husband tolerated me, even though he was a Buddhist guru. In the months leading up to his death, his sex drive returned.

In the morning, you woke up taciturn, troubled, plastered. Don't worry, you'll forget.

What kind of being is this conversation partner? you ask yourself. The answer is in the air, as in Rilke, who asked himself if the air still knew him.—Caroline

I was driving home when, suddenly, I saw images of Persepolis. Ancient palaces and victorious riders; in the corner of my eye, I also could see trees from the Canadian prairie. I became confused . . . What is the meeting point between the past and the long-ago past called? I am going to send you some notes of my Indian friend, who wrote about your country, where he lived for a few years as the son of an ambassador. Everything matters or nothing does. I prefer everything. Every blade of grass like a sword, every star slipping away, every song and scream and whisper.

Try to get started on the "unwritten novels" of your life trajectory. Pages for each twist and turn, each one anticipating the exotic. Have you learned yet about detachment, as the policeman advised? Or how to protect yourself from yourself? To me, you seem like the least detached mammal in the planet's jungle. I'd call you the Nomad, in honor of your lost ancestors. Misanthrope? Yes, you have been affected by our patchwork age. The Nomadic Misanthrope.

It's summer, and I see two fat women—models for Renoir—wash the body of my dead husband. I simply watch. A saintly hypocrite, waiting for the veneration of the crowd. —Caro

When we speak, I understand better the vast distances that separate your life from my microcosm. None of us chose where and when we were born, but do you think we'd choose to be born again if we had the chance? There are ephemeral moments of joy and deep thought that might convince the unborn to allow themselves to be born, but if they knew the end in advance—ashes scattered to the four points of the compass, without a trace—I'm no longer sure they would choose this vanity of vanities. You, exiles, what do you think? And what would those of us who are exiled inside ourselves, we, stationary ones, answer?

In any case, we shouldn't forget that we've mastered only a part of the adventure we've been given.

You ask me what's new in our academic community. I

never ask you about your students. I know them well enough from their dealings with my former husband. A friendly, open, frequently impertinent bunch. All of them raised in excessive freedom. Curious, intelligent philistines. I don't think it was easy for you, especially in the beginning, not with their immature, informal manners. But what about your humble protective bunker of books? Did Eve visit you again? When I ask her, she refuses to talk about it, and I've asked more than once.—Caro

Here's my most recent dream: Papa visited us unexpectedly. Was welcomed with amazement and childish enthusiasm. He was not easy to see because of all the cars, but I caught sight of him, nevertheless. Glowing, immaculate. Mr. John, with his morose manner when someone more important than him suddenly comes into view, slipped in the mud before His Holiness—that's how I imagined it. Everyone understood that it wasn't a bow, but simply an unfortunate burlesque trap set by the recent rains. The image, however, immediately became a painting by Breughel, with Golgotha in the background. Around it swarmed the faithful, along with lizards and snails; I even thought I saw your sister, whom you don't like to talk about.

As I was preparing to get into the greenish-looking car again, an ex-inamorato proposed that we spend a few hours in private. I accepted and found myself in a small, semidark chamber. However, immediately, a band of children overtook us; they were led by a boy and girl, twins who acted as though they were married to each other. They asked me to tell them the plot of a film shown a few days prior on televi-

sion, the one with the two blue squirrels. Like the incestuous couple. The dream evaporated then, as usually happens.
Without a proper ending.—Caro

The beginning of autumn. You spoke marvelously about
that recently deceased friend and about your nocturnal
phone conversations, when he would try to discover the root
of one word or another in your language, words long forgotten in the decades of exile in North and South America. I
ask myself why your country leaves such deep wounds in the
memories of her exiles, which are then smeared over with
the honey of sentimentality.

It's a blank day, I take pleasure in it. I asked my gardener,
Robert, what he would do on a day off, when he didn't have
to work. Sex, drink, rowing, he answered. He did not mention family.

What about your family? Do you ever mention them?
Both parents dead, yes, but what about the brothers, sisters,
aunts, cousins? Is there no one to remember you as you were
before your own memories of yourself, in that first troubled
state of unconsciousness? I ask myself if the loss of my parents and of my brother and husband is also the loss of myself, of that which meant so much to them. I imagine your
father in our forest here, his gentleman's salute to a stranger,
all the while thinking about his wife or daughter, or his affair
with his young sister-in-law, your aunt.—Caro

I just read someone's description of me, in which they
cast me as a hairdresser at a hair salon for the diplomatic

corps. Arms chock-full of heavy bracelets, gifts from my clients, putting on aristocratic airs and pretensions that disgust me.

I dream of an eternal autumn. I am watching them put up new streetlamps outside my house; they look more appropriate for a New Orleans brothel. The brothel wouldn't bother me, given that I've already been described as a hairdresser. The house is an inheritance from my pacifist, abstinent husband; a brothel would be a welcome change. Each property is like a sin, with its own sickly obsessions.

Here I would also mention our erotic interlude. If I can be a hairdresser, I can also uncross my legs from time to time. You've had the opportunity to verify this.

What's the privilege of a woman of a certain age? Technique replaces feeling and becomes potency. I think you you'd agree.—C

The college recently welcomed a therapist: Susan. She promises to heal you of anything: fits of anger, resentments, secrets. Small of stature, hair cropped short, military style, oblique smile. She wears a leather skirt with a lot of chains and baubles, boots, and heavy earrings. Unsparing with the opposite sex: she encourages the young women in her group to stand in the window and leer at the male passerby, to laugh at them. In my youth, at the Catholic boarding school, we were not allowed to look out the street-facing window, so as not to be considered loose women.

Listening to some of the confessions and the many comments made at this therapeutic seminar run by Susan, I feel as if I were in kindergarten again, or at a military school, where everything is regarded in terms of definitive, harsh actions. No middle ground. A bellicose language, overbearing, intense energy, like someone with something to prove. I'm from Switzerland and Canada, as I've told you, and I was shocked by this local simplistic thinking, so sure of itself. Here of all places, where you find so much diversity and where the rhetoric of freedom of choice is ubiquitous. Would this justify the need for a simplistic approach? Nevertheless, the chiaroscuro is absent.—Caro

Protestant or Catholic? Is winter Protestant or Catholic, what do you think? Or, maybe, more likely, it's Orthodox, with drawn-out, unraveling carols, frozen tears, and silver icicles. I feel closer to the Anglo-Catholic option: moderate firm beliefs that in fact sanctify, in code, a kind of uncertainty. I like the grandeur of Catholic discourse, the emphasis on art. But I can't reject Protestantism either, salvation through sin. Calvinism seems more difficult to accept, salvation through grace. We took a detour and, behold, we've arrived again at Dostoevsky and the Karamazov brothers, the mysticism of universal love and neurotic, nocturnal Orthodoxy.

But let's pause a moment with sin, shall we? It brings us closer to God, doesn't it? I've resigned myself to my Buddhism, the adoration of the void. As an atheist, you have the advantage of being able to withdraw into the desert of unbelief. Christmas and New Year can be simply a pretext for parties and relaxing. I hope you were not too disappointed by the one last year, when you met Eve. Will you come again this year? I don't know if she'll come; perhaps you know better than I.

What did I just hear? You're writing an eight-hundred-page novel, one of those "unwritable" ones. That you're in love with a blonde trapeze artist, a former fellow at Keaton College, now in the circus in Moscow. That you're fully prepared to install her in a luxurious dacha, close to the writer's colony your American protector will establish, which he intends to name after Fitzgerald's mad wife. Limited enrollment, beautiful, brilliant, violent young men and women only! I hear that you have a sister who visited you to ask your advice about the Argentinian who has taken her by surprise—the well-known horse breeder. He has a magnificent villa in Buenos Aires, where they'll dance to Piazzolla every day.

I have my ear glued to the ground, as you can see. I catch all the world's rumors. They reach me in the form of an electric shock several times a day, at sunset.

I wish you a pleasant meeting with the sly immigration expert. A vagabond. Always impeccable in the same gray suit, with a red handkerchief in the breast pocket. Don't let his much-exercised courteousness put you off.—Caroline

I understand why you avoid conversations with students about your family, readings, or friends. You fear confessions and importunities. I'm sure that you are still approachable within the limits of decency. Cordial, affectionate, even a jokester—that's the you I know.—C

It was a blizzard, and I was looking for the key to the front door where you had promised to leave it when you abandoned the boudoir of the lecherous old woman. Either you didn't leave it behind or you hid it . . . among Gogol's dead souls.

I will be in the hospital for some time. I should have gone in long ago. Time for the knife thrower's act. I suppose you've gone through something similar. Or did you find that kind of addendum to the dictatorship unnecessary?

Better to speak of the miracles of modern medicine. My niece Ursula, Mike's daughter, looked like a goddess until she was around fourteen. Shared all her secrets with me. She even told me the story of her indelicate deflowering by a classmate, an Italian, Paolo. She was and is possessive and suspicious, clever and egotistical. As she's grown older, she's withdrawn into herself. She became too sure of herself. Later I found out that she's became a self-confessed militant lesbian. Now she lives with a rich Korean economist. She wants a child at any price, she's looking for a sperm donor on the internet. Will it be one of the new business deals of almighty capitalism and absolute freedom, I wonder? A business that is already legal and well organized: along with the sperm, you also receive the generous donor's file, chosen from among the many options you've studied for months. Biographical file: age, nationality, education, looks, medical certificates, etc. You can choose Christians, Jews, Chinese,

Indians, Muslims, atheists, men of all appearances and dialects. The cost is not prohibitive. Nor is it negligible. She keeps thinking about a name for her progeny. Whether it's a girl or boy doesn't matter; a name must be found that works in either case, because at some point, the girl might want to become a boy, or vice versa. A sex change is no longer something that can't be dealt with in our day and age.

I suppose that this new reality, new generation doesn't bother you.

Nor does it me, no. A bad sign, I think.—Caroline

This old troublemaker is in the hospital again. I am being interrogated by a courteous German psychiatrist, who insists on tousling the bedsheets of my former ages. There's an African patient here that I like, he has Paul Robeson's voice and carries on an interminable discourse that combines the Bible with Bahá'í, astrology, and magic. I also like the two quiet Irishmen and my roommate, a beautiful, young Southerner who is reading—who would believe it—*Notes from the Underground*.

I've always believed that accepting reality would be a passive action, an indolent one. I was wrong. It has become an act of mad courage; reality has become fictitious, precipitous, and virtual. All that's left for me to do is to accept it without erasing myself. Perhaps that's also the influence of my former Indian friend. He's taken to visiting again. At one point, I told him that time is an inevitable catastrophe. It passes quickly, you don't even know how or when. Time? Time doesn't exist for me, he answered. Nor for my fellow Indians.—C

I admit, the last time I greeted you I was somewhat un-derdressed and embraced you too enthusiastically. My hand slipped into your pants. But I came to my senses. I admit, af-ter a time I came to my senses and then, together, we played at shyness, its parody. I felt justified in my old woman's élan when you spoke for nearly an hour, asking all the time for more coffee. Globalism: the new perversion of mobility. Your extreme experiences, the camps, the Byzantine social-ism, the transatlantic exile. A privileged destiny! That's what you told me: a privilege. The honor of having been turned away, that is what a thinker from your country used to say. Otherwise, what would this fleeting life be?—Carol

Should I cure my weakness for drink now, at the height of spring? This is what the staff psychiatrists advise. Every-one here seems friendly, a drug addict offered to teach me chess. I can run and use the exercise room, volunteer for gardening or at the hospital's Protestant chapel. The wel-coming Protestant chapel accommodates all of faith's or-phans. It even offers books. I, for one, can't give up reading. Not without reading! I've cohabited and inhabited books all the nights of my life.

Spring is on its way. Slow-moving and capricious. When at last everything is reborn, I will toast the cosmic event with a tall glass full of . . . sparkling water. Clear as vodka. —Caroline

A monotonous summer. For variety's sake, I check into and out of the hospital again and again. Yesterday I heard there about the ten stages of recovery from anti-Semitism. Faith as difference? Seems childish.

Outside it's raining and blustery. My doctor seems worried about my ability to evade death. For now, though, I was thinking of having your grass cut and helping you modestly arrange your garden. I have good Robert, he doesn't ask for much. When you return from your vacation at your sister's, you'll be welcomed by a domesticated, boring landscape, expertly fit for amnesia.

Yesterday, I took my first walk this year along the river, where I often used to go with my official partner. My religious guru, my wise husband. I don't know if I've ever told you that my husband had acceded to the prospect of happiness with an unfaithful partner, but I suppose you've already guessed that on your own.

The red birds have returned and sing their homecoming. I hope you see them, hear them.—Caro

My Indian friend is the son of a diplomat. He has traveled a lot and even visited your country after his Prague childhood. He remembers a novel by Olivia Manning in which he rediscovered images from his adolescence in your Balkan capital. He spoke to me of picturesque villages, Orthodox services, the skinning of a dead horse on a village road, the beautiful national costumes, the music at the Sunday parties around the church, the dusty trucks with refugees from the war, the march of the Green Shirts, those nationalistic mystics, a pogrom which terrified him, the rural landscape, luminous and lyrical.

At the German school, the Evangelische Schule, there

was harsh discipline; two of the teaching staff were in the SS. My Indian friend was friends with a Swedish classmate—they drew the English flag everywhere they could and plotted against their German classmates, who were all puffed up after the victories of the Nazi army. Then he traveled with his family to Ankara, Baghdad, Rangoon. The illness that Auden remembers in *Journey to a War* (1939), reminded him of his student days, after the war. He, too, became gravely ill after a long journey in a military truck. He maintains that interviews with the survivors of Terezin evoke his own despair in the years 1942–1945. Seems somewhat exaggerated, no?—Caro

We are—and I am, still am—on the edge of eternal autumn. Thinning, captive to a puerile melancholy. Did I show you the dusty package with the volumes of Svevo? I've always felt close to his male heroes battling abulia. I'm rereading your French compatriot's *Rhinoceros*. Here, tyranny is more often dissimulated. The poisoned expression of freedom that becomes money, greed, piety, sickness, crime—not necessarily political.

In another envelope, so that you'll remember me, I am sending you fragments from my recent dreams about a couple who find their house (and life) on fire.

Could it be about me? And who could the partner have been?

Caroline Olson

For the stubbornness with which you avoid speaking about your sister, I punish you with my dreams and phantoms.

AT THE PSYCHIATRIST'S

Caroline Olson's favorite shrink, the psychiatrist Vladislaw Weiss, was tall and quiet. Through his silence, he was encouraging the professor to make his confession. "I understand, I do understand," the doctor would repeat after every prolonged silence. After five sessions, however, he had started to become impatient. He would wait for his patient, standing on his long masts of legs, without recourse to the usual ritual. He did not invite the professor to sit down, and he himself did not sit down, giving him to understand that the meeting would be brief. Short and sweet, as one says.

"Yes, yes, I understand. You don't feel like expounding on your biography. It bores you, you don't want any more questions, you won't offer any answers. Psychoanalysis bores you. You just want a pill, that's all. A pill that will put you at ease, that will give you the detachment and humor you need to get on with life. So that you can live simply, without asking yourself any more questions, without having any thoughts, without bothersome memories. A pill then."

He bent down toward the drawer, opened it, and took out the magic pill. It turned out not be a pill, however, but a little book, which he handed to the nomad with an affectionate bow.

"Will this do, sir? This is my pill, Herr Professor. What? Did you expect me to give you Prozac or some other pharmaceutical? No, sir. You take this little book, you read it slowly, at your leisure, you become friends with Ms. Tova and her friend, snail Mischa. You win them over to aid you in your healing. Getting well by example. It's not the usual treatment, as you've probably realized. Neither am I the usual sort of person, as you've also probably realized."

Yes, not at all what one would have expected, given that the good doctor was suggesting the same bizarre treatment Tamar had. His sister, who was both less and more than a sister and with whom, on a dusty street of the American capital, he had discovered the gastropod sent by President Washington, who had lent the messenger his globally popular name, George.

The professor understood with whom he was dealing. He also understood that the historian and chronicler of the circus who had come from the mountains of crystal and ice in the Eastern Lands, the Nomadic Misanthrope, didn't deserve anything more than phantasms. Cryptic charades, stagings, diversions, games with poisonous black glass beads.

The book was in a small format, pocket-sized. He placed it quickly in the right pocket of his jeans and made straight for the door, without taking leave of the wizard. Outside, he sat on the entrance steps to behold the new-old marvel. On the cover, the familiar tawny snail. Half a body and four tentacles on view. Below, a formal presentation of the minuscule therapeutic gospel:

In a work that beautifully demonstrates the rewards of closely observing nature, [the author] shares an inspiring and intimate story of her uncommon encounter with a Neohelix albolabris—*a common woodland snail. [. . .] Intrigued by the snail's molluscan anatomy, cryptic defenses, clear decision making, hydraulic locomotion, and mysterious courtship activities, Bailey becomes an astute and amused observer, providing a candid and engaging look into the curious life of this underappreciated small animal.*[53]

The patient thumbed through the psychiatrist's codex without having the patience to read it. Nevertheless, having come across the word *loneliness* several times, he guessed that this had motivated the doctor to choose the book as a possible form of therapy.

He was unsure whether he had been revitalized by the chance of reading it, or, quite the opposite, if the text only undermined the intensity and novelty of his conversations with his tenant, George. He decided he would read aloud from it every night to the blind, mute, illiterate snail.

Yes, yes, and he'd also have to thank his friend, the ancient, dying Caroline for her tender suggestion that he see Dr. Weiss, the accomplice of snails and other solitary creatures.

EVA ELISABETA LOMBARDINI

It hadn't been a knock at the door; rather a repeated scratching. Modernist, neurotic music. Was it the cat, the homeless rabbit, the neighborhood squirrel, the rebellious spider? A lost bat, perhaps? It was already evening, perfect silence, the time of wandering bats.

"Yes, it's me, you do recognize me? Eva, Caroline's niece."

"Ah, Eve."

The beautiful one had already stepped over the threshold and was now regarding her admirer, smiling.

"Actually, it's Eva. Caroline tended to Americanize my name. It was her style—ironic patriotism. My name is Eva. Eva Elisabeta Lombardini."

"Caroline used to maintain that we had seen each other not just at the New Year's party but after it."

"She was testing you. That's exactly what she was doing. As far as I know, you never rose to her provocations."

"Did she tell you that?"

"Naturally. She was testing me, too. I didn't bite either. And yet, here I am. Lombardini. Elisabeta. And Eva, yes, and Eva."

The professor made a gallant motion, inviting his guest to enter the monastic cell qua cabin. He didn't seem to care that he was in jeans and an old, worn-out T-shirt. Eva, for her part, was already holding above her head the bottle of red wine she had brought as a gesture of friendship.

"I've come so that we can commemorate her. She deserves it, I do believe she deserves it. I know you were close."

"As much as we could be."

"You seemed so shy when I first met you."

"I am shy. And stubborn."

"You're exotic."

"There is no such thing as exotic in this country. The global multitudes. Exiles, adventurers, failures, the persecuted, the wanderers. Misunderstood geniuses."

"Under what category would you file yourself?"

"NM, nomad, misanthrope, as aunt Caroline used to put it."

He had already made room on a chair, had picked up the things piled on it and thrown them on the bed, then the second chair, now there were two chairs at the table and on the table the red bottle and two tall glasses.

"Before we drink, I would like you to explain your three

names. None of them shared with your aunt, Caroline. She claimed she was Swiss and Canadian."

"And so she was. With a brief rest stop in Austria. No big deal, as she would say. She wouldn't even have mentioned that addendum. It was different in my case. For me, Austria remained important. My father, who was much older than my mother, grew up in Tyrol, though he had family all over the place. Turkey, Albania, Italy. But his roots were in Vienna. He almost eloped with my mother, she was only fifteen or sixteen. The family had a fit, and not just because of the age difference. He had introduced himself as Austrian and spoke German perfectly, with a Viennese accent, but they were not sure if he really was a Catholic and not Protestant, Jewish, or God knows what else—Russian Orthodox, or Lebanese Muslim, anything! He was fascinated with Sisi, and they knew it. I, too, consider myself an admirer of Sisi, the famous rebellious empress."

"Rebellious? She had a lot of children as far as I know. Legitimate ones."

"I think so."

"She was called Elisabeta, as far as I know. Sisi was an endearment, a secret name, and that's what it remained, even for posterity."

"My father could never stop telling stories about her. Or eulogizing her. He was incurably in love with Sisi. He knew all the biographical details, the grand mysteries, and could tell you about her charisma, her independence, reading habits, the poems, whatever. You'd wind up completely confused."

Eve stopped answering his questions, and, having sat

down, attempted to open the bottle, twisting its metal cap left and right. The host promptly offered her a corkscrew and sat down beside her, without taking over the task. The glasses turned red with Greek wine.

Yes, she was Caroline's beautiful niece! Her thick, black hair was parted in the middle, hiding her ears. The full, tender lips of a child. Blue eyes, overwhelmingly blue, the alluring neck. The legs, yes, the legs a little too ample but long, like the hands, white and luminous and ready to put on a performance. He had seen all these things the first time they met, too; now, he was merely revisiting them.

They toasted, touching glasses, and the wine in them trembled, complicitous. When she extended her glass, quickly turning then to face her partner, Eva almost seemed to have extended her breast, as well, which swayed proudly under her immaculate blouse. Or, perhaps, it was not she but the chimera which had risen up out of the man and now pitilessly hypnotized him. The single-minded captive chimera enlivened and entranced his solitude, the wasteland he inhabited.

"Sisi, then. It's a good topic for storytelling."

"It's not just that. My father maintained—and he was right—that if Sisi had had real influence, real power in Vienna, Austria would have taken a different path."

"Maybe, though Vienna has also come to symbolize Secession. Creativity, modernism, psychoanalysis, rebel geniuses. In other words, not just hysterical nationalism. But I forgot to ask you what you do, where you work, how you earn a living."

Eva seemed to sense that the exotic one was having a hard time finding his words. They sounded false. She drank again from the red glass, deeply this time, trying to find a natural-sounding answer.

"I'm not sure. I lie in wait for the days. And the nights, especially for them. I try to possess them. Without much success."

"Lonely?"

"Such a pretentious word. It's overused. I'm waiting, that's all. I force myself to be patient. I'm a virgin."

The silence had become alive, mysterious, aggressive.

"It's not what you think. I've spread my legs plenty of times. Maybe not enough, but whenever I've wanted to. Physically I'm not a virgin, nor am I sexually inexperienced. It's something else. Hard to put into words. A kind of waiting, maybe. Yes, that's it, I've found the word on the first try. I'm still waiting."

It was too much! A shameless invitation. Too, too much! He was praying to the chimera inside him to save him. To suddenly put him to sleep, like a demonic kill switch, a kind of posttraumatic absence, the inner fainting of convalescence. But no, the chimera still failed to appear. Sisi would have to be the means of salvation once again.

However, through an abrupt movement of her chair, the stranger suddenly discovered George the Snail slipping down the edge of his glass vessel.

"Ah, I see you're not alone, you have a comrade. How extraordinary! Completely unbelievable! Two exotic creatures, that's what you are! I never would have believed it!"

Before she had finished saying these words, she had already gotten up, was next to George, wanting to make his acquaintance up close, to approach him. She gave him a long, sympathetic look. George did not react; it was hard to say whether he felt the change of energy in the room.

"Where did you find him? Is he another stranger from 'heaven-only-knows-where'? Or an American pureblood? Is he from the old country? Did you bring him here for support?"

The professor gazed at her without answering, allowing the pair's acquaintance to evolve naturally, without interruption.

"I came to see one exotic, and I've found two. What a surprise! I'm sure it's not the only one. Do you have friends? Have you found friends on these shores? Surely you have. The entire world is here, you find kindred spirits, even if not right away. What do you say? I'm not forcing you to confess or provide details. Yes or no will suffice. Can you name one?"

"More than one," the taciturn man whispered.

"Let's hear their names then, go on. What, why are you avoiding the question?"

"Clopidogrel. Losartan."

All quiet. Silence. Muteness. Pause. A prolonged pause. She was bewildered.

"Metformin. Gabapentin."

Eva smiled, intrigued by the seemingly endless enumeration.

"Escitalopram," she heard at last, the name of another one of the exile's friends. Evidently a code name."

"It sounds like a pharmacopeia. Are you ill?"

"No, just old. Incurably so. I get on well with these pals. Co-captains of sorts is how I think of them. Drifters, internationalists. Cosmopolitans, like myself."

DIDACTICA NOVA (II)
The Opinions of the Students:
Exile and Estrangement in Literature

I consider exile to be a radical human experience. Not simply a counterpoint, as Said believes, but the modulation of different symbols. Exile is not just the experience of two simultaneous modes of thinking. The exiled person has at their disposal both their home culture and one or more external cultures that alternate in a reciprocal way. I am thinking chiefly of Meursault, Camus's hero, because his exile takes place at home. What he terms the "arrogant certitude" of the priest is, in fact, a Christian monophony which can tolerate only itself and in which he cannot believe. I find it difficult to think of him as being mistaken. He is only exiled because he is different, like Schlemihl, the wanderer without a shadow, who is different from the others. He does not commit himself to the friendship with Raymond, until Meursault finds himself in total isolation in his jail cell. During the trial, he realizes that he has always been under accusation, isolated from others by the arrogance of those who are so sure of themselves, the ones he calls "the moral majority." The state does not condemn him for killing the Arab. Instead, it sentences him for killing his mother, who, evidently, was killed only by old age. Meursault is conscious of the absurdity of existence. He is guilty only because he has not found a place in society and has not been given the gift of a fairytale featuring seven-league boots, which he would have rejected anyway.

He has no clue whether he possesses a shadow or not. If

he did, he wouldn't sell it, since he's not interested in increasing his income or even in moving to the capital, as has been proposed to him. He wakes up only when Céleste openly declares her solidarity, and he considers the old man's dog as valuable as a wife.

Embittered, Meursault accepts the "amiable indifference" of the world only at the very end of the book. In the end, he connects to the hatred of the faceless multitude, which confirms his own uniqueness.

Meursault lives in a colonial state, a foreign superimposition on a local culture that parallels the superimposition on his life of the justice that condemns him. In the end, Meursault's amorality appropriates the fury of morality. His social exclusion becomes philosophical auto-inclusion, a richer paradox than the counterpoint promoted by Said. Isolation becomes his way of including himself in the human community, while the viewpoint of the "moralist" turns out to be hatred. It is an incredible fact that, on his deathbed, Meursault is preparing for a new beginning. (Jacob)

I would like to expand on our discussion about exile and estrangement, to venture beyond the text, but inspired by the text, through a digression that would consider the problem of gender, which, naturally, could not be addressed in a fairytale from two centuries ago, but which can no longer be avoided in our time. We see this issue each and every moment in the carnival in which we participate. Sexuality has always been a major force in the Bible and in mythology, as in life. Even if it is hidden in the shadows, the theme occupies a central place in our society, and is not a negligible part of buying and selling, which dominate our present time, something intuited perfectly by the author of Peter Schlemihl's adventures in exile.

Buying and selling was a dynamic force even in early capitalism. At that time, the trade in weapons had not yet reached such magnitude, nor was the trade in skin, kidneys, and sperm in existence yet, nor were there sex shops on the main streets of cities. The middleman who offers to buy the shadow for a simple bag of money that never runs out knows why he wears that impeccable gray suit—tailored at the border between black and white, where the shadow itself lives. Taking charge at that time behind the scenes—and not just behind the scenes—of the daily, and, more importantly, the nightly spectacle of history and of migrants, the spectacle subsuming the wishes and dreams and misdeeds of our fellow men and women, the shadow had a vast empire in which to maneuver. The story begins with Peter's exile and ends with globalization and its clearest, most ubiquitous embodiment: money. To this one must add sex, which currently any individual can procure anywhere, including at home, in everyday reality, and online. Little by little, the shadowy conventions have been scattered, they can barely be grasped here and there. The shadow gives them an advantage, but it has been dethroned, humiliated, sold, replaced, falsified, delivered to specialized corporations. Like almost everything else that moves in this world as it hurtles toward its end. And yet, could we live without the chiaroscuro, without secrets and tacit conventions, without hiding places? Everything on view and on the sales counter?

Peter found himself at the point of becoming independently wealthy. His good luck was that ultimately he failed, and he decided to study plants and living things, like his botanist and poet father. But what about sexuality and its mysteries? Can they be ignored? And the relationship to the shadow? And the wandering shadows of the world? The tone of our classroom debate does not have to be overly bleak . . . That would mean forgetting about the ironic nature of hopelessness, about our ephemerality, forgetting that Mr. von Chamisso himself worried that, of all things, it would be the humor that would be lost in his story for putting the Hitzig family children to sleep.

I want to believe that this fact makes up for the rather frivolous and impertinent liberties which I've allowed myself in these comments, expressing my dissatisfaction with a prompt that is altogether too professorial. (Kati)

At the entrance to the hospital, Schlemihl is given the name "the Jew." It's not a mix-up. Nor is it a joke or an insult. He receives a number (12), losing all other identities. Though the story was written two centuries ago, Peter Schlemihl presents us with a new type of exile and alienation in the epoch of globalization, one that comes close to the theme of the "wandering Jew," all too well known. In essence, the author follows the theme of the Jew who has no homeland and no chance to put down roots in a community. The story centers on a new arrival, who has no clue how the society where he was shipwrecked functions and who is not prepared to meet the Man in Gray. Flummoxed, he sells his shadow. Only later does he understand that he will never be accepted in society without a shadow, and that the never-empty bag of money cannot assure his social success. Mina, who entrances him, leaves as soon as she understands what he lacks.

Little by little, the character Schlemihl (in Yiddish this means someone who is naïve, stupidly sincere and infantile, moronic, almost a saint in his innocence) comes to signify the biblical Peter, the Jew who became a proponent of Christianity. He refuses to take back his shadow in exchange for his soul, and risks becoming a pariah, ostracized and excluded, giving up all chance of assimilating into the world which drives him away. His initial foolishness, which seemed like a joke appropriate for a moronic *schlemiel* with his head in the clouds, quickly becomes the premise of a dangerous, long-standing if not eternal drama. The story does not mention God: only people and exile. It's not about a sacred experience, but an unbearable earthly one. "I am alone in my wilderness, as before," Schlemihl states. His effort to live like others do fails. What remains is something that cannot be bought or sold. Even when money seems to speak louder than anything else and makes him complicitous in the process of buying and selling, trapping him again.

If the autocratic and totalitarian regimes exile or kill those who cannot be made to fit their norms, democratic, capitalist regimes find other, more insidious methods to isolate, marginalize, and neutralize such individuals. If anything, they offer the opportunity to travel and see the world, as Schlemihl proceeds to do after he has separated himself from others and found another meaning of exile, but without any relationship to the homeland, national identity, or social acceptance. It seems like the outcome of a typical Jewish experience: entering a new society, following the rules, and inevitably becoming estranged in one way or another.

Chamisso alludes to the particular situation of the Jews in Europe in his time, but also makes a general claim about the eternal cycle of wandering. The Jews were allowed to take on financial roles that brought them prosperity, but not social acceptance. Time after time they were criticized for losing their heritage and sense of belonging (their "shadow"). It is not mere coincidence that *schlemiel* and *schlimazel* come from the Yiddish: a luckless person, a naïve and hapless individual looking for some kind of permanence.

The wanderer Schlemihl finds his place not in a social unit or nation, but in the natural world and its exploration. A necessity especially in today's world, in our world. Internet, cell phones, mass communication, and hyperconnectivity. (Nathan)

Chamisso's story is a moral tale. More important than his former mistake of selling his shadow is Peter's decision to not alienate his soul. Well-being is less important than the shadow (identity), and the latter is less important than the soul. The moral concerns of the text explain the simple nature of the imagery, which is general rather than specific.

The reader is seen as an incidental witness to Chamisso and Schlemihl. An intruder untutored in the requirements of fairytales, a stranger like Peter. After he sells his shadow, Peter becomes an Other, the Stranger, a suspect in a suspect situation. Although the Man in Gray is the puppet master, he is not, in fact, the fairytale's antagonist; rather, that part is played by the people who ostracize Peter and who thereby become the unwitting tools of the Man in Gray. They are in no way obligated to behave like they do, they do it of their own free will. The Man in Gray is glad that others are doing his job for him. He is not the one who harasses Peter. It is society that determines what is normal and acceptable, it is society's actions that estrange and wound Peter. His charitable actions are made public, and Peter feels generous, sure that others will consider him to be virtuous, and will honor and esteem him. Their motivations, however, are hypocritical and Peter does not obtain any moral status. I would have wanted the hero to learn what real suffering means. It is my opinion that a deeper suffering and a more dramatic breakdown would have added to the moral of the story. (Benjamin)

Fairytales promote moral messages to children. Their success depends on their universality, through their fantastic and allegorical elements, free from chronological and spatial references. In the case of von Chamisso's story, both moral critique and the sociopolitical climate make their way into the context. The shadow is a reflection of social status, representing how much space one occupies in the world. The soul is essential to the self. The soul represents the living being, and the shadow reflects its identity. The being exists in space and time, and the shadow connects to space and time by means of the sun. When Peter is alienated from his shadow, he himself becomes a shadow in his social world. Both he and the Man in Gray are examples of the stranger and are often called "poor devils." The Man in Gray uses his social status to cover up identity; he offers social advantages but he himself is dependent on a corrupt hierarchy. In the end, Peter manages without any social relationships, keeping his soul intact, and the Man in Gray continues to manipulate identities. Peter becomes Patient No. 12, meaning one of the twelve apostles of Christ, the rock on which the Church and the faith are built. The story includes an Enlightenment antithesis as well, when Schlemihl retreats into a cave, like the first Christian desert fathers. Not to pray, but to study nature, far away from human barbarity. Reason is the only thing that separates man from animals, who have shadows but not souls. In Yiddish, Mina means "peace-loving," and Schlemihl means a ridiculous, luckless person. The characters are related to established allegories. Chamisso includes himself in the story, like Peter, the botanist, without a shadow, having been forced into exile.

A writer can make a work the shadow of his existence, written so that he can discover who he is. Through writing, Chamisso bares his soul completely, but Schlemihl's entire adventure can also be seen, of course, as the story of a melancholic buffoon, an Augustus the Fool, punished to follow his luckless trajectory. (Alexandra)

The soul against the shadow! A society on the threshold of becoming a materialistic, consumer culture! A fantastical tale! A story for children but with adult themes. A hero, Peter, who sees what others refuse to see. When the Man in Gray takes an enormous lunette from his magical bag, then a Turkish carpet and many other unusual objects, "no one found anything strange about this." The simple style of the story allows one to focus on its message more than its language. The characters fit the typical fairytale mold. Like Kafka's *Metamorphosis,* the story opens with a single major and fantastical event: in Kafka's case the transformation into a bug, in this case the selling of the shadow. When the locals see the shadow is missing, they ostracize Peter, he loses Mina, and he becomes enmeshed in guilt. When he becomes ill, he is identified as Jewish in the Schlemihlium Sanatorium, then he wanders the world with his seven-league boots and becomes preoccupied with nature, like von Chamisso, the author of the story, himself an expatriate from France, exiled because of his upper-class background. The story centers on the changing times in Germany, more specifically on the transition from Kantianism to idealism. German idealism is born from romanticism and the revolutionary politics of the Enlightenment as a response to Kantianism. The fact that an object can be considered independently of its mental premise, is something that is denied by idealism—and so is the idea that the shadow could represent the way we are perceived by others, when in fact it is actually an expression of our existence and does not depend on the social conventions of those around us. But the shadow remains a social point of reference and determines the way Schlemihl is perceived by others; even when he becomes wealthy, society cannot ignore his morally ambiguous status. Here can be seen the conflict between idealism and Kantianism: what is more important, the shadow (how one is perceived socially) or the soul (one's individual existence)?

When Mr. John informs the new arrival that he will need a million dollars for others to take notice of him, he is referring to the values of incipient capitalism: money is the most important thing. Peter is wealthy and ridiculed for his lack of shadow, which is seen as an anomaly. His wealth cannot improve his situation. Peter cannot continue except in the darkness. When his "secret" is uncovered, he loses Mina, he is attacked by Rascal, and he becomes a condemned man, since "a man cannot oppose his destiny." The temporary companionship with the Man in Gray does not help him. The temporary shadow does not help him, and yet, the wanderer rejects the middleman's proposal: he does not give up his soul, and so he definitively loses his shadow and throws away the bag of money that is never empty. "I sat there without a shadow and without any money: in exchange, a great weight had been removed from my soul. I felt glad." The question arises as to what sort of person he will become. He has no reason to feel guilty forever, since he did not give up his soul, but only his shadow which made him like everyone else and made him accepted socially.

He rejects social and human interrelations, and he chooses solitude and nature instead of society. (Christy)

THE PRIVILEGED TRAUMA (II)
Class Lecture

The subtle conclusions reached by Jung and his school seem to be those of someone recently escaped from a totalitarian universe. Pompous if not superfluous, given that the "shadow" to which the captive and survivor of a dictatorship usually refers is the "Informant." Here and everywhere. A completely different embodiment of the shadow than that sought by Western researchers of the psyche, one that is disputed by the personality's own impulses. In a totalitarian regime, outside pressure—generalized suspicion or the imperative of total surveillance—little by little inhibits the dynamics of introspection, leaving the defense mechanisms free to oppose the visible and invisible agents of Power. In this way, a type of Pavlovian mechanism of the functional reflexes is established, to which the individual resorts both in public and in the intimacy of their own private circle. After the fall of European communism, the mechanisms of suppression were revealed: the cases in which intimate friends, or even husbands and wives, served as police informants. For the former captive and experimental lab rat of a dictatorship, exile becomes the much-awaited liberation from one's ever-present Shadow, from the interlocutor-hound, the neighbor at the disposal of the repressive apparatus.

However, what Jung and his followers wrote is not wholly invalidated by this ubiquitous external pressure. It is only codified, and perhaps partially loses its impact. The life force invents its own pragmatic solutions for preservation, isolation, doctoring, duplicity. For the watches of the night, for prompt disguising. In the depths of introspection's ambiguities, the imperative to protect oneself becomes associated with a decisive energy to dissimulate in the exterior world. Paradoxically, masochism can also function as part of this opportunistic mobilization of the survival instinct, by activating the Jungian "dark" side of the self and by cooperating with the repressive powers to accept, if not desire, its unexpected trophies, always offered under suspicious, staged circumstances. Of course, the idea promoted by Jungian psychology that we should not reject our hidden "Shadow" but should opt for inclusion and completion of the self in order to avoid or delay malign admixtures of impulses and the explosion of former inhibitions, in the end cannot accommodate the totalitarian tragedy in its aims. Totalitarianism develops a different set of constraints, which includes not just the "Shadow" who watches at night, in the name of Authority, but also the solidary shadow of a secret, solidary victim whom the duplicitous figure needs in order to reoxygenate his self-confidence.

The exile with the code name "Nomadic Misanthrope" could remember, for example, that at one point, in the studies he consulted on the circus and clowns, he found mention of an unexpected text focusing on *The Apprenticeship Years of Augustus the Fool.*[54] Seen as a luckless and marginalized individual, the subject of the text, a writer, finds in the reader a brotherly witness. A kind of double without whom he cannot maintain his inner defenses, just as the believer cannot long maintain his beliefs without also admitting the existence of so-called specters of faith.

The Jungian vision of Evil as a premise of a potential Good can eventually be applied, even if only with certain risks, to life under dictatorship. It might look like a self-imposed toughening and perfecting of the self who waits. The self develops a secret hopeful code as a reaction to the hostile environment's extreme narrowing of the horizon of possibilities.

If this is so, then, one might also conclude that for the individual who frees himself through exile from the darkness in which he has previously lived and from the homeland's habits of thought, the trauma of exile becomes proportional to the limitations of the universe from which the former captive has emerged. The exile comes to take part in a unique experiment. For the rest of his or her allotted lifespan, he or she can find the positive aspects, the Good, of exile—which is otherwise burdensome and humiliating—and draw from its negative aspects, or from its Evil, the strength to effect a structural change that might consider both such positives and negatives against the frustrations and uncertainties of life "back home."

Yes, and there is something to learn from Jung even in the case of the captive who thrashes about in the traps of freedom and who fails to make such a structural change. In terms of the ambiguities the self must navigate, the doctrines of exilic abundance offer intriguing choices. Of course, the former captive "knows" more than his new neighbors about the nature of illusions and about wandering and the malefic force of suppression; so he gazes on the amorality of the free market and on the compromises that form the backbone of an imperfect democracy as a splendid type of "normality." Moreover, he begins to think of imperfection—with its relatively benign limiting factors—as the natural state of all people, because the compromises which it forces upon one are not those of the dictatorship he has left behind. At the same time, the tribute he formerly paid to despair, in the old places and times of his biography, now protects him against the peddlers of false hopes. (Though this advantage can also become a handicap if it leaves the individual who has found refuge in the free world indifferent to social responsibility and the need to challenge injustice.)

Schlemihl's odyssey does not allow for this sort of excessive, nuanced analysis. It ignores the social and familial priors of the stranger who is cast ashore in a new reality, and it treats exile as its immutable "essence" without revealing any fundamental differences in the experiences of the individual exile. In fact, it even ignores the possibility of a more rigorous scrutiny of the protagonist's "interiority," as though it were something that is naturally inappropriate in a fairytale. Interiority, however, is unavoidable for any wider or more profound understanding of such a drastic, extreme experience. It is bound up with the uncertain human condition, with the experience of being perpetually taken by surprise, of being transformed and uprooted, of having to overcome one's own self, of confronting success and failure, of wearily rediscovering one's own nature in solitude's new beginnings.

Is Schlemihl's adventure meaningful for the expatriate from a dictatorship, or from a tyrannical family, or an environment devastated by poverty, savagery, and fanaticism? Does Peter's drama (as it is rendered) contain the drama of all estranged people, of those who have been dispossessed and excluded, the nomads who have been expelled by History's tempests from this or that refuge? Is there still room in Schlemihl's "dialectic of change," as Brecht called exile, for a leftist—who escaped Hitlerism only to wander under the capitalist torch of freedom? For the dilemmas of the inward-looking person, who is nevertheless subjugated to the violence of the same dialectics?

Old identity documents do not make up a life. Neither can new documents. An official change of identity is only formally symbolic of the internal change the stranger undergoes. A change that little by little erases the footprints (or shadow) of the double, the individual as he was yesterday and long ago. Reduced to the status of a child, the exile must be willing to grow up in a new homeland. The initial shock that heralds the separation will be followed by transitions and transactions that will exchange one set of values for another. In Schlemihl's case, this is underscored harshly and visibly, simply, in the form of the bag of money which is never empty. In reality, however, this change will happen slowly and in fact will involve a complex confrontation. The "exchange period" of values somehow continues to matter . . .

Even if the wanderer's eventual transformation is shaped by a great number of initial conditions, as well as subsequent ones, the differences in the appearance and quality of the "shadow" (and the evolution the latter undergoes) organize the exile's adventure—are in proportion to it and respond to it with varied effects—always and everywhere. The consequences of this for the interior life would offer researchers in Jungian psychoanalysis ample reason to investigate further.

SISI

A century of three days and three nights had passed since the last visit Eva Elisabeth Lombardini had honored him with, when he seemed to hear a scratching at the front door.

Unsure whether he was dealing with an individual or a cat, the professor opened the door cautiously. The specter was there, just a step away.

"Oh, what a surprise!"

"It was a surprise last time. Now it's a mere importunity," the intruder meowed. "I've come to see George. May I?"

"Let me ask him," the professor answered calmly.

He did not wait for George's approval, however, but opened the door with a courtly bow and invited the intruder into his monastic cell.

"Did you come to tell me more about Sisi, your role model?"

"My father's. I only adopted it. I loved my father, so I love her, too. But I didn't come about Sisi. We can talk about her if you want. But I came to talk about your exile. So we'd get to know one another."

"In the biblical sense?"

"Not necessarily. As you wish, monsieur . . . I have no inhibitions of any kind. Just so you know! Only so you know, not so you act. We can talk about anything. No inhibitions. No tricks. Okay?"

"It's difficult without the bottle of red. I see you've opted to do without it."

"I thought I might find one here. Red, green, golden. You're a solitary person, that's what you used to say. That's obvious if we look around. The bottle is only an ally; this time I have the courage to forgo it."

Eva was already in front of George. Her friend seemed to have withdrawn into sleep or into waiting. A good opportunity to scrutinize him. Both the host and the vision who had descended from the clouds did so.

She was less elegant looking than before. Black jeans and a blue short-sleeved blouse that revealed her white childish elbows. Thick hair drawn up in a bun at the top of her head. Lively blue eyes, open wide toward the terrestrial world.

The professor already had a bottle of red Portuguese wine in his hand.

"Shall we have a drink?"

"If it seems necessary . . . Meaning if you'd like to. You can steer the encounter from this point forward. Or the encounters. Of course, I'd prefer to abstain. At least this time. Forgoing the allies. At least today. No bottle!"

"Then, making full use of our sobriety, we should establish the nature of our conversation for the next ten years. Our two five-year plans, to use Stalinist vocabulary. I promise to participate even from the world beyond. Tell me what the first chapter will be."

"The first and the last and those in between should be about exile."

"I don't like to complain."

"So I guessed. I also guessed that you would nevertheless accept me as your conversation partner. Meaning, as a friend. A potential friend. Am I right?"

"Could be. You still haven't told me what you do for a living."

"A kind of journalism. At a TV station. A small weekly show, an hour long, called *Parentheses*."

The professor became mute. He was silent, would be silent forever. At last, he raised his long arms helplessly.

"No, no I can't. I didn't go on TV even in my own country. They didn't want me to there. I didn't meet to their criteria. Here, I don't want to."

"I don't represent the TV station. I am or can become the friend of the exile. The potential friend. Discreet. Very discreet. Mum! Faithful! Trustworthy, I swear! My father was an exile. He always refused to talk about his wanderings. Now I finally have the chance to understand."

"Without knowing, I know that our stories cannot be compared. Your father's and mine."

Silence. Complete and total silence.

"Should I go?"

"Not necessarily. But exile will remain a taboo subject. However, we can empty the bottle of Portuguese wine."

"That's not what I came for. I came for friendship."

"With an old man?"

"With an old exile. To take advantage. Of his solitude. To offer him my friendship. A more detached, more disinterested friendship than my aunt's. Believe me."

The old exile tried to open the bottle of wine, twisting the cap left and right without much success, until, irritated and with an abrupt motion, Eva took the bottle from his hands and twisted open the metal cap.

"Okay, I understand that you don't want me to go."

"I don't. I'm a solitary man, as you said. The neighbors' cat is my only visitor."

He poured the red Portuguese wine into the two glasses he had taken from the cabinet. They toasted and smiled in a friendly way at each other without raising their glasses in homage. They sipped in silence, each looking at his own glass.

"So we'll drink rather than talk. There's nothing more to discuss."

"Yes, there is. Sisi. A rich topic."

"I see you prefer intellectual subjects. Real life doesn't appeal to you."

"Of course, it does. I've been studying the circus for a long time, as I've told you before. Moreover, Sisi is a life, not just a text."

"So about Sisi then. The exile."

"Exile? From München to Berlin and from Bavaria to Austria. Is that an exile?"

"No. Not a geographical or linguistic or religious one, not even an ethnic one. An essential one. Sisi lived in perpetual exile. She wasn't reconciled to life."

"You said she was faithful to the Emperor."

"It seems so, and so I think. The rumors about an affair with her beloved Count Andrássy or the Scottish captain Bay Middleton proved to be groundless. As did those regarding her youngest daughter, Maria Valeria, said to be the illegitimate child of her relationship with Gyula Andrássy. In fact, the little girl is the spitting image of the Emperor. We can talk about the Empress's beauty. The Shah of Persia was stunned when he beheld her, as was Wilhelm II, the German emperor, and the American ambassador. As for her admiration for the exiled poet, the Jew Heine, we can talk about that, too, and we can talk about her prolonged retreats from Vienna, about her Greek lessons and her reading of Homer, about her trips and hunts and morning exercises. We can talk about her humor and irony, or about her frugal eating habits, milk, meat, juice, a few fruits. And about alienation and understanding, about the inevitable worldly exile, which she proclaimed in verse, not just letters. *Eine Möwe bin ich von keinem Land/Meine Heimat nene ich keinen Strand.*"[55]

Eva seemed to know it all, and by heart.

"Or her letter to her friend Count Grunne: *Each ship I see departing, growing smaller and smaller, evokes in me the most intense desire to find myself aboard, whether it is heading to-*

wards Brazil, Africa, or Cabo. It wouldn't matter to me, as long as I didn't have to stay in the same place for long."

The professor listened reverently. When Eva paused to breathe, he timidly intervened with his own addendum:

"Yes, I've learned a lot, thank you. I understand why Sisi fascinates you. Perhaps you didn't know she was a friend of Queen Elisabeta of Romania. Another Elisabeta! 'Mother of the Wounded,' a caregiver, active both philanthropically and as a writer. She helped the composer Enescu, 'the child of her heart,' she gave him musical scores. It's said she even gave him a violin . . . She wasn't an exile exactly, despite what appearances might suggest. Married to the King of Romania, who was a German Catholic who had assimilated perfectly into Eastern Orthodox Romania. She, too, was beautiful, and she published under the pseudonym Carmen Sylva, like Sisi. Poetry, plays, prose."

"I had no idea. Exotic details from an exotic land. Provided by an exotic friend. I hope you're not mad I called you my friend."

Eva poured, and her conversation partner smiled, looking at her.

"Perhaps you don't know about her great Wallachian admirer either. The nihilist Emil Cioran, the Parisian celebrity. Born in Transylvania in the former Austro-Hungarian empire. A pure-blooded exile. He wrote the apologia for exile, called it the aristocratic condition. The threads connect, don't they?"

Eva was silent, thoughtful, ready to be initiated into Eastern European exoticism.

"So, what did your nihilist say about Sisi?"

"I don't remember exactly, I made a note somewhere. Something about the idea of death. They were both obsessed with it. And about her despairing lucidity, something like that."

They had talked and were talking and talking while, to Eve's disappointment, their snail friend remained perpetually indifferent.

It was growing dark, their words softened and shuddered. Eva had gotten up, was at the door.

"I congratulate myself for opening the door. Just so you know, I'll be back. Soon. You don't get to escape that easily."

"Okay, George will be delighted."

With a parting gesture, Eva disappeared.

She returned about ten days later. She didn't scratch at the door . . . knowing that it was always open. She pressed down the handle and was inside, next to George, who was making his rounds on the edge of the glass bowl. The professor was somewhere on the moon, where his real home probably was. Eva did not seem curious about his absence, being wholly absorbed by the slowness of the snail and the tacit resignation with which he journeyed, again and again, around the circumference. When the professor made his appearance from the bathroom, neither his muteness nor his deafness seemed to bother her. In blue cotton shorts and a blue T-shirt. The uniform of a fraternity of solitaries? He was intimidated, it was obvious that he could marshal neither movements nor words.

"Oh, yes, you're not in the habit of announcing your appearance; I'd forgotten. After so many long absences, I'd forgotten. Yes, they were long. I hope you don't mind my casual attire. I'm not sure it's actually casual." The walking stick looked, as if in disbelief, at his shorts, and at the same time caught sight of the bottle in Eve's hands.

"So you've brought allies. It wasn't necessary."

"I don't depend on allies, I feel like talking. I want to be straightforward and alluring. That's all."

"Okay, then we'll dispense with the digressions and stimulants. Yes, even with the stimulants, it'll be clearer that way. So, have a seat, let's get talking."

"I'm settled and American in a country of wanderers and exiles. I'm not a wanderer. I want to understand estrangement. Exile. You'd make a good guide."

"Because I'm a professor? I became one out of necessity. All my life I was a pupil, a student, a reader. You said that I'm solitary. That doesn't bode well for conversation. Your friend George is the only one who knows my monologue. He's discreet, as you can see. He won't reveal the secrets of the castle. All the libraries and bookstores are now full of books about exile. Globalization, exile—it's all in fashion. An enormous bibliography: books, films, songs, anything you like. You don't need me."

"Maybe I do."

"Yes, maybe you do . . . but I am not just a wanderer but someone who's lost. Your aunt used to call me the Nomad."

"Yes, I know."

"And she'd add 'Misanthrope' to that. Probably to rile me up. So that I'd contradict her, prove to her I wasn't one. I didn't succeed. I think you know that. I accepted the categorization; I didn't feel at all offended. Nor betrayed. Nor did I identify with the name. I wander through categories, I've never picked one."

"Perfect! That's true exile. We can talk. With or without wine. That's why I'm wearing a woolen scarf, as you can see. I had the flu. Another exile."

"Without wine. This time, without; I insist. I'm guessing you've exhausted the subject of Sisi, that you're looking for another opening gambit."

It was only at this point that the professor saw the thick green woolen shawl the young Lombardini had wrapped herself in. Young? Yes, relatively young, younger than the Nomad. Elegant, more elegant than she had been the first time. Warning, warning, professor! The intruder has her own tactics! She had done her hair up differently, she had put on light lipstick, nearly invisible around the contour of her half open lips. Through her silken blouse, a glimpse of her bra. But her hands? The professor was obsessed with hands and feet . . . He didn't seem to know the exact nature of Eve's hands and feet. Only her slightly thickened voice, subdued.

"I could take up the thread on Sisi and the Romanian nihilist who adored her. Would you be interested?"

"Anything. I'm interested in anything you choose to reveal."

"I paraphrase books, I don't reveal. As I just said, I'm the perennial student. That's all. And a reader, yes, a reader."

This would have been the moment to pour wine into glasses, to choose and receive the stimulant, but neither of them seemed willing to give in to the temptation.

"Okay then, if you don't want to keep going with Sisi, I'll take up the Transylvanian nihilist again. Putting an emphasis on the differences between them, not on their common points of reference."

"I'd be more interested in the resemblance to you, not to Sisi."

"Okay, here's one. When he was older, Cioran was accosted on the street once by a passerby who asked him: are you Emil Cioran by chance? 'I was,' the solitary man answered. I'd answer the same way. I am approaching his old age. He defined himself as a human fragment. I'd subscribe to that. *If I hadn't taken up writing, I would have become an assassin*—that's what he used to say. In this instance, I don't agree. I'm not courageous enough, I never have been. On the other hand, neither was he, or if he was, it was only in a duel with words. And in his insomnia, yes, a morbid insomnia, incurable, as if it had taken on a life of its own, though it took possession of him. I don't think Sisi suffered from insomnia. I can't complain either, I only have nightmares."

"Sisi was a mother, she gave birth several times. She reconciled herself to her existence in this way. Without appeasing her uncertainties. She had no right to insomnia. She wasn't a man . . . Sisi was a woman through and through. Even mentally. As a man, she might have been like her cousin, Ludwig of Bavaria. She pitied him, but she would have done anything to save him. She wasn't a man despite her private rebellions and her stamina. I'd even say despite her stubborn insistence on being herself, even in an environment of duplicity and alienation. And of rituals, oho, of court and courtly rituals."

"But let's go back to Cioran. He was on a fellowship in Berlin, at the Friedrich Wilhelm University, when he became enamored with Hitlerism."

"Did it happen like that? Just like that?"

"Yes, just so. With Hitler and Hitlerism. Fanaticism, blindness—they fascinated him. The vitality. The intensity."

"In very poor taste!"

"He despised good taste."

"That's not the case with Sisi. The vulgate, vulgarity, they horrified her even in the upper classes. Despite her unyielding nature, she was tender-hearted, enchanting. Do you know what she used to call her favorite dog?"

"I only know what I know. From books. I haven't come across her dog in the library."

"He was called Shadow. They were always together. Inseparable."

"Shadow? That does interest me . . . I read a lot about shadows."

"You read? Books again! Not life."

"Life, too. The dog is life, like his shadow. And Sisi's Shadow. And God, the shadow. All life. During communism, 'the Shadow' was the code name for informants, who stuck to suspects like burrs. Suspects or only persons of interest. Both the followed person and the follower were life."

"But her favorite horse, do you know what Sisi named it? The Nihilist! She was a superb rider."

"The Nihilist? Meaning Cioran?"

"She didn't know about Cioran. And I didn't know either, though I should have."

"Let me get us some water. At least water, if not wine."

Eva closely followed the walking stick's movements, his getting up from the chair, and getting to the kitchen in three large steps. He returned quickly with a carafe and two full glasses.

"Next time, we'll get together at my place. It's more comfortable, bigger."

"Do you have your calendar with you?"

"No, I don't, but I can call to invite you over. Maybe I'll even send a taxi, or come disguised as a driver to pick you up."

"By force?"

"If necessary. Though I'm not that strong."

"You spoke about being insistent. That's a type of strength, maybe. Certainly, of energy."

"Yes, so today we drink water and feast on Cioran."

"He used to say that everyone over forty should be killed."

"We'd both be dead in Cioran's world."

"Words. A machine gun of words. He always talked about suicide, his ideal. He lived to a ripe old age."

"He loved his country, his language—was that it?"

"His country, yes, though in a kind of delirium. He would have liked to see it go mad, too! Language made a captive of him, like any great love. He fought with it, he learned to syllabize and curse in French. It seemed such a pompous language to him. He would swear in the most vulgar Romanian, screaming that he preferred shit to good language. He became a great French stylist. In the Alzheimer's of his old age, Romanian revenged itself on him, wiping from his lost brain the French language, polished for so many years. He died speaking only Romanian."

"An interesting guy, I understand his appeal."

"He never worked a single day in his life. He was so proud! He used to say that his only competition in this would be a whore without johns. He spoke French with a strong foreign accent."

"Was there anything that appealed to him?"

"Yes, Paris. The ideal place to waste your life. That's what he would say. He considered that Romanians were destined to fail. He didn't think there was any place for them beyond the swamp they already owned."

"Was he married?"

"He had an ideal partner, I don't think they had a marriage certificate."

"Lovers?"

"I don't know. There is a small volume of correspondence with a young German woman who admired him. I'll try to find it. Yes, I will give it to you as a present."

"Are you married? You were, but are you? Who is the martyr? And where is she? Does she exist? Is she in jail? Attempted murder? Did she want to kill her husband, her beloved? It's not the neighbors' cat, I hope. She kept circling the door. When I stopped the car, she was circling your door. She ran off, she felt I was a rival. So, are you married?"

The Nomad did not answer but got up from the table.

"My friend is awake. Behold him in his voyage around the world. Around the world in a glass bowl. In your honor, George has taken up his old routine again. His homage to you. Say hello to him, give him a sign. He deserves it."

Eva was already in front of the bowl, admiring her accomplice. The gastropod nomad advanced lazily around the circumference of the container. He didn't seem at all intimidated by the spectators who were hypnotized by his Lilliputian adventure. He advanced, tenaciously, with barely perceptible motions, with a gracious kind of disregard, toward nowhere.

"So, are you married? Do you have a wife, children, a

family? The neighbors' cat didn't tell me anything. She only ran away, as if she were fascinated by your mystery. Next time I'll bring a mouse to tempt her."

"I only have a sister, that's all," the taciturn interlocutor mumbled.

"Is she here, in the land of all possibilities? Or in the past, in the fairytale of childhood?"

"She's here, she's a doctor, we're in touch. Connected. Siblings. At least from time to time."

"Marvelous. Marvelous, so you have someone, not just the neighbors' little white cat. What's her name? What's your sister's name? Her name?"

"Agatha," answered the host, at long last, whispering.

"A beautiful and rare name. So, two exiles, no? I'm surprised that you don't live together, given that you don't have anyone else."

The taciturn interlocutor was silent, closed off, and Eve understood that she had overstepped the sensible limits of an amiable visit and turned to George, accepting the silence in which the three of them then relaxed.

"Okay, it's time to see to my America. Next time, I'll invite you over. It's more comfortable, I promise. You can even bring George, if you don't want it to be just the two of us. I'll come and get you in my car. I'll call you next week to decide on the date of the happy occasion. I know that you won't make a move on your own, that you need it to be inevitable. I'll take on the impropriety. Meaning, the willingness to be impertinent, insistent, as I've said from the beginning. I will call you, and I will come get you. I will bring you back unharmed. Don't count on putting me off! In the end, I'll win. For you, not me. Having specified the terms, I'm leaving now, and I wish you a pleasant evening as I begin to count down the days. Or, rather, I'll begin tomorrow morning. Tonight, I want to sleep in peace, sleep is both dear to me and essential."

Days and nights passed, like ruined centuries. The door had been closed, the neighbors' cat had resigned herself and was hiding in the woods. The Misanthrope had unplugged his phone, to make the temptation go away; he felt safe. Until the afternoon when the American gas guzzler halted abruptly in front of his monastic cell.

The door was closed, and the intruder understood that the ciphered scratchings had no effect and so had begun pounding at the prison gate with her fractious little feet. Again and again and again, let's see who wins! At last, the prisoner gave in. He appeared, astonished but smiling at the center of the wood frame.

"Oh. Was it you?"

"Well, who else? I've been trying to call you for days. It would be good for you to know that I won't let myself be sloughed off. Maybe you haven't forgotten that I've invited you to my place for dinner."

"I haven't forgotten. I'm going back in to change my shirt, and I'll be right back."

He walked back inside, pulled the door shut after him, and, surprise, didn't lock it. He didn't reappear immediately; he had probably run out through the bedroom window, far away, to the neighbor's cat. No. No. Here he is again in the doorway! In a shirt white as snow and ferociously wrinkled. Instead of his shorts, he is wearing devilish black jeans. In-

stead of sneakers, he is wearing—who would believe it!—
stretchy summery men's shoes.

"We'll stop at a flower shop . . . Flowers as homage?"

"Flowers wilt. I prefer Cioran's love letters. You mentioned a little volume."

"The only edition I have is in German. I don't suppose you read German."

"No, I don't, but I'd like you to translate. Instead of flowers. Love's exile. You mentioned that he is the perfect exile."

"So I think."

"And in love? The exile of love! A good topic for dinner. I've reserved a table at a Turkish restaurant. I suppose that their cuisine is something like your country's."

"Yes, it is."

"I'm a failed homemaker. American cooking is like the country itself . . . a rushed improvisation. Pragmatism. That's what they say, that's how it is. Not they, but we, I'm an American after all."

The car headed toward the Pasha restaurant, a small picturesque restaurant where a tall, handsome waiter in livery waited outside to greet them. The reserved table was in a corner. Everything seemed to have sunk down into red velvet. Only one other table was occupied, by a pair of elegant, mustachioed men; they appeared to be ambassadors or elite spies, the two things being one and the same. Three imposing waiters were already standing by the table, which was festively festooned with flowers. Eva and her guest each received a menu bound in red leather. Everything around them was Ottoman red.

"What are we celebrating in this Oriental crypt? Our final parting?"

"After we taste the Sultan's delicacies. A stylized and cosmopolitan gastronomy. Here, you can find both Istanbul's delights and world cuisine. Mainly European. Parisian, Roman, Spanish, and Viennese, yes, let's not forget, Viennese, my father's Vienna."

"Did he bring you here?"

"Naturally. I have no idea how he got the money to pay for it. Maybe it was the symbolic promise his uncertain future made him."

"And how do we get the money to pay for it this evening?"

"You're my guest, don't worry."

"I'm not worried, I'm slightly horrified."

"No point in that. I have a special arrangement here, in memory of my father."

"That only increases my worry."

"I've become accustomed to this indulgence of mine. I don't abuse it. I only wanted to annoy you, to hasten our parting. That's all. It's inevitable, I think. I knew that you wouldn't be comfortable in this setting, with this ritual. That's why I chose it."

"Okay, then I'll order, and you'll pay."

That is how the evening for the ages began: with a kind of prologue-surprise to the surprises that followed. It's difficult to feed the appetite when memories overtake you. Dishes of well-remembered flavors, the last remnants of Ottoman domination over the country of his birth: *yaprak, sarmasi,* the traditional *sarmale* in vine leaves; *kalamar tava,* fried calamari; *patlican salatasi,* the marvelous eggplant salad; *yogurtlu kebab* and *istim kebab,* self-explanatory; *kurzu pirzola,* lamb cutler; *kıyma köftesi,* Moldavian meatballs; and the classic baklava. Cosmopolitan drinks: scotch, martini, raki, cognac, amaretto, white and red wine. The professor chose a Turkish Pinot Noir. He sampled it, was delighted. He waited for the traditional eggplant salad and the lamb and baklava. Eva participated discretely. The Professor's exaltation had opened up a hole in his defenses.

The wine was good, and the two bottles of Bosporus red's sole purpose seemed to be to disregard his fellow diner's silence.

"Oouf, I'm exhausted with so much delight. Can barely breathe. And no doctor's address handy."

"You don't need a doctor, you need to rest. I'll take you home; you'll sleep like a baby."

"*I'm no longer going home on this day . . . A flood before and behind me,* the verse of a great poet-alcoholic."

"One of yours?"

"Yes, we have as many poets as you could ever want. Good ones. We manufacture poets instead of saints. That's the folk saying, we give birth to poets, not saints."

"A superb country! An ideal one! I'd live there."

"Don't rush it. Our poets die young, some in asylums. It's my great luck that I've been neither a poet nor saint. Only a reader. Of the circus. Of clowning! And now, I find myself at a reconciliation dinner in a Muslim restaurant for exiles with the daughter of an exile."

"It's not Muslim, it's American. Turkish cuisine, alcohol of all kinds, forbidden to Muslims."

"You're right. Again! You're not the least bit drunk, neither with wine nor with the charms of a taciturn man."

"Taciturn? Here, this evening, you were a talker. You felt at home."

"Home? Meaning in my mother's belly? Since I've risen

up into the light of purgatory, there's no longer any such thing as home. The placenta is gone. I'm a drifter, wanderer, itinerant, roamer, buffoon, vagabond, circus man. Yes, yes, the subject is the circus, always on wheels, international. The traveling circus on tour through the ghettos of the world. The circus of the world, the circus about which . . . "

"Okay, we're going now. I'm taking you home. Wine has a predictable effect, even when it's Turkish. I'm taking you home."

Eva signaled to the waiter who reacted promptly like a red robot in the red room, now full of elderly gourmands, just as red with voracity. The bill was discretely placed in the client's delicate palm.

"But I've told you, I'm not going home. *I'm no longer going home on this day* . . . "

"Perfect. I'll take you to my place. I've trapped you at last. You kept avoiding it, and now you're trapped. Tormented, tired, alone, and George can't save you. You're alone with me, the game has become serious. Dangerous, deadly."

Eva supported her partner until they reached the car and slowly helped him take his place in the seat next to the driver. At first, the Nomad seemed relaxed, asleep. But it wasn't a long drive, and when they walked through the door of the small, stylish apartment, the guest already seemed to be awake again and to feel like talking. A torrent of words issued forth. About the death trains full of moans and feces, the Stench on Wheels, which he had avoided ever speaking about. He repeated again and again: the Stench on Wheels! A kind of reflex. About Günther and the communist Pioneer summer camp (the German was obsessed with the crimes of the Nazis). About the Botanical Garden in hypercapitalist

Berlin and about the reunion across the ocean with his sister who was trying to escape the sinless sin of incest, and about Peter and the trickster who bought and sold shadows, and about a beautiful, sisterly young woman biblically named Eva (not at all an accident), who was trying to draw him into a new sort of incest, another beginning of the world, and on and on, so many things about the land of all possibilities and of all crap, this place to which he had been exiled for his own freedom and its hypocrisies.

And then again, about the chimera that kept tempting him, though she was actually in love with George, the deaf-mute with whom he had a secret pact, and about a certain Colonel Tudor, whom he paid in dollars to arrange his escape from the lost Homeland, and about Claire, the student with one green and one blue eye, and about his scholarly expedition into the world of the poorest of the poor in the land of the richest of the rich, and about a festive dinner at a diplomatic restaurant, where they served the delicate delicacies of the Ottoman Empire that once had ruled over the planet and would one day rule it again. He spoke, he spoke unceasingly, and as he did so he unwrapped the irresistible Eva of all her outer wrappings and burrowed into her, as if she had been his sister, Tamar.

After the verbal delirium and after their coupling, he fell asleep fully and suddenly. He didn't snore. He woke up with difficulty, late, in a strange room, in a strange world. He opened his eyes, saw the elegant, round table, fell asleep again, woke up, again saw the table covered in lace and the blue paper on it. He rose up, naked, on his aging elbows, then he was on his feet on the little carpet with the childish drawings. He approached the round table with difficulty and picked up the blue paper: "There's food in the fridge. I'm at work until this evening. Phone: 212-767-7778. Tell the assistant that you're my brother and there's an emergency. The home phone number is printed on the phone on the nightstand. This is the encounter that never interested you. If you've risen from the dead, we can return to Pasha's *sarmale*. Wait for me at my place, there are some things around to read."

Messy handwriting, a few missed letters. The professor found the bathroom, the shower, the sink, the towels, came back to life. He would have called for a taxi, but he didn't know the address where he had been shipwrecked. With the pencil that had been abandoned on the blue paper, he added at the bottom of the page: "Thank you for hosting me, I am going to feed George."

Total silence from the East and from the West. Wilderness and amnesia.

After more than a month, Eva received a message: "Your friend has departed from us. These nomads live five years, give or take, but I didn't have the chance to ask George how old he was when I picked him up off the street. I've now prepared him for his leave-taking, he is wrapped in tinfoil. The funeral is tomorrow, toward evening. In the woods nearby. I don't think you can miss it. I hope that, in the world hereafter, he'll find his voice, his sight, his hearing, and his trust."

A short, secular affair. The professor stuck a small blue flag on top of the newly prepared resting place to mark the spot. The two relatives of the deceased then left together toward the Pasha Restaurant to honor the departed him or her. They had decided on light fare along with a bottle of Pinot Noir. A silent and relatively short dinner. When they reached the stratosphere, Eva took out a golden key from her golden purse, opened the magic door and stopped at the threshold, glued to the interior of the door, in the room but without proceeding inside.

"I want you to answer me clearly, do not pause, do not speak in code. Am I wrong to imagine that, without actually evoking it, you need to speak to someone about the Stench that marked you? To talk about obligatory happiness in that totalitarian Utopia? About Jesus and the eternal nature of anti-Semitism? Or the cosmic jump toward the American Circus? Along with so many other things? A postponed confession made to a libertine nun who knows what it means to keep a secret, to keep faith, to keep silent? Am I wrong? Tell me honestly, give it to me in full, be as cynical as you'd like."

Silence. Absolute silence. The Nomad gazed at his dusty dress shoes. When he regained his voice, it seemed a century later, and it was a shy, childish one.

"You are right, of course. I admit it. And I trust you."

"And I'm not Sisi. Or Agatha, Musil's heroine, like your sister."

They embraced. The beginning of a new beginning.

UNWRITTEN NOVELS: APHRODITE'S BROTHER

He had gotten into the habit of conversing with his colleague in the Department of East Asian Languages and Cultures, Ms. Aphrodite Chung. The professor had discovered that at one point she had accompanied an official Chinese delegation to his country as an interpreter, even though she did not speak the language, or, rather, she only spoke languages in the same family—French and Italian. She still had pleasant memories from her exotic excursion: the Balkan dictatorship seemed relatively benign, with a great many fissures of opportunism and the tolerated unavoidability of many humane and natural slips of the cogs of oppression.

One day, Dita, as the Misanthrope called her, opened the bottomless pit of personal memory and told him about her brother, a quasi-genius, and his abrupt fall into mediocrity. He had been the hope and pride of the family: of her father, a famous university professor specializing in the history of China, a venerable and much respected communist, and of her mother, a mediocre actress but frequently featured in official celebrations and paid accordingly, for her Party connections. Their son, Dita's brother, had been considered exceptional since he was little, as had been confirmed by the top marks he had received at school and the superlative praises of his teachers. He was a handsome young man and a bohemian, whose successes came quickly and naturally, effortlessly. Of course, their taciturn father would have liked him to put in more effort and to have clearer plans for the future.

The unspoken tension between father and son seemingly reached its boiling point when the father announced to his son that they were going to visit a renowned expert in classical calligraphy skilled in psychographic predictions of the future. The boy completed the proffered tests without much difficulty and then was asked to wait for his father outside.

The famous calligrapher confessed to the uneasy father that his son's handwriting foretold an inevitable future fall: confusion and lack of power, vice and apathy, debauchery and social failure.

From that moment onward, the son had had to bear constant hostility. Treated as a burden and pariah, he was ignored and humiliated. Naturally, the result was an intense psychic imbalance, deepening into a severe neurosis, which the son tried to escape through drugs, violence, and episodes of a strange kind of servility. An increasingly toxic descent under the horrified gaze of his mother and sister, in the total, glacial indifference of his father.

After long periods of isolation and treatment, the quasigenius ended up in a mental institution, from which he would reemerge from time to time wrecked and empty, incapable of adjusting to everyday life. Returned to the ranks of the disabled, little by little, he fulfilled the premonition and prophecy of the great scribe.

FIONA, THE WIFE OF THE IDEAL HUSBAND

To many—and not just those in the media and popular press, but also those in the universities, parliaments, and charitable organizations—the fall of the Wall that had served as an Iron Curtain and the ensuing spectacle offered a not-to-be-missed advertising opportunity. Fiona Blum-Kovalski, professor of Gender and Sexuality Studies, could not pass up such an opportunity. At Mr. John's garden party, the exile was astonished at the conspicuous glibness with which Miss Fannie caught men's eyes and pretended to be shocked by their admiration. He had not had the courage to approach the seductive ingenue. But it was his reticence, bordering so closely on timidity, that caught the attention of the brunette with wind-blown tresses and the fluid gait of an odalisque.

"You're not from around here," the feline whispered in the ear of the stranger.

The stranger agreed with a slight inclination of the head. No, he was not from around here; in fact, he was just getting acquainted with the language of the locals.

Miss Fannie, as everyone called her, had already taken him by the arm and was beginning to lead him discretely toward the wooded part of the garden. The dizzying progression of events that followed made him feel both uncomfortable and energized. The sunset abetted ambiguous closeness, the moon shimmered among the ancient trees, the ambler already felt the pull of the tidal stream of somnambulists. The pair dawdled amid the shrubbery, moonlight pointing the way. Fannie's graceful, rippling shadow followed in her footsteps when, suddenly, she turned toward her shadowless partner in amazement. She looked at him again, looked around, looked at the country lane, the greenery, the moon, again at the lane, again at the strange, shadowless partner—she had become completely disconcerted by this point—attempted a weak, polite smile and . . . fainted with a brief scream into the arms of the monster. Panicking, aghast in the face of disaster, the fashionable crowd ran toward the place where the incident had occurred.

This had been the Fannie Episode in its first few scenes,

after his first interaction with the Man in Gray. A bad omen of what was to follow later in the stranger's wanderings.

In fact, however, the events in President John's garden had not taken place exactly as they had in the Nomadic Misanthrope's memory. He had caught a glimpse of the slim, brunette, Irish Fiona surrounded by a group of elegant gentlemen to whom she was animatedly expounding on the joy of having a dependable family—of their solidarity in our egotistic and shallow age—of the happiness of having two admirable children and an incomparable husband. Mr. Karel Blum-Kovalski, the aforementioned faithful and tender husband, was a consummate professional both in his chosen profession of engineer and in his role as a family man. His wife admired him just as much as when they had first met. It's rare, isn't it, extremely rare . . .

The Nomad had interrupted this effusion but had only drawn closer to the designated paragon after being summoned by the young wife and model mother.

"Hey, mister, come in closer, closer, we don't bite. Especially not a guest of the president."

"I, no, I'm not . . . no, in no way . . . " the stranger had muttered, drawing closer.

Newly returned from clown college, the wanderer found a new president and the same Fiona. The Eastern European tragicomedy kept offering up new scenes, a *cause célèbre* from which he himself had profited, finally being hired with a full-time salary. This time, he found out that in fact Fiona was a graduate of a prestigious university, held a doctorate in history, and taught gender studies classes, a subject much in demand. Brunette and slim, sociable and sarcastic as he had first seen her, she had the thin, staccato voice of a spoiled child and exaggerated her feline qualities. She wanted—who knows why—to converse with the new hire but, paradoxically it seemed, without according him any greater importance than she might any other unfortunately necessary deviation from her routine.

Then, however, one day she stopped him on the walkway to the administration building, soliciting his help with organizing a conference on the status of women in a totalitarian regime. Did she know anything about totalitarian regimes, was she acquainted with the vast literature on the subject? No, but she was prepared to learn, to make up for lost time. She needed a list of essential books on the subject. She had read about Nazism and communism, she had even read a little about oppressive and misogynistic religious societies, but she needed to know more about the history of Europe, wasn't that so? They sat down on a bench in front of the old neo-Gothic college administration building. The Nomad explained about the socialist laws that ensured the perfect equality of the sexes, about equal pay for equal work, about sick leave and maternity leave, and the positive legal provisions that masked quotidian reality, which functioned beyond and outside the law, condemning women to an eternal, byzantine inferior status.

"I can tell you many stories, too many. You'll also find a few things in the books I'm recommending to you—dates and authoritative commentaries. Women under Nazism and the three Ks—*Kinder, Küche, Kirche*[56]—communism with its interminable meetings and bread lines, obedience, restrictions, and the criminalization of abortion."

The conference organized by Fiona had been a success, bringing together women and even a few men from several countries (especially from the so-called Third World) and receiving ample press coverage. The young professor had given the opening lecture in an elegant long black dress. Both at that time and subsequently, she avoided mentioning that she had received help from the Nomad but did not relinquish her militant advocacy for the family: "However many my professional successes—and I do recognize that I aim for and deserve them—my family comes first. There is nothing more meaningful, nothing that can better legitimize earthly existence than family life! The closest, the defining bond! Companionship, absolutely foundational. I have two children and a husband, and we've been together for a decade. No rifts."

Fiona Blum-Kovalski made such solemn declarations as if she were talking not about a happy personal situation but about a religion. The exile appeared to have been the motivation for this pathetic expression of family solidarity, since Fiona Blum maintained that she hailed from the family of the exile Leopold Blum, and that the name Kovalski, of her Polish husband, himself an exile (though not in Joyce's book) confirmed the authenticity with which the four of them—husband, wife, and children—lived as a united, coherent, happy unit.

"Yes, yes, Fiona maintains that she hails from the family of Leopold Blum, who inspired the Irishman."

It was the voice of Ms. Sally Katz, the blond-wigged librarian, Fiona's friend.

"Jews claim their descent from their mothers," the Misanthrope had objected promptly. "The father is purely incidental, he doesn't count. It's the mother who gives birth, and we begin our earthly exile in her womb. It's Mrs. not Mr. Blum that's Mrs. Kovalski. Karel Kovalski."

"Yes, the ideal husband."

"That's the title of one of Oscar Wilde's comedies. Another Irishman," the Misanthrope hastened to add.

A year after the successful international conference, Sally was also the one who told him about the fabulous transfer of funds made to Mrs. Blum-Kovalski by the foundation of the famous banker Spiros Kantas, who subsidized charitable organizations working in underdeveloped nations. Mr. Kantas, whom Fiona had met at one of the festive dinners given by the college president who had followed Mr. John, had offered the "Irishwoman" the position of executive director of one of his organizations dedicated to literacy and medical aid around the world. The salary had been incomparably larger, and the new president had encouraged the transfer, as he himself depended on the banker's generous donations to the college. He congratulated Fiona, proud of her new role, of her burgeoning international reputation, asking her to stay in contact with the campus.

"Fiona was happy about it," her friend, Sally, commented. "She no longer had to publish her dissertation, publish or perish, or wait years and years for tenure. Just one problem remains."

"She doesn't know any of the African languages?" the Misanthrope had suggested.

"No, that's not the issue. Spiros has the money to pay translators for all the languages and dialects. But there's a lot of travel involved. Long and tiring journeys."

"So, absence from the family. The sacred family . . . " ventured the Nomad.

"Exactly. Fiona is fanatical about family life, as you know. These too-frequent trips are a nightmare. That's what she told me with tears in her eyes. But she can't give up such a rare opportunity."

"Once in a lifetime! If she gives it up, it won't come again."

Then, for a time, Fiona Blum-Kovalski disappeared from the repertory of college gossip. However, surprisingly, she then reappeared in the constant references of Barbara, the secretary, who did not dispense any details, so again it was Sally who had to be consulted.

Sally Katz, however, refused to comment on the reports.

"It's nothing to be ashamed of, believe me," the Nomad assured her. "Adultery is a type of freedom, it rejuvenates marriages. It's a very old spice of life—for thousands of years. It has proven its worth and necessity. Thus, its humanness."

"But it doesn't rejuvenate. It destroys, my dear! That's precisely the problem. It destroys marriages, it destroys the family! We're not in France."

"You're not going to tell me that the Kantas marriage is in danger! And the Kovalski union remains unshaken, even I know that."

"After Fiona blackmailed Kantas, saying she would reveal their relationship, Spiro offered her four million dollars to keep her little mouth sealed shut with the seven proverbial seals," Katz the librarian continued after a time, crimson with fury, her eyes downcast with shame. "At the lawyers' office, Fiona swore she would never again refer to the incident."

"Did someone catch them? Naked, on top of each other, caught in the act?"

"Worse."

"Wounded by a bullet from the ideal husband? Unmasked by an Irish rabbi and a Polish priest, or by the American psychiatrist? Publicly shamed by the teachers of the ideal children of the ideal couple?"

"It's not a joke! The matter is actually quite serious!"

"How serious can an affair be?"

"Very, if one of the partners is too serious."

"Meaning the wife? Mrs. Kantas? The offended party? She has a revolver or a large bank account?"

"Alexandra Kantas is much younger than the banker, she's his third wife. They've been married a few years, and they have blue-eyed twins. But I'm not talking about Spiros's wife. I'm talking about our crazy woman, Fiona, the slut! The one-woman propaganda machine for sacred family! She has lied to all of us shamelessly!"

"She is hoping to establish a new sacred family? To escape the biblical connection to Mr. Kovalski in favor of another more mythological marriage? Greek and atheist?"

"No no no! Imagine this, she asked for the money! The money to keep her mouth shut. Our Fiona! She blackmailed him. She opened her legs, and he opened his wallet and his bank account. Money to keep her mouth shut. She didn't keep it shut. I know, so others must know, too. Now, you know, too, my dear."

"Ah, she sold the secret. She sold the shadow between her legs, the divine mystery."

"It's no longer a secret, I've just told you. She took the four million. Four million! A good price, you must admit."

"Surplus value! Even if the couple itself couples two of the great faiths of Antiquity."

"It's not about that. She kept two million to repair her life, and she gave two million to Kovalski, the wronged husband, to leave her alone. Fiona, our colleague! So smart, so nice, so collegial!"

"And chaste."

"I don't know. She adored her husband, her children . . . A perfect marriage."

"Perfection allows for additional perfecting. Especially if it's also profitable. In the competitive free world, anyone who doesn't have two million doesn't exist. That's what I was told when I came to the Promised Land. Not by Mr. Spiros— for him two million or nine million makes no difference— but by a respected pedagogue, the former president of our college. I was ready to sell my kidneys, my nails, my shadow for a million, but there were no takers. And Fiona, where is she now? She's off to a monastery?"

"She's divorced, or was divorced. Mr. Kovalski took his portion, and Fiona stayed with her Indian woman."

"Indian woman? What Indian woman?"

"You didn't know? Indira Sumar. A researcher here at the college. They've been together for a long time."

"A long time . . . how long? Since she adored her husband or since the money man? And her job? Was she fired or was she promoted?"

"She resigned. She bought a house with Mr. Spiros's money. She's looking for a job. She's not in a rush, she's looking for something suitable. That's what Indira says, that Fiona is waiting for something suitable to turn up."

"She'll write a book, that's what she'll do," hissed the Misanthrope. "A book about the arrogance of the capitalist moneyman and the part of his anatomy designed expressly to humiliate women. It will sell, it will be written intelligently and with pathos. For an acceptable price."

The case deserved further consideration, though the Misanthrope seemed satisfied with this initial evaluation. Cases like this can be found everywhere, you don't have to go to the ends of the earth to discover them. As the eccentric Cioran used to say, if you are, or become, a sojourner, a nomad, a migrant and immigrant, if you have been exiled and/or expelled, it's truly an honor. You can't deny the additional life experiences or incentives that an extreme situation can provide. No, you can't deny the advantage of estrangement, of exile and of breaking the mold. An advantage, yes, an incontestable one.

THE MARTIANS
(GÜNTHER'S EPISTLE TO THE
NOMADIC COMMUNIST PIONEER)

I know you won't answer me. I've gotten used to the whims of the adolescent you've become again. A hermit, yes, one with a phobia of reality. Not just of socialist reality, but of what is apparently its exact opposite, the one to which you've emigrated to find your missing half. I don't condemn you, nor do I pretend to understand you anymore. I only try to adapt to the unusual circumstances that hold us all captive on this planet overrun by monsters.

The news of the aerial attack horrified me. Like so many others, I, too, had the feeling that it was the beginning of the end, and I wondered if you might be among the victims. Desperate, I called your sister . . . I had found your address book, you left it in my Berlin cell. Lo and behold there was her address and even her overseas phone number. The network was still up despite the apocalyptic chaos! And also unbelievably, the doctor picked up promptly, panicked! Scared half to death. I hurried to assure her that I am not one of the invaders, only a senile German, a former apprentice of the Revolution. She was quiet for a long time before she finally agreed to speak with me, still unsure that I really was who I said I was. Yes, she had spoken to her brother just in the last hour, but she didn't know how much longer the phone lines, thrown into chaos by the heavenly curse, would continue to operate. She was happy that you were alive, though it was no longer certain who would remain alive in the hours and days to follow. I thanked her, I asked her permission to call back after a while. She was silent and then hung up. Nevertheless, she managed to tell me that you had refused to cancel your classes at the college, as the dean had advised, wanting to give students the option to go on, and that they had voted for the usual schedule, though they too seemed scared half to death. Probably they felt better together, as a group, than alone. And yet, you cut short the lesson on *Pnin* by half an hour so all of you could discuss the planetary news of the day.

When asked if you had at last made some friends at the

college, your sister replied that you weren't really seeing anyone. But that you met with the students often, even outside of the regularly scheduled class time, attentive to the thoughts and wishes of the new generation.

So, the new millennium! The symbol of post-civilization. New genocides set in motion by earthly and heavenly ghosts. An inaccessible divinity determines one's thoughts and actions, so one becomes completely obedient, follows the heavenly commands. Then . . . disaster. Secular utopia is similar, though more vulnerable to violence than the religious one, which draws on a more powerful mysticism than the earthly utopias we've gotten to know all too well. In the void that grows all around us, "replacers" of all kinds will become more important than we could ever have imagined! Little by little we'll be replaced with rational, refined robots, therapeutically propelling forward the ever-riskier human experiment. What follows will only be the usual rat race in pursuit of money. Then, in the life to come, the comedy of faith. Of course, you know all these things . . . Though, as I understand it, you are still living among books and bookish people, as before. You no longer need a neutral correspondent like me.

The difference between us has become acute and estranged you. Yes, I'm the leftist from the so-called superior race, one of Marx's Teutons, the enemy of my country and of my fellow citizens on the Rhine, the late-blooming adolescent, as you call me. Of course, I no longer deserve any attention from the wanderer chosen by God himself and hated by everyone else, who refuses to question his own biography, humiliations, complete burn-out . . . Anytime you feel like talking to an old man who's younger than you, don't forget that, if necessary, I could act as that much desired sleeping pill. It's hard for me to envy your retreat to the provincial American planet. There's no safe corner left anywhere in this world.

I also can't refrain from telling you that I've already read in the papers the rumor that the chosen people (meaning you and your sister and your dead, both old and new), were warned about the flight of the bats with bombs on September 11? Supposedly this would explain the fact that you are not among the three thousand victims from the first assault . . . Not only were you warned, but you were the orchestrators of the great air show put on by the star and crescent!

It seems you had classes at the college? When did you have any time left for global conspiracies? Your sister is also extremely busy at the hospital and with her marital problems, I gathered. But, naturally, you are all extremely able: the chosen people, chosen for conspiracies and collusion and bank accounts!

Even after all of this, you and your sweet sister refuse to mention the camps! The camps or the Holocaust! Even the post-Holocaust . . . Or the feeling of being perpetually a suspect.

When Colonel Tudor planned his "suffering trap" so he could then perorate about how the times had changed for the better under the rising sun of socialism, you were stubbornly silent. You refused rhetoric. You refused victimhood and false therapy, which I understand. Why are you—both of you—silent? Both of you, in disgust, try to tear off the striped garments in which your neighbors would dress you again: colleagues, bosses, historians, bishops, the ghetto and the elite, friends and enemies.

There hasn't been much talk about the effects of the last month on the attackers and their families or on the multitudes crowded into mosques! Nor about the ravages of illiteracy on the thousands of believers who gather all their information and knowledge about the rules of conduct only on Fridays, only from the mouths of the ayatollahs! They preach the assassination of infidels. Meaning all of us, all of us, not just your libertine little sister or your own—you wouldn't accept forced evacuation into an ethnic enclave overseas, least of all a religious one.

We've known each other since we went to Pioneer camp in Lipova. Fighters for the bright, proletarian future of the planet . . . Your retreat into your snail shell has been in vain! You do know that they'll try to mark you with the extermination number and tie the noose around your throat again. If not literally, at least in the nocturnal literary nightmares which I am sure will go on following you into the future. I know you no longer believe in the Revolution. I know it, but you cannot ignore the demented message of September 11. A hysterical, incendiary warning to the mercantile, myopic, blind world endowed with mischievous spyware. Come out of your shell, at least now! At least let the apocalypse find you awake.

That's what old Günther advises from old Berlin. Scowling like our century, ruined by arrogance.

EVA LOMBARDINI'S JOURNAL

Saturday, September 12—First dizziness, then drunkenness. He loosened his tongue, told stories, commented, joked and then joked again. We howled with laughter looking at the seraglio of long-stemmed and short-stemmed glasses, dumpy and sylphlike glasses which made off with our Turkish meatballs. A torrent of words, a real surprise. What won't a bottle of Turkish Pinot Noir do! Before he got drunk, he would barely respond, occasionally joking but always avoiding any kind of confession. In the end, he went on to talk about the horrors of deportation. "The Stench" that impregnated his mind and body, the moans, death, hell. About the trickster who bought and sold shadows, about his beloved little sister and the despair of all absences. And, behold, unexpectedly Eva appears, Eva the Shadow, biblical Eve, Eve of the *Song of Songs,* the much-beloved woman, the sister-bride.

It was a night of deep kinship and of tender companionship, which he needed so much. In the morning, before departing, he left a conventional note: "Thank you for hosting me, I'm going to feed George." In my dizziness, I thought I was touching the untouchable terrors his sister had experienced. George is the ideal friend for him, an orphan, a wanderer lost in the world, like himself. The snail always asks indiscreet questions, but doesn't ask him to be charming and talkative in response.

Saturday, October 3—Complete silence. Three weeks of complete silence.

I've reread the *Song of Songs,* I've perused books on incest. Incest, that mystical alliance: friendship and limitless intimacy, otherwise untouchable.

Sunday, October 11—I had begun to think that we were rid of each other, and then, suddenly, a message. After a month's absence, I am called back to attend George's funeral.

"I've now prepared him for his leave-taking, he is wrapped in tinfoil. The funeral is tomorrow, toward evening. In the woods nearby. I don't think you can miss it. I hope that, in the world hereafter, he'll find his voice, his sight, his hearing, and his trust."

What kind of trust was the Professor referring to?

After the funeral, it was Pasha restaurant again, again the Pinot Noir, but this time from Oregon. We only talked about snails. A new beginning. We'll miss George.

Thursday, October 15—The world of snails has become an obsession. I've read everything I could find on the internet; I've looked for and acquired books, a new universe is opening up. I've begun to neglect my job, though initially I had thought of doing a surprise program on snails for the weekly show.

Snails have existed on our planet for approximately five hundred and fifty million years, since long before humankind. Their most surprising physical attribute seems to be the calcareous spiral which they carry on their backs and that protects their fragile bodies. The snail moves by dragging himself with the help of a foot-muscle which advances with wavelike movements, gliding on the mucus the snail secretes. Smell is the snail's main sense. Smell and taste are the world in which it lives. The fascination does not end here. Snails are hermaphrodites, but they need traditional partners to reproduce. Some are more male than female, others more female than male: the sexual adventures of these solitary creatures seem heartwarming. Finding an appropriate partner, their initial touches, their techniques of shimmy-ing, kissing, and sex take place over a period of many hours. A charming dance. I saw a lot of videos on the internet. It in-spires you to shimmy along.

The Nomad's friendship with George is not accidental. The enigmatic snail found solutions for a life of solitary wandering just like my nomad friend did. They both have withdrawn into their shells, ignoring the challenges of their environments. The snail has an extraordinary olfactory memory. The obsessive "Stench" remains in the flesh and the brain of the deportee, as well as in George's.

Sunday, November 1, evening—He envies George for his peri-ods of "sleepiness," when the snail shuts the door to his shell and can remain shut in for weeks, months, or even years. I wonder if it's not a solution we've all desired at one point—to absent ourselves from life, to be shut in, to be far away from suffering, misery, or catastrophe, waiting for better times. I know I have . . .

Monday, November 9, evening—Perhaps it's no accident that the circus expert and avid reader assured me that George is a metaphor. Yes, a being, but also a metaphor, as the expert reader repeated.

A surprise! He didn't use to send messages on the com-puter. I can't believe he's reading my thoughts!

"If metaphor is a substitution, George is either a substitute or a substitution, let's not forget his neuter gender.[57] Don't forget this, don't be jealous of George."

A substitute? Substitution? Could this be an indirect declaration of love? Indirect as befits my Nomad. A metaphor, perhaps, but he has changed George's bowl-residence twice recently and has fresh salad in the fridge. Moreover, this is George junior; the former one died five years ago.

A new discovery: Patricia Highsmith's book *The Snail-Watcher,* which is the story of Peter Knoppert, a passionate amateur researcher into the life of snails.

"I never cared for nature before in my life," Mr. Knoppert often remarked—he was a partner in a brokerage firm, a man who had devoted all his life to the science of finance—"but snails have opened my eyes to the beauty of the animal world." [. . .] [Peter] Knoppert [. . .] had happened to notice that a couple of snails in the china bowl on the draining board were behaving very oddly. Standing more or less on their tails, they were waving before each other for all the world like a pair of snakes hypnotized by a flute player. A moment later, their faces came together in a kiss of voluptuous intensity. Mr. Knoppert bent closer and studied them from all angles. Something else was happening: a protuberance like an ear was appearing on the right side of the head of both snails. His instinct told him that he was watching a sexual activity of some sort.

But by that time, a different pair of snails had begun a flirtation, and were slowly readying themselves to get into a position for kissing. Mr. Knoppert told the cook that the snails were not to be served that evening. He took the bowl of them up to his study. And snails were never again served in the Knoppert household.[58]

Subsequently, Mr. Knoppert finds a passage in Darwin's *On the Origins of the Species* on the sensuality of snails. Highsmith tells us *the sentence was in French, a language Mr. Knoppert did not know, but the word sensualité made him tense like a bloodhound that had suddenly found the scent. [. . .] It was a statement of less than a hundred words, saying that snails manifested a sensuality in their mating that was not to be found elsewhere in the animal kingdom.*[59]

Were the two loving snails brother and sister, or at least members of the same family? Does incest exist among animals?

The story has a morbid and apocalyptic ending. The snails who changed Mr. Knoppert's life multiply in catastrophic numbers, occupying and overrunning the whole house and their poor admirer with it. Could we call this an allegory for any passion left unchecked?

Poor Knoppert, the naïve man, could not have anticipated such an ending! And even if he had, he probably could not have stopped it. Is this what the author is suggesting?

Thursday, November 12th—Snails and their adventures have become the favorite topic of our meetings. Jokes scattered here and there: on sensuality, kisses, and sex. Often it facilitates our drawing closer, at other times it replaces it. I don't know if it's a sign of a shared boredom or only a reprise of the process of accommodation.

The nomad first appeared in my life as a curiosity. I know,

I understand myself, I'm susceptible to the unknown, to mystery, and this largely due to my spirit of adventure. What frightens me is that this has all evolved into a more profound part of my life. He has an unpredictable personality, and this fits my bohemian nature; he turns me on intellectually and sexually, but I find it difficult to understand these disappearances into the void (*neither has he passed by here, nor has he smelled aught this year*). Then follows uneasiness, uncertainty . . . I have to find myself again, I hate depending on others.

Perhaps meditation and prayer would help me concentrate. Would having a snail with his humble universe nearby encourage resistance or resignation or, even more simply, a recognition of the joy of being alive?

November 19—Last night I delighted the Professor with my discovery of Jacques Prévert's poem "Chanson des escargots qui vont à l'enterrement."

> *À l'enterrement d'une feuille morte*
> *Deux escargots s'en vont*
> *Ils ont la coquille noire*
> *Du crêpe autour des cornes*
> *Ils s'en vont dans le soir*
> *Un très beau soir d'automne*
> *Hélas quand ils arrivent*
> *C'est déjà le printemps*
> *Les feuilles qui étaient mortes*
> *Sont toutes ressuscitées*
> *Et les deux escargots*
> *Sont très désappointés.*[60]

I recited it well enough, my father would have praised me for my French accent. *Hélas quand ils arrivent/C'est déjàle printemps* [. . .]/*Voilà le soleil.*[61] It's true, the sun comes out.

After a brief pause of admiration, the Nomad headed toward the bookshelf and took out a volume with a multi-colored cover. I felt a hand on my shoulder and heard a mur-mur of words I didn't understand. It sounded lovely, child-ish. He told me it was a superb poem—"Snail Hunting," by Ion Barbu. A mathematician poet actually named Dan Bar-bilian, which to me sounded like an accidental rhyme in it-self. I found a translation on the internet, and the box of marvels opened to reveal a child who had found a snail in the woods. A curiosity and challenge. The boy charmed the snail with a traditional childish refrain:

Melc, melc
Codobelc,
Ghem vărgat
Și ferecat;
Lasă noaptea din găoace,
Melc nătâng și fă-te-ncoace.[62]

In the frigid winter months, he thinks about his friend, but when the thaw comes, he finds the snail has died.

Și pe trupul lui zgârcit
M-am plecat
Și l-am bocit:
"Melc, melc, ce-ai făcut

Din somn cum te-ai desfăcut?
Ai crezut în vorba mea
Prefăcută. Ea glumea!
[...]
Trebuia să dormi ca ieri,
Surd la cânt şi îmbieri,
Să tragi alt oblon de var
Între trup şi ce-i afar."
[...]
Iarna coarnele se frâng,
Melc nătâng,
Melc nătâng.[63]

Poetry is a magical flight among words, a childish curiosity, a nonchalance, a cruel tenderness.

If I can't become a circus acrobat, at least I have to become more playful, funnier.

GÜNTHER'S EPISTLE TO THE PIONEER OF LONG AGO

To the American:

I am waiting to feel better so I can scold you properly. This summons seems inevitable nevertheless: write to your sister! Tamar, Tamara (Mara? Agatha?). She let me know that the last two messages she sent you by certified mail were returned and that you don't answer your phone. She probably thinks that in the guise of your (former) Pioneer leader I have greater authority over you than anyone else, and my intervention might resolve the misunderstanding. I also will take advantage of this occasion to determine for myself, I hope, what grotto you've hidden yourself away in, far from the world that has ceased to interest you when History—which, under our very eyes, continues to struggle in the snare—no longer interests you. That's what you told me when you refused to join in bringing down the Red Wall or in the euphoria its downfall caused, not just in the infamous place itself but everywhere in the world. I thought, however, that the New World might have helped you recover. I've looked into the fact that a snail's life is short, regardless of what you try to do about it. Five years or so say the books, though there are astonishing exceptions. If he's proven a trustworthy friend, you could hope for a longer period of co-habitation. So write to me or at least write to your One and Only. Your sister and better half.

G (of long ago)

DEADLY SHADOWS

The planet's defenses were suddenly overwhelmed by mechanical birds of prey and ruination: large, metallic beasts of the air descended, diving, to shatter buildings and human beings. The shadows turned black, then red, then took on bizarre forms: burning eagles exploding in thousands of giant splinters of shrapnel, like fighter planes. Serial explosions, windows blown to shards, collapsed walls, another, and another, and then yet another. Doors and cabinets and steel tables flying through the air. Burning clothing, burning people, smoke and blaring alarms, screams, moans, and mad flight. The Omnipotent had become angry, his messengers were on a mission to punish the unbelievers who had not heard the appropriate divine warning call.

The room was minuscule, four spectators were watching the television where the event continued to explode in full horror. The Nomad was one of them. Room 224. On the door: Health Department. On the screen, you could see the street and people running haphazardly. The smoke was rising heavily from the buildings that had been transformed into debris and glass and arms torn from bodies. Screams, dust, smoke, flames. Siege and apocalypse. The herald on the screen was communicating warnings rather than information. Was it aliens? Descended from the heavens of the imagination to reclaim control over the universe? There was no time for such questions. For the Nomad was feeling solidarity with those who lived on the bit of earth where he had washed up more than a decade prior. Now he was one of them, yes. He had the right to say, as their president had said years earlier: "Ich bin ein Berliner." Or, more simply: "I am yours," "I am here," "Among you," "With you," "That's it," "I am here," "Like you," "Like you." Though it was only now that he was justifying his new identity, justifying his refuge becoming a home, as an official would put it. A sinister thought clattered through his brain: "They've found me! They've found me!" "They've found me even here!" The birds of death had proved that you couldn't flee any further, or far enough. Far no longer existed, as a concept. Destiny will find you anywhere.

The faraway is nearby, just a step further.

He looked at his watch. It was noon at the end of the world.

In the days to follow, the news was compounded. The TV and radio broadcasts repeated that the relatives of the killers would not concede that their family members were the wrongdoers: the event, it was said, had been orchestrated by the victims themselves. Those imperialists with no scruples, looking for new markets and new colonies and new slaves, for further profit and vile prestige. Naturally, they had been supported by those perpetual conspirators with sidelocks and big bank accounts! In the distant and yet neighboring East, the massacre was being celebrated with much gladness, glorifying the suicides who had given their lives.

The immoral, diabolic civilization that ruled the world would soon fall! It had already fallen.

The Nomad crouched down, overwhelmed by bitter memories. He had a hard time keeping himself from looking for Tamar. A chapter in *Pnin* talked about the death of the beautiful Mira at the hands of the Germans. The young Pnin had been in love with her and could not forget her.

That book had devastated him, not in his first, preliminary reading of it, in his narrow, hard bed, but in the class where he had discussed it, on the very day of the evil attack. After many more nights of insomnia, dead tired, he at last succeeded in falling asleep and slept deeply, as if having given himself up to a much wished-for illness. In the emptiness created by the uncertain hours, by apathy and self-abrogation, as if in the serenity of death, he again encountered the Man in Gray. Unchanged! Time had not had any effect on his appearance or gallant manners. In an impeccable gray suit, with a gray silk shirt and identical lavaliere. Topped by a fine gray silk scarf. He smiled politely.

"I'm glad you recognized me. We parted as friends despite the ultimate failure."

The Nomad was silent. Distraught, he was gazing fixedly at the phantom he did not believe in.

"Last week you dealt with Timofei Pnin. Another patient in our Schlemihilium . . . You didn't know. You haven't paid attention to anyone else during your stay here. Only to your former lover and former friend. But Pnin was there, too, a patient with another bed number and tribe number. Unlike yourself, Pnin did not relinquish his natal shadow, though he was fascinated by his new one which was living with him. As I said, it's a different case, yes, a quite different case. Though similar. Similar, like those of all the patients in the Schlemihilium."

"What do you mean? What failure? What are you talking about?" the sleeper mumbled, not even hearing himself.

"You didn't want to give up your soul. Not even in exchange for a shadow. I wanted to give it back to you. That's what you wished for, but you didn't accept my terms. You didn't accept them, imagine that!" The Man in Gray hurried on with his sing-song charm, pleased that the patient had managed to say a few words, though with great difficulty.

"More b-b-bunk! B-b-barbarous! Blameworthy, blameworthy."

"Not at all, not at all, my dear. That's why I've returned. Not to make a new pact, oh, no! Only to explain the matter to you. Past and future, you deserve to know, to understand.

You fascinated me from the very beginning; I hope you remember. 'You have a very beautiful shadow,' that's how I approached you. I know how troubled you were by our agreement, by our sanatorium, by our charitable organizations. By last week's aeronautical event."

The Nomad crouched down again, as he had when he recalled Mira. Our agreement? Ours? Had the Man in Gray become a pilot? The patient waited for the next blow, the one too difficult to bear given the exhaustion that had laid claim to him.

"Yes, yes, you won't believe it, but that's why I've come. I owe you an explanation. Not money or a Shadow, which won't do you any good now, but an explanation. So that you'll understand what has been and what will be. I owe that to you. Yes, the holy war! It began long ago, but only now has it become visible. The mystical revolution."

The sleepy one who was not sleeping instantly, instinctively, covered his ears with his hands, to no effect.

"You've always thought of me as a middleman. An intermediary. An exchange agent, buying and selling in the name of an invisible boss. Don't object, that's what I am. That's why you accepted the initial bargain: you thought it was unimportant. And you were partially correct. But only partially. Because you didn't know who sent me. Out of fear or indifference. That frivolous indifference, if I may call it so."

The Man in Gray lit a cigar, took off his gray hat, and stood there in his fiendishly black wig.

"Anyone who might have sent me to buy you was interested in souls. Even an emir is interested in souls. Those who flew the planes were also intermediaries, like myself. They had been promised paradise and virgins. I did not need promises and rewards. I am enlightened, I know what will happen; I will be on the winning side at the Last Judgment."

The sleeper who was not sleeping was horrified, had curled in on himself and wished he had Eve's nocturnal protection. He was waiting for his guest to throw off his poor excuse for garments and stand there in his full-length white robe, in his sacramental white hat worn over his fiendishly black wig. The guest would bow down to the ground, he would get on his knees, that's what he would do, he would bow down several times in adoration before the invisible Master, then he would take out the machine gun hidden beneath his coattails, which were as immaculate as the breasts of the virgins who awaited him in the heavens. Who will defend you, weak and weary Nomad? He squeezed his eyes shut tightly, pressed his palms over his ears. So that he wouldn't see or hear anything else. Silence, he heard nothing! The Man in Gray stood motionless in his impeccable costume. A fine professional, well prepared for this verbal exchange. He considered himself an initiate beyond compare.

"In the end, shadows will disappear, you know. They are an occasion for idolatry, they re-create the face of man whom anyone can bow down to, as to a god. Anyone! Both man and the devil. 'Thou shalt not make unto thee any graven image' . . . it's a sacred commandment. We can't compromise, even if the material on which the copy has been engraved is darkness itself. Shadows will disappear, you'll see. They are already forbidden in many places, just as those ancient classical statues are forbidden, with their faces and bodies representing men and women, animals, birds, and fish. Idolatry! I'm sorry to tell you that even double shadows are likewise forbidden, like the ones of the couple you belong to, brother and sister, unseparated inseparables, or even the one of the seasonal placeholder, the American babe with the biblical name. A kind of conjoined twins. Inseparable doubles, that's what the two of you were, the orphans, you and your sister, nasty siblings. Behold, a shadow has slipped in among you!"

No, it was already too much! The middleman had gone too far. The sleeper rose up on his bony elbows to slap the beast. He searched the darkness . . .

Nothing more could be seen, the room was dim, wholly dim, as if it were the dark room of a photographer practicing hypnosis. Patient number 12 collapsed again on the too-small pillow, incapable of crying out for help.

On the following day, or following evening, or even in the following astrological sign, he dragged himself into the shadow of his orphan shadow. Exhausted, staggering, dizzy, as in a fainting fit. The weariness of the previous evening . . . he knew, but he was afraid of what would follow.

Yes, the fear made him dizzy, shook him. The fear of the dark with which he would converse again, without success, incapable of producing more than a timid stammer, unable to unleash the curses and insults and punches he'd prepared for revenge. The villain, the middleman, the lowlife deserved all these things. The Man in Gray more than deserved them, and the Nomad needed to escape the phantom that hunted him.

The night was a torment, but there were no unwelcome guests. And Eva was not there to protect him—she had gone skiing. It was only on the following evening, after he had left the Man in Gray and the nostalgia for his lost shadow had passed, that Figaro, the allusion, the phantom dog, appeared as a trusty companion. He was unrecognizable, scruffy, aged, wasted; luckily he still had his unmistakable reddish-green tongue. Figaro, Figaro, he had whispered, reanimated by the famous aria from his youth. The senile mutt was a clever emissary from the Man in Gray. He understood the trick, in the end: the purloiner in gray was trying to make him sentimental, to wear him down. But too late, it was late, the game has been played, good sir!

"Get out, you mutt!"

The poor canine emissary was thrown out into the street and into the cold night. The patient returned to his sickbed, curled in on himself, in his ancestral uneasiness. At the door he could hear the cries of the poor animal who had been his partner in difficult times, but he decided to ignore them. No, he would put on the gray costume. He fell asleep, or didn't fall asleep, impossible to know . . . The operatic cries did not cease even when dawn blossomed across the window. They were renewed even on the following night and in the following astrological sign. Always the same: languorous, uniform. Toward dawn, they would increase, expanding, like the prolonged howl of a wolf.

At last, he decided to take a risk and open the door, come what may: if he found only Figaro, alone in the darkness, he'd let him in. The dog deserved at least that much compassion for his faithfulness. But what if the hunter of souls were standing there in his suit of gray eminence? Then he'd hit him over the head with a frying pan, eliminating him and his sacred mission forever. He had in his hand the large steel pan, blood-red like buffalo blood. But there was no one at the door! He whistled his signal, familiar to both of them. It was no use. No Figaro! A thick, impenetrable darkness, no living creature stirred. Dense, cold shadows, the frozen mists.

Back in his room, however, the howl of the shadows began anew, sinister. Prolonged, lugubrious, a whole pack of famished shadows seemed ready to spring. He huddled under the blanket, pulled it over his head and stopped up his ears, though he knew it would be no help.

Here, everything can be fixed![64] Mr. John had encouraged him long ago, on that first evening. And that's how it was, there were pills for everything, for thunder, trauma, and timidity, for obesity and melancholy, egotism and impulsivity, stinginess and hatred, laziness, cancer, cholesterol, and baldness. The old lady pharmacist had recommended the latest products to him for putting anyone and anything to sleep: hippopotami, hyenas, hagglers, and highway robbers, that's what the funny old woman had said. Indeed, the triangular green pills worked: the nocturnal howl disappeared, and the Man in Gray now seemed to be held up at the border, no entrance visa, while Figaro likely had found his Count-barber and his own pack on the Milanese stage.

Nights of deep sleep, too deep. Bewildered, the Misanthrope would wake as if it were the beginning of the world. His days, on the other hand, were dominated by the tensions of the time: global terrorism and the eruption of the new century. The papers, radio, television, and mobile phones all claimed that the event with the martyr-airplanes was only the start of a new universal barbarism. A chaotic, accelerated pulse.

Where could one take refuge? the Nomad asked himself. Neither Peter, nor von Chamisso, nor Don Quixote, nor

Samsa, nor Pnin, nor Dostoevsky's idiot, nor Monsieur Meursault seemed willing to answer. The library no longer helped the lost one, nor did the highway patrol seem useful.

He had his moments of solitude on the bench outside the administration building, and on his favorite bench, too, in the garden of the academic cemetery. However, he no longer had Colonel Tudor's phone number or e-mail, to ask him what he thought about the direction the world was taking in the aftermath of communism, or about the futureless future of the fading planet. The daily dose of evening pills protected him at night, his favorite bench calmed his days; he didn't have anything in particular to complain about. The wanderings of the sinner proved better than captivity in the dialectical utopia. All that was left was to reconcile himself with the privilege of being mortal. To wait—without illusions, a reed blown about in the hostile wind—for the coup de grâce.

Meanwhile, he barricaded himself among books. A wholly different type of grotto from that of his friend Schlemihl. Printed bricks, piled one on top of another, next to each other—in the shadows of the letters you'd reach out your hand and instantly be any place you could think of. The world in the pages interested him more than the illusions that followed that certain attack, and that other crime, and that hurricane, and that earthquake thought up by the zealots of earthquakes, or the new flags of the new tribes, of the tropical forests of the earth and the lunar wasteland of the stars that continued to spin around it. Here, on his favorite bench and in his modest hermit's bed, and on the path that led to the well-kept, paradisical cemetery of the elitist college of the New, ephemeral World, the Nomadic Misanthrope negotiated with the unknown. He imagined his future wanderings on the day's chess set, as many as he might still be given.

Resignedly, the mortal wanderer told himself: for the moment, here, just here.

He stretched out on the bed and reached for the telephone to get hold of Tamara. A crying teenager holding the receiver. Not a single word, only the unrestrained, interminable, staccato wail. So, Tamara, dear Tamara was alive. She would save him again. The lack of communication should have been therapeutic—at least for a time—but it hadn't been. As if suddenly, the shell in which he had sequestered himself disappeared, and he stood naked in the tumult of a hostile forest. Tamar knew this but, unlike himself, tolerated it calmly. Crying, rediscovering one's self in tears, dear Tamara.

Carefully, he placed the phone in its cradle. Then he picked it up again and slammed it down vehemently once, twice, nine times.

He could fall back asleep, he had received a visa for sleep.

DIDACTICA NOVA (III)
The Opinions of the Students:
Exile and Estrangement in Literature

The Shadow seems like a metaphor for a homeland, a language, roots, or any other kind of relationship with belonging.

Peter Schlemihl was not born in a given country nor did he claim a certain set of origins, but issued forth from the tides of incertitude itself. He is a stranger from the very beginning. The world in Chamisso's pages is recognizable. An odyssey full of events. It can be supposed that the lunatic to whom we are introduced will reprise his role and will continue to be rootless everywhere his secret proves to be a risk to himself.

The devil in Chamisso's story has no horns or tail. He is a polite gentleman with bourgeoise manners. The gray bureaucrat's suit is emblematic of the banal colorless nature of a shadow. We can ask ourselves, Where is God? For Schlemihl, salvation comes from science. His seven-league boots serve as his education. The boy who sells him the magic pair of boots is described as having blond hair and white skin, a kind of angel. Schlemihl is everywhere and at the same time nowhere at home. He can be found somewhere between the devil and the deep blue sea. (Claire)

As Peter Wortsman notes in his essay on *Peter Schlemihl,* "The Displaced Person's Guide to Nowhere," Chamisso wrote to Mme. de Staël, *I am French in Germany and German in France; Catholic for Protestants and Protestant for Catholics; a philosopher among believers. [. . .] Nowhere am I at home!*[65] A rootless individual without nationality, religion, ethnicity, or culture.

Chamisso's biography is reflected in that of his protagonist. Both the author and his fictive double end up studying the natural world. In the book's closing sentence, Chamisso seems to be the person who is most intimately connected to the narrator's life. Peter Schlemihl is the author's complementary fiction. The lack of a shadow places the author outside human society. In the end, he receives a gift: the seven-league boots seem to be the other aspect of a missing shadow. Exile becomes a kind of freedom. The freedom to travel and to go on adventures. Schlemihl embraces exile, leaving behind his social identity. (Vicky)

I prefer to think about what the story doesn't say but that remains essential for its understanding. Where does Peter come from and why? Was he expelled from somewhere, after a judgment, a crime, an unfulfilled dream? If the Shadow is what Jung insists it is, why does the stranger rush to sell it to an unknown person at the first opportunity? Is it by any chance his hidden self, guilty, ashamed about something that it cannot deal with?

Which is to not say his social, linguistic, or religious "identity," as scholars usually maintain, but his secret, negated, hidden identity? The trauma of a childhood tragedy? Of a former persecution, or exile? Or a case of incest, or a small but unforgettable wrongdoing unknown to anyone? Which might it be? We are not told, but we deduce that it is the psychic baggage of the nomad Peter, and that the shadow is not just what scholarship would indicate. And then, is it an advantage to be rid of it? With all the inherent social risks that would bring?

Yes, Peter loses two chances at love and even marriage, perhaps even more, but doesn't he perhaps become more free in this way? With no money and no reputation, a true pariah, but one who only now becomes interesting?

Even if it's not in the purview of a literary analysis to describe what the text doesn't say, I believe that, at least in this case, this would enliven the discussion in a beneficial way. (Claire, the student with one blue eye and one green one)

Like all exiles, Peter is a captive. A situation with many connotations and a unique ending. The narrative evolves around Peter's discovery of this truth. He realizes that gold does not mean anything, and that love is impossible without a shadow. After he gives up the magical bag (and the rest of his worldly possessions), he gets the magical boots. His freedom of conscience is promptly rewarded with the freedom of movement. In the Schlemihlium, he is respected as a benefactor. He no longer has gold now; but he is applauded for his generosity. Though, later, he seems to become a misanthrope, accompanied only by the little dog, Figaro, and by exotic plants. In the end, he is an exile and a pariah.

In his final remarks, Peter Schlemihl asks Bendel from the Schlemihlium: *Who would play the earthly game of life over again; though it is a blessing on the whole to have lived?*[66]

Trying out the specific themes of the fairytale, von Chamisso adapted his writing style to the problem of exile and estrangement. He confronts the dilemmas of modernity and adds a modernist subtext to them. He consciously proclaims that in the situation of the exile there is nevertheless hope (Jeremy).

If God existed, he would be the Man in Gray.

We have a story about alienation, exile, estrangement, identity, happiness, and about a spiritual journey. The Man in Gray sets in motion the bargain with the shadow as a first step toward taking over Schlemihl's soul. Something that God, too, might try, a God who is not just a passive presence but an active and vigilant one.

In the Old Testament, God puts the faith of the believers on trial. An active God would have to test man's spiritual power and punish sinners, rewarding blameless people. From the perspective of an active God, Schlemihl enters the story as a man whose virtue is unknown and who will be put on trial by God to see to what extreme his sin or ignorance can take him.

Schlemihl does not consider the Man in Gray to be that savior God. The blond boy who smiles when he hands him the boots could be a surrogate for the Man in Gray. His smile could be a sign of divine grace, a blessing. When Schlemihl realizes that he possesses the seven-league boots, he falls to his knees in silent gratitude. Where did all these legendary, mythical objects in the story come from if not from the Man in Gray? The gift of the seven-league boots—an expiation for the sins of the past—is made possible only through a reconciliation with life. An intermediary reconciliation set in motion by the Man in Gray?

The teleological reading of the theme of alienation, exile, and estrangement more clearly underscores the suffering of the exile. The ending of the story amounts to the ideal that Schlemihl can imagine, rather than to a mode of existence in which the soul exists perpetually. To have a shadow, you need to mix with your "fellow man." However, as the last lines of the book make clear, social interaction does not necessarily bring about happiness. At the end of the story,

Schlemihl is literally a citizen of the world but belongs no-where, the only relatively happy ending being that his soul has remained intact.

Though the theological implications of the text can seem off-putting, in the end it becomes clear that the Man in Gray is not the devil or the hunter of souls, but God, who tries the innocence of the common, foolish man. Chamisso seems to believe that it is wrong to concentrate on the shadow as a passport to joining civilization, or as a physical sign of iden-tity. Only by examining what success and social belonging really mean with a skeptical eye, and only by analyzing them through the prism of a higher good for the self, do happiness and survival become one and the same. (Sho)

The shadow can be thought of as an epochal identity, not a national or linguistic one.

If Peter were a Jew and his family name no more than a simple nickname, the whole story would demand another kind of reading. Chamisso considered himself to have no homeland, and he had Jewish friends. His best friend was Jewish, and he wrote this story for his friend's children. The fact that Hitzig had converted to Christianity for "the good of the children" says everything. Chamisso understood this. Being a Christian, Chamisso knew that Jesus is represented by the Church as wearing a crown of thorns with the in-scription "King of the Jews." This was meant as an insult, of course, but it was also the reality.

Peter comes from nowhere, and we don't know why; maybe because of a pogrom, or hooligans' attacks against the kind of shadow associated with Jews, or because of certain accusations of ritual murder, etc. Stories from classic literature. So, where is Schlemihl today, with the story of his shadow and the one who bought it to free him from the baseless blame of the eternal curse and help him with money with which he could defend himself against anything? Money comes and goes, and the danger remains. Better to withdraw into a cave and study bugs and butterflies and tropical plants.

No, the shadow is not a family secret, as in the novel *Amerika,* by Kafka. It is not the sister's unconfessed incest or the rape of the servant, or the money stolen from the safe of the senile grandfather. The curse of the stranger is older, having begun with the renunciation of idolatry and the forever recurring punishment for that renunciation.

That's how I see Schlemihl. It seems like a perfectly justified reading. More up to date than a criticism of rapacious capitalism or money which rules over everything forever . . . The story of the wanderer, who is chased from one place to another and murdered gleefully when the opportunity arises, is the story of the man forced to win his "normal" status through money—a man who fails. (Emet)

The story becomes more and more provocative and enigmatic the more it progresses . . . It is not perfectly structured, it is erratic and lazy, frustrating and undeveloped, but has a kind of interesting feverishness. It is, perhaps, more fascinating than a well-told story.

Peter, as a man without a homeland and a migrant, is not familiar with the labels and values of society. He does not know whom to ask about the Man in Gray, or how to do it, or even whether he is asking the right questions. After he sells his shadow, Peter is treated as an evildoer, because he violates the unspoken rules of the world. The locals know why the lack of a shadow is a serious transgression. As the narrative progresses and Peter becomes wealthier and wealthier, he also seems to become more familiar with the rules of the place, and so less unlike the others.

The magical boots are not only normal, but natural. The seven-league boots represent one of Nature's providential gifts, but their bizarre appearance only serves the arbitrary logic applied by Peter (and Chamisso) over the course of the whole narrative. A quasi-schizophrenia dominates the story. It is what can best be seen in the episodic representation of time.

Peter admits that he cannot recount the nature of this period of time well enough, his literary capacities being inferior to those of Chamisso. Chamisso, the author of the story, employs a postmodern trick before its time.

Emotions are replaced by a more novelistic and maybe more interesting narrative than a simple love story. The ambiguities allow for potentially new ways of defining the characters Mina and Bendel. The only character who maintains a kind of stable identity in the story is the Narrator, who leaves behind him distinct traces. Ironically, it is these lapses that enrich the story.

We have to remember that, at the moment of publication, *Peter Schlemihl* was an original, popular work of fiction, with an unorthodox, humorous approach. It was a great publishing success. We are reminded that a great work of art (as many will call the story of Peter Schlemihl) doesn't

need to be elitist. Innovation does not have to be incompre-
hensible . . . Regardless of whether you are charmed or frus-
trated by the story, it is difficult not to be drawn to it. A rare
thing. (Coleen)

GÜNTHER'S PERSONAL PAPERS:
GOD IN EXILE
"Elie Wiesel: The Writer as Witness to and in Exile,"
by Alan Berger

*Elie Wiesel contends that Judaism speaks of exile in absolute
categories. "Exile," he notes, "envelops God Himself. Language
itself is in exile. [. . .] Not only man, but God is in a state of
exile."*

*Who the exile was appears in tension, both negative and
creative, with who he has become. The cultural collision of the
past with the present can lead to tragedy. The suicides of survivor writers such a Jean Améry, Tadeusz Borowski, Paul Celan,
Primo Levi, Piotor Rawicz, and Benno Werzberger stand as a
stark warning to all about the horror of the Shoah.*

*Elie Wiesel, who kept a picture of Sighet, his birthplace, above
his writing desk, put the matter succinctly, "If we stop remember-
ing," he writes, "we stop being."*

———————

Exile, as noted, is a central way of understanding Jewish existence.

On the personal level, Abraham—the first Jew—is told by God to leave his country, and his kindred and his father's house to a land that God will show him.

The Holocaust was an unprecedented assault on Jews and Judaism. It involved nothing less than a total and complete exile from the ultimate human condition. Unlike the numerous preceding physical expulsions, the Shoah was an ontological event. Jews were exiled from being. Thrown out of history and time, the Jewish people faced extinction for the "crime" of having been born.

The Holocaust is the ultimate manifestation of exile.

Was faith still possible after Auschwitz? If so, what type of faith? Could either God or man ever be trusted?

It is worth recalling that Wiesel on more than one occasion expressed his feeling of frustration at being a stateless person in America, prior to finally obtaining his U.S. citizenship. "The refugee's time is measured in visas. His biography in stamps on his documents. Though he has done nothing illegal, he is sure he is being followed. He begs everyone's pardon: 'Sorry for disturbing you, for bothering you, for breathing.'" As Wiesel later confided, it is no wonder that Socrates preferred death to exile.

———

No wonder then that Wiesel populates his novels with exiles and refugees whose experience stands for all who have been uprooted in modernity. Moving considerably beyond the work of Franz Kafka, who wrote of the dehumanization of the individual and the burgeoning power of the modern state, Wiesel's exiles and refugees do not become insects. Rather, they are stateless.

The author describes his exile from traditional beliefs throughout his memoir. Three pivotal moments stand out in his transformational journey within the concentrationary universe. The first is the soliloquy describing his first night in Auschwitz:

"Never shall I forget that night . . . that turned my life into one long night seven times sealed . . . Never shall I forget those moments that murdered my God and my soul and turned my dreams to ashes. Never shall I forget those things, even were I condemned to live as long as God Himself. Never."

The prisoners are forced to march by the three doomed inmates. One prisoner asks, "For God's sake, where is God?" Wiesel responds, "Where is he? This is where—hanging here from this gallows."

Consequently, for Wiesel, the traditional covenanting God of Sinai who intervened in history to protect the Jewish people no longer remained a valid image. He identifies now with Job and his position. Like Job, he does not deny God's existence but radically questions God's justice. Wiesel's quintessential question, how does one live in a world with an unjust God, permeates the memoir, Night.[67]

From Susannah Heschel's "An Exile of the Soul:
A Theological Examination of
Jewish Understandings of Diaspora"

At the end of the Jewish wedding ceremony, before the groom breaks the glass, he declaims a verse from the Psalms: "If I forget thee, O Jerusalem, let my right hand forget her cunning" (137:5). The breaking of the glass, which is immediately followed by an exuberant "Mazel Tov!" and by music, takes place as a reminder of the destruction of the Temple and of exile from the Land of Israel. Even during the happiest of occasions, the tragedy of exile is presented symbolically, as a reminder that in the state of exile nothing can be perfect or whole any longer. The breaking of the glass underscores the physical break with the land of Israel, transforming exile into the portable homeland of the Jews: both a state of mind and a theological principle.

To be a Jew means to be in exile. Jews not only live in exile (galut), but exile lives in them; exile has come to be the collective condition of the Jewish people and the individual Jew's key to his own self-understanding. Exile is not just a political and theological doctrine, but also an affective state, defining individual Jews' subjective and emotional experiences. The combination of doctrine and affect has given both types of experience their potency and has fortified both through rituals like the breaking of the glass at weddings, the days of fasting during mourning, Tisha B'Av, which commemorates the destruction of the Temple in Jerusalem, and the numerous references to exile in Jewish prayers and different customs, like keeping a piece of the tablecloth or of the rug on the wall to underscore the fact that nothing can be perfect as long as Jews continue to live in exile. On the other hand, as the expulsion of Adam and Eve from Paradise demonstrates, exile is the predetermined condition of all life.

The exile after the destruction of the first Temple in 586 B.C.E., when Jews were deported to Babylon, seems the most important. The emotions associated with this exile are portrayed in Psalm 137, which captures the trauma of the Israelites living in Babylon and opens up an affective pathway that Jews later would continue to deepen in liturgic and political ways up to the present day: "At the rivers of Babylon we sat down and wept when we remembered Zion . . . "

"For our sins were we exiled from our country," the prayer-books repeat. Perhaps it's not surprising that, in the Bible, political possibilities are already tied to religious behavior. Politics turns into theology, and exile becomes connected to sin—an existential state that becomes analogous to Christianity's idea of "original sin," not as the Roman expulsion of the Jews from Israel, but as the human condition of estrangement which then becomes combined with the anticipation of and hope that God will one day send a Messiah.

When the rabbis nudge the political idea of galut towards an existential one, they do not abandon the politics of exile but rather shift that politics towards the domain of theology. The theological transformation of the political state of exile [. . .] eventually leads to the affirmation that God himself is also in exile. The idea is found in the Talmud and Midrash and becomes central to medieval Kabbalistic literature: the Jews are not alone *in exile. God is with them and seeks forgiveness for their sins. It is an idea that sets Jewish theology apart, since it does not correspond to anything in Christianity or Islam.*

From the Bible to the Zohar, the holy writings stipulate that God can be influenced to forgive sins by means of the believer's behavior. [. . .] The Lurianic Kabbalah of the sixteenth century redefines exile as a calamity that is produced at the moment of Creation. [. . .] The desperation of living in a world in exile leads to an even greater calamity, [. . .] to the idea that you can be a Jew without any recourse to Judaism. This was the diaspora's attempt to overcome galut completely, though what this actually meant was that both secular Jews and Sabbateans ended up in an exile devoid of Judaism, as Gershom Scholem maintains. [. . .] When exile loses touch with salvation, it becomes simply a lack both of any hope and of despair.

The traumas of exile become incorporated into the Torah through individual engagement in pious study; through Jews who succeeded in transcending the political medium and economic situation and found shelter in books.

Over time, the Jewish awareness of living in exile has become both more intense and more positive, exile coming to be regarded as an existential state in the Hasidic theology of the late eighteenth century especially.

———————

Exile is less a state of being that must be overcome and more of an existential state that must be investigated for its religious meanings.[68]

RED SHADOWS

The taxi accelerated suddenly, and the passenger was thrown from one side of the car to the other. Though bewildered, he finally succeeded in understanding the driver's admonition.

"*Sir,* do you never take an interest in the person driving? Really? Never?"

The shock was powerful: the car's swerving, the slamming on the brakes. And, floating above it all, the mustachioed man's rudeness.

Yes, the driver had a mustache, that was the extent of what he had glimpsed after he had slammed the door and before he had stretched out on his back, eyes shut, ready to be taken anywhere. And yet, the greatest shock was the language in which the mustachioed one had posed his question.

"Really, *sir,* doesn't the driver deserve any attention? Is he merely a paid servant? Is that all?"

The questions sounded more aggressive in the old tongue than they did in the language of globalization! It was clear that the mustachioed driver and the taciturn and apathetic client were both exiles from the same country. From the same language!

"Don't you recognize me, *sir?* We used to play basketball together once. We were even friends, or so I thought."

The mustachioed one had turned around completely toward his former teammate. The latter had now recognized Pavel Pietraru, called Pupu. Tall and muscular, he had played basketball better than anyone else.

"Of course I recognize you Pupu, and I'm glad. I didn't know you had also come to the land of all possibilities. Or that you were a taxi driver. Not a possibility that had occurred to me."

"The Big Man Above thought of it. The dispatcher."

"Yes, he thinks of everything."

"You haven't changed. I recognized you right away, I was waiting for you to emerge from your apathy. You buried your bald spot in the paper to protect you from intruders. That's how I knew I had no chance. So I stopped the spacecraft to remind you of Pavel Pietraru, called Pupu."

The driver and the client got out of the taxi, embraced, and entered the café with the green sign, *The Acrobat,* where the taxi had stopped. (This happened during the same period when the candidate came to try his luck at the college that Jennifer's uncle had left in favor of Australia.)

The old friend grew silent hearing about the difficulties the Nomad was experiencing: he had forgone his sister's offer of financial help; she was enmeshed in a divorce which was sapping all her energy—and not just financial.

After a silent movie–like moment, the driver proposed that the former basketball player consider the offer of a modest rent-free dwelling in his garage, which had been furnished for desperate situations. Generous, too, in the months to follow, he invited the Nomad to dinner occasionally, chiefly in cheap restaurants in the neighborhood. On one of these sedate occasions, at a sushi bar, he made a surprising confession.

"Your sister is doing well?" he had asked him at a given moment. "Still beautiful?"

Yes, his sister was still beautiful—the reason in fact why the exiled one had plunged, like others, over hills and dales, to defend his wanderer's honor.

"I never met her, but my cousin Nastasia told me about her. Tasia Traikov was her colleague at the hospital and was charmed by her. A doctor at a hospital for children, right? Your sister is a pediatrician?"

"Yes, a pediatrician. And your cousin?"

"A psychologist, a kind of counselor. Though she should have been the one being counseled, she's not a person to give counsel. If you could see her hug the walls, you'd understand immediately. Comes from the Traikov clan, the mogul, the Bulgarian. You've heard of him, I think."

"I have and haven't."

"That's the punchline. The cliché shouldn't apply to this fifth- or sixth-removed cousin of mine. A mogul's daughter has no reason to be afraid of her own shadow. But she's timid. Unsociable, complicated. The famous marriage undid her. You'd never guess the beneficiary of her subtle wiles!"

"I won't even try."

"Hold on to your chair. You're going to fall off it when I tell you."

"I'm holding on to the table."

"That's good. Well! The young Nastasia, Tasia, as we called her, conquered the heir of the Great Stammerer himself."

"My sister didn't tell me anything about this."

"She couldn't have. Nastasia wasn't close to her, or anyone else. She was intimidated by your sister's beauty. Tasia, the daughter of comrade Traikov, became the daughter-in-law of the Tyrant."

"The daughter-in-law of the Tyrant? Really?"

"Didn't you hear the story about the scandalous marriage? It was annulled by the Despot thanks to his wife's maneuvers, that witch. The entire capital was in an uproar. The entire country . . . we lived in the paradise of intrigue and gossip. The lovers married despite the opposition of the all-powerful parents. Two weeks later, they discovered the divorce papers in their mailbox. They hadn't requested them of course. An unexpected present."

"And?"

"Well, love triumphed . . . that's revolutionary romanticism for you. The bitter in-laws had to accept the situation in the end."

"But what did they have against the timid girl? After all, she, too, was from the Nomenclature. From what the papers say, Comrade Traikov was a well-known revolutionary. I would guess Tasia the Kitten didn't do anyone any real harm."

"Not necessarily. Traikov had a wife, a revolutionary herself, who hailed from the elite clan of perpetual revolutionaries: Moses, Jesus, Marx, Freud, Einstein, even Leiba Trotsky."

"You mean to tell me that . . . "

"Yes, yes, the marked ones. The chosen people. Chosen for the pyre.

"Well, she's my cousin. Sixth-, seventh-, eighth-removed cousin. Tasia, the daughter of Comrade Ms. Halevi. It's the mother that counts for the circumcised ones. The father is uncertain, like Our Father who art in heaven."

"That means that you, too . . . "

"Me, too, through my mother and father. I was named Saul, they circumcised me in Greece, in the diaspora. Then, suddenly, I became—meaning I became as if after a revelation—Saint Paul, the revolutionary who overturned the faith of Abraham, Isaac, David, and Solomon and stuck a stake in the decaying carcass of the chosen people."

"You're something of an anti-Semite. Like Saint Paul."

"Paul was not against the Jews. He considered himself to be a Jew, and he left the Jews in peace. But he also did not ask the Christians to respect the Old Testament; he asked them about the new one. That's the key, not his supposed hatred of his former coreligionists."

"That's a novelty! The entire bibliography on this topic points to a different interpretation. And it's an immense bibliography. I assume you know that."

"I know, and I've kept up with everything written on Saint Paul to better understand what I am and what I was. Especially since I landed in this paradise and became a taxi driver. Converted, like Paul, to a new teaching. Yes, I read everything that comes out on the Saint."

"Instead of basketball? Does this explain you giving up basketball?"

"Nothing explains anything, and the dialectic is superseded. I liked the game, that's all. Just as I like to drive taxis, that's all. And to play at being Paul and Saul from Tarsus."

"And Romeo? Romeo the Red, the son of the Tyrant? And Juliette, the sinner? Tasia the Timid? What became of them?"

"They split up in the end. The heir found a less taciturn goddess."

"What does she do?"

"Makes efforts to have a son to replace poor Maxim, Tasia's son. Tasia's son has become the only heir of the Stammerer! The secret service is looking for the link to some global conspiracy. Again with Judas and the thirty pieces of silver."

"What does the Stammerer's son do?"

"Well, he studied in France, like the two sisters. He excelled in science, like his two sisters who died in the Revolution."

"Decapitated?"

"I'm not talking about the French Revolution. The proletarian princesses were beaten to death with clubs. This after their crown-bearing parents were shot in the mob's delirium by a firing squad made up of firefighters and cobblers."

"Cobblers?"

"Yes, our genial Stammerer from the Carpathians, the father of Romeo and the grandfather of poor Maxim, was at one point apprenticed to a cobbler. That's where he proved that the only thing he was really good at was revolutionary activity."

"And now? Where is Tasia? Where is poor Maxim? Why do you keep saying poor?"

"The boy is rather befuddled. They barely escaped the fury of the mob and their thirst for revenge. And do you know where they went?"

"Do I know? I have no way of knowing. Your story is full of traps and shadows."

"Shadows, you say? Sinister prophecies, rather. The mother and son escaped to the Holy Land! Imagine that! Tasia and Maxim arrived there secretly, on a night flight, aided by the Israeli Secret Services who had their own political agenda. This was the presidential heir, of course! The presidential Swiss bank account would one day belong to young Maxim, the heir born of a Jewish mother, like Jesus. The defector was now in the land of Jesus and Jehovah. The unhappy pair had to change their names. Their lives in the new state of the formerly persecuted did not suit them. Nor did the people, to whom they did not want to belong. They found a way . . . or rather, a way was found for them . . . to cross the ocean. Lady Liberty, that Yankee statue! And a new American province, life among former countrymen who had also been exiled. But they bewildered poor Tasia—who in the meantime had become Tess—with their suggestions about social climbing: how to write a book about her grandfather and, more importantly, her grandmother; how to recover her Jewish roots; how to win damages from her former husband; how to reclaim her son's affiliation with the revolutionaries of the world. I send them money from time to time. In the former socialist republic, I had not had any kind of relationship with them."

For the moment, the discussion was at an end. Bored by the subject, he did not try to circle back to the strange destiny of the escapees. However, his sister did later confirm the accuracy of Pavel's description of Tasia, her former colleague at the hospital, whom she had known only vaguely. Only then did the brother truly understand the advantage of no longer receiving news about Tasia from her cousin, her fifth-, sixth-, or sixty-sixth-removed cousin. Paul the taxi driver had disappeared as suddenly as he had appeared. His long-ago teammate was unwilling to look for him; through the simple appearance of the taxi, the latter would have reminded him of the gratitude he still owed him.

The former basketball player reappeared, however, two years later. Without a taxi. He knocked shyly on the door of the professor, who was now employed at the college.

"No, I haven't forgotten you, but Silvia gave birth to a son. A real American, I barely have time to breathe. I gave up the taxi. I'm the administrator of an apartment complex downtown. But here I am again, back to chatting with you."

He smoked a pipe, and the room filled with a pleasantly perfumed smell. The apostle Pavel had grown fatter and moved slowly, sure of himself. He quickly took up his favorite subject.

"This time, I came on Tasia's behalf. Meaning Tess. Tess Thompson. They changed their names, as I told you. It's about Edward, formerly called Maxim, Tess's son and the grandson of the Tyrant who was transferred to hell. Eddy's finished high school. He has excellent grades like his father, the biologist, the son of the Dictator, who escaped the revenge of the masses and remained faithful to his microscope and his stamp collection."

Paul had a blue folder in his hand.

"I've brought you Eddy's school essays. Highest grades. You can take a look at the folder and then decide."

"What should I decide?"

"If you'll help them out. The boy and his mother. Tess,

who worked with your sister, the doctor. I came to ask you if you'll help them."

"How? How should I help him? With what? Money? The grandson of the Dictator? Or is it the grandson of Chaya Halevi, the communist?"

"And the grandson of Comrade Traikov, the great revolutionary, who was eliminated on orders from on high."

"Really? I didn't know, I'm not interested. At all! I'm not interested at all in the history of Bolshevik marriages. Not at all!"

"But what about the fate of a young wanderer? A wanderer, like us. He's talented, smart, poor. Without any kind of protection from the family's past except the false name. No protection from the hounds who are after the Swiss bank account, either."

The professor pushed the blue folder to the edge of the table.

"Is this why you came? You said that you'd come to see me."

"It's a desperate situation. They're desperate, on the edge of the cliff, about to fall into the American void. Yes, I came to see you and speak with you. You're the only one who can help us."

"Help you in the plural sense? Or is this the royal 'we' of your crowned and then decapitated family? I'm a poor untenured professor. I have no power. There are charitable organizations all around."

"Tasia does not want to appeal to charity. She didn't acclimate well to the Holy Land, either. She avoids her coreligionists. She was educated by internationalists and atheists."

"She avoids everyone, as far as I understand. You're probably the only one she confides in."

"That's what I think. I am representing her here, before you. She wants her boy to get into your college. A famous college, yes? He needs a scholarship. They will move here and stay together. I have Eddy's grades, they're very good. You can't turn me down."

"It's hard for me to help you. But we'll see . . . Over time, I've gotten friendly with the new president. A bold young man. I'll put the case to him. Embellish the legend, myth, exoticism of this pair of wanderers. Americans are vulnerable to exoticism."

"Exoticism? What do you mean?"

"Well, the communist Chaya Halevi and the communist Traikov and their daughter, the timid one! And her son with the biologist. And her family ties with the Supreme Potentate! Then the divorce, the flight to the Wailing Wall, the change of identities, the escape to the New World, poverty, desperation! The young president of the college would feel for them. Meaning, he would be intrigued. Everything shrouded in mystery, interruptions, shadows."

"No, no, no! You're not going to start selling the story and have the whole college know, so they'd gape at destiny's marginalized and uprooted pair."

"Uprooted by tyranny, monsieur, not destiny! How else would I make the president interested in their case? I have to intrigue him, astonish him! I sell him a secret, or an anecdote well suited for official dinners. It's my only chance, and it's an uncertain one at that. But I can try."

"On one condition only. That he keeps his trap shut."

"There's no guarantee, even if he promises. The more

you stress the secret aspect, the more the pleasure of gossip increases and becomes irresistible. The only solution is to kill the listener. But then Eddy will have no chance. You need to accept the risk. Especially since it's not yours."

"You've adapted to the capitalist system. Buying and selling."

"I am reminded of it daily. Everything is for sale: organs, sperm, skin. Transplants for other bodies. Anything can be bought or sold. Souls, dreams, weapons, and embryos. A free market, a global bazaar."

The professor hesitated. Of course, he would be looked at with suspicion if he helped the totalitarian system's wandering relatives. He hesitated to reach out to the college president. Then he hesitated some more. Tired of his own hesitations, however, he finally threw all the dice at once and found himself before the president with his mumbled plea.

Despite his wariness, the professor got the scholarship for the secret grandson of the Tyrant from the young president. And a library job for the delicate psychologist Tess Thomson. Pavel was pleased, the smell of refined pipe tobacco filled the professor's office. He thanked him and didn't know how to thank him further. He had not expected his former basketball friend to take his gratitude for the months spent in his garage to such an extreme. And yet, the Professor had only agreed on one condition:

"Before I announce the couple's arrival to the president, I want to see these famous refugees. I can't miss the opportunity, not when it's my chance to see the new communist aristocracy."

"Tess did not profit in any way as a member of the ruling family. Now they're on the lowest rung of the social ladder, just above the abyss. The Utopia's disinherited! They're not guilty of the sins of their parents and grandparents. But they can't adapt to normal life, that's all. You'll see, they're like shadows. Phantom beggars."

The meeting was set for the following Thursday at four P.M. at the Marilyn Café. Though the professor was prepared for all kinds of surprises, the shock was powerful. An ashen mother and a mute son, who stared down at the floor, letting only the briefest of answers escape his lips, at great intervals, his forehead deeply wrinkled. They did not seem at all shocked by the professor's lack of enthusiasm regarding Eddy's schoolboy essays. Nor by the wariness with which the faculty member had approached them. They were only agreeing, resignedly, to a conversation that might help lift them out of squalor and obscurity.

Only at the very end of their time together, when the silence had become heavy, did Tess raise her gaze and smile.

"And Tamar? How is beautiful Tamar? We were colleagues, you probably know this."

"Yes, I know. She remembers, too."

"It was at the hospital where we worked that she met the handsome journalist. I hope she's happy, that they're both happy."

"Yes, they are."

"Send her my good wishes. Tamar is a serene presence, an unforgettable one. She brings joy simply by her presence."

"Yes, that's true. I will send her your good wishes. She'll be glad."

Shyly, the refugees retreated, while the professor remained with his unfinished coffee. He was exhausted by the effort he had made not to see the young Eddy and then to forget him as fast as possible. And behold, he had not been able to. The charged meeting had affected him profoundly. The Tyrant at a young age! The spitting image of his grandfather in the official photographs! A demonic resemblance, difficult to forget, the sudden assault of a phantom who had dominated his distant country for decades. The face cut in straight lines, the concentrated gaze, the fractured and oblique smile, the large hands, matched precisely those of the despot who had become absolute master. He looked like his grandfather in his youth. The young man's shadow was the face of the grandfather projected onto the white wall of the café and into the eyes of the frightened professor.

The night that followed was not at all restful, haunted as it was by the same young, stammering revolutionary superimposed with the effigy of the dictator who was executed by the multitudes. At first, in the handcuffs of the capitalist police. Then before the judges of bourgeoise democracy. In prison, studying the Marxist-Leninist-Stalinist teachings with his cellmates. Then practicing communist speeches on top of the liberating Soviet tanks, a young general tasked with the political education of the People's Army and soon coopted into political office in the single all-powerful Party, the single, united, ruling force of the country on its way to the stainless, sinless future of socialism. And then, its absolute Ruler in the cushioned armchair of the hammer and sickle masquerade, with its crown of bloody red thorns! The grandfather of the present applicant to the nomadic professor's college seemed to have become young again, to have changed his name and acquired a mother who was a former daughter-in-law of the Revolution. Both were now cast away among the skeptics and the speculators.

A night of nightmares: the reel of film featuring the biography of the Carpathian Genius rolled endlessly, portraying the man who had graduated with a degree in propaganda and political activism from the institution owned by the so-called "grave-diggers of capitalism and heralds of Utopia."

In the morning, having awakened from terror, he could no longer recall the difference between Eddy and the grandfather on whom the Devil had heaped congratulatory medals. He knew that he never wanted to encounter the grandson again. He would avoid the couple at any price! He hoped that their real names would not be revealed: that would just enhance the rumors that the professor had been an accomplice to their escape and change of identity.

Cowardice! He was aware of the cowardice of not publicly admitting his role. The president of the college had praised the initiative. "Exemplary, your behavior seems exemplary to me." That is what he had said. "You of all people, who suffered so much under the grandfather's regime. Not many people can overcome their resentments that way."

Okay, the words were a pleasant surprise, but he did not want to have anything more to do with the pair! It was bad enough as it was; he preferred to keep his distance from the disinherited ones.

He saw them from time to time on the pathways of the college, holding hands like a pair of convalescents, and would quickly change course so as not to run into them. Two shadows holding hands. From time to time, the shadows became as red as the Revolution; occasionally, as black as Death, and yet at other times as if they had been parted by a golden cloud. Nevertheless, he was curious about the young man's scholarly accomplishments; they deserved reevaluation. He quickly gave up the thought; he needed to disentangle himself from any connection to the poor refugees, though it was a cynical way of protecting his peace of mind.

Less than nine months after Tess had been hired at the library, the professor's office again filled with the perfumed smoke of Paul's pipe. It was a rainy October afternoon.

"So soon? They just hired her, and now they've fired her! How is that charitable? What does your young president say?"

"I'm not sure, he didn't give me any warning. Nor was he obliged to. I suppose there must be reasons she was fired, I can find out."

And indeed, there were reasons. Tess didn't fit in with her new colleagues, and the new colleagues couldn't manage to establish a real relationship with the taciturn stranger, who was excessively emotional and incapable of concentrating on her new responsibilities, which were not at all difficult. The director of the library had announced to the president that they saw no possibility of improving the situation. Beginning the formalities for establishing citizenship—a recommendation regarding the special qualities of the candidate—these things became impossible given her bizarre estrangement.

The president, however, had proven calm and generous. He seemed to have taken on the charitable responsibility represented by the pair and had found a modest, temporary solution through his secretary, Molly, whose elderly, ill mother needed care.

The misanthropic professor kept his neutrality in the matter; he did not intervene on Tess's behalf. He avoided the pair like the devil's own. He found out from Molly that they ate a pizza a day. Molly also informed him a few months later that her mother could no longer stand the refugee, she simply put her in a bad mood. She dreamed of her at night, a hellish apparition.

When the encounter on the college walkway became unavoidable, the professor stopped, suddenly scared.

Tess had found her voice:

"A pig, this college president! Nothing of what he promised, he did nothing! Nothing! I made an appointment for a meeting with him, but that redheaded secretary of his, Molly, told me that he was overbooked, that I should write to him. I wrote to him about the misery of our capitalist democracy, that I didn't want charity from hypocrites. That I want us to be treated like human beings, that's all! Not like some dirty rags. Let him keep his promise! A job and residency papers! As he promised! He did not respond. Molly, the pious, called me, to tell me that Mr. President regretted what happened, but that he relies on his employees' recommendations regarding employment. That scorpion from the library suggested that I contact one of those refugee aid organizations, who might take an interest in my case if I told them about my family. He, Mr. President, would be willing to put me in touch with a senator who surely would be interested in my case if I don't neglect to tell him about my family and my Jewish family origins. Origins, how about that! It's like communism all over again. Let's look for the origin of evil, let's find the original sin. As if my origins were Jewish! That's what Mr. President would like! As if he weren't well aware I fled the Jewish state as if running from a house on fire and avoided any further contact with them."

The Professor was silent. Tess continued to speak, spoke endlessly, as if making up for her long silence. Now, she could not be stopped.

"I would like to help you somehow, but I'm not sure how. Perhaps I could speak with him again? Explain to him how dire the situation is."

"Explain? The time for explanations is over! We simply fell into his lap, and it really wasn't the right lap . . . That mincing Molly asked me why my son doesn't get a job. All the students make a few bucks in the dining hall, the library, with the landscaping people. That's what the harlot told me."

The Professor was ready to repeat Molly's polite question, but didn't want to prolong the misfortune of the encounter. He thought he should take advantage of the brief pause in the conversation to make himself scarce. That was the ticket. As if he had been caught in a conflagration—look for the emergency exit!

"Of course you can speak to him, but I no longer have any hope. Everyone avoids us like the plague. Eddy's local friends, those he has here, at this great international college, are all from Bangladesh, Pakistan, and Nigeria. Not a single American! That's the full picture, Professor! That's what doesn't get printed in those papers, that all lie anyway. It's the lies of money, let's be clear."

The vehement tone had softened, Tess didn't want to insult her protector. She was smiling, already smiling, as if she had survived a formidable battle. She smiled crookedly, ready for reconciliation.

"The only saving grace might be Congress. When they finally decide to rectify the situation of undocumented refugees and give us citizenship."

And what might you do then, the professor might have asked. Instead, however, he rushed to press the hand of the refugee and made a gesture of sympathy in the direction of the young spectator to the proceedings, who had kept out of the conversation. He seemed either autistic or asthenic, either an imbecile or a genius. And, as could clearly be seen, he resembled his stuttering, sanctified grandfather.

Probably because of this resemblance, the professor had not looked in his direction during the conversation with his mother, and, only at the end, had mimed, in passing, a hypocritical salute. Having read his essays, he did know, in fact, that the heir to the red throne was only a mediocrity. He was neither a complete imbecile nor autistic, only awkward, bored with himself and others, tormented by rather unhappy memories regarding his identity and its metamorphoses, dominated by an overbearing mother, poverty, and the shadows with which both of them continued to converse. The uncertainty of an escapee . . . eternal trembling, avoiding the public eye, waiting for the final tremor.

"Yes, yes, I'd like us to have a further conversation," the professor warned his former teammate. "I met with your relatives, felt both pity and repulsion. For myself, for them. I don't see any solution. Madam Tess refuses the most obvious solution: charity. She also refuses to recognize her Jewish heritage, refuses the possibility of any efforts the little red prince might make, meaning some part-time paid job. None of these options excites the imaginations of the couple, and I'm not senile enough to have any use for a neurotic nanny."

FATA MORGANA

There were mornings, and even evenings, when he would forget about the trees and snails and ants, or the stony sky above. Lured into trap of the printed page, as long ago, when as an adolescent he'd forget all about his dead parents and school and the little girl with blond pigtails in the first row, and give himself up to the impassible block of letters until the small hours of the morning.

Snails and flowers and butterflies, birds and trees, worms and gravestones, stone benches and leafy arbors were not the only things in the cemetery named Eden. There were also spirits and shadows that lived among the phantoms of the departed, unexpectedly rising up—when, how?—on transparent wings.

He had sat down on the bench near the rectangular stone that marked the grave of the Italian teacher whom he had not had the chance to meet. She had been delivered up to the void before he had made his appearance at the college. And yet, nevertheless, perhaps even miraculously, she continued to host him in her birdcage, her home haughtily nicknamed *casa minima.* She came to him in dreams, dozing, and in his somnambulism. A kind of complicity he avoided discussing.

Madam, miss, muse Brandeis, Irma Brandeis, an exegete of Dante, who had become the poet Eugenio Montale's new Beatrice, embodied the myth of Clizia in the version after Ovid, the poet exiled even in the afterlife in Tomis on that bluest Black Sea. In life, the nymph—a woman who had fallen in love with the sun god Apollo—had become Irma, the flower of a biblical sun, a Semitic flower under the hostile sun of new times.

As David Michael Hertz notes in his massive volume *Eugenio Montale, the Fascist Storm, and the Jewish Sunflower,* as Montale's muse, Irma underwent the apotheosis of the suffering nymph who bears the bleeding god through the Levant and the world. The cover of the monograph brings the image of the couple to life: a solid man with a mustache and a delicate young woman with bangs and a candid gaze. A love story immortalized in verse in the Fascist period, the tale links the name of a celebrated poet to that of an American Jew who tried to save him, her Christian, anti-Fascist lover threatened by the scourge that would devour millions of her fellow Jews.

Even if this highly dramatic account found its happy end in poetry (and the collection of 155 of the poet's letters from the 1930s, which eventually, in 1983, were deposited by Irma at the Gabinetto Vieusseux Library in Florence), the American nomad could not help being obsessed by memory's bloody shadows.

Unique feminine elegance and mystical aura, the present-day Nomad had read regarding the corpse beneath his feet. *Her hairstyle and round face recalled the shining yellow pet-*

als and round disk of the sunflower. In his writings, the Italian poet would add a few details that were specific to Irma herself: her hair, her jewelry, her scarf, her sunglasses, the scent of her cigarettes trailing behind her.

Montale could not forget her, as he could not forget Svevo and Saba in the years of the Nazi apocalypse. The invocation of Irma as muse was more than a lyric lament, it was an ardent calling forth of the past into the present: *Bring me the sunflower, let me plant it/in my field parched by the salt sea wind,/and let it show the blue reflecting sky/the yearning of its yellow face all day.*[69] A passionate reader, Irma had looked for the poet in the Florence library. There they embarked on the lively and literary love affair that would obsess both writers for the rest of their lives and inscribe death itself into its final chapters. *I hate Platonism and believe that in life nothing exists besides the fifth of September with variants and additions . . . And if I dream you, I don't dream your Soul, I dream your lips, your eyes, your breast, and the rest which is not silence. I daresay that the rest is the best and Shakespeare knew it.*[70]

From the beginning, Irma's relationship with the poet, who would remain her partner into posterity, bore the fingerprints of the love-magic of a biblical Beatrice from across the sea and her unshakeable Dante. *For me, you have been a great presence half in shadow, just as now you are an immense light,* Montale would write to her after their first meeting.

The Misanthropic Nomad now repeated the verse, sitting next to the gravestone.

Old Mrs. Caro had told him about Irma. Eccentric, baroque, a strange and fascinating being. The Misanthrope felt well protected under the Brandeis roof Irma had built. The inhabitant of the small cabin in which Irma had dreamed was now reading Montale's postmortem poem, watching the snails go by, carrying their minuscule homes. At the death of Doctor Brandeis, Irma's father, Montale remembered that *lontano, ero con te quando tuo padre entrò nell'ombra.*[71] Like a bird of hope, Clizia, the flower, survived the storm:

> Now that the last shreds of tobacco
> die at your gesture in the crystal bowl,
> to the ceiling slowly
> rises a spiral of smoke
> which the chess knights and chess bishops
> regard bemused; which new rings follow,
> more mobile than those
> upon your fingers.
>
> The mirage, that in the sky released
> towers and bridges, disappeared
> at the first puff; the unseen window
> opens and the smoke tosses.[72]

The smoke and the Morgana reappeared in the invisible window at the Annalena Pensione at Costa San Giorgio 54, where Irma had lived in the thirties.

The wanderer of posterity might have said that when, on September 5, 1933, at the Bristol hotel in Genova, the ardor of the young bodies was consummated, "I had not yet been born. The atmosphere surrounding the lovers who would become my parents in a small European market town was still that of fairytale days and nights." In the meantime, however, the Nomad of many decades later had become the seasonal inhabitant of Irma Brandeis's *casa minima,* at the college to which each of them had contributed at different times through their teaching.

"I was born far away, in the years in which Irma had already become the Jewish successor to Petrarch's Laura and Dante's Beatrice," the solitary Eastern European whispered to the snail who huddled on his knees. "In a former Austrian province, though I didn't inherit the 'Austrian eyes' that Montale found in Irma."

Suspected and even accused by the Fascists of being a Jew, Montale remained the lyric captive of his mythical shadow, Clizia, for many years, finding and renewing this shadow in Irma, even after he had refused her proposal to save himself with her in the America of all exiles.

In the years when I was a child lab rat in the Nazi concentration camp, Montale became increasingly philosemitic—rather than just anti-Fascist, as he had always been. And not just because of the Jewish lovers he took before and after Irma. Montale confessed to posterity: *in Milan I'm thought to be Jewish, because of the Svevo case. If it were possible to be Jewish without knowing it, this would be my case.*[73] His letters to Clizia leave no room for doubt that his poetic "motets" were largely inspired by Irma. Above the volcano of time, continuing to resist, a sunflower draws up its shadow, the sign of tormented exile.

A mirage, a failed incest. "We will always be together, regardless of what happens, nothing and no one will part us, regardless of what happens," Agatha had told her misanthropic brother, gazing at night's pillow, the egg-shell that would reunite them, predestined, each time. "And now the Italian one next to whom I will spend my afterlife and my ever after has chosen this place as her final refuge, this Edenic cemetery of the college that has played host to my estrangement," the Misanthrope whispered to the snail who had reappeared on his knees. She's the mirage, the Fata Morgana in the smoke of posterity, the one who lived through the black year of 1938, when I was only two years old and still living in a small Eastern European Semitic enclave.

The *Manifesto degli scienziati razzisti,* (*The Manifesto of Racist Scientists*), published in the *Giornale d'Italia,* in fascist Rome, was a warning regarding what would happen in other cities in Europe. In "La tua fuga" ("Your Flight"), the abandoned poet calls to this blighted city, which he has decided to resurrect in the image of Clizia, the fictional heroine of the age of the scourge. *I write to you from here, from this table/remote, from the honey cell.*[74] *Life that enfables you is still too brief/if it contains you. The luminous ground/unfolds your icon. Outside it rains.*[75]

> *The stars sew with too fine a thread,*
> *the eye of the tower stopped at two,*
> *even the climbing vines are an ascent*
> *of shadows, and their perfume bitter hurt.*

[. . .] This Christian fracas which has no speech
other than shadows or laments,
what does it give you of me?[76]

In the epistolary poem entitled "Notizie dall'Amiata," ("News from Amiata") and in the other fragments inspired by the American runaway in the volume *Le Occasioni* (*Occasions*), dedicated to *I. B.,* the danger that threatens the poet, his muse, and an entire civilization finds its echo in an erotic meditation on the nature of war and religion. The muse read the poems, David Michael Hertz notes: *In January 1941 she borrowed the book of poems that had been dedicated to her from the Sarah Lawrence College library in faraway Bronxville, New York.*[77]

Does the sunflower have its own shadow, though it belongs to the sun? Might its shadow be the perpetual pendulation between sunset and sunrise, the uncertain effluence of the provisory and the ephemeral, the eternal, repetitive act of dissimulation? Irma becomes Clizia, an angelic guest tempering the poet's confrontation with the Nazi void, the *bufera*—a Dantean storm of global genocide—which paralyzed the poet's pen for many years. She is the protective shadow that did not disappear but merely was transformed into a Christian-Jewish emblem, as Hertz notes: *Finally, Clizia becomes (both in spite of and because of her Jewish origins) an unconscious bearer of Christian symbolism and all that it embodies within the context of Montale's poetry. She is the unknow-*

ing salvific Christ-bearer, pagan, Jew, a pan-cultural symbol of good in a pitched battle against evil, and, finally and most important, Christian in her connotations. Montale makes his symbolizing procedure perfectly clear.[78]

"And where was I all along, dear Mr. Hertz?" the exiled Misanthrope asked himself, examining the snail sitting on the page of the book that lay open on his knees. I was saluting the liberating Red Army from the train, returning to the homeland that had betrayed me and thrown me into hell. I was ready to be reborn next to little Tamar, in the beautiful land in which I had been born already and which was now, again, being denied me. What would come next for us, for those of us driven from the East in the years in which, across the ocean, Irma was a translator and promoter of the poems of the man from whom she had parted without really parting?

> *And how much of you is*
> *part of the shipwreck of my people, your*
> *people, now, when*
> *a fire of ice bears into memory the earth which is*
> *yours, which you do not see,*
> *and another rosary I have*
> *not, between my fingers, nor another flame do I carry if not*
> *this one of resin and berries which I*
> *have invested you with.*[79]

So wrote the Italian poet in the years of shipwreck, which had thrown me, the suspect, into a concentration camp. I emerged a shadow. I thirsted after light and peace, ready to stuff myself indiscriminately with books and bloody meat, leaves, ants, snails, and the dreams of lost pigeons.

From the scarlet tribunes, time offered me the lying fairy-tale of the brotherhood of all men and a luminous future. I was vulnerable to stories I hadn't heard. I held on to Tamar in the squalid orphanages of that age. We huddled together between the covers of our schoolbooks. They had to save us! That is how I understood the cruelty of the circus that enveloped us and why I let that fair of terror teach us joy and despair, resignation and cowardice, and at last, wanderlust. And it did teach us, Sir Hertz! That is how we . . . each of us and both of us together . . . arrived in the colorful desert of postcapitalist comfort! An unlikely rebirth for which we are grateful and which disgusts us.

In 1944, the year when Irma was becoming a professor of Italian at the college where we now converse, I barely dared to open my eyes toward the salvific Stalinist tanks. In 1979, when she was retiring, I was glad that the American had succeeded in waking Agatha from her apathy with his love and had given her the gift of new illusions. And in 1990, when Irma Brandeis had found her resting place here, under the stone on which I am now reading the chronicle of her life, I was already nearby, ready to inhabit the *casa minima* of the recently deceased. I had already learned to confuse the shadows in books with those real-life ones, only then to try futilely to separate and define them. In exile, I took up my apprenticeship in shadow-making, my initiation into this final, Edenic exile, the last homestead, which I will share with Irma.

"Nothing and no one will separate us," Tamar used to say. I suppose that, in the end, she will learn to accept Irma, the new Fata Morgana with which destiny has blessed me, as a kind of closing adagio.

Clizia, it's your fate/changed one who the changeless love still serves.[80] The poem "Hitler Spring" shores up the scattered and ruined calendar of time, with the resigned *magnolia's shadow,* as well as the shadow-trace of the angel of fire and ice, who was and remained the "the fragile fugitive,"[81] as the poet puts it. In 1956, eighteen years after Irma left Italy and separated from him definitively, Montale took up again the scintillating, apotheosis-driven Clizia motet in the volume *La bufera e altro* (*The Storm and Something Other*). As Hertz maintains, the lyric deity became a Christian and Jewish symbol with a sacrificial meaning of the millions of victims of the Holocaust.

Her beauty and American audacity may have first captivated the poet in the 1930s, but over the years, her writing, her criticism, and her thought penetrated deeply into the mind of the poet, becoming an essential part of his artistic expression and, eventually, of his trajectory into the larger realm of world literature.[82]

In the end, paradoxically, love offered Montale regeneration, the youthful reincarnation of his mythic heroine. In his last poems, the bewitching young woman returns, luminous, eager for life and ideas. In 1970 he reembodies the person he knew in the 1930s.

The last parting followed: Montale dies in 1981 in Milano; Irma in 1990 in New York. She is laid to rest in the cemetery where, years later, her reader would reclaim her as his own partner. The trees trembling in the wind and the wandering shadows are witnesses, as are the panicked ants, and the tactful and the impenetrable snail now attempting to climb up to the old eyelid of the nomadic stranger.

"In 1944," the Nomad whispers, "when in the East we were scattering the phantoms of war, eager to try out a new Utopia's snares, in faraway Italy the shadows clustered in the wake of each of your footsteps." The Italian poet dedicated his own "1944" to Clizia/Irma, whom he elsewhere called *la mia divina*.[83] The future reader, the man who was shipwrecked on the Hudson River, would listen, years later, to the waves of green leaves whispering the verses of the lovelorn poet. Clustered around him: water, old shadows, the snail, and the wind that had grown silent. *This Christian fracas which has no speech/other than shadows or laments,/what does it give you of me?*[84]

In the Trans-Tristia of the anti-Semitic camps, the shadows of war repeated what Irma intercepted daily at the American Office of War Information, where she worked, preparing radio programs for Italy.

While the Eastern European boy was preparing to return to the places from which he had been driven away, Irma held her place as the muse of the far-off poet; when the young student in Bucharest confronted the slavelike work of engineering and the police state, Irma inhabited the apotheosis of Clizia in the 1956 *La bufera e altro*.

After the war, Irma was already Clizia, the post-Holocaust Jewish poetic symbol. She was another Beatrice, in Dante's ascension toward God and in Montale's lyric ascension toward the Parnassus of modern poetry, in which he glimpsed the agnostic salvation of his own religion and culture, as David Michael Hertz maintains in the monograph which was slipping from the hands of the dozing reader, wounding, in the process, the somnolent snail in his lap.

Wounded, too, by the cruelty of the moment, the Nomad remained by the side of his colleague under the gravestone for a long time. *Mia divina,*[85] under *the magnolia's shadow,*[86] her distant poet had said. The solitary nymph-sunflower fawned between destiny's parchment leaves.

FROM GÜNTHER'S PERSONAL PAPERS: "LONG-LASTING SHADOWS"

After the fall of European communism, our so-called global village was compelled to face a new, ferocious form of aggression: the mystical, militant terrorism of Islamist fanaticism. [. . .] This eruption of terrorist violence coincided with—and in many cases served to propel—a wave of migration all across Europe, along with intense debates about the consequences of population movement on such a massive scale. Migrants reaching the shores of Europe as the result of having fled conflicts in the Middle East and Africa were compared to Jews who fled the Nazi Holocaust.[87]

The current fierce debate in the United States regarding such new migrants recalls "the shameful way we responded as Jews were fleeing Nazi Germany in the 1930s," writes Nicholas Kris-

tof in the New York Times, *when "Americans feared that Euro-*
pean Jews might be left-wing security threats." Kristof reminds
us that "in January 1939 [. . .] a two-to-one majority felt that
the United States should not accept 10,000 mostly Jewish refugee
children from Germany." As a result, the ship St. Louis *was "re-*
turned to Europe where some of its passengers were murdered by
the Nazis." [. . .]

It happens that a remarkable new book, A Brief Stop on the
Road from Auschwitz, *by the Swedish writer and journalist*
Göran Rosenberg, offers a powerful reminder of "the sadly abid-
ing realities" of that time. [. . .] The book follows a tense and
troubled trajectory in the destiny of the young Rosenberg cou-
ple, David and Halinka, both Auschwitz survivors, Polish Jews
who settled after the war in Sweden and became Swedish citizens.
In this intense and revelatory book, their son Göran explores the
parallel between his afterwar life and his parents' own difficult
rebirth in a foreign environment:

> The young man who will be my father alighted from the train
> on an early August evening in 1947. [. . .] This is the Place
> that will continue to form me even when I'm convinced that
> I've formed myself. That's the difference between [my parents]
> and me. They have encountered the world for the first time in
> an entirely different place [. . .] and for them so much has
> already started and already ended, and it's still unclear whether
> anything can start afresh here [. . .] What quickly binds them
> to the Place is the Child, who happens to be me.

The Rosenbergs lost the greatest part of their family during
the war, and their Project became—and would continue to be—
to build a new life and make a successful transition from surviv-

ing to living. *The book lays out their story and a history of their new "Place," their new domicile as migrants, a new home for David and Halinka and a new homeland for Göran and his siblings. Even more important, it investigates their survivors' past and biography.*

The Rosenbergs' biographical nightmare began in the Polish Łódź ghetto camp, which was liquidated in August 1944, and their ordeal continued on their long journey to Auschwitz. The bleak preliminaries are best expressed in the painful and cynical speech made by the Jewish leader Chaim Rumkowski on September 4, 1942. The Germans ordered Rumkowski to dispatch all the underage, old, and sick Jews, a total of some 20,000 detainees. He was forced to urge his people:

> *Fathers and mothers, give me your children! [. . .] I come to you like a bandit to take from you that which you hold most dear. [. . .] We can save the well in their place. [. . .] I share your pain, I suffer your anguish, and I do not know how I shall survive this. [. . .] A broken Jew stands before you. [. . .] I extend my broken, trembling hands to you and implore you: give me the sacrifices! So we can avert the need for even more sacrifices.*

The immediate response of the audience is a wave of suicides and a new type of dementia: "They bark like dogs, howl like wolves, cry like hyenas, roar like lions. [. . .] The ghetto is a cacophony of wild noises in which only one tone is missing: the human tone."

And then? "Survival resumes, as if nothing had happened." "Talk of nothing but rations, potatoes, soup, and so on!" notes the inmate Josef Zelkowicz in his diary. His next diary entry should also be recalled: "During the first twenty days of September the weather was lovely and sunny, with only a few brief showers."

In Göran Rosenberg's book, this terrible episode is followed by essential, unavoidable questions, which constitute an extreme challenge to the reader and to the author's contemporaries: "Can we say that Chaim Rumkowski sacrifices his soul to save the life of the ghetto? Can we say that he enters into a pact with the devil?" These are questions that can be said to torment all leaders—Jewish and non-Jewish—forced to collaborate with their oppressors (be they Nazis or Communists) in the hopes of saving some lives by sacrificing others. Perhaps too eager to serve as tribunal, posterity always harshly criticizes such leaders' actions. Rosenberg's own judgment on this complicated issue however seems exemplary:

> Much has been said about how they should have refused and resisted (as they did in Warsaw at the end, when it was too late anyway), about how they should have let themselves be killed rather than become accomplices in crime. Hannah Arendt calls their actions "the darkest chapter of the whole dark story." [. . .] Primo Levi is one of the few who have earned the moral authority to express an opinion. [. . .] He immediately declares his reservations, citing the unimaginable moral challenge with which Rumkowski was confronted. [. . .] He can see in Rumkowski's ambivalence the ambivalence of our Western civilization, descending "into hell with trumpets and drums [. . .] forgetting that we are all in the ghetto [. . .] and that close by the train is waiting." [. . .] Perhaps he's just expressing his growing sense of powerlessness in the face of amnesia and indifference.

Rosenberg adds: *"In September 1942, Chaim Rumkowski, chairman of the Council of Elders in the Łódź ghetto, is presented with a choice for which I can find no historical equivalent and makes a decision that I lack the authority and ability to say anything about. So I say nothing, I merely observe that in August 1944, the Łódź ghetto is still standing, whereas the Warsaw ghetto is liquidated."*

At the other end of the nightmare, the death factory at Auschwitz manifested a very efficient process of extermination: *"Of the 405,000 people given a registration number on arrival at Auschwitz, 340,000 die. Of the 67,000 Jews delivered from the Łódź ghetto [. . .] 19,000 are allocated to a no-man's-land between slave labor and gas chamber and left unregistered"*—David Rosenberg, father of the author, among them.

> By the end of 1946 there are still 250,000 Jewish survivors in
> European camps for displaced persons waiting for somewhere
> to go. [. . .] The Jewish men from the Łódź ghetto who survive
> the selection on the ramp at Auschwitz-Birkenau, and the
> slave labor at the Büssing factories in Braunschweig, and the
> meandering death transport from Watenstedt to Ravensbrück,
> and the black hole of Wöbbelin, are virtually all transported to
> Sweden through the good offices of the Red Cross in the summer
> of 1945. David Rosenberg. Entered July 18, 1945. Passport
> control, Malmö.

This criminal odyssey of the monstrous extermination of Jews in a Christian Europe took place amid the joyful sound of the "carousel" mentioned in Czesław Miłosz's poem "Campo dei Fiori"—joy accompanied by music and play and the complicity of the "hot wind" that "blew open the skirts of the girls/and the crowds were laughing."

Yet Göran Rosenberg's book also contains destiny's "brief stop" in peaceful Sweden, a welcoming haven for victims. It is a memorable post-Holocaust chronicle that nevertheless contains many implicit warnings for our global present, shaken as it is by conflicts between free and closed societies, dominated by rigid nationalist theocracies, and adhering to medieval dreams of total political obedience.

In his new homeland, the Swedish child of Polish-Jewish origin becomes the inhabitant of another planet: "He knows that Mom and Dad are Jews, and that he and his little sister are too. [. . .] And even if he doesn't know what it means, he knows it has something to do with the shadows." Indeed, this shadow obsession will accompany the narrator to the end, finding its terrible culmination in the shocking suicide of his father, "the wandering Jew" who has tried every possible means of taming his bleeding memory as a member of a hated and hunted minority—first as an inmate in the Łódź ghetto, then at Auschwitz, and then as a survivor, a migrant in transit, a resident alien, and finally a citizen of a democratic, civilized nation ready to receive victims of whatever origin.

Each phase of this troubled and turbulent narrative trajectory reveals yet another dark window for the old-new shadow to slip through. In the beginning, David Rosenberg, the survivor, does everything in his power to gain the coveted status of "normalcy," to forget his lengthy initiation into horror. [. . .] "Despite the fact that immediately after the war, in September 1946, only three percent of the Jewish survivors want to remain in Sweden (while 45 percent dream of Israel, 28 percent of the United

States, eight percent of other destinations, and 16 percent want to be repatriated), despite the fact that they speak the language of Strindberg with the accent of Mickiewicz," the Rosenberg couple prefers to stay in "the Place," and on May 7, 1954, David and Halinka become Swedish citizens.

And yet, "the shadow that follows you all will follow you into this paradise as well." Even relatively small events become warnings and have a pronounced impact on the Rosenbergs' self-aware and sensitive natures: "One winter's day, some children throw snowballs at their kitchen windows and shout 'Jews!' [. . .] The boy hears the snow thump on the window and sees his mother's face go white." Occasionally, too, something happens to thrust the elder Rosenberg back among his previous peers "and their shadows." Then, the decisive ugly moments that follow seem unavoidable:

> *At the factory in the changing room, you try to throw a punch at someone and this someone slams you against a locker so hard you end up with a concussion. This someone had wondered out loud what a person like you was doing among the ordinary workers. Why someone like you was not busy lending money or living off other people. Said he'd never seen a Jew working. After that argument in the changing room your headaches come more often. The headaches and the nightmares.*

It is the beginning of the end, the new beginning of the new end. Medical treatment doesn't seem to help, the shadows dog the patient's every step, he cannot take the decisive leap from surviving to living. Shadows catch him again and again; he is their captive. Now, he has even become the unhappy possessor of an important statement from the medical commission for German reparations claiming that his illness is caused by his need or desire for financial recompense and not because of his experiences at Auschwitz and their consequences.

On February 5, 1960, a certain Dr. Raabe certifies that his patient, on sick leave from his work since December 1959, is living proof of the fact that that there exists a causal link between his ordeal under the Nazis and his nervous illness. On April 26 the disabled survivor is taken to the Sundby Mental Hospital, where he tries to tell the doctors that he worries about swastikas multiplying across the world. After he is released, he returns to the hospital asking for electric shock treatment to overcome his difficulties. Later on, after the shadows finally free him from his unbearable earthly adventure, he is found in the hospital lake. In his last letter to his beloved Halinka, he explains: "I suffer the agonies of hell, and I can't go on."

The chief physician at Sundby Hospital concludes that the shadows that killed his patient had come from the outside and were not his own. The German state was wrong, its victim was right. The shadows of the continent's bloody past did not vanish with the collapse of two European totalitarian systems, nor did long-lived anti-Semitism die out. Instead, the malignancy had revived so as to grow in many places.

What for David Rosenberg, in Sweden, was a "brief stop" in a post-Holocaust world governed by hope and subverted by old and new human shortcomings, became a much longer, ongoing daily struggle for his son, Göran, his father's double in the historical journey to rediscover and bring to life the past. The confusion of the father's last years in Sweden and the son's present, which this impressive book addresses, underscores a mixture of contradictions, the chief ones being the longing for a hybrid, open-minded modern society and the search for identity and belonging. Göran's impulses are sometimes contradictory and become radicalized in a fierce fight for mystical communion with— and sense of the coherence within—a race, ethnicity, and form of religious belief. This inner conflict can be compared with the dilemma faced by the main character in Adelbert von Chamisso's old fairy tale Schlemihl: The Man Who Sold His Shadow: should one surrender one's inner shadow for a more prosperous and free life, or should one keep it as a sacred last refuge, inaccessible to outside influences?

The pages of the book have provoked deep questions, fears, and stimulated the memory of the reader pondering flowers and phantoms in that grand American college cemetery called Eden.

THE SEASHELL

Mollusks with a soft body protect themselves by means of two calcareous valves which make up their external skeleton; the shell of the snail is similar and has the shape of a seashell.

He was holding the scrap of paper with the familiar handwriting he connected to the journal in which he had first seen his obsession for what it was; they were the exact words of that time. After his sister's departure, after four days and nights of tender cohabitation, all he had left was this modest souvenir of words.

"Let's call it a seashell rather than an eggshell. A shell rather than an eggshell. A refuge. A shelter. It seems more appropriate."

"It doesn't matter what we call it. We know what it represents. That's all."

The dictionary definition had only been a pretext for a conversation that seemed difficult to take up again, so many years later, the discussion of the nightly "eggshell" in which their incestuous bodies had enveloped themselves.

Cohabitation in the deepest night for years and decades, from their babyish clinging in their protective hideaway against the dark, to their routine much later, their armor against a hostile world.

"Has our eggshell replaced family itself?"

"Maybe."

"With something else?"

"We're no longer children, or adolescents. Tomorrow we'll be old, you'll see."

"No, that's not true. We are still children and adolescents, and we'll remain old people. You know perfectly well why we couldn't talk about the secret eggshell. We stayed hidden, day and night, not only from others but from ourselves. But is that really why you've come? For a disquisition on our shared past? You want to analyze guilt and defense mechanisms?"

"Past and present. And no, that's not why I came. But we can't put off the conversation any longer."

"The eggshell was our therapy. We had no reason to reject it—have no reason. No matter how often or how rarely we see each other."

"It would finally give us something concrete to free ourselves from. We'd finally be able to talk about trauma and therapy. About the fraternal twins. About our shield against the world and memory itself."

"A shield, yes. Better than a seashell. The nightly watch. The eggshell. The embrace, the entwining. The defense. The trenches where we waited for the next morning."

"The refuge of the orphans who we never stopped being orphans. The lair of exile itself. Wandering, the provisional nature of everything. The two of us clasped together and encased in a single body. The double, inseparable body of the night's own making. Night's children. The gift."

"And the burden?"

"And the joy."

"Guilty? A guilty joy . . . "

"I don't think so. Joy can't be guilty. Only rare, real, and revenging."

The brother found himself again in Eden, ready to begin the day along with his colleagues who in the meantime had become stones. Gravestones. He was again contemplating the trees and the sky, the birds, ants, and snails of the forest that had grown silent. A painful memory.

"I came to talk to you about Luisa. I didn't feel I could write to you about her."

"You mentioned this colleague of yours at the hospital some time ago . . . "

"She's more than a colleague. We've become close. Found an echo in one another."

"What about men? They're not chasing you anymore? I don't suppose they've gone extinct. You've always been a trophy for them."

"Are you jealous?"

"As much as I'm allowed to be."

"You're allowed."

"And Luisa? A surrogate? Like your estimable husband? Or other partners?"

"This is not the time to be sarcastic. This is something else entirely."

"That doesn't make me feel any better."

"You don't need to feel better. That's not the point."

"I would have liked us to live together. I thought you invited me so that we'd be together."

"The danger wasn't only in you but in myself, too. But I wasn't talking about danger; rather about reality. How it's the most important thing."

"Does Luisa know about us?"

"She knows everything. It wouldn't have worked otherwise. I don't like duplicity, you know that."

"And now?"

"We check the knots, the entanglements. Then we doublecheck them."

"Not necessary. As you've just said, everything remains the same. What does Luisa think?"

"She's in agreement. She has no opinion, only agrees. That's how she is. We'll see each other from time to time. Time itself will tell us when. Reality, real life, the most important thing . . . "

"I'll be waiting. I've waited for a long time."

"The time will come. Like destiny. It's inevitable."

"It's our biography."

"Distinct and shared biographies."

"Inseparable and unique."

For a long time, the brother had been staring at the pillow, at the imprint left behind by their two bodies, entwined in each other. There was no trace, and he continued to see the past. The miracle of becoming whole? The secret entwining far from the eyes of the world, the fraternal complicity, the sibling guilt? Secret. Deep. Both resistance and rebellion.

The imprint on the pillow had grown larger. Left alone, the Nomad watched it for a long time, in his hut in the woods. *Casa minima.* Both name and appellation.

FROM GÜNTHER'S PERSONAL PAPERS

My mother was not Jeanne-Clémence Proust, née Weil, and her son was not Marcel reborn. As a child, I did not have the benefit of her maternal kiss before bed and even now, as an old man, this is not something that I eagerly await. [. . .] Nevertheless, the clawing of the past is no less painful when I feel the shadow that watches over me draw near. [. . .] Above, through night's red sky, passes a blind old woman in her paralytic's wheelchair. God dozes in his celestial chair: an old woman, on night's doorstep. [. . .] Among familiar and unfamiliar strangers, hailing from all places, mill my confusions, the final wealth of an exile, which give me back my familiar God.

The walls give way to the land of dreams, and I distinguish the silhouette that is drawn there in the darkness, in the play of shadows.

*The darkness blooms, becomes a forest on the Russian steppe,
I see the nameless pit [. . .] in the woods of Transnistria (Trans-
Tristia), where my grandparents were left behind.*

*Under a stone engulfed in the flames of a Jewish sun, on one
of Jerusalem's crests, rests the man who was once my father. Only
my mother lingers behind [. . .] in the place she had always lived
and that she had always wanted to leave behind.*[88]

Writing in 1789, in Les emblèmes de la raison, *Jean Starob-
inski rightly sees attempts to "reconcile with the shadow" as char-
acterizing the entire sensibility of the seventeenth century. "Not
only do we witness a return of the shadow, but obscurity itself
is proclaimed a universal point of reference: light becomes sec-
ondary, and it is the struggle of contraries that gives birth to its
beauty. Man is not just the place where this cosmic confrontation
takes place, but is the key to overcoming it. He possesses inner
shadows, while his eyes bear a light similar to that of the sun.*[89]

*Taking into account Pessoa's melancholy temperament, his
"metaphysics of autonomous shadows" can be said to reflect a
premise similar in nature to that of works that dwell on the "uneasiness" felt by many generations of individuals regarding their
seldom examined disillusionments. The Portuguese writer compares the reclaiming of the shadow's "autonomy" to the refusal of
the great Socratic admonition to "know thyself" on which a great
deal of Western culture is based.*

However, it would be absurd to see in this coincidence of in-

terests a profession of faith centered on obscurantism (in a book that takes up the invitation to forgo light, whose magic so clearly affected Pessoa in his prose and poetry). We can never spend too much time meditating on the lesson in modesty offered by those who respect shadows; nor should we remain blind to their message. Without ignoring the magnitude of the suffering that shadows embody, I nevertheless believe that they are not symbolic of the diminishment of the plenitude of existence—a plenitude for which we are nostalgic—but of a kind of sensible precaution. Though, of course, this can only be the case on the condition that we agree that no interpretation, no meaning is ever final. As Levinas shows, the last reserves of humaneness (and what writer is more humane than Pessoa?) forbid any violence between human beings—deep-rooted as violence may be in its certainty of possessing the truth as the thing in front of us.[90]

FROM ALBERTO'S PERSONAL PAPERS

Friday

Yesterday, in Paris, I bought a book just for its title: An Exhaustive Treatise on Shadows, *by Abu al-Rayham Muhammad b. Ahmad al-Biruni. Two volumes in octavo, published by Aleppo University in Syria.*

The treatise is an eleventh-century scientific text. The author, a scholar from Central Asia. I don't have the expertise to follow the geometrical annotations, but I am intrigued by observations such as the following: "the second category is that of common people whose hearts are disgusted at the mention of shadows, mores, or sin, and whose hair stands on end at the mere sight of mathematical or scientific instruments." I, on the other hand, am enchanted by shadows. As Goethe says in Act 5 of Faust: *"That is how I become a shadow."*

Saturday

Last night, thinking about shadows, I took Peter Schlemihl *to read in bed. The edition I have (which I received when I was eight or nine years old) has the extraordinary black and white illustrations by George Cruiskshank surrounded by vignettes in ochre. This contemporary of Dickens (whose works he also famously illustrated) manages to capture so well the fairytale quality apparent in Adelbert von Chamisso's book, as well as the horror of the man who loses his shadow. The malevolent force represented by the Man in Gray, who pushes him to that luckless exchange, has nothing of the buffoonery of Goethe's Mephistopheles. He is like a shadow himself, something that pendulates between life and the anticipated grave. As Chamisso says, he looks like "the end of a thread [. . .] the tailor has dropped from his needle."*

For me, as a child, Peter Schlemihl's adventures ended more or less abruptly after the book's seductive beginning, in the middle of the book, when the hero comes to know the final outcome of his numerous adventures: after he exchanges his shadow for a bag that continuously produces gold, suffers because the loss of his shadow causes fear and fury among his fellow men, loses the affections of his beloved, whom he passes on to a servant named Rascal (who tells him "I don't accept gifts from a shadowless man"), and, in the end, refuses to sign over his soul to recover his shadow.

Up to this point, I was enchanted. The rest of the story, de-

tailing Peter's wanderings in his miraculous seven-league boots, bored me.

Now, nearly fifty years later, I know that the real ending resides in those wanderings, in the satisfaction of having refused the last temptation, in the description of Peter as a kindly scholar peacefully researching something at the North Pole.

Monday

Even physically I feel like an Other: someone who has tried repeatedly to grow up a little from that eternal age of eighteen or twenty, someone who has learned nothing, or apparently made no changes, given that the person in the mirror, that Alberto Manguel that others see, is truly myself, yes, but a different me, not the me with whom I identify. To give it a scholarly air, I'd call this illusion: the Dorian Gray Complex.

In the last part of the story, resigned to his fate, Peter Schlemihl travels the whole world with the help of his seven-league boots, seeking scientific specimens for his studies. He visits the frozen regions of the North and crosses the burning deserts of the South, which, being uninhabited, do not expose him to the fury of others. Thus, he becomes capable of offering us his advice: "Friend, if you wish to live among men, learn to respect the Shadow more than you do money. However, if you want to live only with yourself, you do not need this advice."

Later

Peter Schlemihl furnishes me with an epigraph for my journal: "And so it comes to pass that everything I've accumulated

and built is cursed to fall into ruin, to shatter. Oh, my dear Adel-
bert, to what do all these earthly efforts come!"[91]

Luther's translation of the Bible also offers me an unintended
description of what I am doing: if you labor, it is enough; if you
traffic in words, it is a lack. "In all labour there is profit: but the
talk of the lips tendeth only to penury (Proverbs 14:23)."[92]

GÜNTHER'S PERSONAL PAPERS:
TAMAR-AGATHA

Dear Günther,

I apologize for not responding to the messages you sent after our conversation during the apocalypse of 9/11.

My brother, who is so close to you, hasn't sent me a sign for a long time. I became even more worried after the checks I sent him came back uncashed.

For me, you're still Günther, rather than Ulrich in Robert Musil's library—he's my brother's idol, you know, like that of so many other ailing readers. Perhaps he's even one of your idols.

I suppose that my taciturn brother, the great aestheticist of the circus, didn't discuss our former siblinghood with you. It's likely that we'll never known how much of a brother and sister we really are. My mother wasn't too virtuous; it's hard to know with whom or how many others she shared her cursed bed in the camps. My brother's father—who was my uncle, actually—was not the first or the last of her partners. After the death of his wife, he and my aunt, my mother's older sister, became lovers. To simplify, let's concede that my father is also my brother's father, and we only have different mothers. Half siblings, to put it simply, half sinners. Half incestuous! The half that kept us alive and helped us live! Our only lasting happiness after the trials of the camps and their hell. Not much later, they both left us. My brother's father, my mother, and his mother . . . all deceased. We were left alone in the world. Together, we became the Whole. That's how we survived all the squalid socialist orphanages and the dorms of various schools and universities. I didn't want to leave my brother behind when I left the country; what I wanted was to leave myself behind, the person I had been. But marriage was not an entirely successful adventure for me. It wasn't a disaster by any means. After all, I had admired the stranger who had fallen in love with me. Perhaps it happened too quickly—something to do with the psychology and educational style of the country my husband hailed from rather than his own nature.

We split up, or, rather, I left him. It was bad. Those were difficult years for me, but I never gave my ex monthly reports on any of my impasses.

Then I became very ill; that's when Luisa, my colleague, the doctor from Chile, came into the picture. A celestial gift. However, my love for my brother was and is absolute. I don't know what will happen from now on with my exhausted body. Recently, I was glad to discover that here, in this long exile in which all we've had was each other, divided and at odds with one another as we are, he found a partner whom he deeply admires—Clizia. Is this true? They see each other daily it seems, in a mirific park called Eden. The resting place that became the location of their salutary meetings.

I'm not jealous, no, not at all. Rather, I'm resigned. It's likely that this relationship frees him at last of our secret pact, which had both comforted and burdened him for decades. I only want to know if this magical Clizia, whom he names—another one of his literary references!—the Jewish Beatrice, is real. I want to know if this Beatrice is real.

The signs I mentioned, which do not altogether bode well, made me write you. I'd be relieved if I knew that he's still keeping in touch with you and if you could confirm that our Nomad's new interlocutor is truly the proverbial gift he seems to have needed. I'd be especially grateful since it's very possible that the shadows that continue to assault me day after day, worse and worse, will finally succeed in doing away with me.

I thank you, fervently,

I embrace you, as I'd embrace my step- and not-altogether-step-brother,

Tamar.

Contrary to Hannah Arendt's opinion,[93] *unlike Charlie Chaplin, Heine is not at all a* schelemihl, a Taugenichts *(good for nothing) à la mode israélite. No, this character is a role among others, which Heine assumes so that others may shed a tear for his sad fate, since we read poetry to find emotions we may substitute for our own. Heine is not naïve, nor an innocent.* [. . .] *Moreover, Heine seems to subscribe to the following saying:* will alle Deutsche sind doch wahre Peter Schlemihle (Die Nordsee III, p. 223), *or "all of us, Germans, are the true Peter Schlemihls."*[94]

The term "exile" takes its meaning from the Latin exilium, which literally means "outside this place." [. . .] Before all else, what is lost is one's familiar space. [. . .] The place towards which the exile heads takes on greater importance than the place he has left behind. That "other place" of home counterbalances the "outside this place" of exile. [. . .] The acceptance of an irreversible departure bestows a rebel's mindset on the exile.

When he begins to write down his impressions from his long stay on the shores of the Danube, where he had been sent by Augustus for his poem on the nature of love, Ovid tries to find a practical wisdom in exile. He is surprised that former friendships begin to fade and that language fails to give him the necessary words to express his feelings, which confine him to a state of anxiety and obsession for that unique place, Rome. [. . .] Can a man born among the Latin world of the Caesars really be condemned to live among barbarous people? Captive in a hostile territory, Ovid at last resigns himself, consoling himself with the idea that he has been condemned to a relegatio[95] rather than an exilium [. . .] "[for] exile is, in part, a shipwreck. However, not every shipwreck necessarily ends in a drowning."

Edward Said asks himself in Réflexions sur l'exil, why, if exile is so painful, it has been so easily incorporated into modern culture, enriching it and becoming one of its dominant themes. Exile cannot be idealized. [. . .] Exile dehumanizes. There is no saving grace in becoming estranged from yourself. [. . .] Said points to the Jews, Palestinians, and Armenians as an example. When he becomes certain that he will never be able to return home again, the exile begins to create a new world for himself.

Most forms of nationalism begin with this feeling of estrangement arising from the feelings produced by exile.

It can be said that the shadow functions as the hidden face of a personality. It is like a faithful companion, like an external manifestation of inner life, like an echo of the original, that which separates one personality from another. In Adelbert von Chamisso's text, The Extraordinary Tale of Peter Schlemihl, the reason the main character's shadow disappears is ambiguous and is interpreted in contradictory ways. It eventually becomes the pretext for an endless series of encounters in which no one understands why Schlemihl acts the way he does, at least not until the end, when everything is finally revealed.

On the one hand, Chamisso's story can be read as a parable about the human condition after the Fall. The loss of the shadow can be compared to exile from Paradise, and Schlemihl's subsequent life to the long quest to regain Paradise (which, once attained, would bestow a new youthfulness on the human race).

On the other hand, it is possible to interpret the fairytale as a practical lesson about good behavior: don't chase after your own shadow, because you'll discover it to be a stand-in for the vanity of a world you should ignore if you want to have any chance at spiritual fulfillment. These two lessons are not contradictory. It is only necessary to identify the points in the story where one lesson is transformed into the other, when the frantic search for the shadow gives way to the desire to live without it, without the inner transformations that an exile must necessarily undergo.

This epic on the nature of the shadow ends with the conclusion's final lesson, which pits "living among men" against
"living for yourself." [. . .] Schlemihl is shown to be the victim of a process that he does not understand and that makes him
feel never "at home" in this world. He interprets the loss of his
shadow as the sign of the eternal unhappiness that exile produces. But Chamisso's Schlemihl is not just an "unlucky" person,
in the German sense of the word. He is also an individual who
transforms his fate into an opportunity, [. . .] into the chance
to become intellectually edified, despite the series of preceding
disappointments.

When Hannah Arendt compares Charlie Chaplin with Heinrich Heine's schlemihl, she does so in order to associate him to
a pariah, drawing on the metaphor of the Wandering Jew as an
alternative name for someone who is a cosmopolitan, and thus a
"suspect." However, the "suspect" is not just the beggar of whom
we're always suspicious, the individual who sets himself apart
from society by means of his unusual manner of life. He is also
someone who is set apart from the multitude who decides his fate
in advance, by separating him from his own history. When the
multitude jeers at an individual's past, that individual's shadow
is discredited. The individual is oppressed by the weight of the
crowd's incriminations. He can no longer decide how to live his
life. He no longer has the ability to transform his wandering or his
solitude into any form of social position, he falls prey to nostalgia.

In the end, Chamisso's Schlemihl desires to be unknown and
unknowable. He chooses to become invisible and so at once learns

much more about how to live. Applying this idea, the Schlemihl Complex can be used to diagnose those who have believed for too long in the power of the shadow. Chamisso's protagonist does not consider himself truly to lack a part of himself, that part which is usually considered essential. In fact, as if to counteract the despair of an Ovid, Chamisso's Schlemihl establishes a way forward that makes one concede that sometimes it is preferable not to have a shadow if you aspire to live according to your own ideas. The conclusion he reaches is that taking such a decision and living without a shadow would not be justified (in the eyes of the exile himself) if not for the nostalgia he must confront and the necessity of healing of his interior fissures before seeking any reconciliation with society-at-large.

—Olivier Remaud[96]

Dear Mr. Günther von Weissbrot,

I've hesitated for a long time before replying, unsure of who you might be, how you might have come across my name and address, why you might have chosen to write to me, and what you might want from me. To me, the explanation provided—that you wish to expand the scope of the documentation you are working on—seems an exaggeration. You describe the subject of this array of sources as "the Holocaust," but you might as well call it "Günther's Personal Papers," after the name you bear, to differentiate it from the vast archival material already available on the horror.

I have taken your advice and said nothing to the Misanthrope regarding our conversation. I waited for him to take up the matter you allude to in his own time. It's true, we did become friends. He doesn't seem to have many, nor is he easily stirred to self-disclosure. Slowly, he did become more open with me—body and soul. Somehow, I think you like that phrase. He entrusted me with the symbolic key to many of the events that make up his biography. You did not ask me whether I slept with your former friend or how it was, if I rose from that bed sick with pleasure or more self-aware than ever. I never answer questions that were never asked. I will, however, answer the questions that interest me. Those to which—let me be frank—I don't have an appropriate answer.

As for his relationship to Günther: what might have been, what remains between you. It might be said that you no longer have much in common, that you're no longer children. Childish you continue to be, that much I've understood. Each in your own way. Though neither does your disagreement in relation to the Holocaust damage what is left of your friendship, I don't think. One of you, the victim, the Jew, never talks about it; the other, the German, considers himself ethnically complicit with the murderers. Though it's a watered-down ethnicity, rusty; a German of the Germans who have lived in Romanian exile for hundreds of years. Who in the end might be considered already a Romanian himself. Moreover, German guilt isn't what it was a few decades ago; that's the argument of the Germans, to whom, if I understand correctly, you belong, despite having lived for so long in the Romanian Banat region. It's a guilt that should be reconsidered. How? In light of this subsequent attitude. Guilt remains guilt, though, if it is acknowledged and consciously lived through by posterity, it can introduce a new element into the equation: an educational, perhaps religious one, tied in fact to the religion of those who were murdered, which tells us, as

I recently found out from your former friend, that no one has the right to forgive in the name of another. The dead are mute and far away. In any case, the public assumption of guilt is already an enormous step forward, toward Christian forgiveness, which is asked of all of us. In no way have I ever been involved in this tragedy, but I followed the post '68 German debates intently, as a young activist and daughter of my anti-Fascist (though never communist) father. In Berlin I saw the plaques denoting the former homes of the martyrs who were burned alive at Auschwitz. I was deeply moved by this pride, I'd call it an egotistical, self-critical pride, which continues to seem necessary to Germans even today. Especially today.

Is Schlemihl the shadow of his reader? Or have you, Günther, become the shadow of your former friend whom you appear to be obsessed with? Or, following the logic of the poor people living under surveillance in socialism, who each believed they had a double, a paid shadow who was part of the ubiquitous Securitate, are you perhaps the shadow of the Informant? Of the security services, the dreaded Securitate? Or are you Posterity's informant, as our friend seems to think, distrusting both the ever after and the present?

Unsure of the truth, I was willing to talk to you, hoping that you'd slip up and betray yourself. It has not happened yet. A true informant never makes a slip. The Nomad taught me that . . .

Nevertheless, I'm still curious. Perhaps it's because of my hunger for knowledge, for life.

It was also curiosity that drew me into a relationship with your Pioneer friend, beside whom I stand open-mouthed, waiting for this biblical Nomad's next surprise. He's become a skeptic. Indifferent. Though, in the meantime, I, too, have gotten mixed up in these ridiculous matters. These ravings—the shadow and Schlemihl and the all-powerful circus. Maybe it makes up for a lack, or lacks, fills a hole. Time seems to be embodied, like my own life, and I am grateful to him. It's not just that, of course, it's much more, barring professions of faith. I'm not capable of the that, it's not in my nature, which is intractable and slippery.

To sum up. I had no idea who you were and why you decided to choose me as an accomplice. I did not say anything to the Misanthrope, I merely prodded him to tell me more about his childhood and communism's childish ideals . . . After a long and tacitly agreed-upon period of waiting, I finally managed to become his confidante. And—to appeal to formal definitions—his lover, his bedfellow, his nocturnal nymph. To a man who is neither very young, nor very outgoing. Hence, it has not been a very active relationship, though a pleasant one. A seasonal lover, nothing more, taking the place of his absent sister. His destiny's sister: irreplaceable. We're all jealous, aren't we? His sister is more than a sister. He spoke to me of the Pioneer camp when he was thirteen and of his friendship with the instructor, Günther, who, as impromptu censor, had agreed to read the letters of the red-scarf teenagers to their parents. To check if they met the requirements: don't tell your parents anything about the polio epidemic. They had all been terrified of that new, invisible enemy to the proletarian cause. I understand that, even as an adult, you're still that impassioned, insistent, and blindly faithful Pioneer, this being the real reason the Misanthrope ended his friendship with you.

You must know, of course, that he's become an incurable skeptic regarding the ability of the human species to better itself. He had studied and continues to study the history of the circus, allowing himself to be charmed by the caricatures of those who surround us, both the funny and the tragic ones. To him it must seem the only possible response to this tragicomedy of vanity. He has not yet convinced me of the appropriateness of this position, though we are close, as you intuited. Nevertheless, despite being unconvinced, I've become his representative, a stand-in for him in his absence, his withdrawal into his incurable solitude.

Here, we come to the Schlemihl, his friend from long ago, his current friend. He, too, is an unwilling buffoon, if we think carefully about his successes and failures. Both ridiculous! You are correct in thinking that Schlemihl's ghost is a faithful companion of his; he sees in the exile Peter an example of today's subservience to money. He constantly reminds me that Jesus, the fictitious savior of humanity—that's what he says, "a fictitious savior"—was aware of the very human day-to-day life in long-ago Jerusalem, when he overturned the tables of the moneylenders and drove them away along with their shady business. Another not very funny circus . . . My friend, or should I say, our friend, found in Schlemihl an imaginary companion. He had the yellow booklet with him when the socialist guard confiscated it at freedom's border. Having arrived in the capitalist paradise without that travel guide, he found another copy. I don't think you gathered how important that famous botanist's fairytale was to him. Charmed by the circus and its clowns, our Misanthrope is the advocate for them and for all the exiles of the world. Beginning with Adalbert von, whom you well know. Another convert to Berlin, as you, my own correspondent, Günther, was forced to be.

Money and money again; we have daily proof of this irresistible trick. It's one of vanity's ubiquitous and highly efficient talismans, which works both on children and on those of all ages. That's what our Misanthrope maintains, and he's right. There's still no solution. A smart guy, our Nomad. He understands and is silent. Silence, his most powerful weapon. I can only draw him out of it with difficulty, even I . . . with my womanly charms. I confess, they're not always effective. The magnet between my legs isn't as new as it used to be, what can I do. Though it's not ready for the junk heap, not yet, anyway . . .

I suppose that it's for these all-too-human details that you've written to me four times. The pretext, of course, was to inquire about your friend's health and successes. But, now that I've responded, let me respond to this manipulation, too: that dear man is no longer what he used to be. He has a cane like a crippled man, scratched glasses, friends at the pharmacy. Yes, he says that pills are the only thing he has left, his only trusty friends, always there for him. But he's alive, I swear; I stay with him out of love, which is not always the same thing as being in love. I've learned a lot from him. From his biography, not just his bibliography. I would never leave him for an American, I've had enough of them.

The Nomad is a unique specimen, the Man Without Qualities!

Perhaps you've never read Musil, his favorite author. I was only able to swallow the first volume of the trilogy. Rather bookish and lewd. But engrossing, I concede that.

We live in constant hunger for each other, I swear. Both discrete, taciturn, intertwined, moribund. In constant despair, chiefly in our childish embrace which is wordless and soundless. He often makes sarcastic jokes, as is his habit, and I try to match them with my cosmopolitan glibness. I tell you these things in preparation for the words that will end our chatty conversation.

Here, at the end, a message for his sister. She keeps asking him to join her. He insists that I get to know her, maybe so that she'd finally be convinced that he's landed on his feet. Between someone's feet! It matters, yes, especially if one is rheumatic and needs to keep warm. I don't want to know her, it makes no sense to speak with ghosts. I'm well aware that eventually he'll return to her when the bell tolls. I only want to warn her: the apple of our eyes doesn't want a funeral. He no longer wants one! He's lived long enough in the country of all possibilities, where each individual is entitled to his own opinion and choice. And to personal happiness. He doesn't want a coffin or a grave. She must get used to the idea. Accept it, not try to negotiate with him about it, because he'll give in, as he always does. He wants to be cremated, burned, and that's that. I think the word crematorium gives him life. It seems the best option to him. I say this only as a joke. A sinister joke. So, she, his better half, the shadow Tamar from the camps, or Musil's shadow from books, or what have you, will not be able to share his coffin as they had planned and sworn on a midsummer's night.

He's changed his mind. The Nomadic Misanthrope has changed his mind, and it's his right to do so! My lover prefers something else and is prepared to argue for his right.

Says that she should understand, feel the long reach of that option. Because they were burned alive on the same pyre.

Essentially, that's the message. Maybe our conversation hasn't been useless after all.

In short, here are a few answers to the questions that have tormented you.

In friendship,

Eva

THE POTENCY OF THE SUNSET

A weekly walk through the woods, always concluding with a meal at the Turkish restaurant. Nighttime encourages conversation. They would go to bed late, embracing like siblings. He would take care of the morning, waking up first, taking a shower, and returning with two large black coffees.

On the kitchen table the notebook was always open to the same page. "Man is a shadow's dream"—Pindar. Further down, a quote from Giorgio Agamben's book, *The Time That Remains: A Commentary on the Letter to the Romans,* with a note scribbled nervously in blue pencil: "For St. Paul, shadows are the earthly prefigurations of the divine truth."

The days with Eva were followed by those without her. The Nomad was bewildered by solitude and the telephone's matching hostility. It had grown silent forever. Tamar no longer answered his calls. Neither today, nor yesterday, nor the day before yesterday, the daytime or nighttime, the morning or evening. He had the habit of calling on Friday evenings and would answer any call on the first ring, never complaining. Preferred an unhurried conversation, the unspoken signs of affection. His voice had aged recently, there were long, questionable pauses. The Nomad would be unable to make a sound. Regardless of what he might try, there was no way of correcting this.

In the end, Eva intervened. "Why don't you go to her if you're so set on it, go on. The old and new curse has gotten the better of you. I'll come along if you think it will help." After a few days, without any further questions to him, Eva bought two round trip tickets and took him to the airport.

It was raining heavily. The clouds were furious, exploding in black spasms. The airport, then another airport, a taxi, then the impervious front door. He searched his pockets and finally found the key. The door suddenly became welcoming, as long ago, and stepping through he saw the crumpled-up note on the table: "See you soon in the vastness of distance!" The paper stiffened, the thunder came more frequently, left him breathless. His shirt was wet, as were his hands and his bald spot. Noah's flood had found its final victim. "You were right. Our love has been the highest possible form of love for another." Desert, cold, fear. Further down, Luisa's name and telephone number . . . Should he call Luisa? Her, of all people . . . Destiny seemed to be beating him hard, ceaselessly, without any . . . And then vertigo.

A melodious voice. "Yes, it's me." Cold. A timid, truncated, tremulous volume: "Next year I'm going to have a baby girl. Named after her." Cosmic fury, devilish, demonic, demented rain screaming across the gutters. Had Tamar been given up to the clutches of old, blind Noah, the archangel of the deluge of garbage and horror? The end of the world! In the end, an end! A prodigious, wild explosion.

"No, no, you don't understand. Suicide! They ruled it a suicide! Reality, the eternal enemy . . . you should have guessed. Haven't you known for a long time? The abiding enemy. You stayed between book covers, suffocating, buried alive, you lost the thread long ago, very long ago, before you ever lost your sister . . .

"Suicide, you hear me? Free at last, you hear me? Your ears work, do you hear the thunder? Has the thunder finally gotten through to you?"

An infinite moment, as long as the apocalypse itself. The dead man mumbled the lament of loss, exhausted, extended, unfeeling on the incestuous bed, under the hidden death's head. The final cold. I've brought with me the desert, my sister, my own desert, which should have been our own. You called to me, and I came. Curse and blessing. The well-known, devious, lying reality. The macabre, murderous darkness of the Hooked Cross. The hatred that never left us alone. The poisonous, necessary initiation, the forever damned concentration camp to which we pay perpetual rent. My wandering through the book from which I couldn't part . . . Incest? Agatha, our code name, didn't interest you, nor were you willing to connect with the exile Schlemihl, or with the destiny of those who have no shadow or ideology—those like him and me. The only one of my accomplices you consented to was the mysterious, transcendental snail.

"Our love was an orphan's whimper," that's what you used to say. Should I call Herr Musil on the intergalactic phone? Would Herr Robert Musil untangle the Gordian knot, or would he only give it shade and substance?

———

He fell asleep, having returned defeated from the shore that fell away into the darkness, not having found the slippery liminal place, the bank, finding himself again curled up beneath the sacred, sovereign rain. Proof that the madness continued and would continue forever, infinitely, in the hazy infinity where the new queen of light, Tamar, reigned. The eternal, everlasting, all-powerful sister, inexhaustible in her childish charms, stronger than poor, old dame Reality covered with sores.

The guards were in their places, as in the Death Camps. In his sleep, the prisoner begged his sister to answer, she who was rocked in the waters of the ocean. The rain gurgled forth the celestial call, Tamar knew and took part, as long ago.

Under the sounds of fraternal rain, the Nomad mumbled alone for two days. Sunset became dawn but the answer did not come, or came, had come, was at the door and had a voice ready to tame the senile old frog. The night had uncharmed all its doors, murmured an almost shy beginning, or no, no, it was only the failed attempt of the wind to take part where it had no business and found nothing of interest. A seasonal putting on of airs, that was all. And yet, there it was, the scratching of a hound. Death holds a golden key even for a rusty, senile lock, like the Nomad's mind, for all the fictional locks. In a moment, he will be in his sister's—the angel's—bedchamber.

It was Eva, who would have thought it, not sleep, nor Tamar, it was Eva standing before him speaking in the dream's voice. "I was sure you were here! I found the address on the envelope with those two identical keys. Here I am, your personal emergency service! To save you, I'm the only one who can wake you up from this, I'm the only one left. There's no other way out. War veteran. Now saved. Queen Sisi saves the one who wanders in the clouds, walks in books." Her hands were cold and satiny, as Lifesaving Services demanded, and her voice, too, followed the rules imposed in the case of emergencies and life-and-death situations.

"Open your eyes, let in reality. Eva wins again. The defense mechanisms are useless, nothing can defend you, you are in salvation's grip, as you were destined to be long ago, since forever, no literary trick can protect you, no avoidance tactic remove you, no, not a single one, you remain the captive you've always been, and you will open your bookish infant's eyes and come to know the inevitable.

"Know and submit, you cannot be asleep forever, not yet, not yet, Tamar is waiting and will wait for you as long as it takes, as she always has."

The somnambulist moved, and the spell was broken at dawn. He could no longer refuse, no, no he could not, the satiny hands gripped him, there was no escape. "You'll feel like yourself again soon, that's how children are, even old children, there is no escaping it. Already, one eye open, you can no longer hide in your dead faint," the bony hands grip the satiny hands of the savior, the bewildered man rests in agony's arms.

Eva tidied, opened the windows and the armoire with drawers where everything had its set place. On the second day, the student Eva had hired to pack up the books, letters, citizenship and divorce papers appeared. The eradication of an individual biography and the shipping of the relics to Berlin, to comrade Günther, took three days. Everything came to an end, ended for the time being, until the following ninth of July, when the ritual for the reunion with Tamar would be repeated on her birthday, as the pair had established when they had promised to never separate even though they had to part.

The nomadic brother was already on the steps of the plane. He was returning to the land of the living, to the caves of a cannibalistic reality from which he would never free himself.

HINENI

Rather than returning home from the concert, the poet stands glued to the spot in front of the Czernowitz Armenian Church, gripped in his exchange with the Divine.

"*Hineni,* here I am!" the poet repeats, a statement made more than eight hundred times in the Hebrew Bible, the answer to a question that exiles have been asked for millennia. The fact that it is answered in front of an Armenian church and not a synagogue, as one might have expected, attests to a pious expansion of the old covenant. We find the statement in the conversation between Abraham and the Omnipotent, before the sacrifice of Isaac is to take place, as well as in the conversation between Moses and God in front of the pyre—or burning bush—always underscoring the absolute obedience of the believer.

"*Hineni,* here I am!" finds multiple echoes in the Bible. It is the prayer that the poet, transfigured, repeated during the night of his celestial encounter, to the stupefaction of the audience scattered in the darkness. He will repeat it, again and again, at the core of each poem. It is not only a mystical reaffirmation but also the highest justification for poetry.

The fact that God himself has been exiled, as some commentaries on the sacred texts attest, humanizes the divine presence wandering among His worshippers. (If man is conceived in the image and likeness of God, exile's contradictions are no longer irresolvable.)

In the Parisian night, Paul Celan converses with his guest, the Polish poet Zbigniew Herbert, silently, the sacred illumination of speechlessness overspreading both writers. Both would recall their long hours of silent companionship as the most extraordinary of adventures. The Bukovinean poet would repeat the miracle of the night he shared with his fraternal wanderer during many of his nocturnes in exile, in Bucharest, Vienna, and Paris. The Seine waited for him, as did the infinite waters of uncertainty.

In the end, Celan would throw himself into the jaws of the watery abyss, consecrating his lyrically tormented covenant. It is not at all certain that his tenebrous destiny found its final resolution in this way, but the denouement confirmed an inevitable spiritual sacrifice.

Transnistria. Was it salvation, through a mother's death, from everything that might have been and was no longer allowed?

> "*Do you hear me? Do you hear me, Tamar?*"
> *The abyss's answer fulfilled in death.*

"Do you hear? Do you hear me, Tamar?"
The phantom's echo, the abyss's answer,
the ravaged waves, waters of the last twinning,
suffering and solitude,
black and uncertain the curse of silence.

Vain to take refuge, young Pesach, *in the breath of the old Kaddish.*
The tragedy of a final burning, Holocaust, spectacle,
free ticket to posterity,
the shadow of the sacrificial Jew watches.

Pesach? *The word led straight to the gas.*
Don't forget anything, don't forget death.
You are Paul now. Holiest Paul,
meaning Pesach, the millenary,
in the dark corner of the Greek synagogue,
at the crucifixion of the great transgressor, Yehoshua,
in the church of the new religion of the saved.
Hineni, *here I am. No eschewing*
believers and enemies,
heretics and killers of the Most Holy,
transfigured nuns and desert fathers in trances,
poets seeking the shore,
the Bukovinean migrant Celan
with his compass good for the global workshop of sacred
   reparations,
suitable for the next procession
of the exiled without documents and domicile.

A prolonged pause is the silence,
in the fog of the pseudo-divine desert.

The voice of no one, a first step
towards conversation?
The shadow leads to self-seeking,
to the belief in a repeated interrogation,
the rhyme, the meeting of the poet
with himself in the sovereign dusk of incertitude.

Tamar! Hineni, Hineni!
I am here, still here, exhausted and culpable,
the poet flings his plume to his forbearers
bleeding, still bleeding
in the mass grave long as the whole world,
wide as the world's cemetery.

"Look around:
See how things all come alive—
By death! Alive!
Speaks true who speaks shadow."[97]
"Near are we, Lord,
near and graspable.
Grasped already, Lord,
clawed into each other, as if
each of our bodies were
your body, Lord.
Pray, Lord."[98]

Celan in mourning looks for links,
returning, repeating the fragment born in hesitation,
from a slaughtered mother, the adored, slaughtered mother.
A black and mute, cracked sky

ravenous for tragedy.
In the shadow of the lost,
the exile transcribes the murmur of the puddle of blood,
fresh, always refreshed by the gloom.
Hineni? *An arrow suddenly brought back*
from the dead, in the zenith
of the murderous chaos.

Hineni? *Where are you? Tamar?*
We are here where destiny has forgotten us,
shadows walking and talking,
difficult to despoil, impossible to despoil.
We are here, here for ages, forever,
the storm does not defeat us, nor the biblical curse,
we are here,
with our childish, uninterrupted cries
continuous, without a cure.
We murmur desperation, the whimper Tamar,
the biblical sister beneath the prodigious wave.

Yes, the light of the lonely world,
liquid, enchanted nights,
a moment's lost tears repeating in trance
brother Pesach, brother Paul,
they have found you, in the flood they have found you,
in the Seine they have found you, deathless phantom.

Here, together, in night's watery cemetery,
at last, brothers of the endless moment
drunkenly, the green wave returns the celestial dusk.

THE COLLOQUIUM (I)

It had been an usual day in the gentle autumn light. Without any real reason, he had grown more tired. A sort of lethargy, a kind of let me be so I'll let you be. The morning visit to Eden had been shorter than usual. The silence of the morbid paradise weighed on him, he had withdrawn quickly toward eternity's gravestones. The solemn, solitary trees, the snails making their slow and languorous rounds. Sunset had found him on a bench in front of the central dorms. A building in the style of British colleges of a century or more ago. Classes hadn't yet started, the campus was empty. Silence. He closed his eyes, felt anesthetized. Yes, he had been lucky: little by little, his wanderings had offered him calm and resignation. The light was fading, the sunset offered itself up in a kind of perverse harmony. He was no longer sure. He felt a presence next to him and opened his eyes: no one. Again, just the same: no one.

After a time, his invisible neighbor's tricks no longer worked: he appeared! Tall, bony, in a leather jacket, a silver medallion around his neck. Small head, bushy, black hair. Large, indolent eyes. He guessed—suspected—that appearance but did not look at his neighbor. He stared straight ahead, toward the horizon. Could he speak to him? Would he answer?

"I've waited for you for a long time. I was afraid of our meeting," the professor murmured.

Absolute silence, no answer. The stranger refused to speak, as if he didn't feel the weight and offensive nature of his presence.

"You said that you'd lost—meaning sold—your shadow. For a bag of money that only brought your trouble."

Silence, absence, emptiness. He no longer knew if his interlocutor was there, next to him, or hidden among the graves. He didn't have the courage to look at the narrow bench, to convince himself that he was alone once again. He continued to look into the distance, toward the inaccessible horizon, and to speak to himself if there was no other way. Was his guest deaf and dumb?

"I lost her, too, though not entirely. I gave her up at the border, in exchange for a new home. Freedom's home. And yes, I won . . . Not money, I don't have money. But freedom, yes. Relative, as freedom always is. I had known it even then, when I left Comrade Colonel Tudor. Then at the airport, when they searched me, just in case I was carrying instructions to build the atomic bomb. Naturally, they found nothing. The only thing they took was my little yellow booklet by Mr. Chamisso."

The stranger continued to refuse to answer.

"I'm honored that we've found each other again here."

His Honorable Holiness Peter did not move, had not come back to life. He, too, was gazing into the distance, into the void, he did not know that someone was sitting next to him, on the same bench.

"I'm happy that you're here," the professor insisted.

Beginning to be annoyed, in the moment that followed, he turned, at last, toward the intruder who—behold!—had disappeared. He had disappeared just in time, again, without providing any answer. Humiliated by the farce?

"Wandering is not just a catastrophe. That's what I wanted

to tell you. It is also potentiality, it's worth trying. Though I know that everything I tell you, you already know. But it is important that you listen to me. That you contradict me, so that I can learn something from your neuroses."

On the following day, again no one. Nor on the one that followed. The Nomad did not manage to encounter his conversation partner again, though he waited a good few hours for him, on the same bench.

It was only on a Thursday afternoon, again toward sunset, that the professor felt a shadow in his vicinity once more. He didn't have the courage to look, to see if his guest had truly reappeared. He had frozen in the same stance of waiting, looking into the distance, toward nowhere.

"I went to the meeting," the stranger whispered evasively. More of a nightmare than a dream. A confidential meeting with Mr. Schlemihl, the shadow. "Was this what you hoped for? Well, it finally happened. I went through this, as through so many other things. Dressed to the nines, however, and preceded by the eulogy given by a renowned botanist and poet who was a friend. Friend? What am I saying. The Author, in fact, that much even I understood. You won't believe who was in the audience."

Without any warning, the guest had slipped into a more formal mode of address, the second person plural. It meant that he was adhering to protocol and could become more daring.

"I am a new researcher in genetics," the professor heard the thin, squeaky voice of the shadow coming from his left. "Dogs are faithful, cats are sly, elephants are family-oriented.

I even know about parrots and fish. I'm not interested in human beings, or no longer interested, not since I listened to Schlemihl. He gave an absolutely convincing speech. This was Monsieur Ionesco's opinion, too. Even the depressive Cioran was nodding along. Even the pathetic Fondane, freshly returned from Auschwitz, still pallid and confused. Many of your fellow Romanians were there. Meaning, your former co-citizens. Before your wanderings."

And who else participated? The professor didn't have the courage to ask.

"Well, many exiles did. It was a subversive meeting, that's what I was told. Mr. Nabokov attended, Sir Joyce, Herr Mann with his brother, Herr Brecht, and Brodsky. Celan, the Bukovinean who became a shadow, held his pills tightly in his fist splotched with rashes. The talkative Quasimodo kept interrupting. Many Spanish who had been driven away by Franco were there. Weak, the whole lot of them, and tired, aged, drained of strength. And a few ladies, yes. Your sister, Tamar, who would not accept being called anything but Agatha—even I made the mistake. She was with an elderly woman, Ms. Irma, the poet and muse of the Italian poet, the college's former Italian teacher. She no longer had the sparkle or freshness she had at her burial, when she was lowered, carefully and adoringly, into Eden's basement. And Lispector, the Brazilian from Ukraine, arm in arm with old Neruda and old Lampedusa. Followed by the Armenians, the Turk Hikmet, the ancient Ovid, and that ballerina who wrote verses, I've forgotten her name, I didn't even recognize her—the ruin she had become. A lot of the beau monde. I was nearly done in with emotion. I might have hidden in shame, but I had to see and hear, so that I'd have something to report."

Hearing these words, the professor took courage, come what may, and turned to face the squeaky voice, convinced that no one was there. But there he was, behold, the ghost had not disappeared. The young man with the equivocal smile and a yellow shirt that said "University of Iowa" in large gold letters was wearing red shorts. Large feet, shoeless, hair that had been dyed scarlet, a small, green backpack.

"I've been waiting for a long time, but I was afraid of this torment," the old man confessed.

"Yes, yes, I understand," the youth murmured.

The grayness of the dusk scattered the light, but the voice continued invisibly.

"I see that you've adapted to the new banality."

The Iowan silhouette dimmed, then suddenly flew away with the magical boots of the fairytale. The professor was used to the magic of transatlantic flight, he no longer marveled at anything, but he couldn't resist asking the air his question.

"Have you kept in touch with the Colonel? Colonel Toma or Tudor, I'm sure you remember."

"No, I didn't fall into that trap."

The voice had grown thicker, viscous.

"Too bad, you might have learned a lot. He's set things up for himself, he's a rich man now. An import-export agent! An important figure in the transition period, the one toward the democracy of prosperity. Newly minted prosperity, more valuable than the Party's fourragères. As you can see, the match can be won even at home, not just in exile."

"The proud little gnome who smoked Kents?"

"He no longer smokes anything. He follows medical advice, takes good care of himself. But he still keeps a collection of expensive cigars. Even poor Tess gave us something of a surprise, after she returned with her darling to her native shores, which she feared so much."

"Tell me, please tell me, I'm actually very interested in this. I know that you became depressed on account of that depressed lady."

"I did and I continue to be, uncertain of what my former friend, the one I played basketball with, got me mixed up in. I felt guilty for having avoided the unsavory couple. Tess, the shy, solitary, neurotic, delicate woman who had escaped the lair of murderers without being able to forget them. My former rugby or basketball friend told me recently that the Dictator always had a special plane—donated by the Americans—ready to go if he needed to save himself. There was no more time. They asked him to bring his former daughter-in-law with him, the un-Jewish Jewess, with her little innocent babe still drinking his mother's milk. They needed them in the West, naturally. Tess, the innocent, caught forever in the cursed snare of religion? If the half-wit, the ghostly son, had managed to get a scholarship, an academic diploma as his mama wished, everything would have turned out differently and just as poorly. But now he's on his last legs. Tess has metastatic cancer and refuses to see a doctor. The forty-year-old son can't let go of his mother's hand, day or night, come what may, even the apocalypse. They both carry the ancestral virus of the cursed people from whom they tried to free themselves. A complicated tale, perhaps we'll untangle it sometime, but I'm tired now."

Tired and tireless, entangled, untangled. He had disappeared.

GÜNTHER'S PERSONAL PAPERS

The late medieval story of Fortunatus [. . .] *is thought of as an ancestor of the modern novel for its realistic accounts of people, events, and places.* Fortunatus *unfolds a profoundly moral and thought-provoking view of the world, illustrating the problems that the possession of great wealth is apt to bring and how human desires untempered by reason can lead to self-destruction.*

Peter Schlemihl, *like* Fortunatus, *has aspects that could appeal to children, but it primarily embodies unsettling questions about alienation and identity that belong indubitably to the province of adulthood. However, some of these anxieties were put back into the sphere of childhood by Hans Andersen in his story "The Shadow," which was clearly influenced by Chamisso's tale.* [. . .] *The story, like Kafka's* Metamorphosis, *depends on a single event that transgresses reason, before and after which the narrative proceeds in a perfectly matter-of-fact manner until a further element of fantasy—the accidental acquisition of seven-league boots—comes in at the end.* [. . .] *The fictive Peter Schlemihl addresses his story to his friend Chamisso, whom he addresses five times as Chamisso and twice as Adelbert in the course of the narrative. The story also refers explicitly to Fouqué's* Der Zauberring (The Magic Ring) *of 1813, which Schlemihl dreams is lying on Chamisso's desk, along with the works of Haller, Humboldt, Linné, and a volume of Goethe.* Der Zauberring *was the latest novel of Chamisso's friend Fouqué, while Albrecht von Haller, Alexander von Humboldt, and Carl von Linné were among the leading scientists of the day. Indeed, the various scientific works that Schlemihl declares himself to have writ-*

ten at the end of the book probably represent a kind of homage to Humboldt's explorations and publications in the field of geography and botany. [. . .] The suggestion that Schlemihl's manuscripts will be deposited in the University of Berlin on his death is a graceful acknowledgment of the very recent founding of the University by Alexander's brother, Wilhelm.

Goethe may well present the synthesis of science and literature with the unnamed volume from his extensive works. We may imagine that volume to be the first part of Faust, published in 1808, with its Mephistopheles stalking anonymously through the pages of Peter Schlemihl. But the man in the grey coat is more urbane than the figure of the wandering scholar in whose guise Mephistopheles first appears in Faust, though his grey coat may recall the diabolical grey monk who first fills that role in the sixteenth-century Historia von D. Johann Fausten. [. . .] The man in the grey coat offers Schlemihl a choice of typical fairy-tale devices, among which feature the magic napkin of Roland's squires (referring to a Volksbuch that Musäus also refashioned), a mandrake (probably alluding to a story by Foqué), and the wishing-cap and magic purse of Fortunatus. Chamisso thus cleverly splices the fairytale world with popular literature of the day.

The fact that many features of Schlemihl's story reflect key aspects of Chamisso's own life has led to an understandable, but unfortunate emphasis on biographical interpretations of the story, but Chamisso himself was careful to avoid answering questions about the meaning of the story's symbolism.

The author's introduction comes in the form of a letter written by Chamisso to his friend Julius Eduard Hitzig, another member of the literary circle in Berlin that included Fouqué and Hoffman. *The letter declares the work to have been put into Chamisso's hands by "A strange man with a long gray beard, wearing a black worn-out* kurtka, *with a botanical case suspended at his side, and slippers over his boots, on account of the damp, rainy weather, who inquired after me, and left these papers behind him. He pretended he came from Berlin." This letter figures in most editions of Chamisso's story and forms part of the playfulness of the story itself, claiming factuality for something that is transparently a fiction. Hitzig, in a letter to Fouqué dated January 1827, describes how, when he first read Schlemihl to Hoffman, the latter "was beside himself with delight and eagerness, and hung upon my lips till I got to the end." Hoffman's reaction not only displays his own affinity to Chamisso as a writer, but is a splendid testimony to the inherent fascination of the story.*[99]

THE COLLOQUIUM (II)

A normal day, gentle and autumnal. In Eden, the silence of a morbid paradise. The gravestones, the impassive trees, the deaf and dumb solitary snails. The sunset had found him again on a bench, next to Irma. Irma's shadow. Irma, the ghost. The professor waited for his interlocutor, sure that he, too, was impatient to continue the conversation, which had ended on a touchy point. He shut his eyes and was numb. Surely the urgency with which he waited and invoked his guest would at last produce him.

After many days, he finally felt the neighborly presence close by, but did not have the courage to check. He shut his eyes, opened them, reality confirmed it: the stranger seemed to be close by; he, too, preoccupied by Clizia's gravestone.

"You're Schlemihl, aren't you?" the professor dared to force destiny into speech.

He turned his head in a weary manner, certain that the vampire would disappear. He didn't.

A tall and bony young man. A leather jacket and short boots. The silver medallion around his neck. Long, bushy hair.

"Do you remember where we broke off our conversation?"

Silence, as he had expected.

"I was afraid of meeting you, though I've gotten more used to the idea recently. I'm honored by our meeting."

He continued to look off into the distance, ready to continue the much-delayed discussion.

"Wandering is always something you have to try for yourself. It's not just a catastrophe, and you know this. All options deserve close examination. It's important that you listen to me, that you contradict me even, so that I can learn from your silences and your secrets."

They were sitting in the same place, on the bench, in the uncertainties of dusk. He wasn't in a hurry, he didn't have any reason to be, didn't have any reason to be pleased by what was happening. Evening was beginning to envelop the landscape. He glimpsed the shirt with the large red letters proclaiming "University of Iowa." Shorts, red hair dyed scarlet, a small hiking backpack.

"My wandering's gift to me was your shadow. A guide, I'd call it."

The young Iowa man nodded, and the bright red forelock nodded along, approvingly.

"Let's continue our discussion about wanderers. It's not mere chance that, at the sanatorium that bears your name, they gave you that other certain name. It wasn't just about your appearance. Though I didn't understand what bothered you about it, why you then ran away from your cursed identity. Or why you now complain about the miseries your fellow men caused you. Have you seen Cioran? He used to maintain that it's an honor to be repudiated, exiled, rejected. And Mr. Fundoianu, by the way, Mr. Fondane-Fundoianu Wechsler, said something even more fantastic. You didn't mention him as a guest at the lecture. Perhaps you haven't even heard of him. His name is on the Auschwitz monument! Benjamin Wechsler and his sister, whom he couldn't part from. And then there is another certain someone who can't part from his sister . . . "

The stranger was smiling thinly. He shifted his backpack and put it down next to him on the bench. He turned condescendingly toward his contentious conversation partner.

"I know something about these creatures. Not too much. I'm in the Genetics Department at the university. As I've told you before: dogs are faithful, cats are sly, elephants are family-oriented. I also know about parrots and fish. Less about human beings. They don't really interest me."

"That's a mistake. A big one! A big mistake. They're the most interesting of God's creatures."

"God?"

"Fine, fine, the Goddess's. Nature's, rather. Let's get back to Benjamin. The poet Fondane-Fundoianu was not ashamed of his identity. *'Ulysses, you're a Jew,'* he used to curse in the dark. *'You're a Jew, Ulysses!'* he once shouted on a sacred Friday, after Mr. Cioran had left, who also pretended to be a metaphysical Jew. '*Did you hear that?! Metaphysical!*' But if you're not also physical, it's useless, you can't understand anything from all this debacle. There you have it, that's metaphysics . . . how can you go on living in this pretentious farce . . . "

Suddenly, his neighbor's breath cut out, along with his squeaky voice. Again there was no one next to him! An empty place! The yellow shirt and the green backpack had disappeared along with the young Iowa man. Find him there, take him here. Nowhere. But the monologue continued.

Much later he heard: "Nevertheless, let me ask you a question. I have a question."

The question wasn't forthcoming, however. The old, lonely man's need to converse seemed pointless; he didn't have anyone to speak to, nor anyone to answer him. The Iowa silhouette had disappeared into the void, along with his magic boots of transatlantic flight. The Nomad had learned not to be surprised by anything anymore; earthly or heavenly wonders no longer made any impression on him. He alone was responsible for the questions and answers. He was talking to himself, let's not stare at him. He was waiting for the return of Schlemihl, the student, and was preparing for their meeting by talking to himself, or to the walls.

"Do you think I'm responsible for the rumors regarding the legend of Schlemihl, the moony Jew with his head in the clouds? You shouldn't think that, even children know the legend. And not just the children of Hitzig, the lawyer. My only sin is that I got involved in the dispute about the history of the circus, in all that talk about the buffoon who maligned the memory of Saint Peter. Regardless of whether we like it or not, at a certain point, he too was among the sidelocked wanderers. Until he got his act back together again. His actions already of a Christian nature . . . It's true, like an idiot I got involved in that business about clowns, maintaining that it was possible that von Chamisso had thought of that hypothesis. Many of his friends came from nomadic lineages. He even wrote about them sympathetically. A philo-Semite, despite his noble heritage. How could it be otherwise? All unexpectedly specterlike: you come out of nowhere, Herr Schlemihl! We're not told where you hail from, nor who you are, whom you've left behind, why you ran from one place to another without any clear coordinates. A suspect, a perennial suspect. No readily available documentation regarding your God or your creed. It would have mattered, could have been essential. Let's just tell it like it is: it would have been the only identifying element that mattered. Even today, for many it is still the only real form of identity. So, not a single word about this, you keep your little mouth shut. But the greed for gold, who is that supposed to represent? Who is quick to give up not just his shadow but even his shirt for a bag of gold? A fiendish bag, a perpetuum mobile that produces coins and newly printed banknotes, what else is there to add! Who are we talking about here? What do you think, Mr. Schlemihl Iowa?"

Schlemihl Iowa continued to absent himself, and Professor Nomad continued to converse with himself. He did so as if he were a long-ago Schlemihl, and a present-day Schlemihl, and a future one, of all times and all places.

"Are you going to accuse me of hating my wandering brothers? Or, quite the opposite, insist that I feel solidarity with them? What do you think? I've gotten used to both situations. I don't plead for anything or anyone anymore; like any misanthrope, I am simply participating in a logical, objective debate. Any legal mind would confirm it. All it is is a kind of memorandum to my reading habits, that's all! And the Bible is just a book! That's all, just a book. That's how I read it, that's how I've written about it, even in my essays on the buffoons and on Schlemihl, the sad, Semitic buffoon. It's a 'laugh until you cry' story, as you well know. The wanderers' humor, sweetly bitter, mixed like all the admixtures of the people who were driven away."

The act and scene were repeated several times. The man was speaking with himself, since the students were on vacation and no longer crowded around the clown. Was he addressing anyone?

As expected, nature, Mother Nature, finally provided the solution, or the salvation, as one might call it: the autumn had grown tired of good weather, and the rains and winds began in earnest. It became difficult to leave one's warm refuge. There could be no talk of walking to Eden to converse with the dead.

The professor was forced to retreat to his office to wait for visits from the students, or whoever else might chance to intrude.

After a weeklong wait, Schlemihl Iowa reappeared, again setting in motion the mumbling undertones.

"It's raining, Prof! Noah's flood, the real deal. Ugh, I barely made it."

He was wearing a black kurtka and cape, as in the book,

and he seemed beaten down by the hostile elements. He picked up the thread of the conversation again, after he had hung up his cape and umbrella on the hat stand. Refreshed by the presence of Noah's shadow, he shook himself, and took up the old dispute.

"So. Let's go back to von Chamisso, our good father. A wanderer like us. One of our neighbors in the fairytale for Hitzig's children—that convert, that generous, kindhearted suspect. A kind of Itzhak, that Hitzig, yes. Taking much care with the futures of his heirs, having converted to Christianity, the faith of the Jew Jesus, the undying, daily unresurrected in the churches of his followers, wearing a crown of thorns with the inscription 'the King of the Jews.' Mr. Chamisso empathized with those wanderers! With Hitzig's and Job's brothers, with Moses and Mary the virgin mother, unconverted, suspected by both Jews and Christians, as by so many of her friends and ours, who wear masks among the wanderers and are suspected of being circumcised. Let's be clear. Adelbert was not among them! That was not his justification, those were not his people, but only his brain: the thinking part in which he again found allies among the expatriated. Meaning, those who had learned to converse with their identities, rather than submit like deaf-and-dumb snails . . . How could the poet Chamisso not sneak in an allusion or raise a doubt regarding Peter Schlemihl's identity? Named after Peter, the apostle of Christianity, and after Schlemihl, the unlucky lover of the rabbi's wife, the ghetto's main village idiot, before his head and phallus were cut off? How could he not, young Iowa, how could he not?"

The discourse came to an end, at last! Horrified by his guest who confused him with a fairytale's fictional character, the professor no longer had the strength to make a sound. He was exhausted and frightened of what was surely to come, the fairytale terror.

How long would he have to listen to his own thoughts being spoken by a strange and hostile voice? Misanthrope, Nomad, miserable, babyish loafer, tormented and mortal vagabond astride a ghost, astride a broomstick, how long will you let this parody go on? No alarm rang, however. The actors were given a break. The surprise had no place from which to appear: the official little room for office hours was less favorable to disputes than the susurrating forest of Eden.

"How, tell me how, Herr Iowa? Herr Heine, the Poet, affirmed that all Germans are Schlemihls. He forgot to add that he was not a pure-blooded German but was wearing borrowed clothes. And his friend and your countryman, now considered to be an anti-Semite, Monsieur Emil Cioran, the Parisian insomniac, considered himself, as I've told you, to be a metaphysical Jew. Evidently a pleonasm, the Transylvanian nihilist was clueless."

A pause to breathe and gather strength. Sit quietly, you good for nothing. Both the conversation and its concerns will settle. Your ticker's just had a lapse: a defective eight seconds' worth.

"I've been delayed both on account of this tiresome weather and because of that meeting on the nature of the shadow. It was scheduled to take place long ago and then rescheduled repeatedly, because the invitees were always busy. It finally took place, and a few people came, I even took their picture. Celan and Desnos, Don Quixote, the rider, Herr Musil's Man Without Qualities, Monsieur Montaigne, the card player, Mr. K, the voyager. Even Count Pessoa, with his lyrical alternates. All obsessed by exile and the shadow and its macabre adventures. Much was said, much was left unsaid, no one could bear to leave. And you wouldn't believe it, even your name was mentioned. Twice! In regard to your essay on humor and in connection to the wandering people, from Abraham to Einstein and Schlemihl. Yes, yes, even Schlemihl, the man without a country, the suspect, Mr. Chamisso's representative, the representative of the poet and savant, who was also rootless, was mentioned. In support of your thesis regarding the general hatred of circumcised nomads, who are always accused of getting rich, provoking revolutions, or of causing all the world's evils, the opinion of several great men was cited: Luther, Dostoevsky, Hitler, Joseph Vissarionovich,[100] and this king, and that queen, and her lover, and the famous Haman of Persia. Many others. Some refused to admit that our Lord Jesus Christ, who was sent to save us, was also of the same privileged and sinful race destined to suffering. The privilege of suffering! With or without a shadow! Isn't that the fundamental state of nomads who live in the shadow? They will always be identified as deficient—always be said to have a missing finger, two different colored eyes, bad teeth, a nose too long or too crooked. The shadow is not an invention, everyone on earth has one, with no effort on their part. Only Peter Schlemihl, the evangelizing Apostle, had given his up, like a ne'er-do-well."

The Professor was silent. He hadn't said a word the whole time. Amazed by what was happening, he felt—why?—guilty. He had fervently awaited the reunion with the young geneticist, whom he had baptized Schlemihl Iowa in his mind, and behold, the nomad had nothing better to do than say what he himself, the professor, thought but had avoided confronting, with an old man's cowardice. Cowardice lying in wait for him in this and that perverse corner of his earthly peregrinations, not part of today's journey, or yesterday's, but of the journey he undertook in Colonel Tudor's time, the colonel whom he didn't have the courage to confront over his disgust with minorities. And then, too, long before this Tudor, long before, waiting beneath all the persecutions, at all the meridians where the death of the malicious, wandering people was demanded—cowardice.

He had risen from his upholstered swivel chair to take his leave from the shadow who had disappeared. He, too, it seemed, tried to distance himself, vexed by who-knows-what tormented shadow. The professor hadn't yet succeeded in regaining his composure when the door opened again: the wanderer from the Genetics Department entered like a whirlwind, sweaty from his mad dash back. Yes, yes, he had forgotten something.

"I forgot to mention the electronic gadgets with which even children know how to guess your secrets and quickly sell them, not just to the police, but to Jehovah's enemies, who multiply exponentially every day, every moment, in all the hidden corners of the warring planet.

"Did you believe in the post-Auschwitz illusion? Never again, never! Never! Is that what the survivors shouted? What about those who had set it motion and helped run the crematoria? Did you really think it wouldn't happen again? Why shouldn't it happen again? That's what you ask yourself, isn't it, and you don't have the courage to shout so that even the dead can hear, so that even Herr Hitler and Comrade Joseph Vissarionovich and this or that Emir, and the Shah, and His Highness Haman and all his relatives can finally hear.

"Why don't you tell the truth, why don't you shout it from the rooftops, you old, worn out sage? After all, you don't have long to go until you reach your eternal home! It's close by, with its snails and ants and arrogant trees and Irma the seductress and the eternal silence, which you dreamed about again in your professorial nightmares. Why don't you shout it, you exile, why not, you unlucky one, masked one, trickster, perfidious being? Why, explain why, gather up your courage at last! You have nothing more to lose, shake off the self-made armor of the prisoner and drifter, free the planet's paradise of your wanderer's shadow!"

It had grown quiet. The unwelcome guest retreated at last. The door was wide open for anyone who might be passing by to contemplate the professor's balding head, which was now at the same level as the table, or his body, which was also hunched over the table, over the room. Alone, alone, as he deserved. An eternal orphan, a stranger forever, a suspect forever, forever a renegade, as he deserved. Yes, there was silence again. No other voice from another world could be heard. Only the fitful breath of the captive, of all captives, of all those driven from one hiding place to another, forever cursed to never have peace, regardless of what hole they might crawl into.

Despite his balding head touching the table, the professor nevertheless was able to distinguish at last a murmur. It came from who-knows-where. Maybe it came from inside himself.

"Twitter, have you heard of this word? Twitter! E-mail,

have you heard of that? Facebook? Text messaging? Mobile phones? You can use them to receive letters and take pictures. Yes, there are others, many others, though I understand you're immune. Meaning dead, in the other world, not in this one. Not like Agatha, no, she can master all these devilish inventions, maneuver them with dexterity and pleasure. Of course, she had that American journalist to teach her. An expert in cosmic communication. It's called "virtual." That's how she, too, entered the present—from the virtual. But now you can no longer reach her, even if you'd like to. So you'll stay here with your lyrical Irma, in your multidenominational, multiethnic cemetery. And you'll talk to the deaf-and-dumb snails, sing in your sleep to the birds of the sky, and at last you'll stop complaining about exile, estrangement, persecution, genocide, solitude, isolation, infirmity, and the refugee's entire menu of options."

"I'm not complaining, I won't complain at all, I don't like complainers, and I can't stand being a victim."

"Well, you see, monsieur? You've put your finger directly on the ancient wound. You're full of yourself in your exaggerated modesty, you don't want to reveal anything, put yourself out there. As if you were in possession of who knows what treasure. Exiled not because you're far from your native shores, but because you've become assimilated into this category of bizarre angels of history, that's why! Shaped according to your own nature, not your particular situation."

"Is that so? Is it so?" the professor mumbled confusedly.

"Yes, just so. Better said, *even* so. Of course, you were exiled, deported, driven away once and then again and again, you live in a world that continues to exile itself, but that's not all. Your structural make-up, monsieur! The ancient makeup! Which you are only willing to speak about to yourself, in your head, so as not to give yourself away. So that the hunters won't find you, those men driving their packs of mad dogs. You grew up in a world where those like you were envied or humiliated or both. Better to keep your head down, you thought, stay hidden behind your mask, in your lair. But it was pointless, they quickly found you. Comrade Colonel was only one of the many guards who specialized in uncovering identities. Identification and extermination. Ethnic cleansing."

The professor had fallen asleep with his balding head on the table. Alone, alone, alone, no ghost to harass him. He could finally allow himself to fall asleep and forget, such were the blessed gifts of the void.

He was no longer listening, the Professor was no longer listening. He had tired of these self-flagellatory meetings in the tradition of his ancestors and of the long-ago prophets and those of more recent times. The poor man had fallen asleep with his balding head resting on the cold desktop. He was happy, had reached the age of sleep and of senility. He enjoyed sleeping deeply, for many hours, as many hours as possible, and feeling rich in dreams and nightmares and sensual snores. The true gift of the dark, of the tired. The true salvation.

He mumbled. *Hineni,* here I am, I am here. I am ready.

Notes

Quotations from published sources are indicated by italics in the text, and the sources are cited below.

1. Adapted from correspondence between the author and the National Geographic Society's Genographic Project.

2. After "The History of Migration," exhibition text, Red Star Line Museum (Antwerp: Red Star Line Museum, 2000).

3. The main character, who will accompany the reader like a shadow, comes from the story *Peter Schlemihls wundersame Geschichte* (1814) by Adelbert von Chamisso. Multiple English translations of the German text are available. For a recent translation, see: Adelbert von Chamisso, "Peter Schlemiel," in *Tales of the German Imagination: From the Brothers Grimm to Ingeborg Bachmann,* ed. Peter Wortsman (New York: Penguin Press, 2012).

4. A reference to Nicolae Ceaușescu and Elena Ceaușescu. Beginning in the 1970s, when the cult of the leader reached its apogee in Romania, the state apparatus began to refer to Ceaușescu as "the Most Beloved Son of the People," a moniker that, like the appellations "Genius of the Carpathians," and "an Exceptional Person of this World," was often added to his official designations. Elena Ceaușescu, around whom a similar personality cult developed, became known as "the Mother of the Nation," but was often ridiculed for her homely appearance with designations like "Bitty."—Trans.

5. A play on words. The Romanian adjective "amar/ă" translates as "bitter."—Trans.

6. Robert Musil, the author of the novel *Der Mann ohne Eigenschaften* [*The Man Without Qualities*], 2 vols., trans. Sophie Wilkins and Burton Pike (Vintage, 1995).

7. For the English edition of the novel, the translator, in collaboration with the author, has chosen the online *Oxford English Dictionary* as the source for the definitions of all the words listed in this chapter. When a definition was not available in the *Oxford English Dictionary,* the online *Merriam-Webster Dictionary* was used.—Trans. "exile, n.1." *OED Online.* June 2021. Oxford University Press. www.oed.com/view/Entry /66231. Reproduced with permission of the Licensor through PLSclear.

8. "wanderer, n." *OED Online.* June 2021. Oxford University Press. www.oed.com/view/Entry/225440. Reproduced with permission of the Licensor through PLSclear.

9. "wander, v." *OED Online.* June 2021. Oxford University Press. www.oed.com/view/Entry/225437. Reproduced with permission of the Licensor through PLSclear.

10. "Wandering albatross." *Merriam-Webster.com Dictionary.* July 2021. Merriam-Webster. https://www.merriam-webster.com/dictionary /wandering%20albatross.

11. "Brazilian wandering spider." *Merriam-Webster.com Dictionary.* July 2021. Merriam-Webster. https://www.merriam-webster.com/dictio nary/Brazilian%20wandering%20spider.

12. "wandering, adj." *OED Online.* June 2021. Oxford University Press. www.oed.com/view/Entry/225442. Reproduced with permission of the Licensor through PLSclear.

13. "refugee, n." *OED Online.* June 2021. Oxford University Press. www.oed.com/view/Entry/161121. Reproduced with permission of the Licensor through PLSclear.

14. German: "After a happy [. . .] a happy however arduous a journey [. . .] however terribly arduous a sea journey for me, personally, [. . .]."—Trans.

15. German: "After a [. . .] terribly arduous sea journey, for me, personally, we reached the port at last."—Trans.

16. Antonio Damasio, *Looking for Spinoza: Joy, Sorrow, and the Feeling Brain* (London: Harvest / Harcourt, 2003), 229.

17. Ibid., 233–234.

18. Ibid., 249–250.

19. German: "A happy but arduous journey."—Trans.

20. Wortsman, 349.—Trans.

21. For the description of this thrilling expedition, see Adelbert von Chamisso, *Reise um die Welt in den Jahren 1815–1818* (Leipzig: Weidmannsche Buchhandlung, 1836). The quotations in the present chapter are taken from the novel about Adelbert von Chamisso's life by Hans Natonek: *Der Schlemihl. Ein Roman von Leben Adelberts von Chamisso* (Stuttgart: Behrendt Verlag, 1949). No page numbers are given in the original Romanian edition.

22. Natonek.

23. A reference to the so-called Hep-Hep Riots, a series of violent riots against Jews, which took place in 1819, in the German Confederation, in response to Jews' increasing demand for civil and political rights. The origin of the pejorative phrase is disputed. Some scholars believe it is a taunt that refers to the Crusader cry *Hierosolyma est perdiata,* or "Jerusalem is lost," while others argue that it is a sheepherding exhortation adapted by anti-Semitic rioters hunting their victims. See "Anti-Semitism: The Hep Hep Riots," *The Jewish Virtual Library,* American-Israeli Cooperative Enterprise, April 11, 2022, https://www.jewishvirtuallibrary.org/hep-hep-riots.—Trans.

24. "I think of the times when, the world's school inviting / Our early friendship [. . .]" Adelbert von Chamisso, "To my old Friend, Peter Schlemihl" in *Peter Schlemihl,* trans. Sir John Bowring (New York: Denham & Co., 1874), 17.—Trans.

25. "I am forced to leave Europe, he said to Hitzig."—Trans. See Natonek.

26. *La nausée (Nausea)* is a novel by Jean-Paul Sartre.

27. "The shadow, considered on a plane that is situated behind the opaque body that produces it, is nothing other than the section of that plane through the solid that produces that shadow."—Trans.

28. "[The shadow] thus originates from this solid, [and] it is this solid that is in question in the marvelous story of *Peter Schlemihl.* [. . .] He wants us to profit from the lesson which cost him so dearly, and his experience cries out to us: Think of the solid!"—Trans.

29. The excerpts quoted in this chapter come from Thomas Mann's 1911 essay "Chamisso," in *Essays of Three Decades,* trans. H. T. Lowe-Porter (New York: Alfred A. Knopf, 1948), 241–258. ISBN 978-3-10-048225, Thomas Mann, Späte Erzählungen © 2022 S. Fischer Verlag GmbH, Hed-

derichstr. 114, D-60596 Frankfurt am Main. English translation by H. T. Lowe-Porter, copyright © 1947, copyright renewed 1974 by Penguin Random House LLC; from ESSAYS OF THREE DECADES by Thomas Mann, edited by H. T. Lowe-Porter, translated by H. T. Lowe-Porter. Used by permission of Random House, an imprint and division of Penguin Random House LLC. All rights reserved.

30. French: "Melancholy is the happiness of being sad."—Trans.

31. Misha Lemonade (also known as Misha Sparkling Water): two of Mikhail Gorbachev's nicknames making fun of the 50 percent price increase of alcoholic beverages—known as "Gorbachev's Prohibition"—a policy which the USSR adopted from 1985 to 1987.

32. A reference to the swastika, known in German as the Hakenkreuz.—Trans.

33. "After a lucky [. . .] but very arduous trip," the first sentence of Adelbert von Chamisso's *Peter Schlemihl's Wundersame Gesichte* (*Peter Schlemihl's Marvelous Tale*).

34. Ruth R. Wisse, *The Schlemiel as Modern Hero* (Chicago and London: University of Chicago Press, 1971), x–xi. Republished with permission of Ruth R. Wisse; permission conveyed through Copyright Clearance Center, Inc.

35. Ibid., Appendix, 125.

36. Ibid., 125–126.

37. The statue, sculpted by Jean-Antoine Houdon in the early 1790s, can be found in the rotunda of the Virginia State Capitol in Richmond.

38. Mariana Codruț, "On Poetry," *Areal* (Pitești: Editura Paralela 45, 2011), 8. Translated from the Romanian by the translator. Reprinted with permission.

39. Maxim Gorky, "Soviet Literature," in *Problems of Soviet Literature: Reports and Speeches at the First Soviet Writers' Congress,* by A. Zhdanov, Maxim Gorky, N. Bukharin, K. Radek, A. Stesky, ed. H. G. Scott (New York: International Publishers, 1935), 44.

40. Benedetto Croce, *European Literature in the Nineteenth Century,* trans. Douglas Ainslie (New York: Alfred A. Knopf, 1924), 61.

41. Hermann J. Weigand, *Surveys and Soundings in European Literature,* ed. A. Leslie Willson (Princeton: Princeton University Press, 1966), 210–221. Permission conveyed through Copyright Clearance Center, Inc.

42. Adelbert von Chamisso, "147: An Hitzig: Gunnersdorf September 1813, furz nach der Schlacht bei Dennewiss," in *Werke,* vol 3. (Leipzig: Weidmann'fche Buch handlung, 1852), 382. Translated from the German by the translator.—Trans.

43. Herbert Feinstein, "Buster Keaton: An Interview," in *Interviews,* ed. Kevin W. Sweeney (Jackson: University of Mississippi Press, 2007), 135. The main character in the film *The General* is a locomotive mechanic.

44. Tony Thomas, "Interview with Buster Keaton, (1960)," ibid., 107.

45. George Sadoul, "A Dinner with Keaton," ibid., 153.

46. Hans Christian Andersen, "The Shadow" in *Hans Christian Andersen: The Complete Stories,* trans. Jean Herscholt (London: British Library, 2005), 294–303.

47. "The Shadow (fairy tale)," *Wikipedia* (Wikimedia Foundation, 2021). Accessed November 20, 2021, https://en.wikipedia.org/wiki/The_Shadow_(fairy_tale)

48. Excerpted with permission from Jun'ichirō Tanizaki, *In Praise of Shadows* (New Haven: Leete's Island Books, 1977), 18–21.

49. Adelbert von Chamisso, *Peter Schlemihl* (London, Paris, and Melbourne: Cassell & Company 1889) [Project Gutenberg, 2002], https://www.gutenberg.org/files/5339/5339-h/5339-h.htm.

50. Ibid.

51. Ibid.

52. Rabbi Elijah ben Solomon (1720–1797) was known as the "gaon" (excellency, sage) of Vilna (Vilnius); he was a principal opponent of Hasidism.

53. Flap-copy text excerpted from Elisabeth Tove-Bailey, *Sound of a Wild Snail Eating* (Chapel Hill, NC: Algonquin Books, 2016).—Trans.

54. Norman Manea, *Anii de ucenicie ai lui August Prostul* (Bucharest: Cartea Românească, 1979) (3rd ed., Iaşi: Editura Polirom, 2010).

55. "I am a seagull from no country / No strand do I call my home." —Trans.

56. German: "Children, kitchen, church."—Trans.

57. A play on words: in Romanian "substitute" is a masculine noun and "substitution" a feminine one.—Trans.

58. Patricia Highsmith, "The Snail-Watcher," in *Eleven Short Stories* (London: Heinemann, 1970), 3–4.

59. Ibid., 5.

60. "Two snails are on their way / To bury a dead leaf. / They've painted their shell black / And have veils round their horns. / They set forth in the night, / A lovely autumn night! / Alas, when they get there / They find that spring has sprung / And the leaves that had died / Have all come back to life / And the two little snails / Are well disappointed." Jacques Prévert's "Chanson des escargots qui vont à l'enterrement." Trans. San Cassimally, "Snails Going to the Burial of a Dead Leaf," in *Medium,* Medium Corporation, August 2, 2018, Accessed: December 14, 2021, https://medium .com/the-story-hall/snails-going-to-the-burial-a-dead-leaf-683653f8cb5e. Used with permission. Original French poem © Éditions Gallimard, www .gallimard.fr. Used with permission.

61. "Alas, when they get there / They find that spring has sprung / [. . .] / But here comes the sun." Ibid.

62. "Snail, snail / Curling pale / Balled and striped / And locked up tight; / Let the yolk of night come forth, / Sluggish snail come out to sport." Ion Barbu, "Dupa Melci (1921)," in *Barbu: Opera Poetica,* ed. Mircea Coşolenco, vol. 1 (Bucharest: Editura Cartier, 2002), 9. Translated by Carla Baricz.

63. "To his stringy little self / I bent down, / I wept and cradled: / 'Snail, oh, snail what went wrong? / From your sleep you've come unstrung! / You believed the words I said / They were false . . . They joked you dead. / [. . .] / As before you should have slept, / Deaf to song you should have kept, / Pulled the varnished shades of dream / You, the world, and they between.' / [. . .] / In the winter antlers fail / Sluggish snail / Sluggish snail." Ibid., 16–18.—Trans.

64. Peter Wortsman, "The Displaced Person's Guide to Nowhere," introduction to *Peter Schlemiel: The Man Who Sold His Shadow,* by Adelbert von Chamisso (New York: Fromm International Publishing Corporation), ix–xv.

65. Ibid.

66. Adelbert von Chamisso, *Peter Schlemihl: From the German of Lamotte Foqué* (London: G. and W. B. Whittaker, 1824), 160.

67. Alan L. Berger, "Elie Wiesel: Writer as Witness to and in Exile," in *Exile in Global Literature and Culture,* ed. Asher Z. Milbauer and James

M. Sutton (New York and London: Routledge, 2020), 102–109; permission conveyed through Copyright Clearance Center, Inc.

68. From Susannah Heschel, "An Exile of the Soul: A Theological Examination of Jewish Understandings of Diaspora," in *Diaspora and Law: Culture, Religion, and Jurisprudence Beyond Sovereignty,* ed. Liliane Feierstein and Daniel Weidner (forthcoming, de Gruyter Press). Used with permission.

69. Eugenio Montale, "Bring Me the Sunflower," in *Collected Poems, 1920–1954,* by Eugenio Montale, trans. and ed. Jonathan Galassi (New York: Farrar, Straus and Giroux, 1998), 47. Original Italian: "Portami il girasole" from *Ossi di seppia* © 2003 Arnoldo Mondadori Editore S.p.A., Milan; © 2016 Mondadori Libri S.p.A., Milan. Published by arrangement with The Italian Literary Agency. Used with permission. Translation copyright © 1998, 2000, 2012 by Jonathan Galassi. Reprinted by permission of Farrar, Straus and Giroux. All rights reserved.

70. David Michael Hertz, *Eugenio Montale, the Fascist Storm, and the Jewish Sunflower* (Toronto: University of Toronto Press, 2013), 62.

71. "Long ago, I was with you when your father stepped into the shadows."—Trans. See Eugenio Montale "Lontano ero con tue padre . . . " *Le Occasioni: 1928–1939,* ed. Dante Isella (Turin: Einaudi, 1996), 65.

72. "New Stanzas" by Eugenio Montale, translated by Ben Johnson and James Merrill; from COLLECTED POEMS by James Merrill, copyright © 2001 by the Literary Estate of James Merrill at Washington University. Used by permission of Alfred A. Knopf, an imprint of the Knopf Doubleday Publishing Group, a division of Penguin Random House LLC. All rights reserved. Original Italian poem "Nuove stanze" from "Le occasioni" © 2011 Arnoldo Mondadori Editore S.p.A., Milan, © 2018 Mondadori Libri S.p.A., Milan. Published by arrangement with The Italian Literary Agency.

73. Ibid., 93.—Trans.

74. Quoted ibid., 150.—Trans.

75. Eugenio Montale, "News from Amiata," trans. Irma Brandeis in *Irma Brandeis' Translations of Montale* (Washington University Digital Gateway) http://omeka.wustl.edu/omeka/exhibits/show/merrill-poetry -mss/jm-muse/montale-muse. Original Italian poem "Notizie dall'A-

miata" from *Le occasioni* © 2011 Arnoldo Mondadori Editore S.p.A., Milan, © 2018 Mondadori Libri S.p.A., Milan. Published by arrangement with The Italian Literary Agency. Used with permission.

76. Quoted ibid., 150.

77. Hertz, 157.

78. Ibid., 198.

79. Eugenio Montale, "Iride," in *La bufera e altro,* ed. Ida Campeggiani e Niccolò Scaffai (Milan: Mondadori, 2019), trans. Carla Baricz. Original Italian poem © 2019 Mondadori Libri S.p.A., Milan. Published by arrangement with The Italian Literary Agency.

80. Eugenio Montale, "Hitler Spring," trans. James Merrill in *Poetry* (October–November 1989): 10–11.

81. Eugenio Montale, "L'Ombra della magnolia," in *La bufera e altro,* ed. Ida Campeggiani and Niccolò Scaffai (Milan: Mondadori, 2019), 311–315. Copyright © 2019 Mondadori Libri S.p.A., Milan.

82. Hertz, 270.

83. Eugenio Montale, "Mi pare impossibile," *Altri versi e poesie disperse,* ed. Giorgio Zampa (Milan: Mondadori, 1981), 73. Copyright © 2003 Arnoldo Mondadori Editore S.p.A., Milan; © 2016 Mondadori Libri S.p.A., Milan.

84. Montale, "News from Amiata."

85. Montale, "Mi pare impossibile."

86. Montale, "L'Ombra della magnolia."

87. This section comprises fragments from Norman Manea, "Long Lasting Shadows," in *The Los Angeles Review of Books* (January 7, 2016). http://lareviewofbooks.org/article/long-lasting-shadows/. Reprinted with permission.

88. Norman Manea, "Gheara II" in *Întoarcerea huliganului* [*The Hooligan's Return*] (Iaşi: Editura Polirom, 2006), 202–204.

89. Max Milner, "Creativité de l'ombre," in *L'envers du visible: Essai sur l'ombre* (Paris: Seuil, 2005), 83. © Editions du Seuil, 2005. Reprinted with permission.

90. Ibid., 436.

91. "In this way, from the very beginning, the work on which I was meditating and which I was going to accomplish was condemned to remain unfinished. Oh, my dear Adelbert, to what end does mankind la-

bor?" Here, the translation follows the Romanian edition: Adelbert von Chamisso, *Extraordinara poveste a lui Peter Schlemihl,* trans. Petru Manoliu (Bucharest: ESPLA, 1956), 102.

92. Manguel's author notes about the tale of Peter Schlemihl appear in the German edition of his reading journal, under the date "November 2002." See Alberto Manguel, *Tagebuch eines Lesers* (Berlin: Fischer Taschenbuch, 2007), 115–120. © Alberto Manguel c/o Schavelzon Graham Agencia Literaria (www.schavelzongraham.com). Used with permission.

93. See Hannah Arendt's discussion of Heinrich Heine and the *Schlemihl* as the Lord of the World of Dreams, in "The Jew as Pariah: A Hidden Tradition," *Jewish Social Studies,* vol. 6, no. 2 (1944): 99–122.

94. Anne-Sophie Astrup, "Le voyage identitaire des reisebilder," in *Heine voyageur,* ed. Alain Cozic, Françoise Knopper, and Alain Ruiz (Toulouse: Pres Universitaires du Mirail, 1999), 113–128, here 126.

95. Relegatio: a relegation. In ancient Rome, a milder form of exile, which could be temporary and did not entail the loss of Roman citizenship or of one's wealth and goods.—Trans.

96. Fragments paraphrasing Olivier Remaud, "Lexil et le complexe de Schlémihl," in *Un monde étrange. Pour une autre approche du cosmopolitisme* (Paris: PUF, 2015), 99–113. Used with permission.

97. Paul Celan, "Sprich auch du," from *Von Schwelle zu Schwelle.* Copyright © 1955, Deutsche Verlags-Anstalt (Munich: Penguin Random House Verlagsgruppe GmbH). English translation: "Speak You Too," from SELECTED POEMS AND PROSE OF PAUL CELAN by Paul Celan, translated by John Felstiner. Copyright © 2001 by John Felstiner. Used by permission of W. W. Norton & Company, Inc.

98. Paul Celan, "Tenebrae," from *Sprachgitter,* 1959. Copyright © S. Fischer Verlag GmbH, Frankfurt am Main, 1959. All rights reserved by S. Fischer Verlag GmbH (978-3-10-010502-8). English translation: "Tenebrae," from SELECTED POEMS AND PROSE OF PAUL CELAN by Paul Celan, translated by John Felstiner. Copyright © 2001 by John Felstiner. Used by permission of W. W. Norton & Company, Inc.

99. From David Blamires, *Telling Tales: The Impact of Germany on English Children's Books, 1780–1918* (Cambridge, UK: Open Book Publishers, 2009), 135–145.

100. A reference to the dictator Joseph Stalin (1878–1953), the leader

of the Soviet Union and general secretary of the Communist Party from 1924 until his death. During his time in power, Stalin expanded the reach of the USSR to include the Eastern European satellite states, collectivized agriculture, and was the force behind Soviet totalitarianism and the so-called Red Terror of the 1930s.—Trans.

NORMAN MANEA is Francis Flournoy Professor Emeritus of European Studies and Culture as well as Writer-in-Residence at Bard College. Deported from his native Romania to a Ukrainian concentration camp during World War II, he was again forced to leave Romania in 1986, no longer safe under an intolerant Communist dictatorship. He has received major Romanian, American, and European cultural distinctions. He is the Laureate of the Romanian National Prize for Literature and has been awarded the distinction of Star of Romania by the Romanian government; he is also the first Romanian writer to be granted the American MacArthur Fellowship. His works have also been awarded the Italian International Nonino Prize, the French Medicis étranger Prize, the German Nelly Sachs Prize, the Spanish Palau Fabre Prize, and the FIL Literary Award in Romance Languages; and he has received the Literary Lion Medal of the New York Public Library. Member of the Berlin Academy of Art and of the Royal Society of Literature in Great Britain, he is decorated by the French government with the title of Commandeur dans l'Ordre des Arts et des Lettres.

CARLA BARICZ is the assistant editor and translator of *Romanian Writers on Writing: A Writer's World Anthology* (San Antonio: Trinity University Press, 2011). She has translated the work of a number of Romanian writers, including Max Blecher, Ion Budai-Deleanu, Florin Mugur, Octavian Paler, and Dan Sociu.